PRAISE FOR ENTER THE DUKE

**NERWA Readers' Choice Awards Finalist
Golden Quill Finalist
Maggie Award of Excellence Finalist**

"Could not put this story down.... Ransom and Maggie were perfect for each other and the sparks fly throughout the entire book! It gets really steamy at times. I usually hate secret baby tropes, but this one was perfectly executed and I loved it!" -Candace, *Goodreads*

"I adored this book, it's one that gave me a fuzzy feeling of hope inside, showing that through all adversity, you can get to where you want to be." -Maggie, *Goodreads*

"A highly charged story with great characters that will take you through on an adventure and back again." -Lori, *Goodreads*

"Seeing Rhys' journey to redemption will put a smile on your face and some tears in your eyes. Maggie and Rhys are so right for each other....If you love second chances with a lot of hope and redemption, then read this book." -Angela, *Goodreads*

"[Callaway] was able to take this villainous rake and have me sympathize with him...The way he opened himself up to his heroine Maggie was wonderful and I felt invested in their relationship...The chemistry between our heroine and hero was HOT." -Jan, *Goodreads*

ADDITIONAL PRAISE FOR GRACE CALLAWAY

"Readers looking for a good historical mystery/romance or a historical with a little more kink will enjoy *The Duke Who Knew Too Much*." -*Smart Bitches, Trashy Books*

"*Her Husband's Harlot* is a pleasing, out of the ordinary read." -*Dear Author*

"Grace Callaway writes the way Loretta Chase would if she got kind of dark and VERY naughty." -Nicole, *Goodreads*

"Grace Callaway's book is the first in her 'Heart of Enquiry' series, and this excellent brew of romance and intrigue and emotion is also *Stevereads* best Romance novel of 2015." -*The Duke Who Knew Too Much* named the #1 Best Romance of the Year by *Stevereads*

"I discovered a new auto-buy author with [*M is for Marquess*]... I've now read each of Grace Callaway's books and loved them—which is exceptional. Gabriel and Thea from this book were two of the best characters I read this year. Both had their difficulties and it was charming to see how they overcame them together, even though it wasn't always easy for them. This is my favorite book of 2015." -*Romantic Historical Reviews*

"Erotic historical romance isn't as plentiful as many would think, but here you have a very well-written example of this genre. It's entertaining and fun and a darn good read." -*The Book Binge*

"Grace Callaway is a remarkable writer." -*Love Romance Passion*

GAME OF DUKES

The Duke Identity

Enter the Duke

Regarding the Duke

The Duke Redemption

The Return of the Duke (June 2020)

HEART OF ENQUIRY

The Widow Vanishes (Prequel Novella)

The Duke Who Knew Too Much

M is for Marquess

The Lady Who Came in from the Cold

The Viscount Always Knocks Twice

Never Say Never to an Earl

The Gentleman Who Loved Me

MAYHEM IN MAYFAIR

Her Husband's Harlot

Her Wanton Wager

Her Protector's Pleasure

Her Prodigal Passion

CHRONICLES OF ABIGAIL JONES

Abigail Jones

"See that there is no one to fight, only an illusion to see through."
  -Bruce Lee

This book is dedicated to my husband and his childhood idol.

Enter the Duke

Book Two

GRACE CALLAWAY

PROLOGUE

DORSET, 1829

"This is no place for you, Miss Goode," Paul Foley said.

His thin, spare features settled into disapproving lines as he surveyed the dockside tavern. Neither the dimness nor the smokiness could hide that this was a disreputable place. The patrons were rowdy, the drinks cheap; the air was thick with the smell of unwashed bodies and roasting meat.

In her eighteen years, Maggie Goode had been in worse places. She wiped down the sticky counter in front of her friend and gave him a reassuring smile.

"I'm grateful for the work, Mr. Foley," she said. "The Crown 'n Anchor pays two shillings more a week than Mr. 'Arper did."

"I suppose that explains your choice to leave the butcher shop," he replied with a troubled sigh.

Leaving Harper's butcher shop hadn't been her choice, a fact she wasn't keen to share.

"Can't say I mind leaving behind the blood 'n guts," she said brightly.

At that moment, a patron began spewing his guts out nearby,

his cronies roaring with laughter as they jumped out of harm's way.

Mr. Foley's greying brows rose over his spectacles.

"Least there ain't blood," she said with a shrug.

She'd started at the Crown and Anchor a fortnight ago. As she'd been working since the age of thirteen (and before then, she'd helped her departed ma, a dockside washerwoman), she'd gotten the lay of the land quickly. Friday nights like this one were boisterous. Local men and passing sailors arrived, their week's wages burning a hole through their pockets.

"This is no place for a young lady," Mr. Foley insisted.

The fact that he considered her a "lady" was one of the things Maggie liked about him.

She'd first met him when he'd wandered into Harper's butcher shop. His spectacles and rumpled garb had marked him as a scholarly gent. In a cultured voice, he'd confessed to having a hankering for a roast supper yet knew nothing about cuts of meat or how to prepare them. Before Mrs. Harper, the butcher's wife, could swoop in and sell him a costly beefsteak he would undoubtedly ruin, Maggie had told him the name of a local cook looking for work.

The relief in his faded blue eyes had almost made up for the flogging she'd later received from Mrs. Harper's sharp tongue.

To Maggie's surprise, Mr. Foley had returned to the shop a few days later, this time with a list in hand from his new cook. His visits became a weekly event, and Maggie learned that he was a bachelor in his fifties. He'd taken up residence in the village to pursue his study of fossils, which were plentiful here on the Dorset coast. She'd been shocked at the amount that Mr. Foley claimed his fellow collectors would pay for old bones.

As Ma used to say, some folks had more money than sense.

Unfortunately, Maggie came from a family that was infamous for having neither.

There goes another No Goode was a familiar refrain in the village.

The Goodes were notorious for being hot-blooded and feckless. Maggie's father had died when she was young, breaking his neck during a drunken ride. Her older brothers carried on his legacy through their tavern brawls and shady money-making schemes. Delilah, her older sister, got entangled with one dishonorable fellow after the next.

Take care o' your siblings, Maggie. They ain't got your sense. On her deathbed, Ma's voice had been weak, yet urgency had lit her green eyes. *Most o' all, don't let your Goode blood lure you into sin. Don't be like me and Delilah, looking for a prince to sweep you off your feet. For us Goodes, there won't be no fancy violins, flowers, and faerie tale endings. But if you work 'ard and be a good girl, maybe you'll find the respectability that we ne'er did.*

More than anything, Maggie craved respectability.

She dreamed of one day opening a flower shop. Ma had had a way with flowers, and she'd passed that love onto Maggie. Maggie couldn't imagine anything more wonderful than to work surrounded by fresh blooms and foliage, her favorite roses scenting the air. As a successful proprietress, she'd dress in spotless bombazine and learn to speak proper-like, too (with Mr. Foley's help, she was already working on refining her accent).

Then people would no longer look down their noses at her. She would prove that a Goode could make something of herself. She'd start a new family legacy, one that she'd be proud to pass onto her own children...

"Oi ain't paying you to be idle!"

At the shouted words, her dream dispersed like a dandelion puff. Mr. Marsh, owner of the tavern, was a short man with an even shorter temper, and he was scowling at her as he drew ale into tankards. "Can't you see the pool o' vomit on the floor? Quit palavering and clean it up!"

"Yes, sir," Maggie said hastily. In order to attain her dream, she needed this job. She turned to Mr. Foley. "Can I get you another ale afore I go?"

"Thank you, no. It's getting late, and I'd best be going." Mr. Foley left his stool and a generous tip. "Adieu until next week."

Fetching a mop and bucket, Maggie went to take care of the mess.

After that, she wove through the noisy room, replenishing drinks and platters. Along the way, she wiped down tables, collected dirty vessels, and dodged wandering hands. Her last stop was the table in the alcove next to the back door.

She approached warily as the pair of brutish newcomers sprawled in the seats were well into their cups. From their salt-chapped hands and Cockney accents, she guessed they were seamen passing through. Their florid, leering faces spelled trouble.

She took a breath, pasted on a smile. "Good evening, sirs. What'll it be?"

"What're ye offerin', dove?"

This came from the sandy-haired man seated to her right. Her skin crawled as his piggish eyes roved over her, lingering on her breasts. The lout on the left had a striped kerchief wound around his neck, and he was looking his own fill, licking his thick lips as he eyed her bottom.

Not for the first time, she cursed her appearance. Why couldn't she be a respectable-looking female—a slender blonde, say, with an angelic blue gaze? Instead, all Goode women were cursed with wavy reddish-brown hair, full curves, and green eyes, a combination that proved to be a lightning rod for randy bastards.

She kept her smile fixed in place. "The ale and meat pie are some o' the finest in the county."

"Reckon ye 'ave more than that to offer a man," Striped Kerchief said, winking.

"Food and drink are all I serve," she said firmly. "Now if you be needing time to decide—"

He reached out, grabbing an unruly tress that had escaped the knot at the back of her head. When she tried to pull free, he stabbed his fingers into her hair, yanking her face to his. Pain shot through her scalp.

"What I need is a good ruttin'." His breath puffed hotly against her cheek. "And ye look like just the wench to give it to me."

Her insides lurching, she snapped, "Let me go, you blighter!"

"Saucy wench, eh? I like lively sport." He nodded toward the nearby door, which led to the alleyway behind the tavern. "Let's get to know one another be'er."

Maggie raced through her options. She was no missish female, and if this were any other situation, she'd have walloped the blighter. Her ma and brothers had taught her to defend herself: she could wield a frying pan like a weapon and knew how to disarm a man with a well-placed knee.

But she didn't dare create a fuss. Not here. Mr. Marsh had made it clear that any bar maid causing a ruckus would be sacked, a threat he'd carried out twice since she'd started working here.

After the fiasco at the butcher's shop, she couldn't afford to lose this job, which she'd been lucky to get, given her family's reputation. If she was dismissed from this position too, she might never find work in the village again. And her dream of the flower shop would be forever out of her reach.

The bastard yanked again, and she gasped, "All right, I'll go with you. Just let me go."

I'll run for the bar. The bastards won't be bold enough to rape me in public.

The instant the pressure on her scalp eased, she jerked away, ready to bolt. Her back slammed into a beefy chest. Pig Eyes— he'd crept up behind her. Before she could cry out, his thick hand smothered her breath.

"No need to put on airs, wench," he hissed in her ear. "Blind man can see ye make yer living on yer back. Come out back wif us, and we'll make it worf yer while."

Panic thumped in Maggie's chest as Pig Eyes locked an arm

around her waist, dragging her toward the back door. He was giving her no choice. Job or no job, she would have to fight back—

"Beg pardon," a deep, aristocratic voice said. "I must ask that you release the lady."

Despite Maggie's predicament, she couldn't help but gawk at the man who stepped into their path. He was the most dashing gentleman she'd ever seen. His exotic hazel eyes gleamed beneath dark, slashing brows. Shadowed by the brim of his fine hat, his face was chiseled and strong, his golden skin a virile contrast to his snowy cravat. His tall, lean figure was garbed in understated elegance, and his lord of the manor bearing could only come from centuries of blue-blooded stock.

"Get out o' my way," Maggie's captor snarled.

"I'm afraid that's not possible. You are absconding with the serving maid, and I am in want of ale." The gentleman smiled wryly. "Or what passes for ale in this establishment. At any rate, for the sake of my thirst, I must insist you release her."

Pig Eyes faltered at the banter, his hand falling from Maggie's mouth although he kept her trapped against him. She wasn't sure what to make of her would-be champion, whose pleasant drawl was laced with a quiet threat. She sensed the restrained power beneath his polished façade, and it set off a strange, quivery feeling in her stomach.

She knew instinctively that only a fool would challenge the man.

Striped Kerchief surged forward. "Ye can shove yer fancy words up yer fancy arse."

Aye. Only a fool.

Maggie's breath held as the brute threw a punch. The gent dodged the attack easily, catching the bastard's arm with one gloved hand, twisting it behind the other's back. Quick as lightning, he used the limb as leverage, forcing his opponent onto the ground, his polished boot planting into the other's back.

Striped Kerchief groaned and struggled but could not free himself.

Pig Eyes pushed Maggie aside, readying to help his comrade.

"If it were me, I'd choose another alternative." With his free hand, the gent pulled out a pistol. Cocked it. "I'm a fastidious sort, but if I must, I'll make an exception. Luckily, my valet has a knack for removing blood stains."

Pig Eyes's gaze widened. While Maggie doubted he knew what "fastidious" meant (to be honest, she wasn't sure herself), the rotter definitely understood the meaning of the loaded pistol.

Raising his hands, he stammered, "Don't w-want no trouble."

"Make your apologies to the lady. Be quick about it," the gentleman said sharply.

"S-sorry miss." Pig Eyes wet his lips. "A misunderstandin', it was."

Out of the corner of her eye, Maggie spotted Mr. Marsh charging toward them like a bull.

"No 'arm done," she said in a panicked rush.

"And you?" The toff directed his inquiry to the man still trapped beneath his boot. "Will you apologize to the lady, or shall we go another round?"

"Meant no disrespect," Striped Kerchief gasped out.

The gent released him. "Begone."

At the command, the ruffians hustled out the back door, disappearing into the night.

No sooner had the door closed then Mr. Marsh was upon them.

"What's going on 'ere?" The proprietor jabbed a stubby finger at Maggie. "You be the cause o' this trouble, girl?"

Her heart thrashed against a cage of fear. "N-no, sir, I weren't doing nothing—"

"Oi should've known better than to 'ire a Goode," Mr. Marsh spat. "Ramshacklum drunks, slommocks, and drawlatchets, the lot o' you!"

Maggie willed back the humiliating tears. As if it weren't enough that her dreams were crashing down like a house of cards, her shame was being aired in front of the gentleman who'd gallantly defended her. She prayed that he didn't understand the local vernacular Mr. Marsh used to describe her kin: a "slommock" was a slattern and "drawlatchet" a lazy person. "Ramshacklum" meant "good for nothing"—and was a common prefix to her family's name.

She couldn't meet the gent's eyes, didn't want to see the all too familiar disdain.

"You are the owner of this establishment?"

The gentleman's curt words cut off Mr. Marsh, who sputtered, "Aye, sir. And you may rest assured that this slommock won't be bothering—"

"She wasn't bothering me. Quite the opposite. In point of fact, she was lending a hand."

At that, Maggie peered up.

Mr. Marsh squinted. He clearly didn't believe the gent but also didn't want to offend an obviously well-to-do customer. "With what?"

"I wished for a seat in the alcove and offered to buy the occupants a drink in exchange for their table. They, however, took offense." As the gent shrugged his broad shoulders, nary a wrinkle appeared on the deep sapphire superfine. "Your employee here... Miss Goode, is it?"

His unexpectedly gentle tone eased some of the knots in Maggie's midsection.

"Yes, sir," she whispered.

"Rhys Jones, at your service." He inclined his head.

Maggie dipped her knees in an awkward curtsy.

"Miss Goode saw what was happening and tried to intervene. Alas, even her gentle diplomacy could not dissuade the two brutes, and I had no choice but to respond. Now that the unpleasant business is concluded,"—Mr. Jones's commanding tone indicated that he was done with explanations—"you may fetch me a bottle of your finest brandy and a collation. A round for the house as well. Forthwith."

The cool dismissal propelled Mr. Marsh into action. "Yes, sir. Thank you, sir." To Maggie, he barked, "Well, don't just stand there like a loplolly. Bring the gent 'is bit-an'-drop!"

She rushed off to collect the food and drink. In the kitchen, she snuck extra slices of ham onto the platter while Cook was looking the other way. It was little enough but the best that she could do to thank her rescuer.

When she returned, Mr. Jones had settled in at the table. He'd removed his hat and gloves, and in the candlelight, his brown-black hair gleamed like a luxurious pelt. He wore it a trifle over-long, the thick waves framing his patrician features. He looked to be a few years older than her, perhaps in his early twenties. His brilliant hazel eyes and golden-hued skin added a foreign flair to his English bones.

She wondered about his heritage. Working in a dockside town, she'd seen sailors from all over the world. But she'd never met a man as striking and unique as this one.

For all his worldly refinement, there was also a restless, untamed quality about him. She felt an odd tingle watching his hands idly play with the supple leather of his gloves. She remembered a story her mama had liked to tell her, about a dashing pirate prince who ruled the seas, defying kings and rescuing damsels in distress. If she closed her eyes and imagined that make-believe prince, she would see this man.

"Ah, you're back. That was quick."

His friendly tone made her duck her head, a stray strand brushing her cheek. She wished she'd taken the time to neaten herself before returning. Not that it would have made any difference.

She was an ill-kempt, gawky tavern wench. He was male perfection, lounging in his chair as if it were a throne. He was above her in every way, and the only reason he'd done her a favor was because he was a gentleman in the truest sense.

Keeping her gaze on the items she unloaded from the tray, she said in a low voice, "I wanted to thank you, sir, for what you did. I swear I didn't—"

"You are not to blame for the brutes accosting you," he said briskly. "Nor for the actions of your relations, whatever your idiot employer might believe."

Startled, she saw that his handsome face showed no sign of mockery.

"You're the first one who's e'er said that to me, sir," she said honestly.

The only one who's e'er seen...me. Just me.

"I'm an expert on distancing oneself from family." Before she could puzzle out the meaning of his words, he tasted his brandy. "First-rate. Amazing, isn't it, how the finest French imports can be found in sleepy coastal villages?"

She was fairly certain he was referring to the smuggling that was as common as fleas in these parts, but she could hardly admit that the Crown and Anchor dealt in ill-gotten goods. Or that her brothers were oft times the purveyors of said goods.

As she chewed on her bottom lip, debating what to say, he laughed. The sound was rich and vibrant, warming her insides like a posset.

"A discreet thing, aren't you?" His lips curved faintly. "Something we have in common."

That this elegant prince of a gentleman would think they had anything in common made her speechless. She felt giddy, as if she'd partaken of the bootlegged brandy. Flustered, she reached to straighten the platter she'd placed on the table.

His hand moved at the same time; their fingers collided. A sharp spark crackled between them. It danced over her skin, jolting her nerve endings. She jerked her hand away, her lips parting in shock.

His long, black lashes swept up. Up close, she saw that flecks of green were buried in his golden-brown irises like emeralds amongst pirate's gold. His gaze flashed; she'd watched a storm once, standing on a cliff overlooking the sea, and she felt as breathless now as she did then.

His long-fingered hand cupped the brandy glass, the amber liquid swirling.

"Pardon, Miss Goode," he said.

His well-bred manners and raw charisma were a potent combination. A hot, pulsing urgency awakened inside her. When she wetted her lips, his gaze followed the motion.

"Folks be calling me Maggie, sir," she offered shyly.

"Well then...Maggie." If he wasn't already the most beautiful man she'd ever seen, his slow smile, which revealed a mesmerizing set of dimples, would have made him so. "Call me Rhys."

❧　I　❧

DORSET, 1838

"Welcome back, Your Grace," Quince grumbled.

Despite his dark mood, Edward Rhys Hugo Jones Cavendish, the Fifth Duke of Ranelagh and Somerville, felt a tug of amusement at the butler's sour greeting. It had been over nine years since Rhys's last visit to his Uncle Horatio's Dorset estate, and Quince hadn't changed much. Unlike a fine wine, the curmudgeon did not improve with age: he merely got older and crankier.

Rhys tossed his hat to the stooped grey-haired servant. Quince snapped it out of the air with a flair that betrayed his past as a juggler with the famed Astley's Amphitheatre. Rhys's recently deceased uncle had been an adventurer and explorer, and he'd surrounded himself with characters as colorful as he, himself, had been.

"I've readied the master's chamber," Quince said, as if he'd completed one of the labors of Hercules. "Your valet can bring your things up."

"I'm traveling alone." Rhys gestured at the two valises he'd carried in. "These are my bags."

Quince's rheumy gaze travelled up Rhys's polished boots and buff trousers, past his claret frock coat, pausing on his neatly trimmed beard and mustache. Facial hair was a daring new style that Rhys had picked up on the Continent; Quince's expression conveyed his belief that it ought to have been left there. While the servant's behavior was bloody impertinent, Rhys was used to being stared at and couldn't be bothered to issue a reprimand.

Given his mixed-blood heritage—he was the product of an English aristocrat and a Chinese merchant's daughter—he'd been an object of curiosity all his life. As a boy, he'd been bullied and rejected by his peers for being different. As a man, his "exotic" looks had made him popular and sought after, thanks to the English fetish for all things Oriental.

Five years ago, when he'd become a duke at six-and-twenty, his celebrity had soared into the stratosphere. Indeed, the *ton*, with their predictable tediousness, had given him a moniker: "Ransom," a contraction of his title...and an allusion to the way he captured ladies' hearts. In his opinion, the latter characterization missed the mark entirely. For in his interactions with the fair sex, the heart was the one part of the female anatomy that he took pains to avoid.

Whatever the case, he found himself immune to social scrutiny. It wasn't as if anyone saw *him*, after all. All they saw was the image he presented to them—that of a charming, worldly, and indolent rake. These days, when he stared into the looking glass, that image was what he saw of himself.

"Who's going to keep you looking fancy?" the butler asked suspiciously.

Rhys gave the other's crumpled, stained livery a sardonic glance. "I'll take care of myself."

It wasn't by choice. No gentleman would *choose* to take care of himself. But necessity was the mother of invention, and being on the flit from cutthroat moneylenders had made Rhys quite inventive: he could tie his own cravat and trim his own facial hair. Mortifying, but true.

Rhys's troubles were, in part, inherited. When Phillip Cavendish, Rhys's sire, had died five years ago, he'd left his heir with a title and mountain of debts. Phillip had not believed in fiscal management, a concept he'd deemed "vulgar." Combined with his love of extravagant living, he'd done the estate irreparable damage.

His deathbed words had been as spiteful as the man himself. *You've been a disappointment from the time you were born—a weakling and a mongrel. You and your mother have tainted the bloodline. What's the point in preserving the well when the water's been poisoned?*

Rhys had been determined to save his legacy, if for no other reason than to prove his father wrong. He'd thought himself so clever to come up with a plan to rescue the estate through investments. Using his modest inheritance from his mother, he'd turned a neat profit. Buoyed by his successes, he'd risked more and more, eventually borrowing money to make money. Like any gambler, he thought Fortune smiled upon him...until she gave him the cold shoulder.

Thus began his spiral downward.

Now Sweeney and Garrity, two of London's most notorious usurers, held his vowels in their blood-stained fists. Thanks to their rates of interest, his debts had gone from large to astronomical. Now he owed them fifty thousand pounds apiece.

While some might think that a duke would be above such troubles, Rhys had discovered that his title meant nothing to cent-per-cents determined to collect. Power came from wealth, and he was penniless. His father had sold off anything that wasn't nailed down or entailed; his ancestral lands had been literally run into the ground and would take years to become profitable again —years that he didn't have.

Another duke might be able to depend on influential connections to lend a hand, but Rhys had quickly discovered the perfidy of his so-called friends. The only thing the *ton* loved more than a rising star was a falling one. Men who'd envied his popularity with the ladies were the first to cast him from their circle. One by one, doors to exclusive clubs slammed in his face.

He oughtn't have been surprised. His popularity was akin to the craze for chinoiserie: once the fad was over, the currently *à la mode* objects would be tossed into the rubbish bin. He meant no more to his acquaintances than an Oriental vase or carpet...and probably less.

Acceptance was an illusion. The truth was that he'd always been an outsider.

The only thing of value Rhys had left was the title itself, which could be bartered for a dowry. It would have to be an enormous dowry, and Rhys would have to be willing to submit to the shackles of matrimony. The memories of his parents' union made his gut clench.

The last thing he wanted was a marriage of convenience.

Desperate times called for equal measures, however, and he'd briefly courted an heiress. After the affair had ended in disaster, he'd seen the light and exercised his final option: he'd fled London.

He knew he couldn't run forever. Indeed, he'd instructed his man-of-business to keep an eye out for any suitable heiresses that might pop up. In the meantime, a new opportunity had presented itself and brought him here.

A fortnight ago, he'd received a letter informing him of Horatio's death and the inheritance awaiting him at Journey's End. Glancing around the shabby antechamber, he doubted any bequest from his eccentric uncle could cover his debts, but perhaps there would be enough to replenish the dwindling stash that was subsidizing his flit. Being a realist, he knew he couldn't avoid marriage forever, but by Jove, he would stave it off for as long as he could.

"You'll be wanting supper, I suppose?" Quince said begrudgingly.

"Later." No sense beating around the bush. "I understand my uncle left instructions for me?"

The butler sniffed. "There's a letter in the study with your name on it."

"Excellent. I know the way."

It was difficult to get lost in the small manor, which if memory served, contained a parlor, dining room, and study on the ground floor and a smattering of bedchambers on the floor above. Rhys headed to his destination, his boots thumping on the worn floorboards. The corridor to the study was lined with cabinets bursting with artifacts from Horatio's expeditions. Glazed porcelain from China stood next to burial masks from Egypt; the shelves were crammed with everything from Indian silks to shells from the Caribbean to ivory carvings from Africa.

Rhys had visited here twice before. As a child of twelve, he'd found solace and escape in Horatio's curiosities. As a man of two-and-twenty, he'd been bored by them...or, more precisely, he'd been distracted by other things.

Memories of a cinnamon-haired bar maid pervaded his loins with pleasant heat. Ah, Maggie. She'd been a comely wench with big green eyes and bigger tits topped with the sweetest cherry nipples. A hot-blooded man by nature, he'd never had an encounter as passionate as the one he'd had with her. The hunger they'd unleashed in one another had been astonishing. In fact, they'd barely reached the room of his lodgings: that first time, he'd taken her right up against the door.

He wondered idly whether she still lived in the nearby village. Even if she did, she'd probably married a farmer and had a pack of brats by now. Better to stick to his fantasy Maggie, the one who, he wasn't ashamed to admit, still fired up his bedtime imagination from time to time.

He found the study at the end of the hallway. The scent of

dust and exotic incense stirred up an uneasy mix of reminiscence and longing. He remembered the first time he'd crossed the Persian rug of his uncle's sanctum. At twelve years old, he'd been sent to spend the summer with his father's younger brother.

Standing by the mullioned windows, backlit by the sun, Horatio had seemed larger than life. He'd shared Phillip's tall, broad-shouldered Cavendish frame and aquiline features, but that was where the resemblance ended between the brothers. Rhys recalled his shock when Horatio had trod over and greeted him with a hug.

Rhys's father had never touched him. Not with affection.

Despite being brothers, Uncle Horatio and Rhys's father turned out to be as different as night and day. Horatio, who chafed at the dictates of convention, went by the less recognizable family surname of Jones, and his world had been one of adventure, exploration, and joy. For that one magical summer, he'd given Rhys a taste of happiness...before disappearing for the next ten years.

You could be counted upon for fun, Horatio, old boy. But you just couldn't be counted upon.

Rhys poured himself a glass of brandy from a dusty decanter and walked past the windows overlooking the garden. The leafy labyrinth had once been Horatio's pride. Now, in the fading autumn light, the hedgerows looked overgrown and tangled with weeds, dead leaves littering the graveled path.

Folding his long frame into Horatio's chair, Rhys surveyed the desk's cluttered surface with bittersweet fondness. The eclecticism was signature Horatio: exotic writing implements, a heart-shaped bottle of ink, and a Japanese wooden box vied for space. He dug through the items to find the letter addressed to him. He opened it, revealing Horatio's spiky penmanship.

My dear Rhys,

*If you are reading this, then I have departed upon my greatest adventure.
Having lived life to its fullest, I embark on this journey with no regret,
save one: you, my dearest nephew. I was not there for you when you
needed me most, and by the time our paths crossed again, it was too late.
The breach between us could not be healed.*

Rhys felt a pang at his uncle's acknowledgment. After that
summer at Journey's End, Rhys had returned home to a dead
mother and a one-way ticket to Eton. During his tumultuous
years at the boarding school, he'd penned dozens of letters to
Horatio: all of them had gone unanswered. When Horatio had
finally sought Rhys out again, Rhys had reached his majority and
had little use for his absentee uncle.

He read on.

*In truth, you were already too far along the path that led you to become
the man you are today. A man who has forgotten the joys of adventure
and discovery. A man who no longer marvels at the wonders around him.
A man who is deadened by cynicism, duty, and banality.*

   A man much like your father.

Rhys's jaw clenched. *Devil take you, Horatio.*

Horatio knew the state of affairs between Rhys and Phillip—
knew how much Rhys hated the bastard. Indeed, Rhys had done
everything in his power to distance himself from his sire. Whatever his father had desired him to do, he'd done the opposite.

His Grace wanted a dutiful heir whose morals were beyond
reproach?

Rhys had taken off on a Grand Tour that had lasted *years*
instead of months. He'd spent his early twenties drinking, dueling,
and bedding his way through the Continent. He'd refused to have
anything to do with his sire's rabid Toryism and politics in
general.

Moreover, Horatio had some bloody nerve casting judgment

when all *he'd* ever done was take off on one carefree lark after another. At least Rhys had tried to take on the responsibilities of the insolvent dukedom his father had left behind...even if he'd proven a miserable failure.

He forced himself to continue reading.

You're probably judging me a hypocrite, and you'd have the right of it, dear boy. Responsibility has never been my forte. I've been accountable to no one and nothing but my own conscience...which leads me to you. I haven't been the best uncle, Rhys, but it is my hope that the inheritance I leave you will, in some small way, compensate for my shortcomings....

Rhys sat up in his chair, hating his eagerness. His pounding desperation.

First off, Journey's End is yours. I'm afraid it's not worth much—if indeed you can find a buyer. But there is value in sentiment, and I hope you will keep this haven where we have shared good times.

Rhys was going to start looking for a buyer straight away. Sentiment did not pay off debts or appease cutthroats.

Now onto your true bequest.

During my travels in the Caribbean, I came upon a chest of jewels washed ashore. Emeralds, sapphires, and diamonds, jewels fit for a king. (Indeed, from the markings on the chest, I believe the intended recipient may have been Louis XIV, to fund his armies during the War of Spanish Succession.) I've had the jewels valued: they're worth over half a million pounds.

The amount was staggering. Enough to pay off Rhys's debts five times over. Heart racing, he read on because there had to be a catch...

I leave them to you, my nephew—if you can find them.

...and there it bloody was.

To wit, your inheritance is a treasure hunt. Follow the clues to find the gems. And remember this: nothing worth having in life comes easily. It is my greatest hope that, in your search for the jewels, you will also find your way.

Your loving uncle,
   Horatio

P.S. Your first clue lies in the Japanese puzzle box on the desk.

Rhys slammed the letter onto the blotter, rattling the items on the desk. To come so *close*...only to have his uncle leave him high and dry yet again. To turn his life-or-death situation into a damned game.

Did you expect someone to actually take your corner? His inner voice sneered. *If you've learned anything, it's this: the only one you can depend upon is yourself.*

God knew that was no consolation. He'd let himself down more times than he cared to count.

He curled and uncurled his fingers before snatching up the puzzle box. Grimly, he studied the smooth, lacquered sides: no visible keyhole or opening. For an instant, he was tempted to smash open the blasted thing...but a memory stopped him.

When it had come time for Rhys to leave that summer, Horatio had handed him a puzzle box just like this one. "To entertain you on your journey back to Northumberland, nephew."

"I don't want to go home," Rhys had whispered.

Secrets and shame had festered inside him, yet he hadn't known how to release them. How to purge the fear that had made his insides churn and his hands clammy.

Swallowing, he'd begged, "Let me stay with you, Uncle, *please*. I shan't be any trouble. I'll go on expeditions with you, be your apprentice—"

"You must do as your father says." Horatio had ruffled his hair. "The sole heir to a duke can't go gallivanting about. That's the prerogative of younger sons."

"I don't want to be the heir!"

"You don't have a choice in the matter."

The heretofore unknown firmness in Horatio's tone unearthed feelings Rhys had long buried.

"You don't want me. You're no different from the duke. I hate you both!" He'd shouted the words and thrown the puzzle box with all his might. It had bounced along the gravel drive, the sound of something delicate smashing inside.

"Have a care, lad," Horatio had said quietly. "Puzzle boxes cannot be solved by force. To do so will only destroy what is within."

The memory fading, Rhys stared at the object he currently held. A hammer was out of the question: the clue inside was likely fragile, easily destroyed if not accessed through the intended means. Swearing under his breath, he examined all sides of the box. He found near-seamless panels, four on each side. In order to open the blasted thing, he would have to slide those panels open in a specific sequence...out of over a thousand possible combinations.

Solve the puzzle box—or find an heiress to marry. Those are my goddamned choices.

With a frustrated growl, he tossed back the rest of his brandy and got to work.

❁   2   ❁

"*Blooming hell.*"

As soon as the words left her lips, Maggie Foley regretted them. The sound echoed off the cabinets crammed with fossils and old bones, but luckily there was no one to hear her. Unluckily, this was because Foley's Emporium of Natural Wonders was devoid of patrons, an all-too-common state of late. Even so, she knew better than to give into a bad habit.

A lady does not curse, no matter the circumstances, her late husband's voice chided her gently.

It made Maggie feel even worse. She owed everything to Paul Foley. He had given her and her daughter Gloriana his name, a comfortable life, and the greatest gift of all: respectability.

Her marriage had been one of platonic respect. A meeting of the minds rather than the flesh. That was the way Paul had wanted it, and she'd been so grateful to him that she would have accepted any terms. With his help, she'd transformed from a frowsy bar maid to a reputable matron.

Yet here she was, letting him down. Not just with the unlady-like swearing.

"Is something amiss, Maggie?" Paul's sister, Hypatia Foley, stuck her head out from the green curtain that separated the backroom from the rest of the shop.

A handsome spinster in her early forties, Hypatia had come to live with Maggie and Paul five years ago, after completing her last post as a governess. She and Maggie had become fast friends. Patty shared her brother's slender frame and narrow face. Whereas Paul's gaze had been light blue and dreamy, hers was navy and shrewd behind her small gold spectacles. Silver was beginning to thread the chestnut curls beneath her frilled cap, and she had the no-nonsense air of a life-long bluestocking.

Before answering her sister-in-law, Maggie counted to ten. It was a trick Paul had taught her to curb what he called her "impulsive nature." Along with elocution and etiquette lessons, he'd instructed her on how to tame the Goode recklessness that ran in her blood...the wicked urges that had nearly led to her downfall.

The memory of her greatest mistake nudged into her thoughts; with ease borne of practice, she pushed it aside just as quickly. She was no longer that ignorant, stupid girl, susceptible to a rake's advances. Through her reformatory efforts, she'd gained control over her impulses...most of the time.

During her marriage, there'd been times when her Goode impulses became too strong. When she'd yearned for more than a chaste peck on the cheek, the polite bidding goodnight before her husband doused the lights. Over the years, she'd discovered furtive, disgraceful ways to tend to her own needs. Her wantonness shamed her, a continuing reminder that she would never be a true lady.

She shoved aside the ignominious fact and forced a smile. It came out as more of a grimace, but it was better than her initial urge. Screaming in frustration was never becoming. She smoothed out the letter she'd crumpled on the counter.

"I've received another letter from the creditors," she said.

Patty arched her brows. "How bad is it?"

A respectable lady does not indulge in an excessive display of emotion.

"It's not the best news," Maggie hedged.

Patty came over to the front counter. She'd been cleaning out the backroom, which was crammed with objects Paul had squirreled away over the years. Her purpose had been to salvage any items of value that could be sold to keep the shop afloat. If the rusty sword and skull (*Monkey?* Maggie wondered) she held were any indication, Foley's Emporium was sunk.

Patty set the objects down on the counter with a clunk. "Have they given you a deadline?"

Maggie chewed on her lip. "I have until the end of the month to settle the debts."

Debts she hadn't even known existed until she'd received a visit from a creditor after Paul's death. Unbeknownst to her, Paul had leveraged Foley's in order to invest in a mining scheme. The scheme had come to naught, and now she had to pay five hundred pounds or she would lose the shop. Her sole means of supporting herself and her family.

She tried to calm the flutter of panic.

"My brother didn't exactly leave his affairs in order, did he?" Patty muttered.

Maggie secretly agreed...and felt a stab of guilt. How could she be so disloyal? If it hadn't been for Paul's kindness, she would have wound up an unwed mother with a bastard child. He'd saved her from disgrace, given her a life better than any she could have imagined. She was Mrs. Hippolytus Foley, the widow of a gentleman, and her daughter Glory was a bright, educated girl.

Maggie owed all of that to her husband. She *had* to make a success of Foley's Emporium, which had been his dream and life's work. Not to mention the source of her family's livelihood.

"We'll make it work somehow," she said resolutely.

"The motto of women since the beginning of time." Patty's tone was dry. "We'd have a better go of it if that blighter Bill

Bancroft wasn't poaching our customers. Worse than a thief in the night, he is."

Maggie agreed with Patty's assessment. The owner of a competing business, Bancroft had tried to buy Foley's Emporium before Paul's body had even grown cold. When Maggie had refused the paltry offer, Bancroft had proceeded on a campaign to put Maggie out of business. He'd spread rumors that, without Paul at the helm, Foley's would no longer be able to carry out the fossil finding expeditions for which it was known.

This was rubbish, of course. Given Paul's progressive ailment, he hadn't been able to explore the caves for years. Instead, he'd taught Maggie the tricks of the trade, and she'd been the one who'd done the fossil hunting, the one who'd discovered the complete plesiosaurus skeleton that had brought Foley's to the attention of avid aristocratic collectors.

She had given the credit to her husband, but Bancroft knew the truth for he'd seen her exploring the caves on her own. Yet he continued to spread the lies. Because Maggie was a woman, the patrons believed him. They'd begun to jump ship like panicked rats, taking their money with them.

May that bastard Bancroft rot in hell.

Drat...that was her second blasphemy. And in less than ten minutes.

She composed herself by fiddling with the bouquet on the counter. For years, she'd livened up the shop with her arrangements. Her small, cheery bouquets were made up of blooms she'd picked from her garden or foraged from the wild, as Paul had deemed buying flowers a needless expense.

Since his death, she hadn't had time to tend to her garden. Nonetheless, she'd managed to find some silky yellow gorse, winter honeysuckle, and fragrant sprigs of pink wood calamint in the fields by her cottage. She'd added some fresh foliage and wound an old ribbon around the plain glass jar that served as a vase.

It was a small thing, but the simple beauty of the bouquet calmed her.

"Once our patrons realize that Bancroft doesn't know a fossil from a farthing, they'll come back," she said. "And we haven't lost all of our clients. Don't forget that our most valued one is due to pay a visit next week."

"If only I *could* forget." Hypatia sighed. "Of all the clients that had to stay on board, why did it have to be that cheeseparer?"

"Mr. Pickering-Parks is a favored patron of this establishment," Maggie said primly.

"Seeing as he's our *only* remaining patron, I suppose that's no lie."

The bell over the door jingled. Maggie's business-woman's heart beat faster. A *customer*.

She turned, a welcoming smile pinned on her face…and barely suppressed a groan when she saw her sister sauntering toward her. Merciful heavens, a visit from Delilah was the *last* thing she needed. Especially with Patty present. Her sister and sister-in-law were mortal enemies.

"So 'ere's where you be 'iding, Maggie." Dressed in a low-cut sateen frock more suited to a lightskirt than the widow of a successful fishmonger, Delilah smirked at Hypatia. "Oh, 'ello Hypatia. Didn't notice you standing next to 'em old bones. You blend in so well."

"And you stick out like a sore thumb." Patty sniffed the air. "I say, does something—or someone—smell fishy around here?"

Delilah growled.

Maggie's temples began to throb. "I haven't been hiding, Delilah. I've been working."

Delilah turned back to Maggie. In some ways, it was like looking in the mirror for her older sister was the same height and shared her reddish-brown hair and green eyes. Yet Delilah's face was harder, distinctive lines fanning from her eyes and bracketing her mouth. Ever since Maggie could recall, Delilah had been peeved about something...and that something was somehow always Maggie's fault.

"Not on your looks, that's for certain." Delilah's lips curled with disdain. "Why are you still wearing those widow's weeds? Your husband cocked 'is toes afore mine did, and oi been out o' mourning for months."

It was true that Maggie could have transitioned out of mourning. The reason she continued to wear black was more economic than sentimental: when Paul died, she'd saved money by dying her old dresses black instead of buying new ones. Now she had no lighter colors to wear.

Since she didn't think her sister actually cared about the state of her wardrobe, she asked, "Is there something I can do for you?"

Eyes narrowing, Delilah snapped, "You can clean up your mess is what you can do."

"What mess?" Maggie asked with a sigh.

"Our brothers, Jeremy, Jacob, and Jimmy, that's what. They've been sniffing at my 'eels for 'andouts e'er since you cut 'em off."

The rare point of contention in Maggie's marriage had been her family. Paul disapproved of the Goodes and refused to interact with them. Yet Maggie couldn't cut herself off from her own kin; what little pin money she could save, she'd given to her brothers, who were forever short of the ready. Since Paul's death and the revelation of her own debts, however, she'd had nothing extra to give.

"I told you giving your brothers money was a mistake," Patty muttered.

Like Paul, she disapproved of Maggie having anything to do with the Goodes.

The throbbing at Maggie's temples increased. "Patty, would you mind giving my sister and me a moment alone?"

"Yes. This be *family* business," Delilah said cattily.

With a huff, Patty strode into the backroom. Maggie would

have to smooth her sister-in-law's ruffled feathers later. *I'll deal with one crisis at a time.*

"I didn't cut our brothers off," she said. "I simply have no money to give them. The shop...it hasn't been doing well, Delilah."

"Well, serves you right. Thought you were so much be'er than the rest o' us marrying that snobbish bone collector. Should've married a real man like my Wilson; he might 'ave spent his life knee-deep in fish, but he brought in the blunt, 'e did."

Indeed, Maggie knew that Wilson had left Delilah with a comfortable living and a large house in town. "If that's the case, why don't you help our brothers?"

The instant the words came out, she regretted them.

Delilah's face turned scarlet. "Why should oi share what's mine? Unlike those worthless gits, oi worked 'ard for my life."

By working hard, Delilah meant on her back and with all and sundry...but Maggie kept that uncharitable thought to herself.

"Then don't help them," she said. "But don't blame me if I cannot."

"O' course oi be blaming you," her sister shot back. "Think you're be'er than the rest o' us, with your fancy speech and fancy life. You ain't e'er done a real day's work in your life."

The unfairness of the accusation tore through Maggie's restraint.

"I've been working since I was *thirteen*. I helped our mother with the dockside wash when she was alive. After she died, I tried to support the family by working at the butcher's—but *you* got me sacked by having an affair with him!"

Chest heaving, Maggie could still recall her shame when the butcher's wife had screamed at her, calling her the sister of a harlot. She'd found herself tossed out the door—with no references, either.

"Can oi 'elp it if old 'Arper wanted a bit o' a tickle? 'E wasn't getting any married to that old prune." Delilah slapped a hand on her hip. "We can't all be perfect angels like you."

If only you knew how imperfect I've been, Maggie thought wearily. *I'm the last one who deserves to judge anyone else.*

Her temper fizzling, she said, "Let's not argue any more. If our brothers pester you, tell them to find me. I'll talk to them and do what I can."

"You'd love that, wouldn't you? Showing me up once again. Saint Margaret to the rescue."

With that parting shot, Delilah flounced out of the shop, knocking over a basket of fossils on the way.

Exhaling, Maggie went over to clean up the mess. She knelt, picking up the spiral-shaped fossils that she and Glory had gathered on the nearby coast of Charmouth. The fossils made excellent commemorative gifts and sold well to tourists.

If only someone would come into the store and buy some...

The bell jingled again. She looked up hopefully.

Her heart plummeted when she saw Mr. Snelling, the village schoolmaster, marching purposefully toward her. Since Maggie and her siblings had been taught by Mr. Snelling (or "Old Smelly," as Jeremy had dubbed him), she was well acquainted with the wrathful look on his moon-shaped face. He'd never liked any of the Goodes, whom he labelled as troublemakers: unfortunately, he'd cast Glory in that category as well.

Rising, Maggie noticed absently that he looked a bit different today. His head seemed larger than usual in proportion to his small, stout body.

"Good day, Mr. Snelling," she said, feigning a smile. "How can I help you?"

"It's about Glory," he said sternly.

Uh oh. "Has she, um, done something wrong?"

"The questioning of facts, the constant fidgeting, the fighting with the other children." His voice shook with anger. "And that is only scratching the surface."

Maggie had heard all these complaints before. "I apologize, Mr. Snelling, but you know it has been a difficult time for Glory since her papa's death—"

"Yes, I understand. But this time the girl has gone too far," the schoolmaster thundered.

"What are my niece's supposed offenses, sir?"

This came from Hypatia, who had emerged from the back-room to join them. A former governess, she had strong views on the education of children and described Mr. Snelling's methods as "backward." As she'd explained to Maggie, Glory was an uncommonly bright child, who became bored when not challenged. And boredom led to mischief.

When Paul had been alive, Hypatia had generously taken over Glory's education, but since his death, she'd been needed at the shop. Glory had had to return to the village school. The transition had not gone well.

"Glory challenged my authority." Mr. Snelling bristled. "I was teaching a lesson on divine creation, and she had the temerity to interrupt. To argue that creatures were not created as God intended but had *transmuted* over time to adapt to their environments. Only the whispers of the devil could cause such blasphemy to leave a child's lips!"

"Or Jean Baptiste Lamarck," Hypatia said coolly.

"Who?" Snelling demanded.

"The French naturalist. Author of *Philosophie Zoologique*. I introduced Glory to several of his interesting hypotheses."

"That explains it," Snelling snapped. "He's worse than the devil—he's French."

Patty looked at Maggie, her eyes aiming heavenward. "Given that Glory and I were examining the fossils she'd collected, it seemed only right to discuss Lamarck's theories."

"I understand." Facing Mr. Snelling, Maggie said, "I apologize if Glory offended you, sir. She can be a spirited child, it's true, but I assure you she meant no harm—"

"Meant no harm?" the schoolmaster yelled. "The damned brat stole my *wig*."

The realization struck Maggie. *That* was why Snelling looked different: the patch of hair on the top of his head was gone. A horrified giggle rose in her throat.

She slapped her hand over her mouth just in time. Hopefully, she looked appalled rather than on the edge of laughter. "I-I'm so s-sorry..."

"After class, I kept her sitting in the corner with the dunce cap," he said through his teeth. "She was supposed to be contemplating her sins. I may have nodded off at my desk for a moment; when I came to, she—and my wig—had vanished."

"*Dunce cap?*" Hypatia said, outraged. "Of all the antiquated, detrimental—"

"We will find your wig, Mr. Snelling." Maggie cut off her sister-in-law. As much as she disagreed with Snelling's methods, provoking the village's one and only schoolmaster would do Glory no good. "It will be returned to you first thing in the morning and with Glory's apologies."

"It had better. Or your daughter will have to find herself a new school." He stormed off, the door slamming behind him.

Maggie rubbed her hands over her face. "Don't say it, Hypatia. It doesn't matter if he's an idiot, and Glory's right. She still can't go insulting people and stealing their wigs."

"I was going to offer to look for her," Patty said somberly. "I doubt she's coming here after that incident."

"I know where she's gone," Maggie said.

It was where Glory always went.

"The cliffs," Patty agreed. "I'll come with you."

"Someone has to stay and mind the shop."

"To keep out the hordes?" Patty gestured to the empty room. "Thus far, the only visitors we've had are your sister and Snelling. One shudders to think who might show up next."

Patty had a point. Moreover, Maggie knew that reining her

daughter in would be no easy task. For Glory was as headstrong as she was clever, and since Paul's death, she'd been running amok.

Onto the next crisis.

"I could use the reinforcements," Maggie said gratefully. "Let's go."

3

"Damn and blast, Horatio. Is this really necessary?"

Rhys's words echoed off the rocky walls. His lantern flickered, the darkness of the cavern closing in even more. At high tide, the place would be flooded with seawater, and he hastened his steps.

Briny, humid air plugged his nostrils as he made his way through the winding passage. Unbidden memories swamped him: the water closet in Eton, the suffocating panic of being locked in the stinking blackness by laughing bullies. The concealing darkness of the wardrobe, the frozen panic of witnessing his sire's rage and his mama's sobbing despair...

To this day, he did not like enclosed spaces. He wondered if his uncle was aware of that fact. If this was yet another test to see if he was worthy of the supposed fortune Horatio had left him.

Could have spared you the trouble, old boy, he thought grimly. *I already know I'm a failure through and through.*

Nonetheless, he forged on. It had taken him two days—and a goodly amount of brandy—to crack open the Japanese puzzle box. Inside, he'd found a piece of paper-thin porcelain that would have indeed been smashed to smithereens had he chosen to break open the box with a hammer.

The next clue had been painted upon the fragment:

At the heart of Journey's End.

Recalling that Horatio had called these seaside cliffs the "heart" of his estate, Rhys had made his way down to the pebble-strewn shore. He'd spent yesterday exploring the golden sandstone structures until he'd found the hidden cavern he was presently sweating in.

"Some heart. More like the damned bowels, I'd say," Rhys muttered.

The darkness grew more smothering. Even with the lamp, he couldn't see more than a yard ahead of him. The passage narrowed with each step forward; his brow misted as his shoulders brushed the rock on each side. A draft came out of nowhere, a ghostly hand pinching out the lantern's flame.

Holy hell. He fumbled in his pocket for the tinderbox. As he did so, his shoulders lodged against the rocky walls. He cursed again, struggling to get free, finding himself wedged in the stony vice. He forced himself to calm. To think over the thudding panic. Twisting his torso clockwise, he felt a little give. He continued turning, little by little...until he could wrench himself free.

Jewels or no jewels, he wasn't perishing in this rocky grave.

He stumbled back the way he'd come. It seemed to take a lifetime until the sunlight hit his face. He staggered onto the beach, bracing his hands on his thighs, gulping in the fresh sea air.

"You look like you've seen a ghost!"

The child-like accents stirred the hairs on his nape. Turning, he saw a girl standing several feet away, staring at him with undisguised curiosity. Skinny and freckled, she looked about eight or nine. She wore no bonnet, her auburn plaits swinging as she skipped toward him, a basket in one hand. The hem of her serviceable frock was splattered with dirt and sand.

"Were you in the cave?" she asked.

"Er, yes," he heard himself say.

Her eyes were golden-green and thickly fringed. They studied him from an otherwise plain little face. "You were scared, weren't you?"

He stiffened. "I most assuredly was not."

"You were," she said cheerfully. "I can tell. I'm an excellent judge of people."

Was the impudent chit accusing him of lying? Of lacking *courage?*

Scowling, he said, "Now see here—"

"*I'm* not scared of the cave," she said—or boasted, rather. "I go in there all the time. I'm not afraid of the dark or anything else. Mama says I'm fearless."

Mannerless, more the like, he thought darkly.

He took further stock of the chit. Her dress was worn but decently made, and her accents had the clear, precise ring of education. Shabby gentility, he concluded. The daughter of a clergyman, perhaps.

Whoever the father was, he'd do well to take the hoyden in hand.

Rhys said in his most ducal voice, "You are trespassing on private property."

"Papa had the permission of the previous owner to explore the cliffs whenever he wanted. Papa is a famous fossils scholar—or was, rather." Her gaze lowered to her sandy half-boots. "He died."

Rhys's annoyance faded. Now he felt like a perfect boor.

He cast about for the right thing to say. He made it a habit to avoid children and pets; both fell under the category of "Messy and Inconvenient." For an instant, a memory surfaced of his childhood pet—he shut it out. No use thinking about the past.

At any rate, he was a fastidious man and didn't care for dirt and disorder. Children, in particular, could be sticky...like a half-eaten sweet clinging to the sole of one's boot.

He'd never understood the appeal of fatherhood; certainly, he had no desire to be the kind of father his own had been. As he did like the act of procreation, however, he'd learned to take the necessary precautions. The bar maid, Maggie—strange, that he should think of her twice in a short span—had been a notable omission...a fact he chalked up to their mutual impatience.

Donning a sheath had been the last thing on his mind while he'd screwed her up against the door. Luckily, they'd only spent the one night together. Anyway, the experienced women he'd known had had their own prophylactic remedies.

Looking at the downcast head before him, he realized that he should say something.

"My deepest condolences," he said. "I'm sure the loss must be...difficult."

The girl's head swung up. "How do you know? Have you lost a father?"

Confronted by those perceptive eyes, he found himself answering, "Both parents, actually."

"How old were you when your papa passed?"

"Six-and-twenty."

"I'm eight-and-a-quarter." Her head tipped to one side. "Do you miss him very much?"

He hesitated. No one had directly asked him that question before. "Not so very much."

Her eyes widened. "Why not?"

"He and I...did not always get on."

An understatement, to be sure. Phillip Cavendish had hated his heir and only child, the possible reasons for this being many and varied. It could have been because Phillip had been forced to marry Yu-Yan, Rhys's mother, after Yu-Yan's father had saved his life. Or because, as a child, Rhys had more resembled his Chinese mother, being small and slight—a "weak mongrel" in his father's eyes.

Or Phillip's hatred of his own child could have simply been due to the fact that he was a cruel, bitter bastard who'd never cared about anyone but himself.

"Were you a bad boy?" the girl asked gravely.

You're a taint on the Ranelagh and Somerville line. A disgrace. You'll never amount to anything.

Rhys smiled humorlessly. "My sire seemed to think so."

"It isn't easy being good all the time." Her tone was knowing. "I try, but it's much more fun being bad, isn't it?"

He couldn't disagree with that. Although he probably should in the presence of a tot.

He settled for, "Regrettably so."

"The truth is, I did something very bad."

He doubted it. He wasn't good at much, but he was an expert on behaving badly.

"Can you keep a secret?" she went on.

"Probably not."

"I stole the schoolmaster's wig." She confided in him anyway. "But he's an idiot. He doesn't even know about Lamarck's theory of transmutation."

"Well, then. He must be an idiot," Rhys said.

He'd never heard about Lamarck's theories; God willing, he never would. He'd always been more athletic than academic. He enjoyed boxing, riding, and other gentlemanly sports.

She nodded, her face blazing with indignation. "And he wanted *me* to wear the dunce cap!"

Being no stranger to dunce caps and idiots, Rhys felt a tug of commiseration. "I'm afraid you'll discover that the percentage of those with bacon for brains in the world far outweigh those with functioning intellects."

She looked at him...and giggled. "You're funny."

"I endeavor to amuse. Now if you'll excuse me—"

"I have to go too. I have to get into the caves before the tides rise."

He stared at her. "Surely you're not planning on going into the caves alone?"

"I am. I'm a fossil collector." She flipped open the lid of her basket to show him the contents. He saw an assortment of stones in unusual shapes and colors. "I just found these ammonites and bezoar stones. They'll fetch several shillings a piece at our shop."

Curiouser and curiouser. "Your family owns a shop?"

Her thin chest puffed out. "Foley's is one of the most famous fossil shops in Dorset. Well, next to Mrs. Anning's. Her shop is more famous, but ours delivers a better value." She sounded like a newspaper advertisement. "Gentlemen, some of them *lords*, travel from London to buy our goods. The very rich ones hire Father to go on expeditions to find fossils for them..." Her face fell. "Or at least they did until he died."

The kernel of a plan that had begun to sprout in Rhys's head came to an abrupt halt. Right. The father was dead, which meant that Rhys couldn't make use of the man's cave-exploring abilities. Too bad. But maybe there were other locals whose skills Rhys could employ for such a purpose. Yes, that was the ticket. Why undertake something unpleasant when one could hire someone else to do it?

"I'm not supposed to know the shop is in trouble, but I overhear things. Aunt Patty says little pitchers have big ears. But don't big pitchers also have big ears? I've never understood the saying. Anyway," she chirped on, "Mama is going to save the shop. And I'm going to help her."

"Indeed." Rhys was only half-listening, his mind brewing a plan. "By the by, would you know the names of other reputable fossil hunters in the vicinity?"

"Mrs. Anning in Lyme Regis is the most famous." She paused, her gaze shrewd. "But my mama, Margaret Foley, is just as skilled. And she charges a better price."

"You're recommending female fossil hunters?"

"*I* am a female, and I find fossils." She pointed emphatically at her basket.

"Right." Rhys didn't bother to hide his skepticism.

The girl huffed out a breath. Then she tossed her basket onto

the sand. In the next instant, she dashed toward the nearest cliff...
and began to *climb* it. Her agility was as astonishing as it was terrifying. He got over the shock and ran over.

"Get down this instant," he shouted—yes, *shouted*, for the chit
was halfway up the rocky wall already, so high up that he couldn't
be sure she heard him. Devil take it, if she fell...

She reversed direction and descended. Ignoring his
outstretched arms, she jumped down, landing nimbly in the sand.

"What were you thinking?" he bit out over his thundering
heart. "You could have broken your neck—"

"Only if I *fell*," she said, smug as you please, "which I never do
because I'm an excellent climber. Billy Pinkleton—he's ten—challenged me to a tree climbing contest, and I bested him. He wasn't
too happy about it." A flicker passed through her eyes, before she
lifted her chin again. "Anyway, what do I care what Billy Pinkleton
thinks? He has bacon for brains, just like you said. I showed him
that girls can climb as well as boys. Mama says women might be
smaller than men, but we're more flexible and agile. Which makes
us perfectly suited to fossil hunting."

Rhys continued to glower at her...although he had to admit
that she had a point. Women *were* smaller and more flexible, and
given that Horatio could have hidden the second clue anywhere in
the cave, those qualities could come in handy. And if the mother's
acrobatic skills were anywhere near the daughter's...

"Where can I find this mother of yours?" he asked.

The girl's glance slid over him again. He could practically hear
coins tipping onto a scale as she took the measure of his Bond
Street garments. He found himself reluctantly amused by her
clearly conniving mind. Like recognized like, after all.

"Because Mama is sought after," she said, tapping her chin,
"she is *terribly* busy. But since I am introducing you, I am sure
she'd be willing to take you on an expedition for a discounted
price. Say, one hundred pounds?"

He had to give her points for her brazenness. Before he'd

gone on the run, he'd sold off the remainder of his personal possessions and had a thousand pounds left in his stash. He'd planned to live off that money for as long as he could. The fact that he was worried about spending a hundred of it—a paltry sum that, in the past, he'd lost on a hand of cards without blinking—was galling.

If you find the jewels, you'll be living like a king. Who gives a damn about a mere hundred quid? This Mrs. Foley could be worth her weight in gold.

He pictured an older version of the girl. Lean and tough, a plain, masculine woman with a no-nonsense air about her. One who'd have no qualms entering a cave to fetch him the next clue.

"You have a deal," he said.

The girl's breath came out in a whoosh. He blinked as her smile transformed her skinny little face, showing the unexpected promise of beauty. A pair of rather charming dimples peeped out.

She beamed. "You won't regret it, sir!"

"I'd better not," he muttered. "Now where can I find Mrs. Foley?"

"You can find her right here." The girl pointed to a pair of women marching toward her, their cloaks and black skirts whipping in the ocean breeze. "Here she comes!"

"Gloriana Foley, I want to speak to you!"

At the pleasantly husky female voice, Rhys's blood quickened. There was something oddly familiar about those cultured tones. He gazed intently on the approaching pair, one tall and narrow, the other shorter and curvier, both of their faces hidden by their bonnets.

"I'm going to get it now," the girl—Gloriana, apparently —muttered.

"Chin up," he advised. "And let me do the talking."

As the women neared, he summoned his most debonair smile, the one that never failed to make a lady's fan (and other parts, he'd been told) flutter. Mrs. Foley might be a hardy, pickaxe-wielding cave explorer, but she was still a female, and it never hurt to pour on the charm.

"Good afternoon, madam..." He trailed off as recognition slammed into him.

Cinnamon curls peeped beneath the bonnet's black brim. Tip-tilted emerald eyes stared at him. And below...his gaze locked on a pair of breasts, which possessed an exquisite roundness even a shapeless cloak couldn't conceal. They surged upward as if in invitation, and heat shot into his groin, his body reacting before his mind could piece together words.

"Maggie?" he asked stupidly. "What are you doing here?"

$$\maltese \quad 4 \quad \maltese$$

Maggie's heart knocked against her rib cage.

Blooming hell...it can't be...

The brilliant leonine eyes that had haunted her dreams and nightmares stared at her now. The years had not diminished Rhys Jones's looks, she saw numbly. Indeed, his boyish perfection had been honed into the potency of a man in his prime.

His face was leaner, with hollows that highlighted his sculpted cheekbones and golden skin. His thick brown-black hair was still worn a bit long, and her fingers tingled with the memory of those liquid-silk waves slipping between them. He now sported a mustache and trimmed scruff on his jaw. The dashing ring of hair emphasized the sensual shape of his mouth and made him look more piratical than ever.

His physique was tougher, more muscular than she recalled. The breadth of his shoulders strained his tobacco frockcoat, the sinewy line of his long legs extending into tall, polished boots.

He was still the most beautiful man she'd ever seen. The devil in disguise.

"Do you know my mama?"

At her daughter's innocent inquiry, the present came crashing back like the waves against the shore. An undertow of emotions sucked her under: bewilderment, yearning, mortification. She struggled to breathe, frantic thoughts dashing against her skull.

Dear heavens...Glory. Must protect her. Can't let him find out.

Rhys was still looking at her, only now his dark brows were drawn. His gaze traveled between her and Glory. The golden hazel eyes flickered...with speculation?

Fear cleared her head. Reminded her exactly who he was and who she was—or had been, rather.

Shame thumping in her breast, she told herself that she was no longer that foolish wench. A girl who'd been so dazzled by a handsome gentleman that she'd given up her virginity with no thought to the consequences. Who'd proven that she was a trollop, a Goode through and through. Who'd woken the next morning to find herself in the room of an inn, alone...

With a fifty-pound note left on the table. For services rendered.

The memory of the humiliation centered her. She had no one to blame but herself for the choices she'd made. Yet she'd paid the price in full, and now she'd made a life for herself, one of gentility, and she'd stop at nothing to protect Glory from her past mistakes.

Seeing her daughter's expectant look (and Patty's curious one), Maggie knew she had to manage the situation. She put a cork in her emotions and schooled her expression.

"I believe the gentleman once visited the shop," she said in her most professional tone. "Mister...Johnson, was it?"

"It's Jones." His face was inscrutable. "Rhys Jones."

"If you've been to Foley's," Glory said to him, her brow furrowed, "why didn't you mention it earlier?"

Maggie's breath held, but he said, "It was several years ago and slipped my mind."

Thank God the man was a good liar. Then again, she oughtn't to be surprised. A rake like him must have ample experience with running into women who'd shared his bed. Who knew how many wild oats he'd sown up and down the English coast?

You were stupid enough to be one more notch on his bedpost.

The self-disgust that constricted her insides was tighter than any corset. "I do apologize, sir," she said brusquely, "but I have patrons waiting in the shop. Come, Gloriana—"

"Wait, Mama," Glory burst out. "Mr. Jones *is* a patron. He wants to hire us. And he's promised to pay us *one hundred pounds* to find fossils for him. Didn't you, sir?"

He bowed. "You drive a hard bargain, Miss Foley."

"That will help the shop, won't it, Mama?" Glory said.

Maggie's throat cinched at her child's triumphant smile. Surely God would not be so cruel.

All she wanted was to give her daughter a childhood with the things her own had lacked: respectability and security. Thanks to Paul, she'd succeeded in giving Glory a good name and a life of decency. After his death, she'd tried to hide the financial woes, wanting to protect her girl from adult worries. Apparently, she'd done a shoddy job of it if Glory knew that the shop needed saving —and had had the wherewithal to bargain for a one-hundred-pound fee.

Dumbfounded, she watched as her daughter beamed at Rhys Jones. The man who'd seen Maggie as no more than a whore, who'd bedded her and left her...with a bastard.

As panic thrummed in Maggie's breast, she told herself that, save for the color of their eyes, Glory and Rhys didn't look much alike. No one would suspect the disgraceful truth—which she planned to take to her grave. Although she'd told Paul about the circumstances that had led to her pregnancy, she'd never told her husband the identity of her lover. Being a true gentleman, Paul had never pressed her for a name. And when she'd given birth to Glory, she'd been relieved that the girl had taken after her...mostly.

Seeing the bold gleam of gold in her daughter's green eyes had, at times, unnerved her. Luckily, with her own eyes being green, nothing had seemed untoward. No one had ever questioned that Gloriana was Paul's child—and she had been, in the ways that mattered.

I won't let anyone take that away from her, Maggie vowed fiercely. *Or from Paul.*

Even if Rhys suspected that Glory was his, he likely wouldn't give a damn. A rake like him probably had by-blows littered across the countryside.

"Is this true, sir?" Hypatia's hopeful inquiry refocused Maggie's attention. "You wish to retain the services of Foley's?"

"Miss Foley, here, has been extoling the virtues of your business," Rhys said.

He oozed charm. The dimples that had led to Maggie's downfall were in full display. But more than his good looks, it was his manner: even on a windy beach, with sand upon his boots, he was confident and charismatic, lord of all he surveyed.

Once, Maggie had found his princely manner irresistible; now it aggravated her.

"And whom do I have the pleasure of addressing?" he asked.

"Dear me, where have my manners gone?" Sounding flustered, Patty said, "I am Miss Hypatia Foley. Mrs. Foley was married to my brother."

"*Enchanté*, ma'am."

Patty blushed like a debutante.

Nip this in the bud. You must protect Glory, get her away from that man—now.

"I'm afraid our services are not available at present," Maggie said brusquely. "Autumn is our busy season. You'll have to find someone else."

Rhys's dark brows inched upward.

"I was told that you are the premier fossil hunter in the district." His relaxed tone did not fool her; his power was not a blunt instrument but a subtly honed scalpel. "I wish to hire the best for the project I have in mind."

"And we are not too busy, Mama," Glory said, sounding puzzled. "I heard you telling Aunt Patty that we need more customers. And I've found us a perfectly good one—"

"I'll not work for the likes of him."

She immediately regretted her rash words. Rhys's jaw clenched, and she fought to regain the composure she'd worked on for years. Why did this man's mere presence make her feel once again like a wanton, ignorant bar maid—a dashed *No Goode*?

Hypatia gave a discreet cough. "I am certain what Mrs. Foley means to say is that we would welcome the patronage of a fine gentleman such as yourself." Her elbow connected not-so-discreetly with Maggie's ribs. "Isn't that true, Margaret?"

Maggie's mind raced through possible excuses to turn down Rhys Jones without rousing further suspicion. To swerve away from the disaster that was approaching head-on like a runaway carriage.

"Generally, yes," she said, thinking quickly. "In this case, however, I have promised my services to another client. He is arriving this week, in point of fact."

"You cannot mean Mr. Pickering-Parks," Patty said under her breath. "He is far from a sure thing, and he never spends more than fifty pounds tops. Every cent of which he'll quibble over. You'll have plenty of time to help Mr. Jones."

Blooming hell.

Desperately, Maggie said, "I must be selective in who I choose to take on—"

"I begin to see the problem," Rhys said.

She did not like his mocking drawl. Nor the dangerous glint in his eyes.

Warily, she said, "I'm glad. Then we will be on our way—"

"How much?"

She blinked at him. "I beg your pardon?"

"How much blunt will it require to...engage your services?"

His unsubtle innuendo shredded the last vestiges of her self-control. *How dare that bastard bring up the past—humiliate me once more?*

She lifted her chin. "Nothing *you* can afford, sir."

"Try me." Irritation edged his tone.

"Really, Margaret—" Hypatia began.

She held up a hand to cut the other off. "Contrary to what some may believe, money does not buy everything. I own a respectable business, and I will only work with *respectable* gentlemen. Good day to you, sir."

She knew she'd gone too far when hellfire blazed in Rhys's eyes. A muscle leapt in his jaw. He vibrated with barely leashed power, like a stallion at the starting gate.

She marched past him and took hold of her daughter's hand. "We are leaving, Glory."

"But Mama—"

"*Now,*" she said severely. "For once, you will do as you're told."

Glory's bottom lip poked out. Her expression went from bewildered to sullen.

Maggie would deal with hurt feelings later. She herded her daughter down the beach, Hypatia following in their wake. She was all too aware that Rhys Jones remained unmoving behind them.

A thrill of fear shot up her spine, her heart thudding with unwelcome knowledge.

I may have won this skirmish...but the battle has only begun.

❦ 5 ❦

Two nights later, Maggie paused before the door of the Flag and Mast's finest suite. She looked this way and that. She'd worn a hooded cloak to conceal her identity, but there was no one to see her in the shadowed corridor, and no one had seen her climb the back steps to this private wing of the inn.

Memories of her shameful exit down those wooden steps nearly a decade ago flooded her.

Buck up, and do what you came to do.

Still, she hesitated. Had been hesitating ever since she'd received the imperious summons this morning. Scrawled in a bold, masculine hand, the note had been short and to the point:

I'll be waiting for you where we had our last meeting. Midnight. Don't be late.

She'd been strongly tempted not to come. To ignore Rhys Jones's command. But knowing him, he wouldn't leave her be until he'd had his say, and she didn't want to risk another public encounter with him. Tonight, she would make it clear in no uncertain terms that she wanted nothing to do with him. That this meeting would be their last.

Raising her fist, she knocked on the door before she lost her nerve.

Her heartbeat measured out the moments before the door opened. Rhys filled the doorway. He was in his shirtsleeves, his silk cravat tied in a loose knot that had probably taken his valet hours to perfect. His forest green waistcoat, which had a subtle paisley design, fit like it had been sewn onto his lean torso. His trousers skimmed the long, muscular contours of his legs. She caught a whiff of his scent, a blend of sandalwood and clean male musk.

Instant, mortifying awareness quickened her blood. She kept her shoulders back, her gaze level.

He bowed and stepped aside. "I wondered if you would come."

"You left me little choice." She swept in, glad that the wobbliness of her knees didn't show. When he closed the door, she pushed off the hood of her cloak.

Ignoring her barb, he said with a charming smile, "Make yourself comfortable."

He gestured toward the sitting room, which boasted a cheerful fire and matching striped chairs, a cozy woolen rug upon the floor. A feast had been laid out upon the table, which was set with two places.

She didn't budge. "We can talk here. Whatever you wish to say shouldn't take long."

He studied her for an instant before drawling, "If memory serves, you and I didn't make it past the entryway the last time, either."

The memory scorched through her: her lips fused to his, the desperate, sizzling hunger. Everywhere he'd touched, pleasure had bloomed. His hands had framed her hips, lifting her against the door, and suddenly she'd felt his hard, thick flesh driving into her. Invading her, pushing the air from her lungs. He'd surged into her again and again, the stretching burn fading as her core liquefied with bliss...

His footsteps broke the spell of the past. He'd gone ahead to the table and was filling glasses with wine. Huffing out a breath, she followed.

He held out a glass to her.

"None for me," she said. "I must insist you state your business."

He sipped his wine before saying, "Is Gloriana mine?"

Although she'd prepared herself for this eventuality, the directness of his question took her aback. The years of refining her composure came to her rescue.

"How *dare* you, sir." She prayed the quiver in her voice would pass for indignation. "Gloriana is my husband's daughter. The child of a gentleman. For you to suggest otherwise is an insult."

He looked at her. She returned his stare. Ruddy color rose on his lean cheeks, and she didn't miss the flash of relief in his tawny hazel eyes.

"I assure you I meant no insult," he muttered and took another swallow of wine.

"The fact that you ordered me here for no reason other than to impugn my honor *is* an insult." *Keep it up. Throw him off the scent so that you can get out of here.*

"My question arose not from ill regard but from necessity, given certain facts of life." His broad shoulders hitched; the blasted man made even a shrug look elegant. "I am relieved to hear my concern was groundless."

Oh, I'm certain you are. She ought to be relieved that he was giving up so easily yet, for some reason, it irked her.

"I pray you will not mention the matter again." She used the loftiest accents that elocution lessons could buy.

"You have my word," he said with feeling.

"As a courtesy, I also ask that you refrain from *any* mention of our past association." Recalling one of Paul's many teachings, she added, "A lady's reputation is her greatest asset, you know."

She feared she may have spread the haughtiness on too thickly when Rhys arched a brow.

"Really? Because you managed to do quite well for yourself without one." His tone was wry. "Or, rather, in spite of the one earned by your family."

The familiar shame heated her cheeks. To have him comment on her lowly origins was beyond humiliating. The night they'd spent together, in between the fornicating, he'd asked about her family. About why her employer had denigrated them. He'd seemed so sincere and interested that she'd told him the truth.

She'd even divulged her goal of owning a flower shop. In the ensuing years, she'd berated herself endlessly for her naïveté. For allowing herself to be seduced by the first charming stranger to show her any attention. For giving him her virginity and the knowledge of her deepest dreams...only for him to leave the next morning without even saying goodbye.

In the end, she couldn't even fault him. He'd made no promises. She had no one to blame but herself for being dazzled by a rake; in her darkest moments, she felt like she'd deserved the payment he'd left on the table. She'd acted like a whore, after all.

Swallowing, she said, "It is ungentlemanly of you to throw my family in my face."

"I'm merely pointing out the fallacy of your assertion. Your greatest asset is not your reputation. Your strength lies in your work ethic and determination, your ability to see things through."

She blinked at him, unsure what he meant. Was he paying her a *compliment*?

"Trust me, as a man who lacks work ethic and any useful abilities," he drawled, "I have a great respect for them in others."

He can't be serious about his lack of abilities. Is he making fun of me? Does he think I'm still a witless tavern wench, too stupid to understand his jokes?

"In the past two days, I've had the chance to ask around about you," he went on.

Her shoulders stiffened. "You had *no* right—"

"Settle your feathers, Maggie," he said easily. "My interest was professional, not personal."

"You may address me as Mrs. Foley." *When in doubt, revert to proper comportment.* "I don't wish to be of interest to you in any capacity."

"And I don't wish to have to shave twice a day. We can't always have what we want."

Catching the brief quiver of his lips, she narrowed her eyes at him. His expression was smooth as honey. But the glint in those hazel eyes...was the cad *laughing* at her?

"Now, Mrs. Foley," he said, "I have a proposition for you."

Her temper flared. The *nerve.* "You can take your proposition and stick it—"

"A *business* proposition," he said. "I'm willing to pay to have a cave explored, and you're a cave explorer who needs money. A match made in heaven."

"I said it before, and I'll say it again. I ain't..."—anger wreaked havoc on her speech, and she caught herself in the nick of time —"...I *will not* work for the likes of you."

"What is 'the likes of me', exactly? Truly, I am curious." Plucking an almond from the nut dish, he popped it into his mouth, as if he had no bloody concerns in the world.

"You're a rake," she said flatly. "You have no principles. All you care about is your own amusement."

He studied her, his gaze unreadable. "Well, I'll grant you two of the three. I do seek out amusements because boredom is tedious. And if enjoying life's pleasures makes me a rake, then so be it. But I must disagree on the matter of principles. I live by them. Three, in point of fact."

"Really?" she said scornfully.

He counted them off on his fingers. "Loyalty, honesty...and well, I've forgotten the third, but it'll come to mind, I'm sure."

Something in his tone raised her suspicions. "Do you find this amusing?"

"I'm not bored." The corners of his mouth tugged upward.

"Why, you insufferable blighter—"

"Before you go on, I'd like to point out that it was your wish for this meeting to be brief. Pointing out the flaws in my character will take far too long and postpone getting to the business at hand."

"We have no business!"

"On that, we disagree. You have something I want, and I have something you need."

"You have nothing I need," she shot back.

"I have five hundred pounds. The amount you owe Rotherby's Bank."

She was stunned. Couldn't stop herself from gaping at him. "How do you know that?"

"I also know that your dead husband used your shop as collateral," he said, not answering her question. "That you have until the end of the month to pay off your debt or Foley's Emporium belongs to the bank."

"You...you can't...this is an invasion of privacy!" she sputtered.

"I consider it research." He studied his nails, buffed them on his waistcoat. "The point is, we are in a position to help one another."

Despite her whirling anger, she couldn't deny the truth of his words. At least on her end. Five hundred pounds would allow her to keep Foley's, provide for her family, and preserve Paul's dream. She forced herself to take a calming breath. Then another before she trusted herself to speak.

"What would I have to do for the five hundred pounds?" she asked bluntly.

"Spoken like a true proprietress. No, don't get cross," he said, reading her well, "I meant that as a compliment. The short of it is, when my uncle Horatio Jones died, he left me an inheritance. His estate and, er, something else."

Surprise percolated through her. Horatio Jones had been a local eccentric who'd reputedly traveled the world. No one in the village knew much about him as he'd taken off for long stretches. When at home, he and his staff kept to themselves. As Paul had secured Jones's permission to explore the caves on his property, Maggie had been to the cliffs at Journey's End, but she'd never met the owner.

She didn't know that Mr. Jones had any family. And Rhys hadn't bothered to mention the connection the night they'd met. Then again, why would he share personal information with a wench he'd casually tupped?

She forced herself to concentrate. "For five hundred pounds, you want me to hunt for fossils in the caves at Journey's End? I've been in those caves, and I'm telling you there are no bones worth that sum in there."

"I'm not after bones."

"What then would you have me looking for?"

Rhys gave her a measuring look. "I need to have a fossil hunter I can trust before I answer that question. Do we have a deal?"

He extended a long-fingered hand. Her palms tingled with the memory of those hands touching every part of her. Of her touching him. Of them skin to sweat-slickened skin...

Her breathing hitched. His magnetism pulled at her, warred with her capacity for reason.

But she wasn't the same naïve fool she'd been nearly a decade ago. Back then, she could chalk up her reckless behavior to ignorance and youthful impulses; if she trusted him again, knowing what she did about him, she'd have nothing to blame but her own moral character. The weakness that ran in the Goode blood.

And while her judgement when it came to men might be lacking, her business acumen was keen: there was something shady about Rhys's proposition. Why would anyone pay five hundred pounds to have a cave explored? As tempting as the money was, she'd be signing the devil's bargain. For she'd have to work with Rhys Jones, be near him, this man who knew too much about her past...and who could expose Glory as a bastard and ruin her future.

The terrible risk tipped the scales and made up Maggie's mind.

"Look for someone else," she said.

"I have been looking." Impatience colored his voice. "Mrs. Anning is away on an expedition and unavailable. Yesterday I met with your chief competitor Bill Bancroft."

She couldn't resist the temptation of asking, "And?"

"He's an oily bastard. I wouldn't trust him farther than I could toss him."

She couldn't help but feel the tiniest bit of satisfaction at the spot-on description of Bancroft.

"While I cannot give Mr. Bancroft my vote of confidence," she said justly, "Mr. Shelley in Axmouth runs a reputable business. I wish you luck, sir."

She turned, heading for the exit. Her hand was on the knob when his planted on the door, keeping it shut. She whirled around—only to find him close.

Much too close. Her pulse throbbed against the tender skin of her throat.

"This arrangement will benefit both of us," he insisted. "Why won't you consider it?"

Her spine pressed into the door. A mistake—for her body remembered the last time it had taken this position. The hard door against her back, an even harder Rhys sandwiching her, moving inside her, pleasure bursting in his wake...

"Because I want nothing to do with you," she managed.

"You didn't use to feel that way." He was close enough for her to see the shards of green in his golden-brown irises. "I know you asked me not to bring up the past, but I feel I must. We were friends once, and I thought we parted on good terms, but I think you are angry with me."

"I'm not angry." She wouldn't give him the satisfaction of knowing that he had any power over her.

"Good, because you have no reason to be. What happened between us, it was by mutual consent. You wanted me as much as I wanted you."

If he'd spoken in anger or frustration, her defenses would have leapt to her rescue. But his honesty and directness seeped through the chinks in her armor. She might not be clever, refined, or beautiful, but there was one thing she prided herself upon.

Margaret Foley was fair.

The protective cloak of anger shed from her, leaving her shivering with shame.

"You're right," she said...because he was. "You are not to blame for what happened. You didn't force me to share your bed. I made the choice, and I have to live with it."

His hand cupped her cheek, and the gentleness of his touch made her swallow. She ought to pull away, but she couldn't. She hadn't had this sort of touch in so long. Not since the last time... here, with him. However wrong it was, his heat soothed the aching emptiness inside her. Stirred up the need that her body had never allowed her to forget.

"Sweeting, you seem to think ill of our past while I have nothing but fond memories. No 'fond' isn't the right word." His thumb stroked down her cheekbone, and God help her, her insides trembled like an aspic. "Whenever I have thought of you, and it has been more often than I'd care to admit, I have remembered your sweetness, generosity, and passion."

He thought of me...often?

His smoldering gaze seemed to penetrate her innermost recesses. To feed that hidden, dangerous flame that a marriage based on mutual interests and respect had never managed to douse. His thumb stroked along her jaw, her chin, her heart beating in her throat as he caressed the side of her neck. This was wrong, so wrong, and yet...her lips parted.

He lowered his head toward hers, and her eyes closed.

The first touch of his lips melted away reason. No pressure, just a gentle coaxing that unspooled the protective binding she'd placed around her needs. Layer after layer peeled away as the kiss deepened. The taste of him hit her like a drug after years of abstinence. She craved his flavor, that of sin and temptation.

A needful moan broke from her lips, and he soothed it away with his tongue. With each lick, each seductive nibble, she became more lost, desire diminishing her thoughts, need magnifying sensation. Her awareness became his mouth against hers, his hard, lean body pressing her into the door. She tilted her head back for more of his kiss.

His growl vibrated in her throat and then his tongue was inside her. It was like setting a match to kindling: her desire burst into flames. He thrust deep into her mouth, and she opened to him. Welcomed his deliciousness, savored it. The more she had, the more she wanted. Her hands gripped his head, the soft, thick pelt of his hair sliding between her fingers. Her breasts surged against his chest, and even with layers between them, she could feel his rock-hard contours, his unyielding masculinity.

His hands cupped her hips, urged them closer to where he was harder yet. Hard and huge. His bulging desire melted her core, humid heat trickling from her sex. Heavens, she was hot, hot everywhere, and she leaned into the fire...

"By God, you're sweet," he groaned against her lips. "Even sweeter than I remembered. I can't wait to get inside you."

His words slammed upon her consciousness like a door upon fingers. Pain jolted her. His speech was dirty, carnal, the sort a gentleman would never use with a lady he respected. When he'd bedded her years ago, he'd used similar wicked words, and she'd been aroused by them because she hadn't known any better. But now she did.

How he talks shows what he thinks of you. You're just a harlot to him. A trollop.

Horrified awareness shot through her: she was pressed up against the door, draped like a ha'penny whore over Rhys Jones... the man who'd made a whore of her before. Who'd nearly ruined her life. Who *could* ruin her daughter's life if he asked too many questions, got too close.

What the blooming hell am I doing?

Mortified, she shoved at his shoulders. "Get away from me."

"What's the matter—"

"Let me *go*." She pushed harder, and after a heartbeat, he stepped back.

His lean face had the flush of passion, but his eyes were measured. "What is happening here, Maggie? Did I do something wrong? Did I misread—"

"I am *not* some trollop for you to use at your convenience." Despite her churning shame, she kept her chin up. "I am a respectable widow, and I deserve respect."

He stared at her. Pushed his fingers through the dark waves of his hair, a gesture of infinite male frustration. "I do respect you."

"If that is true, then you will prove it by staying away from me. I don't want to see you again, Mr. Jones. Good night."

She groped for the door handle behind her. She half expected him to stop her, but he just stood there, his hands braced on his hips, his expression unreadable.

She turned the knob, pivoted quickly, and fled.

While she still could.

$\maltese$ 6 $\maltese$

IN THE HOURS BEFORE DAWN, RHYS WAS UNABLE TO SLEEP. He lay naked in bed, his hands laced behind his head, the sheets tangled at his waist. Staring into the shadowed canopy, he let his mind wander. In the twilight hours, it was easy to slip into a reality of his choosing.

In his fantasy, he and Maggie had just finished kissing. She had her back against the door. She leaned against it in a posture both shy and provocative.

"Take me, Rhys," she breathed.

She beckoned him with her kiss-swollen lips and heavy-lidded eyes. He wanted to kiss her again, to partake of that feminine flavor that was hers and hers alone, but he wanted something more. He reached for the pins that confined her hair, plucking them out one by one. He was rewarded by the cascade of cinnamon waves, the scented strands slipping like silk through his fingers.

She smelled of roses and spice. Everything nice.

His cockstand showed his appreciation.

He took her mouth again. She was every bit as hungry for the kiss as he was, and the mating of their mouths grew carnal, ferocious. Licking, sucking, tongue against tongue. Ah, God, she made him greedy. Made him feel as if he hadn't had a woman in years—and he hadn't, not one like Maggie. Never one like her.

He unclasped the cheap velveteen cloak, pushing it off her shoulders. It pooled at her feet, and the rest of her garments soon joined the heap. He stripped her down to her chemise, the thin layer exposing her to his rapacious gaze. Her tits were full and round, their cherry tips budded against the linen, begging for him to have a taste.

He bent his head, drew the delicate fruit into his mouth. Her gasp of delight went straight to his groin, and his bollocks drew tighter, his cock turgid with need. He suckled her through the linen, his tongue flicking her nipple, laving it over and again. Her fingers slid into his hair, and pleasure shot down his spine as she tugged, holding him at her breast.

As if he'd ever want to leave. But he did…only to give her other breast the same attention he lavished upon the first. As he licked and nibbled, he squeezed the firm mounds, appreciating how they overflowed his palms.

"Please, Rhys, hurry. I can't wait."

Her panted pleas were a siren's call. Who was he to resist? He grasped the hem of her chemise, shoving it up to her hips. The sight of her shapely legs threatened the integrity of his trousers: his erection butted into the placket like a battering ram as he gripped one smooth, firm thigh, just to the side of her sweet thatch.

The hair on her sex was a shade lighter than that on her head and a piquant contrast to the pink petals they guarded. She had the prettiest pussy. He slid a finger along her slit and found a dream come true. She was wet and wanting, creamy for him. His thumb skated upward to her hidden pearl, and her hips bucked.

"What do you want, Maggie?" he growled. "Tell me."

She wetted her lips. Lips as pink and plump as the ones he was petting. "I want you inside me."

Imagining her breathy admission, Rhys couldn't resist any longer. He gripped his rearing cock, the crown already bulging, slickened by his fantasies. He thrust into his fist as if it were Maggie's cunny, tight and lush and greedy to be fucked. From the village gossip, he'd learned that her dead husband had been an elderly scholar, and he couldn't imagine she'd had much satisfaction from a dried-up old stick.

He frowned. He didn't want to think about Maggie with another man. With anyone but him.

He focused instead on taking her up against the door. His fingers dug into her plush hips as he lifted her against the wood then impaled her upon his raging shaft. She moaned, her hands clutching his shoulders as her cunny stretched to take his invading meat. He pulled out and slammed in to the rhythm of their panted breaths. Her tits bounced as he plowed her, tunneling deep into her small, succulent hole. She took it all and begged for more.

"Take me, Rhys. Make love to me. I want you."

Her sweet urgency made his stones swell with heat. His biceps flexed, his fist working like a piston. He gritted his teeth against a groan as he climaxed in hot bursts.

After cleaning himself up, he lay back against the pillows. He felt relaxed...but not replete. The respite of the physical release soon faded, and he was left again with his old friend Restlessness. Only this time, he wasn't feeling on edge because of boredom—quite the opposite. His mind was absorbed by Maggie, who, he had to admit, held his attention as no woman ever had.

He'd first been drawn to her sexually. Their carnal encounter had heated his imagination for years, and their kiss two nights ago had demonstrated why. The sexual alchemy between them was more powerful than any he'd known...and he'd known a lot, in the biblical sense.

He'd had lovers aplenty, and back when he'd been flush, he'd kept his share of mistresses. In truth, a paid arrangement had suited him well. He believed in hiring experts for the job: professionals who understood that there were to be no messy emotions involved. If a paramour hinted that she wanted more from him, she was served her *congé*, along with a generous parting gift.

He didn't have many principles, but he believed in honesty: he never promised anything he couldn't give. A woman who expected him to be her champion, her hero, or, God forbid, her love was destined for disappointment.

He'd failed to protect the ones he'd loved; he'd been failed by those he'd counted upon. Love created expectations that always led to pain and disillusionment, and he wanted no part of it.

None of his former lovers had complained that he gave only a part of himself. They'd been happy to share his bed and be seen on his arm. His popularity with the gentler sex had fed into the *ton*'s image of him; scandal sheets and wags had extolled the latest exploits of "Ransom the Rake," endowing him with prodigious stamina and an unattainable heart.

The fact that they'd glorified his casual dealings with women had amused him.

His interest in Maggie was different, however. He'd first been drawn to her sexually, yes, but now he found himself fascinated not only by her physical charms, but by...her. The surprising edges to her personality. Whereas he'd been attracted to the old Maggie's shy sweetness, he was intrigued by the new Maggie's sharp tongue and prim and proper manner.

He wanted to know why she dressed and acted like a nun. Why she held such a grudge against him when he'd not done her any harm—and, make no mistake, he *was* relieved that he hadn't gotten her with child. He didn't need that sin to join all his others. For all his faults, he believed in taking responsibility when due, as any man who called himself a gentleman should. She'd accused him of not respecting her when that was untrue.

For devil's sake, he trusted her enough to hire her. Having interviewed some of her competitors, he'd concluded that Maggie stood head and shoulders above the rest. Mr. Shelley, the shop owner in Axmouth, had said that she had an integrity uncommon in the business.

Rhys admitted to himself that his interest in Maggie was more than professional. He also wanted to explore the sexual attraction between them. The timing was less than ideal. It was, in truth, terrible: his rational mind told him Maggie Foley was a distraction he didn't need.

His cock wholeheartedly disagreed.

A compromise was possible, he reasoned. As long as he was clear about what he was offering her—the pleasure of the moment, no strings or promises—why couldn't they enjoy a liaison? They'd done so with great success in the past.

Clearly, it wouldn't be easy convincing her to fall into bed with him again.

The words from his uncle's letter came back to him. *Nothing worth having in life comes easily.* Seducing a woman probably wasn't what the old boy was referring to...but Maggie was definitely worth having.

Thinking and releasing his seed were taking their toll. Rhys's eyelids began to drift downward. As he sank into sleep, his dreams were of her.

$$\text{※}\quad 7 \quad\text{※}$$

MAGGIE'S TEMPLES THROBBED IN RHYTHM TO THE DRONING tones of her prized client, Mr. Nigel Pickering-Parks. He was short and portly, facts that his bright tangerine waistcoat did little to conceal. Although Maggie was no arbiter of fashion, his tailor clearly wasn't either, for the rest of him was garbed in an orange-and-brown striped worsted to match the waistcoat. It looked as if autumn had vomited upon him.

Perspiration glistened along Pickering-Parks's thinning hairline, and he mopped his brow repeatedly with a handkerchief. He'd lumbered into Foley's a quarter hour ago; it felt as if he'd been there forever. She'd tried to steer him toward the issue of the commission he'd promised her, but, like a mule, he plodded along at his own pace. There was nothing she could do but follow.

Her stomach growled; knowing the ordeal that lay ahead with Pickering-Parks, she'd been too nervous to eat breakfast. She snuck a glance at the long case clock in the corner. It was half-past noon; Hypatia had gone to fetch Glory from the schoolhouse, and the two would soon be returning to the shop.

At Maggie's insistence, Glory had apologized to Mr. Snelling for taking his wig, and as punishment, taken on extra chores at home. To reward the girl's compliance, Maggie had promised to take her to the market today. Since Paul's death, she'd been preoccupied by the demands of the business, and she looked forward to spending a few carefree hours with her daughter.

She'd done the right thing to protect Glory from Rhys Jones. If only she'd done a better job of protecting herself...the memory of his kiss washed through her, and she wanted to kick herself for being so stupid. For acting like the trollop she'd been all those years ago.

"I say, are you listening to me?"

The annoyed expression on Nigel Pickering-Parks's chubby face snapped her back to reality.

"Of course, sir," she said hastily. "You were, um, talking about a set of fossils?"

A good guess since he never talked about anything but old bones.

"Indeed." He sniffed. "As I was saying, several years ago, a magnificent set of fossils was stolen from under my nose. An ichthyosaurus. A complete set, no less. A jewel of a find, sirrah, and it slipped through my fingers. The devastation I suffered should come as no surprise."

It did come as no surprise for he'd told this tale during every single visit. At *least* once.

Maggie suppressed her impatience. "I am sorry to hear of your loss," she said as gravely as if he'd lost his kin. "But rest assured you'll be in excellent hands when you commission Foley's to do an expedition for you. I personally know of a local site that has yielded several outstanding specimens—"

"You are not listening," Pickering-Parks said. "I cannot entrust my reputation as a fossil collector to your shop. That is what I'm here to tell you."

Maggie's stomach sank like a boulder. *Blooming hell, I can't afford to lose this idiot too.*

She regrouped quickly. "We've earned your trust in the past.

Why, recall the excellent pterosaur skeleton that we secured for you less than two years ago—"

"That *Mr.* Foley secured for me. Your husband was a gentleman of quality and noted fossils expert, thus worthy of my commission." Pickering-Parks stared down his nose at her...which wasn't very effective given that they were nearly of a height. "But things, obviously, have changed."

A lady never loses her temper. Keep a lid on it.

It took every ounce of her willpower to brighten her smile. To not snap at the condescending buffoon who'd never lifted a finger in his entire life and tell him that she, Maggie Foley, was indeed worthy of his commission because *she* had found the damned bones he'd bought from her husband! For weeks, she'd mucked about the nearby cliffs known as the Spittles. Soaked by rain and mud, she'd dodged several landslips as she searched for fossils. Luckily, one cascade of rock had cleared a section of the cliff, revealing the pterosaur's remains.

Rash words burned on the tip of her tongue; she held them back, swallowing the burn. One, she would never desecrate Paul's reputation. Second, Pickering-Parks wouldn't believe her even if she told the truth. Third, she *needed* his present commission and couldn't afford to offend him.

She inhaled through her nose. "What if I were to offer you a discounted rate?"

Greed gleamed in his small, wide-spaced eyes. "How much of a discount?"

Lord above, if the man had a passion for anything other than fossils it was pinching pennies.

"Twenty percent," she said, "off our standard fees."

Foley's standard fees ran around a hundred pounds for a personalized expedition that promised all finds to the patron. Even without the discount, she wouldn't make enough to pay her debts off by the end of the month. Yet if word got out that Foley's was once again fashionable with the society gentlemen, then perhaps more clients would sign on.

Some money was better than none. Maybe she could persuade Rotherby's bank to take a payment in lieu of the total sum, especially if she could prove that she had other commissions waiting. It was a small chance, but what other alternative did she have?

Her mind flashed back to Rhys's offer, his kiss...and she shut down that line of thought immediately. No way could she work with him. Like the devil, he seduced the lustful weakness in her blood. Just one kiss from him, and all of her hard-won respectability had flown out the window.

Since she couldn't trust herself around Rhys, there was only one solution: she had to stay far away from him.

"I'll pay fifty percent," Pickering-Parks declared. "And not a penny more."

She wondered why life always seemed to trap her between a rock and a hard place.

"Be reasonable, sir." She tried not to sound desperate. "I cannot make a profit at such a sum."

"That's not my problem. And if you don't want my business, Mr. Bancroft certainly does. Made a point of finding me at my lodgings. He told me your business was a sinking ship. Bancroft is a reputable gentleman...and one willing to give his patrons the proper discount."

Pickering-Parks's smug smile and the mention of her nemesis made her hands curl. Just when she thought matters could not get any worse, the tinkling bell over the door announced another visitor. The sight of the dark auburn hair and handsome, grinning face increased the pounding at her temples.

Oh, blooming hell. What does Jeremy want?

Her youngest brother Jeremy never came to her unless he wanted something. And that something was never good. She forced herself to remain calm as he sauntered over to the counter.

He cut in front of Pickering-Parks, ignoring the man completely (if only she had the luxury of doing the same).

"Hullo there, Maggie." Jeremy flashed a charming smile. "Need to 'ave a word with you."

"As you can see, I am with a customer." She knew her pointed words would be futile.

"You don't mind cooling your 'eels a bit, do you, guv?" Jeremy winked at Pickering-Parks, who sputtered. "Got to talk with my sister on a matter o' great importance."

"It'll have to wait, Jeremy. Come back later and—"

"Now's the only time oi got." Before she could stop him, Jeremy rounded the counter and took hold of her arm. Like all the Goode men, he was tall and strapping, and she was no match for his strength as he tugged her toward the back office. "This won't take but a minute. Oi'll 'ave you back afore this fine gent even knows you're gone."

When Jeremy, or any of her siblings, set their minds upon a thing, resistance was useless. If she dug in her heels, he'd only create more of a fuss and make her look even more unprofessional in Pickering-Parks's eyes.

"Please excuse me, Mr. Pickering-Parks. If you'd like to peruse the shop for a moment, I'll be right back," she called.

She shook off her brother's hold and led the way into the backroom, pulling the curtain closed behind them. Patty had made progress organizing the space; neat stacks of labeled boxes stood against the walls. To establish some sort of authority, Maggie went to stand by Paul's desk.

Folding her arms across her chest, she said, "What do you want, Jeremy? Be quick about it."

"'Ow's that a way to greet your own dear brother?" He shook his head mournfully. "Forgotten, 'ave you, 'ow Ma's deathbed wish was for you to be a good girl and look after your kin. Well, oi fault that dead 'usband o' yours. Looked down 'is nose on us Goodes and taught you to be 'igh in the instep, too."

Jeremy wasn't wrong: Paul *had* despised her family. He'd refused to have anything to do with them and advised her to do the same. Yet she couldn't bring herself to cut ties completely, even when faced with her brothers' schemes and her sister's dramatics. Thus, she'd found herself in a constant tug-of-war between her family and her husband.

Sighing, she repeated, "What do you want?"

"It's not what *oi* want, Maggie, but what oi got to offer *you*."

Jeremy wanted something, all right. And that something was definitely not good.

"It's like this." He pitched his voice low. "Jacob, Jimmy, and me, we got a special shipment coming in Friday at midnight, and we need someone to keep watch. Easy job, ain't nothing to do but keep your eyes peeled for any unwanted guests to the party. Seeing as 'ow your dead 'usband left you in dun territory, we thought we'd do you a favor and let you 'ave the job."

"*Let* me have the job?" she said with rising ire. "I don't want any part of a smuggling scheme. And if you had any brains, you wouldn't either!"

"For God's sakes, lower your voice." His eyes darted to the curtain. "Are you wanting to bring the excise men down on our 'eads?"

"I'm wanting you to 'ave a lick 'o common sense." Anger rubbed the polish off her speech, and she threw up her hands. "When Ma was alive, she ne'er approved of such goings-on. Not when Pa did it, not when you and the other boys joined in on it. Besides telling me to look after you sorry lot, do you know what else she said to me on 'er deathbed, Jeremy?"

"What?" he said warily.

"That you all put 'er there with your nonsense!"

For an instant, Jeremy looked shamefaced. Like the little brother who'd cried when Mr. Snelling had forced him to wear the dunce cap in front of the class for misspelling a word. And

Maggie thought maybe, just maybe, she'd gotten through his thick skull.

Then his expression hardened. He stepped toward her, and she retreated, the back of her legs hitting the desk. Her brothers had never hurt her, but they were big men and could get intimidating when angered or in their cups.

"If you want to get down from your 'igh 'orse and lend a 'elping 'and to your own kin," Jeremy sneered, leaning into her so that she had to bend back, "then we'll be at Crip's Cove, Friday night. But if you're too hoity-toity, we'll take care o' the business ourselves."

Before she could tell him to bugger off, a deep voice sliced through the room.

"Step away from the lady. Now."

Her gaze bounced to the doorway. Rhys stood there, his face set in foreboding lines.

Jeremy pivoted, facing him. "Who the bloody 'ell are you?"

"I'm the fellow who's going to teach you a lesson if you don't leave Mrs. Foley be." Rhys's tones were quietly lethal, his big hands fisted at his sides.

"You and what army?" her brother unwisely taunted.

Regaining her senses, Maggie pushed past Jeremy to stand between the men. "Stop it. There will be no brawling in my shop."

"You know this bastard, Maggie?" Jeremy said, eyes narrowed.

"He's a customer." She drew a breath. "Now I have a shop to run—"

"Oi won't take up any more o' your precious time," Jeremy said mockingly. "Seeing as 'ow you care more for your old bones than your own blood."

He stormed toward the exit, his path blocked by Rhys. Maggie's breath held when Rhys paused a moment longer than necessary before stepping aside. Jeremy yanked aside the curtain with enough force to tear it (just what she needed, another thing to fix). Seconds later, the slam of the front door shook the walls.

"Blooming hell." She massaged her pounding temples.

"Your brother's a right sod, isn't he?" Rhys remarked.

"He's been...under duress of late." She had no idea why she was defending Jeremy. Maybe it was because she was buffle-headed from skipping breakfast.

"Be that as it may, he doesn't have the right to treat you that way. Are you all right?"

Her pulse stuttered at his protective words. At the concern in his hazel gaze.

"Jeremy would never hurt me." She folded her arms around herself. "Why are you here? I thought I made things clear when we last spoke."

"You did. That's why I came. To apologize."

Her heart flipped. "For what?"

"For not showing you the proper respect. The respect that I do, indeed, have for you."

His words and expression were sincere. She didn't know how to react, how to stem the tide of warmth that flooded her. At that instant, the front door slammed a second time...and brought her to her senses.

"Blooming *hell*." She dashed around Rhys to get through the curtain.

She looked around the empty shop...saw her empty future.

Pickering-Parks was her last hope, and she'd lost him.

"Maggie, what's the matter?" Rhys asked.

"My last patron left," she said in a shaking voice. "He was poached by that *bastard* Bancroft."

Desperation cinched her throat. Her last customer was gone, taking her livelihood with him. Her brother was furious with her. And her ex-lover, whom she needed to stay far away from, was standing right behind her. She was struck by a sense of unreality. For a mad instant, she didn't know whether to laugh or cry.

At least things can't get any worse, she thought wildly.

The door opened. Glory skipped in, chaperoned by Hypatia.

"Hello, Mr. Jones," the girl exclaimed. "I was hoping to see you again!"

Numbly, Maggie watched as her daughter dashed straight to Rhys. Glory dimpled when he bowed, returning his greeting with the best curtsy Maggie had ever seen from her.

"Good afternoon, ladies," Rhys said.

"It is indeed! Mama and Aunt Patty are taking me to the fair." Glory's eyes shone with excitement. "Would you care to join us, Mr. Jones?"

Rhys looked at Maggie, the intensity of his gaze making her heart thump against her ribs. For an instant, the mask of the insouciant rake slipped: he scrutinized her with a keenness that made her shiver with dread...and a strange sort of longing.

"Thank you," he said. "I'd enjoy the company."

"Hooray!" Glory clapped her hands together gleefully. "This will be great fun!"

Maggie did not share her daughter's enthusiasm, yet uninviting Rhys would only draw undue attention. Her best course of action was to spend the afternoon with her ex-lover and the child they'd made together and pray that no one noticed the truth.

Panic increased her lightheadedness. At the same time, against her will, she felt a constriction in her chest...the threads of a tattered dream tangling around her heart.

$$\maltese \quad 8 \quad \maltese$$

THE FAIR TURNED OUT TO BE JUST A SHORT STROLL OVER FROM the shop. Clustered around the town's Market House, the event was in full swing when Rhys arrived with Maggie, Glory, and Hypatia. Strings of paper flags fluttered in the ocean breeze. Purveyors had set up stalls on both sides of Broad Street, luring potential customers over with samples of foodstuffs and household items. A fiddler played a lively country tune, children gathering around him.

Despite the cheerful setting, the outing did not get off to a promising start.

Upon arrival, Glory made a bee-line for a hawker selling brown-spotted puppies. She alternately cajoled, begged, and whined at her mother to have one. Rhys had to admire Maggie's patience as she explained firmly and repeatedly that a puppy would be too much work.

With a sulky look, Glory turned to him, saying loudly, "I'd wager Mr. Jones likes dogs."

A memory ignited of Bailey, the foxhound he'd had as a child. Bailey had been his faithful companion and only friend—until the day his sire had shot the dog in front of him. With ease borne of practice, Rhys shut out the dark swell of emotion.

"I don't," he said.

Glory frowned. "But *everyone* likes dogs. Except Mama," she accused darkly.

"I have nothing against dogs in particular, but I don't like the care and attention that is required by a pet." *Nor the pain of losing one.* "I prefer freedom above all things."

"Spoken like a true bachelor," Hypatia said with her dry-as-toast wit.

"But *I* don't mind the work," Glory argued.

"Your mama does." He saw no point in honey-coating matters. He'd never understood why some people talked down to children, as if they were stupid, which, he knew, Glory was not. "She has a shop to run, house to keep. Not to mention a little girl to raise. Don't you think that is enough without adding a pet to the mix?"

The mutiny faded from Glory's gaze; she looked abashed. As he'd gleaned from their first encounter, while headstrong and perhaps a trifle overindulged, she was clever and responded to reason. At heart, she seemed like a good, loyal child. She'd proven it back on the beach when she'd negotiated a hundred pounds out of him to help her family.

"I don't need a puppy, Mama," she said contritely. "May I go ahead and find the cheesemonger?"

"I'll go with her," Hypatia said.

Glory darted like a goldfish through the sea of people, her aunt following faithfully in her wake. Rhys continued at a more sedate pace with Maggie, noting her drawn-up shoulders and the tense line of her mouth. Although she was doing her best to hide it, she was distressed...and who could blame her?

He thought of her brother Jeremy's uncouth treatment of her and regretted not planting a facer on the bastard. Then there was the worm Bancroft poaching her customers. Not to mention the debt that threatened her family's survival. All of this, and she still walked along, her bonneted head held high, her spine ramrod-straight.

He felt a surge of respect—and an urge he knew better than to give into.

You have no business wanting to protect her, he told himself. *You know where that will lead.*

He saw his mama, the purple marks glowing on her porcelain skin, her eyes red-rimmed behind her shining black curtain of hair. *Go, Rhys, go...*

He saw himself kneeling next to Bailey, unable to stop the bleeding or the dog's pained whimpers. *I'm sorry, boy,* he'd sobbed. *It's all my fault...*

His throat thickened. No, he couldn't risk getting involved—for Maggie's sake as well as his own. Everything and everyone he'd gotten close to he had failed to protect. Because of him, they'd paid the ultimate price...and he'd learned the futility of getting too close, of caring too much. With ruthless will, he locked away the anguished memories.

Better to be Ransom the Rake, charming and carefree.

"You didn't have to come. I'm sure a simple country fair is hardly to your taste."

Maggie's low voice drew him back to the present. He realized that she'd glimpsed his expression, his reaction to the past, and misinterpreted the cause.

"There's no place I'd rather be," he said smoothly.

He told himself that his attraction to her was acceptable as long as he kept a clear head. As long as expectations were clear and no undue attachments formed. His plan was two-fold: to persuade Maggie to work for him and share his bed again. Given her mistrust of him, the tasks were Herculean. Yet he was determined to succeed.

Her worn black half-boots continued to trudge forward. The slant of her bonnet conveyed that her gaze was on Glory and

Hypatia, who were tasting samples at a cheesemonger's booth up ahead.

"I'm sure you have better things to do," she said.

"I enjoy Miss Glory's company." In truth, he found himself strangely taken with the girl. He liked her pluck and independent spirit. "Her mama's as well."

"I neither want nor need your flattery." Maggie's pace quickened.

"What about my business, then?" He lengthened his stride to match hers. "As it seems you have lost your last customer, I might be your last hope."

"You'd like that, wouldn't you? You're no different from Bancroft and all the rest. Ready to pounce and take advantage of a woman when she has no options left."

Her heated assertion took him aback. Surprised him into taking hold of her elbow to halt her.

She faced him, her shoulders proudly drawn back. Yet beneath the brim of her dark bonnet, her brilliant green eyes were shimmering. She was close to tears, he saw with some shock. To see a strong-willed female like Maggie struggle to keep her composure hit him like a punch to the gut.

"Everything is in shambles, and the last thing I need is trouble from your quarter." Her voice shook with emotion. "Why won't you just leave me be?"

It was, undoubtedly, the wise thing to do. But he...couldn't.

"Wait here a moment," he said.

He knew she was in a bad state indeed when she simply pressed her lips together and didn't reply. He headed toward Glory and Hypatia.

"Mr. Jones!" Glory's greeting was muffled by her mouthful of cheese. She pointed at a blue-veined morsel on the tray of samples. "You must try this one. It's my favorite so far!"

"The miss has fine taste," the aproned cheesemonger said,

beaming. "Our Blue Vinney is the finest in the county. Help your-self, sir."

"None for me." Rhys handed the proprietor a few coins. "Wrap up whatever she wants."

Glory's eyes widened. She immediately began to sample the other cheeses while the cheesemonger provided a description of each.

Hypatia frowned at Rhys. "Sir, you needn't—"

"Mrs. Foley is a trifle peaked," he said in a low voice. "I will be securing her refreshment at that tea shop we just passed. Gibson's, I believe. You and Miss Glory must join us when you're finished here."

The spinster's gaze was acute. "Pickering-Parks didn't come up to scratch?"

"He did not," Rhys confirmed. "Mrs. Foley also had a visit from her brother Jeremy."

"It never rains but pours," Hypatia muttered. Then she nodded. "Take your time. I believe Glory and I will finish making the rounds of the market before joining you at Gibson's."

Maggie didn't know how she ended up having tea with Rhys. One minute she'd reached the end of her rope and was unraveling in the middle of the street, the next he was ushering her into Gibson's Tea Room. Inside, she passed several people she knew, and all of them, especially a local gossip by the name of Mrs. Mulligan, wanted to know the identity of her companion.

As if attuned to her exhaustion, Rhys had taken over, handling the situation with his usual suave charm. He'd told Mrs. Mulligan that he was a relation of Horatio Jones and had taken up resi-dence at Journey's End. He'd also made clear that his interest in Maggie was in a professional capacity as he wished to explore the caves his uncle had left him.

Now they were seated in a quiet alcove away from prying eyes. Rhys ordered a lavish menu, even though Maggie had no stomach for food. Mrs. Gibson brought the tea first, depositing the pot on the flowered tablecloth and discreetly leaving them to their conversation.

The problem was Maggie didn't trust herself to speak. Her thoughts and emotions were a jumbled mess. And none of the tricks Paul had taught her were working: she *couldn't* compose herself, and that fact worsened her agitation.

"Maggie." The soft command in Rhys's voice compelled her to look at him. His hazel eyes were warm and intent. "Tell me what is going on in that head of yours."

"You don't want to know." She took a sip of tea, hoping it would settle her nerves.

"I wouldn't ask if I didn't. Now tell me why you've lumped me in with that bastard Bancroft."

So that's it. He feels wronged. That's why he wants to know what you're thinking.

"I apologize," she said instantly. "I was overwhelmed and spoke out of turn."

"What is overwhelming you?" he asked.

God, if he'd only told her to calm herself, the way Paul had. Or ignored her state of mind, the way her family was wont to do. But instead, he was being *understanding*...a response that she had little experience with and no defenses against.

She concentrated on dumping more sugar into her tea. "It's nothing I cannot manage."

"Like your brother Jeremy? Pardon my saying, but you did not seem to be managing him very well. What did he want from you?"

To be a lookout for the smuggling ring he and my other brothers have put together. To risk my neck—or risk theirs.

She stirred in another spoonful of white crystals. "He asked a favor, that's all."

"He wants you to do something you do not wish to do. And he was not above using guilt to manipulate you into doing it."

The accuracy of his assessment made her spoon rattle against her cup.

"It is a family matter." She lifted her chin. "It's complicated."

"And the business with Bancroft, I take it that is complicated as well?"

"No, *that* is simple." Anger loosened her tongue. "Bancroft is a scheming, snake in the grass who has been poaching my customers. He means to put me out of business with his lies. And my customers are nodcocks who take him at his word just because he's a man and I'm—"

"A woman?"

"Exactly!" The word left her in an explosive breath. "It's blooming unfair!"

"I agree."

She stared at him. "You do?"

"Any rational person who'd met Bancroft would know he's not to be trusted," Rhys said calmly. "You're head and shoulders above the competition."

"I found the plesiosaurus skeleton," she blurted.

"Beg pardon?"

"The remains of a prehistoric reptilian sea creature. *I* found them." A dam broke inside her, the words flowing out. "Everyone thought Mr. Foley did the fossil finding, and it's true that he taught me all I know, but in the last five years, I was the one doing the work. Because of his ailment."

Rhys's eyes sharpened. "Your husband had an ailment?"

Don't talk about Paul's physical problems. You're treading in deep waters. Retreat.

Swallowing, she said, "The point is, everyone thinks that Foley's Emporium can't stay in business now that he's gone, but that is untrue. I've been finding fossils for years, and I will continue to do so, if only the collectors would give me a chance."

"But you aren't getting commissions because of the lies Bancroft has been spreading."

"Precisely." She leaned forward, uncaring that her elbows were on the table. "And he, of all people, *knows* that I'm fully capable of finding fossils. He's *seen* me mucking about in caves on my own!"

Rhys frowned, as if he were about to say something, but Mrs. Gibson arrived with tiered plates of savories and sweets. Maggie's stomach gave an ignominious growl. Since she'd been too nervous to eat before meeting with Pickering-Parks, her last meal had been supper the night before.

Rhys filled a plate and passed it to her. Suddenly ravenous, she dug in. The food tasted heavenly. She plowed through a mincemeat pie, some biscuits and cheese, and was working her way through a fluffy sponge layered with jam and whipped cream when she caught Rhys looking at her.

He was leaning back in his chair, his own food untouched. His lips were tipped up at the corners. Dimples showed above his manly beard.

"Hungry?" he said.

Suddenly embarrassed, she finished the bite of cake. "I haven't eaten anything today."

"Feel better now that you have?"

She did feel better, she realized. And not just because of the food.

She blew out a breath. "Why are you being like this?"

"You'll have to be more specific."

"Like *this*." She waved at the food, then at him. "Having tea with me. Listening to my complaints."

"I enjoy your company."

The food had helped to clear her head. She felt stronger again, more in control. Looking around the room, making sure no one was within earshot, she said, "I'm not going to bed with you again."

"Well." He arched a brow. "No one's ever going to accuse you of beating around the bush."

"I'm serious. If that's what this is about, if you're being...*nice* just because you think I'll succumb to your charms again, you can forget about it." She lowered her voice to a hush. "No matter what you think, I'm not a whore to be used for your pleasure."

"I don't think that." His voice had an edge of impatience. "But I'm curious why you think that I do."

"Isn't it obvious? We shared a bed the night we met." Despite her flaming cheeks, she forced herself to go on. "The morning after, you left fifty pounds on the table—for services rendered."

His eyes widened slightly. To her fascination, ruddy color tinged his cheekbones.

"I meant that as a gift not payment in kind," he muttered. "If I'd had some other token of appreciation on hand—a trinket or the like—I would have left that instead." He dragged his fingers through his hair, leaving the dark waves in sensual disarray. "I'm not usually ham-handed. I wasn't prepared for a rendezvous that night; I certainly meant no offense."

His obvious discomfort and explanation helped to soothe her injured pride. But they didn't change the consequences of that night. The life-altering choice that she'd made.

"Regardless, I am not the woman you believe me to be," she said.

"And what sort of woman is that?"

Because it felt good to air the thoughts that had long been festering inside her, she told him.

"A trollop. Ignorant. Slatternly...and stupid."

Like my mother and sister. A No Goode through and through.

He stared at her. "*I* think that?"

She gave a prim nod.

He swore. The ungentlemanly word jarred her, made her blink.

"This is going to be more complicated than I realized," he said grimly.

"What is?"

"Convincing you to work for me because it is in both our best interests." He narrowed his eyes, his fingers drumming on the table. "And convincing you to go to bed with me for the same reason."

Her heart catapulted into her ribs. "I already told you I'm not that kind of woman—"

"I know what kind of woman you are." He cut her off with a look. "Passionate. Honest and hard-working. Responsible to a fault."

Her jaw slackened.

"What I *don't* understand is why you've allowed your family's behavior to taint your image of yourself," he went on. "Why you've complicated things to such a degree that it will take a miracle to solve the Gordian knot of your mind."

She had no idea what a Gordian knot was, but it didn't sound flattering.

"If I'm so complicated," she retorted, "why don't you leave me be?"

"I can't." Before she could make sense of her surging hope, he said, "I need you to search my cave." He paused as she struggled to sort out her jumbled emotions. "We'll have to take this one problem at a time," he said decisively. "Business first, pleasure later."

His arrogance was unbelievable. "Now listen here—"

"You don't want to feel cornered, to work for me because you have no choice. I appreciate that. We'll have to work around it," he said. "Make sure you do have options."

"How, pray tell?" She couldn't keep the sarcasm from her voice. "I've been trying for months to improve business, to no avail. People won't hire a business headed by a woman."

"Leave it to me."

She exhaled, trying to hold onto her patience. "You cannot just command people to patronize my shop. You may be lord of the manor in whatever world you live in, Rhys, but here, you're no...why are you smiling at me like that?"

"You just called me Rhys." His smile deepened, his strong, white teeth flashing against his beard. "I take it we're back to first-name terms...Maggie?"

Blooming hell.

Before she could think of some way to salvage her pride, the door opened, and Glory flew in with Hypatia at her heels.

"This has been the best day!" she crowed, clambering into the chair next to Rhys. "Thank you for the cheese, Mr. Jones. I chose some of *each* kind!"

Maggie frowned at him. "You needn't have given her money. I would have bought her whatever she needed."

"I didn't give Miss Glory money," he said innocently.

"He didn't, Mama," Glory said, also innocently.

Settling beside Maggie, Hypatia clarified, "He gave it to the cheesemonger."

With a flash of intuition, Maggie realized that what had seduced her years ago wasn't just Rhys's dashing good looks or rakish charm: it was his unexpected kindness. His attentiveness to her. His ability to make her feel special...seen.

Yet the past had demonstrated that, purposefully or not, he could hurt her. Hurt her badly. With just a kiss, he could lay waste to her hard-won respectability and unleash the wanton in her blood.

Could she trust him to help her now when her family's future was at stake?

Could she trust...herself?

❀   9   ❀

"IF YOU BOUGHT ME A DOG, MAMA, I WOULD TAKE CARE OF IT. You wouldn't have to do a thing," Glory said in a wheedling tone. "I'll feed it and train it and let it sleep with me."

Sitting on the side of the bed, Maggie swept a reddish-brown lock off her daughter's face, letting her palm linger on the girl's freckled cheek. It hadn't taken long for Glory to resume her campaign for a pet.

"You know the answer, dear," Maggie said. "Now no more arguing. Time for bed."

Glory wrinkled her freckled nose. "I'm not sleepy."

"You will be as soon as you close your eyes."

If Glory didn't get a full eight hours of rest, she'd be grumpy and restless come morning. The last thing Maggie wanted was another visit from the schoolmaster.

If only I could afford to have Patty stay home and instruct her instead of Snelling. If only I could give Glory the dog she wants, be a better mama. If only…if only.

"But I'm eight and a quarter. Jenny Pinkleton is only eight, and her mama allows her to stay up as late as she wants."

No stranger to her daughter's negotiations, Maggie said firmly,

"Mrs. Pinkleton can do as she pleases in her house. But this is mine, and you'll do as I tell you."

"Father let me stay up as late as I wanted. I wish he were here," Glory said with a pout.

Pain stabbed Maggie's heart. Glory hadn't spoken much of Paul since his death. In their own way, the two had been close. Given his age and infirmities, Paul hadn't been able to keep up with Glory physically, and when closeted in his study with his bones, he'd tended to forget all else. Yet whenever he'd spent time with Glory, he'd been a doting father.

Maggie had been grateful for Paul's kindness to Glory. Although sometimes, she'd thought with secret guilt, he'd given the headstrong girl too much freedom. For Maggie, it hadn't been easy being the parent who set and enforced the rules. She thanked God every day for sending along her sister-in-law, who'd acted as Maggie's second through countless duels with her obstinate daughter.

Her mind veered to Rhys and the way he'd handled Glory yesterday at the fair. His natural ease with the girl and the positive way she'd responded to his authority had filled Maggie with equal parts wonder and unease...and a sprinkling of guilt.

For the first time, she was forced to wonder if she was making the right choice in keeping Glory's true parentage a secret. But what choice did she have? She didn't want Glory labelled a bastard.

And if Rhys can't tolerate the loss of freedom inflicted by a pet, she thought wryly, *what on earth would he do with a child?*

Reassured, she set the thoughts aside and studied her daughter. She wanted Glory to be able to speak freely of her grief over Paul's death, lest it fester inside.

"Do you miss your papa, my dear?" she said.

"Yes." Glory's bottom lip pushed out. "He allowed me to do what I wanted. *He* loved me."

The blade twisted in Maggie's chest. She said quietly, "Right now, your father is watching from Heaven. He would want you to be a good girl: to obey your mama and try to sleep."

Glory huffed and turned on her side.

Maggie tried again. "You need to be refreshed and attentive for school on the morrow."

"I don't need to be attentive; I know all the lessons," came Glory's petulant reply. "The lessons are for bacon-brained babes. I hate them. I hate school."

Maggie knew there was no point trying to reason any further. Suppressing a sigh, she touched her daughter's shoulder. "Sleep well, my darling."

By the time she reached the door, she heard the first snippet of a snore.

She made her way past the other two small bedchambers and headed down the narrow stairs of the small cottage. On the main floor were the kitchen, Paul's study, and the parlor, which served dual purposes as dining and sitting room. Maggie found her sister-in-law in the last chamber.

Loose chestnut curls tumbling over her chintz wrapper, Patty was reading on the settee. She had a pot of tea and two cups on the table in front of her.

"Abed at last?" she inquired, setting her book on her lap.

"At *long* last," Maggie said.

She dropped into the armchair, which creaked in protest. Like much in the cottage, the chair needed to be fixed up, but there had never seemed to be time or money for renovation, even when Paul was alive. Looking at the faded floral wallpaper, scratched-up furnishings, and threadbare rug, Maggie thought ruefully that the only style she could lay claim to was "shabby gentility"...which was still better than what she'd grown up with.

Thinking of her family, as she'd been doing on and off throughout the day, knotted her insides. She couldn't help but cast a look at the battered clock on the mantel.

Nine o'clock. Three hours until her brothers would be bringing in their shipment.

And I still don't know what I should do.

"What is the matter, Maggie? You've been woolgathering all day." Above her spectacles, Hypatia's brows were raised. "Now that Pickering-Parks has come to heel, I would think you would be relieved."

"I am relieved," Maggie said quickly.

This afternoon, when Nigel Pickering-Parks had appeared at Foley's and put down a commission of one hundred pounds, Maggie had barely been able to conceal her shock. She'd gathered her wits sufficiently to thank him. Unable to stop herself from looking the gift horse in the mouth, she'd hesitantly asked what had changed his mind.

To which Pickering-Parks had declared, "I have it on the authority of a true gentleman that your services are in high demand. The *crème de la crème* of fossil hunters, he called you. Told me that he'd offered you five hundred pounds to do an expedition for him, and you refused. Well, I fully expect you to honor our initial agreement of a hundred pounds for I shan't pay a penny more."

Thus, Maggie knew the reason for Pickering-Parks's change of heart: Rhys.

You don't want to feel cornered, to work for me because you have no choice. I appreciate that. We'll work around it.

She hadn't taken Rhys seriously. Now she was forced to realize that he was behind her windfall. That he'd secured her a customer...in order to give her a choice.

With Pickering-Parks's money, she could make a payment to the bank. And she'd have an easier time drumming up more business when it was known she had a commission in her pocket. She wouldn't need to accept Rhys's proposition out of desperation.

He had given her that freedom despite it being detrimental to his own cause.

He'd given her more, too. Called her "passionate," "honest," and "hard-working."

To top it off, she didn't even have to question his motivations because he'd been so blatantly honest about them. *Business first, pleasure later...*

Last night, she'd tossed in her bed, tortured by sensual memories. Of the pleasure Rhys had once shown her and that she hadn't experienced again until he kissed her at the inn. The desires she'd been bottling up for years popped free like a cork, effervescent need spilling through her veins. She hadn't been able to stop her hands from wandering to her breasts, from caressing the budded tips until the ache expanded in her core, and her fingers had drifted lower and lower...

"There you go again."

Patty's exasperated words yanked Maggie from her reverie.

"Apologies," she mumbled. "I have a lot on my mind."

Between an ex-lover, brothers who smuggle, a brilliant and relentless child, and the world's most irritating patron, it's a wonder I don't have bats in the belfry.

"Does it have to do with Mr. Jones?"

Maggie's face warmed. "Why would you ask that?"

"Come now, I may be a spinster, but I am not stupid." Patty set her book aside and reached for her tea. "I see the way the man looks at you. His interest is not purely professional."

Her throat tight with shame, Maggie said, "I'm sorry."

"Sorry? But why should you be?" Patty's brows knotted.

"Because it's...unseemly." *You're a trollop, a No Goode.* "I'm a widow."

"Precisely. You're a widow, not dead," came her sister-in-law's blunt reply. "Paul has been gone for a year. It's time you came out of mourning."

Maggie's fingers twisted in her dark skirts. "I don't know that I'm ready."

"Suit yourself." With her legs curled beneath her and chestnut hair flowing over her shoulders, Patty looked more like a mischievous schoolgirl than a spinster. "But if I had a tall, dark handsome gentleman who looked like a pirate prince pining after me, I'd shed my widow's weeds in an instant—and my unmentionables as well."

"*Hypatia*." Maggie gave a horrified giggle.

"Oh, don't be such a prude. You cannot deny Mr. Jones has a certain *je ne sais quoi*." Patty gave a lazy wave. "You know how fond I was of Paul, but my brother was a stickler, wasn't he? Now it's just the two of us here, and I find it entirely too tiresome to bind myself up in niceties. Being able to speak one's mind is so freeing, don't you agree?"

Maggie thought of how good it had felt to share her true thoughts with Rhys. She gave a slow nod. Reaching for the teapot, she filled the empty cup and said, "Would you care for more tea?"

"Yes, but that's not tea. Not only tea, anyway."

She brought the cup to her nose, her eyes watering at the heady fumes. "You've been drinking *brandy*?"

"I found it when I was looking for a book in Paul's study." Patty waggled her brows. "Cigars, as well."

Laughing, Maggie set down the cup. "You are incorrigible."

"And you, my dear, need to have some fun." Patty continued sipping.

"Patty..." Maggie hesitated. "Do you ever wish you'd married?"

"No, because I never met the right man," Patty said matter-of-factly. "Only one reason would compel me to wed."

"And that is?"

Patty's brows rose. "Why, love, of course."

As always, Maggie respected the other's clarity and forthrightness. And she felt a pang. The truth was, as much as she'd tried, she had not loved Paul. At least, not in the manner a wife ought to love her husband. She'd admired and respected him, done her best to be a helpmeet...but that was not the same as love.

To be fair, Paul had seemed perfectly content. He'd not asked for her love, nor had he offered his own. He'd wanted a relationship based on the meeting of the minds, and Maggie had been so grateful to him that she'd have gone along with any arrangement he proposed.

For the first time, she found herself wondering if her marriage had made her happy...and her guilt compounded.

What right do you have to such thoughts? Paul saved you and Glory. If it weren't for him, you might be in a workhouse—or worse. Glory could have ended up a No Goode...

At the thought of her family curse, Maggie glanced anxiously at the clock. Nearly ten o'clock now. Her brothers must be at Crip's Cove, readying to haul in their shipment. Knowing them, they'd be armed with a half-baked plan and too much bravado. They were bound to get into trouble.

Take care o' your siblings, Maggie. Her mother's voice acted as her conscience.

"You're as fidgety as a child in a classroom. What *is* the matter, Margaret?"

Maggie was tempted to confide her worries but, when it came to the Goodes, Hypatia had always sided with Paul. The spinster disapproved of Maggie's family and wanted to keep Glory away from their influence. Maggie understood, yet she loved her siblings, numskulls and miscreants though they were. With Goodes, blood did run thicker than water.

She couldn't let her brothers get tossed into gaol.

If I leave soon, I can go to Crip's Cove and try to talk Jeremy and the others out of their idiotic scheme. Convince them that there is a better way.

"It's been a long day," she said. *And about to get longer.*

"I'm rather fatigued myself." Yawning, Patty rose. "I think I will finish my book in bed. Will you be heading up?"

"Not quite yet." Maggie forced a smile. "I have some matters to take care of first."

Rhys didn't know why he was riding to the Foley cottage in the starlit darkness. Some instinct had told him to come here, even though it was too late to call. He'd hoped that Maggie might seek him out after receiving the news of Pickering-Parks's change of heart, but she hadn't. Like some moonstruck calf, he hadn't been able to stop thinking about her...so he'd saddled his stallion and come to find her.

This plan was asinine. He ought to turn around. Find her in the shop tomorrow morning.

As he was about to retreat, he spied movement ahead of him. A rider on an old nag emerged from a drive a few yards away, and Rhys instinctively halted his own horse by a clump of bushes. The rider pulled the hood of her cloak over her hair which, even in the moonlight, had a telling red gleam. With a furtive look at the cottage behind her, she urged her mount into a lumbering trot.

Where the devil is Maggie going this time of night? His gloved hands gripped the reins as the possibilities raced through his head, not one of them good. If she had a lover, why hadn't she mentioned it? If she wasn't meeting a lover, didn't she know the danger she courted, a lone female riding in the dark?

With a sense of foreboding, he followed her.

He kept a safe distance, the cover of darkness and overgrown shrubbery making it easy to conceal himself. Whatever her mission was, she was so intent upon it that she didn't look back. The growing roar of waves told him they were nearing the water, and she continued east for a quarter hour, ending up at an isolated stretch of coastline.

On the beach, she dismounted, leading her horse into a cove beyond his view. When she re-emerged, she was without her mount, and lamp in hand, continued on foot, heading north. He waited until she rounded a bend before heading to the cove she'd exited. There, he found her mare tethered to a washed-up log;

securing his own horse, he raced after her. Not wanting to give himself away, he didn't use his own lamp, instead relying on the shifting glow of the moon to light his way.

He stuck close to the jutting cliffs. Within them, mouths of darkness gaped; the stirring in those caverns hastened his pace. The beach narrowed to a thin strip, the water lapping at his boots. His tension grew with each step.

Bloody hell, what is she doing here? This was no place for a lover's tryst; the other unthinkable explanation made his gut clench.

Up ahead, he saw a dancing orange flame—a bonfire. He stopped behind an outcropping of rock, watching as Maggie approached the brawny male figure standing by the fire.

"Well, oi'll be. Maggie, my girl, looks like you be a Goode, after all."

Rhys recognized her brother Jeremy's triumphant tones.

"Made it just in time, you did. Jimmy and Jacob are 'bout to bring the shipment ashore, and we'll need you to keep a lookout while we unload the goods."

Devil and damn. Rhys balled his hands. *Smuggling? That's what the bounder wanted her to help him with?*

"I'm not here to help." Though hushed, Maggie's tones were clear and crisp. "I'm here to talk you out of this idiotic plan. The excise men have increased their patrolling of the waters, and the three of you are like sitting ducks. If you leave now—"

"Don't be daft." Jeremy's tone heated with ready anger. "We got blunt invested, and we ain't leaving without our brandy."

"No amount of blunt is worth rotting in gaol over," she shot back.

"Oi ain't got time to argue with you. Now you either 'elp—or get out o' the way."

Before she could reply, shouts came from the direction of the water. Rhys spied two men knee-deep in the waves, an anchored boat just beyond them. Each man was hauling a rope of floating casks.

As Jeremy ran over to help, Rhys caught a bobbing movement on the horizon. Was there something in the waves? He squinted, trying to get a better look. The moon suddenly broke through the clouds, splattering pale light over the ocean—and the object.

Men on a lighter. Moving with determined speed toward the beach.

Bloody. Fucking. Hell.

Rhys broke into a run toward Maggie, shouting, "Excise men, they're coming!"

$\maltese$ 10 $\maltese$

MAGGIE JOLTED AT THE SOUND OF RHYS'S VOICE, THE SIGHT OF
him running toward her.

Then his words sank in.

Blooming hell...

"Run for it!" Jeremy's yell blasted through the darkness.

Dazed, her gaze bounced to her brothers, who were cutting themselves loose from the cargo. They scrambled onto the beach and sprinted away from her. Paralyzed, she saw the boat nearing the shore, a lamp flaring as a shout went up.

"Stop where you are! In the name of Her Majesty the Queen, we place you under arrest for the illegal import of goods!"

Rhys grabbed her hand. "We have to *go*."

His touch vanquished her shock.

"Follow me," she said. "I know a place."

He jerked his chin, and she took off in the opposite direction of her brothers, going back the way she'd come. She couldn't tell if the loud pounding in her ears was that of her heart or the excise officers giving chase or the waves against the shore, but she kept moving, didn't look back. She felt Rhys's steady presence behind her. When her half-boots lost purchase against ocean-slicked rocks, he caught her.

"Keep going," he growled in her ear.

She didn't stop until she found the place she'd been looking for. The cavern, that even in the dark, she knew like the back of her hand since she'd spent hours there hunting for fossils. As she headed toward the opening behind an outcropping of rock, Rhys's hand wrapped around her elbow.

"They won't find us in here," she whispered. "The entrance is hidden, and the tunnels inside are deep and winding."

After a brief hesitation, he nodded.

She led the way inside, darkness enclosing them like a tomb. She didn't dare light a candle until they were deeper into the cave, so she used her hands to guide her along the familiar rocky walls, following the twisting tunnel that would take them to safety.

At points the passage narrowed, and she could hear Rhys's harsh breaths behind her.

"All right?" she whispered.

"Fine," came his clipped reply.

Minutes later, the passage opened into the place she'd been searching for. Fumbling in her cloak pocket, she found her candle and tinder box. In the flaring light, shadows danced across the cave's walls and high ceiling.

"We can wait them out in here. Even the high tide doesn't reach this far..." As she turned to Rhys, she trailed off at the anger blazing on his countenance.

"Are you insane?" he bit out. "What the *devil* were you thinking taking part in a smuggling operation?"

"I wasn't taking part in the smuggling; I was trying to talk my brothers out of it." Even to her own ears, her rationale wasn't very sound. "Jeremy told me his plan, you see, and I couldn't just do nothing—"

"Yes, you could. If someone says they are going to jump off a bridge, you do not jump off with them. You do not risk your neck trying to save theirs." Hands bracing his hips, Rhys glowered at her. "You stay at home where you are safe."

She knew he was right. Her plan hadn't been one of her most brilliant ideas. Impulse had driven her rather than reasoning.

"We're Goodes," she said on a resigned breath. "We stick together."

For several heartbeats, Rhys stared at her.

Then he exhaled and muttered, "You're shaking."

She was, she suddenly realized. Now that the after-effects of the chase were wearing off, she felt the icy dampness of her skirts seeping into her. Her teeth chattered.

Rhys began to pull off his boots.

"Wh-what are you doing?" she asked.

"Getting out of my wet things," he said flatly. "You'll do the same if you don't wish to freeze. To conserve heat, we'll sleep on your cloak and use my greatcoat as a blanket. With any luck, we'll make it through the night without catching our deaths of cold."

Of all the things Maggie had imagined herself doing that night, lying in a dark cave in the arms of her former lover was not one of them.

At first, she'd lain stiffly beside Rhys, trying to avoid any contact between her body and his. She'd tried to stop her chilled limbs from shaking. A minute later, his arm had closed around her shoulders, tucking her firmly against his side.

Before she could utter a protest, he'd said gruffly, "For God's sake, I'm not going to take advantage of you. I just want to keep you warm. Now close your eyes and rest."

Thus, there she was, clad in her shift and drawers, on her side plastered against his hard form. Her cheek was pressed against his warm, muscled chest, his heartbeat a steady, lulling rhythm beneath her ear. On the one hand, she had to admit his tactic worked wonderfully: she was no longer cold but warm. *Very warm.*

Yet sleep eluded her. Rhys's closeness had a stimulating effect on her senses. She was all too aware that his state of undress matched hers: only his fine linen shirt separated her cheek from his firm pectoral muscle, and her stocking-clad leg lay next to his hard, trouser-clad thigh. His hand rested on her hip. His heat permeated her, his spicy musk filling her nostrils.

Thoughts entered her head. Dangerous thoughts. Thoughts she had no business having.

When she willed herself to stop thinking about them, they grew stronger. Memories assailed her: the flexing of his back muscles beneath her palms. The blissful shock of his manhood stretching her, pushing her deeper and deeper toward the heart of pleasure. She recalled the exquisite spasms that had rippled through her, followed by his primal sounds of satisfaction...

For heaven's sake, stop thinking like a harlot, she told herself desperately. *Go to sleep.*

Something that Rhys seemed to have no trouble doing. Beneath her head, his chest rose and fell in the rhythm of sound slumber. Unlike her, he wasn't being kept awake by lustful urges.

The last time she'd had this physical closeness with a man was with Rhys. Never before and never since. The blackness spun around her senses, cocooning them from logic and good sense. She felt like a sleepwalker wandering through a fantasy. The yearning in her grew and grew...until restraint crumbled.

In the dark, her fingertips found the open vee of his collar. His throat was a strong, corded column beneath her feather-light touch. She skimmed upward over the masculine bump, finding the bristly jut of his jaw and chin.

The pleasant scrape raised shivery goose pimples on her skin. She lightly traced the wicked, sensual ring of hair around his mouth. Their first time together, he'd been clean-shaven, and now she had an unholy curiosity about how that beard and mustache would feel against her skin...

"Enjoying yourself?"

His voice, the warmth of his breath against her fingers, jerked her back to reality. Her hand still hovered by his mouth, and she snatched it away...but not quickly enough. He caught it, rolling in a swift movement so that he was atop her.

It was too dark to see his face. She could only feel his hard, virile power surrounding her. Swamping her with desire.

Don't do this. Her mind resisted her body's clamoring need. *Don't act like a whore.*

"You promised," she managed. "You said...you wouldn't take advantage."

"I won't. The choice is yours." His voice was husky, sin and temptation wrapped in velvet. "Tell me to stop, and I will."

She realized that, while he hung over her, he wasn't holding her in place. He'd deliberately taken his own weight. His fingers were loosely linked with hers against the softness of her cloak, and she could pull away if she wanted to. Stop everything...if she wanted to.

I don't want to stop.

She blurted, "I'm not a harlot."

"No, you aren't. And I don't understand why you would think that you are." His hand found her jaw, cupping it. "You're a beautiful, hard-working, passionate woman, Maggie. I respect you."

She wished she could see his eyes. Confirm the sincerity in his deep tones. "Truly?"

"Truly." His thumb trailed over her bottom lip. "I respect you, which is why I must be honest about my desires and what I have to offer. What I want from you, what I can give, is the pleasure of the moment. Nothing more, nothing less."

The pleasure of the moment. Oh, how she *wanted* it. Yearned for it with every fiber of her being...but she couldn't make the same mistake twice.

Her good sense rallied. "There cannot be consequences..."

"Ah. I have a solution for that."

She could picture the sensual curve of his mouth.

"Not with me at the moment, but there are many ways to make love, Maggie. Ways to find pleasure without me spilling my seed inside you."

Her entire being shuddered at his bluntness. At the image and sensations his words evoked.

"Will you allow me, sweeting?" he murmured. "Will you let me make love to you, to pleasure you without consequences?"

Could she trust him? The truth was, all those years ago, he hadn't broken a promise to her: he'd never made any to begin with. Since his return, he'd been looking out for her. He'd defended her from her brother, taken care of her at the fair, even won her a commission. Tonight, he'd risked his neck to save her and her brothers from the excise men.

Now he was offering to see to her physical needs, with no strings attached. There would be no consequences; no one would know. And he couldn't hurt her again because she was no longer a fool and knew exactly what she was signing up for.

One night of mindless pleasure.

She wanted him. Wanted him so badly. For years, she hadn't let herself have what she wanted.

Why not take what he offered, the pleasure she'd been denied for so many years?

In the darkness, temptation was irresistible.

"Yes," she breathed.

In the next instant, his lips were upon hers, and she moaned at his delicious taste. The addictive male flavor she'd been craving since he'd kissed her at the inn. Hunger overwhelmed her, and she parted her lips to take more of him in, greeting the sensual thrust of his tongue with a parry of her own. He groaned, and she slid her fingers into his thick hair, holding him in place so that she could feast some more.

His lips went to her ear, and she shuddered as he suckled on the tender lobe. He trailed hot kisses down her throat, and she'd been right about his bristle, it scraped against her sensitive skin, leaving a wicked burn in its wake. Her neck arched as his kisses continued on, over her chemise-covered breastbone, his lips in the valley between her breasts. Her bosoms surged, the hard tips pushing against the thin linen, begging to be freed.

His finger brushed over her lips, her throat, hooking the neckline of her shift. She felt a tug, heard the sound of rending fabric. Before she could protest the destruction of a perfectly good undergarment, his hands covered her bare breasts, the possessive squeeze making her squirm with wanting.

"God, I love your tits," he said thickly. "They're the perfect handful."

She'd always thought herself too abundant in this area, but when he hefted the mounds in his palms, the pleasure *was* perfect. Her body felt made for what he was doing. She moaned as he skillfully played with the engorged tips, rubbing and pinching. Fire streaked from her breasts to her sex. Her insides bloomed with heat.

"You're so responsive. So sweet." His voice purred with masculine approval. "I want to kiss your breasts. Would you like that?"

"Yes." It seemed the only word she was capable of saying to him.

The first, hot swipe of his tongue drew a moan from her. The second made her back arch off the blanket. When he took the aching peak into his mouth, her mind went as still and dark as her surroundings. Sensation replaced thought and desire, caution. Pleasure was the guiding force, the flame that lit the moment.

He tongued her breasts, going back and forth. The need in her burned and raged, growing unbearable. As her legs shifted restlessly, his thigh suddenly thrust between them, the sinewy ledge applying friction exactly where she needed it...

She gasped as the fire in her exploded, showering her with bliss.

"Did you just spend?" He sounded both surprised and smug. "From me kissing your breasts?"

"Um..." Blushing, she couldn't think of a good way to answer the question. One that wouldn't make her seem like such a wanton. "It's been a while since I... That is, I haven't, well, you know..."

"That's bloody splendid."

Her cheeks grew hotter. "You needn't sound so smug."

"This isn't my smug voice. I'm saving that for what happens next."

Curiosity got the better of her. "What happens next?"

"I thought you'd never ask."

She felt her drawers being lowered, then whisked off her legs. He kissed her quivering belly, his tongue dipping into her navel. When his hands clamped onto her bare thighs, pushing them wide apart, she froze.

Surely he didn't mean to continue kissing her...*there?*

Even in the dimness, she knew she was spread for him, and the vulnerability made her wriggle in his grasp. "Rhys, what are you...?"

"I wasn't too creative the last time, was I?" he muttered. "A shortcoming I intend to make up for tonight."

The sinuous slide of his tongue made her shriek in surprise. What he was doing...it *had* to be a sin. But, sweet heavens, she couldn't summon the words to make him stop. He held her open, his carnal kisses melting away her resistance. Her head fell back, her hands clenching her cloak as he masterfully stoked her flames.

"Goddamn, your pussy is sweet." His words were hot against her humid flesh. "Like a ripe peach. Even more delicious than I imagined."

He'd imagined doing *this* to her?

"I'm going to eat you," he rasped, "and lick up every drop of juice when you come for me."

She didn't know what inflamed her more, his torrid words or questing mouth. He found the quivering bud of her desire and wooed it with his tongue. With teasing flicks and lashes, he took her higher and higher, to a place beyond reason, a place ruled by passion and passion alone. When his lips closed over her nub, suckling hard, she hurtled over the edge again with a shocked cry.

"By Jove, you're beautiful," he said, his voice ragged.

His weight left her, and she felt instantly bereft. She heard the swish of his clothes being shed, then he was back atop her, the contact of skin on skin reviving her spent nerves. His carved hardness was an erotic contrast to her soft curves. The granite slabs of his chest titillated her nipples, the ridges of his abdomen rubbing like a washboard against her belly. His manhood was a heavy iron bar against her thigh.

"Ah, sweeting, you feel fine." His voice was gravel wrapped in velvet.

"So do you," she managed.

"Let's see if you like this."

He moved, and she gasped as his massive shaft tunneled through her folds. He did it again, not entering her, but rather rubbing his rod along her intimate seam. Her wetness lubricated his movements. Breathing harshly, he pushed against her, spreading her petals with his hot, pulsing staff. When he slid against her exposed peak, she jerked, moisture gushing from her core.

"That's right, love, rub that creamy pussy against my cock," he coaxed thickly. "Make my prick nice and wet while I fuck your pretty pearl."

His wicked litany and the lunge of his hips made stars flash in the darkness. "*Rhys.*"

"Right here. Come again—this time with me."

His lips closed on her nipple. The hot, fierce suction accompanied the steady plowing through her slick sex. Her fingers slid into the rough silk of his hair, holding on as, unbelievably, pleasure surged once again. She cried out as her crisis hit for a third time.

"Bloody hell, yes," he groaned. "Feel me, sweeting."

His cock rocked against her pussy once, twice, and then a shudder wracked his large frame. Wet heat exploded against her belly, flooding her navel and dripping down her sides. The scent of his fulfillment hung richly in the air.

After tenderly wiping her clean, he cuddled her close, pulling his greatcoat over them both. His lips pressed against her temple.

Enveloped in his solid warmth, she listened to the pounding of his heart. Of her own. And before the consequences of what she'd done could begin to spin in her head, sleep blissfully claimed her.

❧ 11 ❧

RHYS BLINKED IN THE DARKNESS. THE DISORIENTATION TURNED into satisfaction as he remembered where he was and who was with him. His morning cockstand reared to instant readiness. Then he frowned, realizing that his arms were not full of a warm, curvy woman.

The place next to him was empty.

He sat up, his greatcoat falling to his waist. "Maggie?"

He heard the faint resonance of footsteps. A minute later, a glow pervaded the cavern, revealing Maggie, fully dressed and holding a candle. Even after the night's adventures, she looked delectable. Her cinnamon hair had lost all its pins, cascading to her waist in shiny waves. Her eyes were luminous and watchful.

"You're up," she said.

Nothing coy or flirtatious in her tone. Despite the scorching intimacy they'd shared, she was as proper as a governess. For some reason, her primness made him want to smile...and do unspeakable things to her.

"In more ways than one." He dropped his gaze to his lap, where his erection tented the wool. "Shall we put it to good use?"

The dimness couldn't hide her charming blush.

"We cannot afford to tarry," she said crisply. "The tide is low so we can depart. I scouted outside and didn't see any excise men."

Right. It was good that one of them was thinking with their head rather than their...other head.

He rose, grimacing as he tucked away his aroused flesh. He got dressed, and they headed through the tunnel. Her efficient navigation soon led them back to the outside world.

It took his eyes a moment to adjust to the brilliant sunrise spreading over the sky. Gulls called to each other, the sounds carried on the fresh, invigorating breeze. He inhaled deeply.

"I didn't see footprints going toward the cove where I tied my horse." She started walking in that direction. "The excise men must have left after netting the cargo. That is, unless they gave chase to my brothers..."

Hearing the tremor in her voice, he fell in step beside her. "I wouldn't worry. Your brothers took off like rabbits at the first sign of trouble."

And they left you behind. An ember of anger smoldered in his chest. Christ, what sort of men involved their sister in their shenanigans and then left her unprotected?

"They were frightened," she said quickly. "I'm sure they weren't thinking properly."

"If their choice of activity was any indication, they weren't thinking at all. And neither were you for helping them."

She stopped to glare at him, her cloak whipping around her, her hair a pagan tangle around her face. "You're not my lord and master. I don't have to answer to you."

"On the contrary, you do."

He didn't know which of them was more surprised at his declaration. Yet he couldn't stop the damned protectiveness surging through his veins. By God, in the nine days since he'd found her again, she'd suffered blow after blow. She'd been abandoned by her smuggling kin and mistreated by patrons and competitors; simultaneously, she'd dealt with the demands of running a shop and a household.

Any other female of his acquaintance—or male, for that matter—would have buckled under the pressure. Or at least turned to drink and other vice as he, himself, had when his fortunes had circled the drain.

But not Maggie. She didn't yield. The woman was responsible, stubborn, and loyal to a fault.

She needed someone to protect her—from herself.

Being a hero isn't exactly your forte, his inner voice reminded him starkly.

He'd failed to protect his mama and even his dog from his sire's brutality.

In more recent memory, his attempt to rescue his erstwhile fiancée Tessa Todd had also ended in disaster. She'd run off with a fellow named Harry Kent; masquerading as a bodyguard, Kent had wooed her from beneath Rhys's nose. Rhys had caught up with them and exposed that Kent was, in fact, a policeman investigating her cutthroat grandfather. True, Rhys's actions had been motivated by mercenary rather than emotional reasons—he'd only wanted Tessa for her dowry—but at least he'd been honest with her...unlike that bastard Kent.

Even so, Tessa had turned on *him*, breaking their engagement and making him look like the villain. Now she and Kent were happily wed. As far as Rhys was concerned, the love-sick fools deserved each other.

Life had taught him time and again that emotional attachment led to pain. The lesson was simple: you hurt the ones you loved, and they hurt you in return. Whether it was intentional or not didn't matter because the end result was the same. Thus, he would have to guard against the strange, foolish longing Maggie stirred in him. A longing for something he'd never experienced and never would.

On the other hand...he could still look out for Maggie. It was the gentlemanly thing to do, after all. He and Maggie were both mature adults, he reasoned; they could work and sleep together without getting unduly attached. As long as they were honest that this was just a temporary, casual affair, no one would get hurt.

Indeed, he thought, his mood brightening, there was much to be gained for both of them. Professionally...and personally.

Unfortunately, Maggie hadn't yet reached the same conclusion. Hands braced on her hips, she declared, "You have no right to interfere with my life. Last night changed nothing between us."

"I beg to differ," he said smoothly.

As if his brain had been percolating all along, he had the perfect plan.

"Beg all you want." She started moving forward again, and he found the way she was stomping through the sand absurdly adorable. "You said so yourself that it was only a night of pleasure. No strings attached."

"You don't have to answer to me because we're lovers." He paused for effect. "You have to answer to me because I'm your employer."

She whirled to face him, her expression incredulous. "I never said I'd work for you!"

"But you will."

"Pray tell, what makes you so certain?" Her beautiful, tip-tilted eyes shot sparks at him.

If he knew anything about her, it was this: she was proud and not one to default on a debt.

Ruthlessly, he played his winning hand. "Because you *owe* me, Maggie."

His words cut through her defenses with the precision of a scalpel. It sliced through her anger, her incredulity that he would assume himself to be her employer, and cut to the quick of her.

That was the way of truth.

The fact was she *did* owe him. For securing her the patronage of Pickering-Parks. For sounding the alarm and saving her brothers. For saving...her.

Last night, it had been so easy to surrender to passion. To yield to temptation in the dark. In the light of day, she saw that she'd taken a dangerous risk to allow him back into her life, even in the capacity of a casual bedpartner.

With throbbing shame, she recalled how easily she'd succumbed to him. Her eager reaction to his lovemaking and naughty words. She'd abandoned her principles, showed herself to be a wanton...and now she would have to pay the piper and *work* for the bloody man!

If I wasn't so indebted to him, I'd be sorely tempted to punch him in the nose.

Humiliated heat crept up her cheeks.

He curled a finger under her chin, lifting her eyes to his. "Why are you blushing?"

She batted his hand away. "I'm not blushing."

"Your face is pinker than the sunrise. You're thinking about our lovemaking, aren't you?"

"It was a mistake."

"It was bloody perfect." He planted his palms on the rock on either side of her, his eyes glittering like rare pirate's treasure. "The mistake is what's going on in your beautiful head right now."

Her traitorous heart skipped a beat at being called "beautiful."

"You don't know what I'm thinking," she said in clipped tones.

"You're regretting that we made love. You think the fact that you allowed me liberties makes you somehow not respectable." He paused. "And you're tempted to do me bodily harm."

She stared at him. "Now you can read minds?"

"I can read yours. Devil take it, what will it take to get it through your head that there's nothing wrong with honest passion between two consenting parties?"

"You said wicked things to me." The accusation burst from her. "Words you would never say to a lady you respected."

He frowned. "What words?"

"*I* am not going to say them!"

His eyes lit with understanding. Unbelievably, his mouth twitched.

"What is so amusing?" She would have crossed her arms in annoyance, but he had her caged. She settled for a hard stare.

Unfortunately, that only made his dimples appear. His exceedingly attractive dimples.

"Was it my use of the word *pussy* that offended you?" he inquired. "Or that I adored *eating* it? Or mayhap it was the fact that I wanted to fuck your delightful little pearl?"

"*Hush*." Even though she knew no one was about, she whipped her head left and right just to be certain. "You can't say such indecent things in public."

"I don't, usually. I also don't say them to disrespect a lady. I reserve such language for partners whose honesty in sexual matters I admire and respect."

The blasted man had an answer for everything. She couldn't deny that his sincerity mollified her. Yet she had to ask, "How many ladies have you said such things to?"

He threw back his head and laughed.

She pushed at his shoulders; it was as effective as pushing at a boulder. He swooped in and kissed her until the air was sucked from her lungs. She felt lightheaded, her knees losing their starch. She would have fallen had he not held her upright against the stone.

"Darling Maggie," he murmured. "You're adorable always. And especially when you're jealous."

"I'm not jealous," she lied. "Why should I care what you say to your other lovers?"

"Why should you indeed? To be clear, however, there will be

no other lovers while you and I carry out our liaison. For me or for you."

His fierceness surprised her as much as his words.

"We're not having a liaison," she protested.

"I just kissed you until we were both breathless," he pointed out. "I'm hard as a pike, and I'd wager your, ahem, unmentionable parts are not unaffected."

Seeing the laughter in his eyes, she scowled. "Why are we even having this discussion? You don't want a relationship. For heaven's sake, you can't even tolerate a *pet*."

"For you, I'd make an exception." His eyes were still smiling. "More to the point, you and I understand one another, do we not? We're adults, capable of enjoying the pleasure of the moment while it lasts. We need not subscribe to the tedious conventions of relationships."

"We sleep together until one of us bores of the other," she said dryly. "Have I got that right?"

"Don't forget about the exclusivity."

"If it's just about tupping, why do you even care?" she said in exasperation.

A faint line etched between his brows. "I didn't say it was just about tupping."

"Yes, you did. Although you used a euphemism." She raised her fingers in the air, mimicking quotation marks. "'*Pleasure of the moment*'?"

"It's true that going to bed with you is the very definition of pleasure. But your company offers other rewards as well."

She didn't bother to hide her skepticism. "Such as?"

"I enjoy bantering with you. I admire your intelligence and determination, the fact that you don't kowtow to anyone. I like that you're generally sensible and practical. And then there's that prim exterior of yours." His voice roughened. "It excites me, knowing the sweet, generous passion that lies beneath."

Her pulse throbbed in her throat as she stared at him. No one had ever said such things to her. No one had even *noticed* those things, she was sure of it.

"Have I made you speechless, my sweet?" He cupped her jaw, his thumb skating over her bottom lip. "May I take your silence to mean that we're having an affair?"

Tell him no. Tell him it was just one night and a mistake.

Yet her senses still hummed from their lovemaking. She felt replete, both invigorated and relaxed. An affair with Rhys would assuage the fleshly needs she could no longer deny. Moreover, when they were together, she didn't feel as if her impulses were wrong or wanton or coarse.

With him, she felt...beautiful.

And therein lay the danger.

"I...I'll think about it." Before she could regret her decision, she marched on ahead.

"Fair enough. We'll take things one day at a time. Get to know one another better." He caught up with her in an easy stride. "Speaking of which, I'm curious about your aversion to intimate words. Did your husband never use them during lovemaking?"

The question caught her off-guard. The idea of Paul expressing intimacy—verbal or physical—was unthinkable. He simply hadn't been that sort of man.

She would die before admitting that to Rhys.

"My marriage is none of your business," she stated.

"Discretion is one of your many estimable traits," he said easily. "As it happens, I'm in need of a fossil hunter whom I can trust. One who will keep my project confidential."

Damn the man. His manner was smoother than a drink of chocolate. And as difficult to resist.

Sighing, she said, "What is the job, precisely?"

"Are you signing up for it?"

She mentally weighed her options, even though in her gut she already knew which she would choose. After all, she *did* owe him. And taking the job would solve her most pressing problem.

"You'll pay me five hundred pounds as promised?" She searched his face for any sign that he might renege. "If I say yes to your job, I'll have to delay my work for Mr. Pickering-Parks. Knowing him, he'll walk away, so I'll be losing his commission if I take on yours."

What a relief it'll be not to have to grovel to that cheeseparing buffoon.

"Five hundred pounds upfront," Rhys said. "If you come back to the house with me, the money is yours to collect today."

At long last, financial security for her family was within reach.

One by one, the reasons to refuse his offer had dissipated. Her initial anger at him had faded; indeed, she realized that her anger had mostly been at herself. With regards to Glory, he'd seemed to take Maggie's denial of his paternity at face value and showed no signs of knowing that Glory was his. Even if he did, Maggie doubted that he would do anything about it.

A child would interfere with his all-important freedom. More significantly, she knew that his rakish exterior hid a core of gallantry. Her intuition told her that the man who'd charged to her rescue time and again wouldn't expose a little girl to the pain of being a bastard.

Maggie was honest enough to admit that the real threat was to her own well-being. Spending time with Rhys would make her want things she couldn't have. If she were to work with him, have an affair with him, then she would have to guard her emotions.

She couldn't open herself up to hope. Couldn't confuse kindness and pleasure with...love.

I can do this. And, for once in my life, I'm going to enjoy the moment.

Drawing a breath, she stopped. Held out her hand. "I'll take the job."

"Capital." Lips curving, Rhys shook her hand...and then brought it to his lips. "And I can be assured of your discretion?"

"You have my word." She tugged her hand free, her knuckles tingling. "Now what are you hiring me to do?"

Juxtaposed against the dawn-streaked sky, his dark hair whipping in the wind and eyes roguishly agleam, he looked like a gentleman outlaw. Elegant and ruthless. Capable of stealing not only booty—but a woman's heart.

An awareness of peril shivered through her as he flashed a charismatic grin. "As to that, sweeting...have you ever gone on a treasure hunt?"

$$\maltese \quad 12 \quad \maltese$$

On his way to the study the following afternoon, Rhys was intercepted by Quince.

"This just arrived for you." As usual, the butler was as cheerful as a dirge.

Rhys took the letter from the salver. He frowned, recognizing his man-of-business's handwriting. "By the by, I'm expecting a guest. Show Mrs. Foley to the study when she arrives."

"Yes, Your Grace."

"Er, about that. As I've mentioned, I wish to remain incognito during my stay. When Mrs. Foley is here, be sure to forgo the formalities. To her, I am simply Rhys Jones."

If the butler had any curiosity about Rhys's request, he showed no sign as he shuffled off. Then again, his former master had also chosen to prune himself from the illustrious family tree. Continuing to his study, Rhys felt the increasingly bothersome prick of guilt. He wasn't lying to Maggie for he was, indeed, Mr. Rhys Jones.

Yet he hesitated to share that he was also the Duke of Ranelagh and Somerville. First, he was hiding from cutthroats;

the fewer who knew who he was, the better. Second, he had a strong hunch that Maggie would not react well to their differences in station. The more time he spent with her, the more he understood her insecurities. Time and again, she'd thought he believed her to be less than a lady, which couldn't be further from the truth.

He knew countesses who couldn't match her dignity and duchesses who didn't have her pride.

Perhaps that was why he'd also neglected to mention the fact that he was in debt and on the flit. His past embarrassed him. He wasn't keen on revealing his weaknesses and tainting Maggie's image of him, as it were.

Stop being a namby-pamby fool, he told himself crossly. *You'll tell her what she needs to know when she needs to know it.*

Entering his study, he went to the desk. Locating the letter opener next to the heart-shaped bottle of ink, he slit open the note from Newton.

Your Grace,

Per your instructions before you left London, I have been making inquiries on your behalf. I am writing to inform you that I have located a possible candidate to meet your requirements: Miss Gretchen Sharpe, only child and heir to Mr. Thomas Sharpe, an industrialist from New York.

The Sharpes understand your terms and are eager to negotiate an advantageous arrangement for both parties, pending a personal audience with you.

Please let me know how you wish to proceed.

Your servant,

Arthur Newton

Holy hell. Rhys had almost forgotten his instructions to his man-of-business. Prior to leaving—all right, *fleeing*—London, he'd told Newton to keep an eye out for any heiresses with fortunes sufficient to cover his debts. He'd assumed that plump dowries were in short supply and that he'd likely sent Newton on a fool's errand.

Apparently, he'd underestimated both the prevalence of heiresses and his man-of-business's diligence. He shouldn't have been surprised at the latter: Arthur Newton was as reliable and loyal as they came. Rhys had once done the man a favor, and Newton had been paying him back ever since. And now Newton had found a solution to Rhys's debts.

The problem was that it involved exchanging one kind of hell for another.

I kept my end of the bargain marrying you, you Oriental bitch.

His father's venom reached through the years, dragging him back into the darkness of his mama's wardrobe, the hiding place he'd found in a panic. He wasn't supposed to be there: the duke had made it clear that his mama's suite was off-limits.

At twelve, however, Rhys was starting to resent His Grace's cruel and autocratic ways. Yesterday, the duke had sacked Miss Yardley, Rhys's most recent governess; when Rhys had protested, his sire had turned on him.

You're already weak, boy, His Grace hissed. *I won't have you turn into a needy milksop. Let this be a lesson to you: a true man doesn't need others.*

A lesson His Grace had inflicted on Rhys countless times. Yet this time, Rhys had rebelled, some instinct leading him to search out his mother. In those rare, brief times he'd been allowed to see her, she never spoke, at least not in a language he understood. But she would sometimes smile, and he thought her beautiful with her hair as smooth as black glass and eyes of translucent amber.

He didn't know why he'd come. Why he thought that seeing her might make things better.

Now you will keep your end and provide me my spare, his sire raged.

His mama's weeping seemed to fill the wardrobe. His insides turned to ice as she made a sound like that of a fatally injured animal...like Bailey's last whimper.

Spread your legs, you stupid cunt, his father roared. *Spread them, I say—*

Rhys locked away the memory. He knew how the scene ended.

The notion of domestic life—of allowing anyone too close—chilled him. Yet he'd come to grips with the reality that he might have to marry for money. If he was forced to wed, he'd vowed not to be the kind of husband and father his own had been.

But now he had another option. He had the inheritance from his uncle—and with Maggie's help, his hope of finding it soared. Even though theirs was just an affair, she distracted him from his woes. He enjoyed her company as much as her luscious body.

With her, he didn't feel as...alone.

While he wanted to tell Newton to forgo the whole heiress business, he knew he couldn't. He had to prepare for the possibility that he might not find the treasure. Or what if he did, but the treasure's worth wasn't as impressive as Horatio claimed it was? Miss Sharpe's dowry might be Rhys's last hope, the only thing standing between him and two murderous moneylenders.

Rhys believed in hedging his bets. Especially when he was betting on himself.

Thus, he settled for a compromise: in his reply to Newton, he instructed the other to delay the Sharpes for a fortnight. If he hadn't made progress on the treasure hunt by then, then he probably never would. He'd give himself two weeks, then he would reassess and do what needed to be done.

Two weeks of freedom. Two weeks to find those legendary jewels.

Two weeks to be with Maggie.

He'd just finished sealing the missive with wax when he heard voices in the hallway. He rose as Maggie followed in Quince's tow like spring on the heels of a bleak winter. It mattered naught that her hair was once again restrained in a prim knot or that she wore drab widow's weeds or that a battered leather tool bag was slung across her body: her radiant sensuality halted his breath.

By Jove, it had only been a day since he'd had her, and he wanted her again. Right here. Now.

Chiding his own lack of self-discipline, he dismissed Quince and bowed to her. "You are a vision of loveliness."

She flushed, looking uncomfortable—as if gallantry of any kind was alien to her. It made him want to shower her with compliments and gewgaws, the things ladies took for granted. He realized that he hadn't given Maggie any gifts...unless one counted the damnable fifty-pound note he'd once carelessly left her.

The memory made him cringe. With increasing discomfiture, he recognized that he was in no position to give her diamond necklaces or carte blanche at the modiste, the kind of presents he'd given lovers in the past. Nonetheless, he made note to get her some token of his esteem, even if a trinket was all he could afford at present.

"Thank you." Her smile was shy as she set her lumpy tool bag down by the desk. "Your home is very grand."

This place, grand? It was a dump. He thought of his family seat in Northumberland, a sprawling estate of several hundred acres. His sire had run the place into the ground, and Rhys hadn't the means to restore the once gracious country house or its surrounding lands.

A startling, unbidden image flashed in his head: Maggie standing amidst the flourishing gardens of his renovated estate, dressed in a stylish gown. She wore the prior duchess's exotic jewels; they were the only things he had left of his mama, and out of stupid sentiment, he couldn't bring himself to sell them. A strange, wild sensation thumped in his chest—before he firmly suppressed it.

"Uncle Horatio wasn't much for domestic matters," he said. "Runs in the family."

Her head tipped to one side. "Do you have an estate of your own?"

He was treading on thin ice, yet he didn't want to lie to her. "There's a family property in Northumberland. My parents lived there when they were alive."

"Glory mentioned that your parents had passed. I'm sorry to hear it."

"Don't be. My father was a bastard, and we never got on," he said flatly.

Her lashes swept up, her tip-tilted eyes wide. "And your mama...were you close to her?"

As a rule, he never spoke about his mother. But something about Maggie's honest curiosity compelled him to answer.

"Not really," he said curtly. "She was Chinese, the daughter of a merchant my father had dealings with. Our communication was limited since she did not speak English. She was frail, and I did not see her much; she died when I was twelve."

He waited for Maggie's reaction. Would she be repulsed by his mixed blood? Titillated? He was used to those responses.

"My mama passed when I was thirteen." The verdant empathy in her eyes caused an odd constriction in his chest. "I still miss her."

"I imagine the feeling of loss is proportionate to the degree of one's attachment." Another reason to avoid entanglements, he reminded himself. They were messy to begin with and invariably resulted in pain.

She nodded, then said hesitantly, "Was it difficult?"

"As I said, I was not close to my mama."

"Not that. I meant being...different."

Her acute observation cut through his calluses to the tenderness beneath. The sweet pain jolted him, made his brows draw together.

"I didn't mean to pry," she said hastily. "It's just that being a Goode, well...I understand what it's like to be judged for something beyond one's control."

In her eyes, he saw a reflection of himself unlike any he'd seen before. He felt laid bare, exposed. He didn't care for the feeling.

To distract her, he reached out and tucked a stray tress behind her ear. His fingers trailed lazily down her silken jaw and neck, to the throbbing pulse above the high neck of her serviceable gown. A flush suffused her cheeks.

"I've found that being unique has its benefits," he said in deliberately drawling tones. "Scarcity of supply increases demand, after all."

"I'm sure that's true for you." Her eyes looked a bit glazed. "But we can't all look like a pirate prince."

He blinked. "You think I look like a *pirate?*"

"Well, um, a regal one. A gentleman outlaw, that is." She jerked away, clearly flustered. "With your coloring, eyes, and beard, you look civilized yet roguish. Like you're capable of carrying out dashing misdeeds while gallantly rescuing a maiden in distress..."

For once, he was speechless. He stared at her in mute fascination.

Now beet red, she snatched up her tool bag, muttering, "We ought to get going before the high tides reach the caves."

"Allow me." He took the bag from her, his brows rising at its heft. "By Jove, are we planning to live in the cave for a week? What have you got in here?"

"Just a few tools for excavation," she said. "It pays to be prepared."

He slung the bag on his shoulder, wondering how the hell she managed to carry the weight on her own. "If this bag is any indication, I'm sure we will be—even if the plague hits."

~

As Maggie led the way through the winding cavern tunnel, Rhys close behind her, she realized that for the first time in years, she felt...alive.

In part, it was because she was finally free from the looming cloud of debt. She'd gone to Rotherby's bank this morning and plunked down the five hundred pounds Rhys had paid her. Now no one could take away her shop: her family's livelihood was secure.

But it was more than freedom she was feeling. Making love with Rhys had uncorked a bubbling vitality: she felt like a sleep-walker who'd suddenly come awake. Her roused senses hungrily soaked in all that she'd been missing, from his spice-tinged virility to the heat of his nearness.

Her heart pumped; impulses swirled in her veins.

Flushing, she couldn't believe she'd told Rhys that he looked like a pirate. Luckily, he'd seemed more amused than offended. With each exchange they shared, she glimpsed another facet of him. He'd never spoken of his family before, and she couldn't help but feel sympathy for a boy who'd clearly had a strained relationship with his father and a non-existent one with his mother.

The more she learned about Rhys, the less he seemed like a carefree rake. Despite his charming exterior, there was darkness in him. She recognized those shadows of loneliness—because they haunted her too.

Don't let your emotions get involved, she lectured herself. *Concentrate on the job he's hired you to do.*

Having explored the caverns before, she knew the present underground passage connected three separate caverns. They'd searched the first two and found nothing; now they were on their way to the third. Here in the final stretch the tunnel would reach its narrowest point.

"You may have to duck and walk sideways to fit through the next section of the tunnel," she advised. "We'll be coming upon the last vestibule soon."

"Capital."

Something in his tone made her look more closely at him. The flickering light of the lamp revealed the sheen of perspiration on his face. He looked...queasy?

"Is everything all right?" she asked.

"I'm fine," he muttered. "Let's move on."

"If you're not feeling well, we can head back—"

"We're not going back." His jaw clenched. "I'm not traversing this blasted tunnel again."

It dawned on her. "Do you have a fear of closed spaces?"

"They're not my favorite places." Lines of unease deepened on his forehead.

She thought back to their escape from the excise men. "You didn't seem to have a problem when we spent the night in a cave."

"I didn't have time to have a problem. We were running for our lives through that tunnel. The cave didn't bother me because the ceiling was high. And you distracted me." He quirked a brow. "Care to do so again?"

Her belly fluttered. At his flirtatiousness, yes, but more so at the fact that this big, confident fellow had a weakness. The fact that he was trying to hide his unease behind a devil-may-care façade was rather endearing.

She couldn't resist teasing him. "We *could* make love right now, but we might run out of air. And one doesn't want to make excessive movements due to possible avalanches. Being buried in rock would be a terrible way to go."

Above his cravat, his throat worked. "Unfair, sweeting. Bloody unfair."

She hid a grin. On impulse, she took his hand.

"Come along, dear," she said in the manner she would use with a frightened child. "I won't let anything happen to you, I promise."

His hand engulfed hers, squeezing hard. "Have your fun now,

pet. But know that I'm a man whose personal motto is *quid pro quo*."

She tugged him forward, continuing the conversation to distract him. "Quid pro...what?"

"It means tit for tat."

"You won't be able to scare me with closed spaces." She turned sideways to fit, and with a grimace, he followed suit. "I've spent too much time in places like this."

"You have an unusual passion." His hand gripped hers like a lifeline.

"It's not a passion. It's my livelihood."

"You don't enjoy collecting fossils?"

"I don't *dislike* it. There are worse jobs one could have, and trust me, I've had a few of those. Fossil finding has its merits. But is it my life's dream to scavenge for old bones and preserved fecal matter?" Her shoulders hitched against rock as they continued to walk sideways through the tight channel. "Not really."

"When you put it that way." Amusement colored his voice. "Tell me, what is your passion?"

Their lovemaking blazed in her memory. She bit her lip.

His husky laugh echoed through the passageway. "Besides that, you lusty wench. What I meant was, if you had the freedom to choose, what would you most enjoy doing?"

She glanced at him. "I'd open a flower shop."

"Ah, yes...you mentioned that the night we met."

He actually listened to me and remembers what I told him all those years ago?

He proceeded to astound her further. "The arrangements at Foley's. Are they yours?"

She couldn't believe that he'd noticed them. "I wanted something to brighten up the shop. I couldn't justify the expense of buying hothouse blooms, so they're mostly wildflowers—"

"They're lovely. You've a way with flowers, Maggie."

His compliment slid through her like a hot toddy. "I learned from my mama. She didn't have an easy go of it, being left to raise me and my four siblings after my papa died. But she used to say to me, *Maggie, my girl, don't forget to stop and smell the flowers.*"

"Pragmatic yet fanciful." He was looking at her as if he'd just figured out a puzzle. Then his gaze shifted beyond her. "About bloody time."

They'd reached the end of the tunnel, which now widened into the final cavern. Maggie held her lamp up higher, revealing the striated brown walls and dome-shaped ceiling that nature had miraculously created.

"This is the last cavern," she said. "Let's split up to look for the treasure."

Rhys nodded and they circled the perimeter, going in opposite directions. She held her lantern aloft, running her fingers along the rugged surfaces. As she worked, she wondered again why Horatio would hide Rhys's inheritance in a cave. Rich folks did have more money than sense, it seemed.

"Maggie—I've found something."

She hurried over. Rhys had set down her tool bag and was attempting to pry loose chunks of rock from the wall using his hands.

"This section looked different from the rest," he said intently. "I think someone packed this rock in there."

Crouching, she rummaged through her tool bag, extracting a small pickaxe. "Here, try this."

He struck the tool into the wall, and rock came free. On the second hit, more rock showered to the ground. On the third try, he exclaimed, "By Jove, I think I struck something."

"Careful. You don't want to damage whatever it is." She took out a brush made of stiffened horse hair. "Here, let me clear the way."

Leaning in, she employed the brush with the same care she

used when extricating delicate bones from rock. Plumes of gravel and dust dissipated, revealing a carved mahogany surface.

"It's a chest," she said with surging excitement. "And it's large."

"Allow me."

She stepped aside to give Rhys room. Gripping the sides of the wooden box, he yanked it free in a cloud of dust. The chest was as wide as his torso and nearly as long. He set it down on the ground with a clunk; they both knelt beside it.

"It's heavy." Rhys's exhilaration was palpable. "Let's see what's inside, shall we?"

Her breath held as he reached for the brass clasp and flipped open the lid.

In the red satin interior sat a folded piece of paper.

Scowling, Rhys snatched up the note and scanned it. "Devil take it."

"What is it?"

"Another damned clue."

Peering over his shoulder, she read aloud, "*See with your heart, not your eyes.*" She frowned. "What does that mean?"

"Bloody hell if I know." He ripped off the satin lining, his scowl deepening when all that was revealed was the box's wooden sides. "Horatio and his damned games. He's probably laughing his head off from behind the pearly gates—unless he ended up in hotter climes. Would serve him right."

His words simmered with frustration, yet Maggie sensed another emotion as well. A feeling she was well acquainted with: desperation.

Softly, she ventured, "This inheritance...it's important to you, isn't it?"

His gaze swung to hers, then away just as quickly. Yet she caught the flash of battered pride.

"I have debts. Significant ones." He appeared fixated on the scrap of paper, which he was folding into precise squares. "The situation is of my own making, and I had hoped to find the solution in this cave." His lips twisted with self-derision. "But I've failed once again."

Her heart squeezed with empathy. She understood too well the helplessness of not having enough money. Of feeling that one's survival was under constant threat.

"You haven't failed." She touched his arm, wool-covered steel flexing beneath her fingertips. "You've found the next clue, which is what your uncle meant for you to do, isn't it? 'Tis a treasure hunt after all. You simply must persevere, find the next clue, and the next...until the prize is yours. And it will be, if you don't give up."

He aimed a brooding look at her. "You believe that?"

"Yes. And you won't have to go at it alone. I'll help you."

"Our deal was for you to search the caves. You've held up your end," he said curtly. "I cannot afford to pay you more."

"I'm including my ongoing services as part of our bargain."

His brow furrowed. "Why would you do that?"

Clearly, he wasn't used to being offered support. While she'd made the offer on impulse, she knew that it was the right thing to do. He seemed so alone in his troubles; she couldn't stand for him to lose hope. Especially when he'd given her the means to solve her own financial problems.

"Two heads are better than one." She employed a crisp tone, sensing that his pride would balk at any hint of compassion. "When we at Foley's take on a client, we like to see the job to the end."

"Ever the consummate professional." The ring of his irises turned to molten gold, the emotion there causing a flutter in her belly. "I won't take your charity, however."

"It's not charity—"

"You'll take a cut," he said firmly. "Five percent of whatever we find."

Relieved that he was accepting her help, she nodded. "We shouldn't linger. The tide will be coming in soon."

He helped her to her feet. He didn't release her hand but, rather, brought it to his lips. The tender brush of his bristle and the raw wonder in his eyes halted her breath.

"Let's go then, sweeting," he said hoarsely. "We've work to do."

❃ 13 ❃

Dusk was falling by the time they returned to the manor. Dumping the useless chest in the study, Rhys invited Maggie to stay for supper.

"I'd like to stay," she said with clear regret. "But Glory and Hypatia are expecting me."

"All right. Let's go."

"Wait...you're coming home with me?"

He frowned at her astonished tone. "I'm not going to allow a woman to ride home unescorted. In the dark, no less."

"I do it all the time."

He did not find the notion reassuring. "Being a widow, I'm sure that was unavoidable."

"I did it even when my husband was alive," Maggie said.

God's teeth, hadn't anyone ever looked out for this woman? Her dead husband plummeted further in Rhys's esteem. While Rhys wouldn't win any prizes in chivalry, he would not let her take unnecessary risks.

"He's not here. I am," he said. "You'll have to do with my escort."

When Maggie looked as if she might argue, he forestalled her by taking her face in his hands and doing what he'd wanted to do since her endearing offer to help him. He kissed her.

Her "Oh" of surprise gave him the entry he desired. His lips courted hers, his tongue exploring her honeyed cavern. She was the essence of sweetness. Her warmth and generosity warmed him to the marrow.

She sighed, her head tipping back to give him more access.

Finally, he had to break off the kiss. Running his thumb over her plush, kiss-swollen lips, he murmured, "We'd better go."

Her eyes had that dazed look. The way it took them several moments to come into focus was bloody glorious. He adored the way she lost herself in their passion, the way primness gave way to sensuality. The blush that spread over her cheeks was lovelier than a sunrise. She pulled away, patting her hands over her hair and brushing her somber skirts.

"Yes," she mumbled. "We ought to—"

"Sweetheart." He curled a finger under her chin, bringing her flustered gaze to his. "If I had my way, I'd sweep you off to my bed and make love to you all night. My cock is throbbing like the devil, just from the touch of your lips against mine. But your family is waiting, and I don't wish to cause them worry."

Her eyes darted to his groin, widening. Even Bond Street tailoring could not hide the prominent bulge of his erection. He was so aroused that he could feel his pre-seed dampening his smalls—damn, from a simple kiss.

She wetted her lips, and the pulsing in his bollocks grew. Then she dazzled him with a smile, his breath catching at the purity of her beauty.

"You're right, we should go," she whispered.

He kissed her on her nose, and they proceeded to her cottage without further ado.

Upon their arrival, the front door of the snug stone cottage was flung open before they reached the front step. Glory scampered out, her cinnamon plaits bouncing over her shoulders.

"Hello, Mr. Jones," she said breathlessly before addressing her mother. "Mama, thank goodness you are home! Aunt Delilah is here." Her nose scrunched as raised female voices came from inside the house. "Aunt Patty isn't too pleased about it."

"Merciful heavens," Maggie muttered. "How long have they been at it?"

"Aunt Delilah arrived a few minutes ago, and she was in a state," the girl supplied helpfully.

"She's always in a state." Maggie sighed, turning to him. "Thank you for the escort. If you'll excuse me, I must talk to my sister—"

Before she could finish her sentence, a woman emerged from the cottage. Even in the falling light, Rhys saw that she shared Maggie's coloring and build. Her features were coarser, however, and her eyes lacked the alluring, tip-tilted shape of Maggie's. She would still be considered an attractive woman, had her personality not stamped itself upon her face.

Bitter lines bracketed her mouth. Her eyes were squinted with spite, and her application of paint was far from subtle. Her bright pink frock was scanty on top and boasted an excess of ruffles, ribbons, and pleats on the bottom. Juxtaposed against Maggie's somber dignity, she had the look of cheap wares.

Her gaze landed on Rhys, and her demeanor altered. Coyness smoothed out her peevish lines. He couldn't say he found it an improvement.

"Well, Maggie, was wondering what was keeping you. Now oi can see for myself." Her sooted eyelashes fluttered as she held her hand out to him. "Oi don't believe oi've 'ad the pleasure?"

He touched her as briefly as possible. "Rhys Jones, ma'am. I'm a patron of Foley's."

"The name's Delilah Wilson." She sidled up to him, and in doing so, "accidentally" brushed her breasts against his arm. "Oi be Maggie's sister...and a widow."

By Jove, the woman has the manner of a ha'penny whore.

He looked at Maggie, whose cheeks were stained with embarrassment. She avoided his eyes.

"What do you want, Delilah?" she asked in a low voice.

Delilah's coyness dropped from her like dung from a cow. She whirled to face her sister.

"Oi want you to fix the problem you caused," she snapped.

"I didn't cause any problems for you."

"Oh no?" Delilah slapped her hands on her hips. "Then why is Jeremy setting up camp in my 'ouse? Says 'e needs a place to stay on account o' 'is ship not coming in the other night."

Maggie inhaled, clearly trying to hold onto her temper. "That is not my fault. I tried to help him—"

"Clearly you didn't because now 'is lazy arse is on my settee! Oi ain't got room for that git!"

Rhys winced. Delilah's voice scratched over his eardrums like a fork over china.

"Please be reasonable." In contrast, Maggie kept her tones soft and controlled. "With Mr. Wilson gone, you've an entire cottage all to yourself—"

"That don't mean oi got to take our ramshacklum brother under my roof!"

"I would take Jeremy in, but our rooms are all occupied—"

"You could share with that precious girl o' yours. Or is she too spoiled for that?"

Seeing Glory shrink back at her aunt's venomous tone, Rhys felt a surge of anger. *How dare the bitch frighten a young girl?* He strode over to Glory, placing himself between her and her aunt. From behind him, she slipped her small hand into his.

"Glory could bunk with you or that uppity ape leader you call a sister-in-law," Maggie's sister griped on.

"Better an ape leader than an ill-bred fishwife." The retort came from Hypatia. She now stood in the cottage doorway, menace glittering behind her spectacles.

Delilah sized her up, and Hypatia returned the favor. For an instant, Rhys wondered if he was going to have to break up a brawl between the two women.

Then Delilah turned to Maggie. "Are you going to let 'er talk to me like that?"

"This has naught to do with Hypatia or Glory, so leave them out of this," Maggie said. "The point is that you have two spare bedchambers—"

"You *are* siding with her!" Delilah spat. "Well, ain't that a surprise. Miss 'Igh-And-Mighty lording it o'er the rest o' us."

"I never lorded it over you." Maggie's voice trembled. "Over anyone."

"Always thought yourself be'er than the rest o' us. Always the babe and Ma's favorite," her sister sneered. "Well, yer fine manners and fancy speech don't put food on the table, do they? Maybe you ought to 'ave made your bed with a man like mine. My Wilson might've been a fishmonger, but 'e knew 'ow to keep a woman 'appy. Knew 'is way 'round Cupid's Alley, 'e did. The man could rut like a stallion all night long an' still go to work come morn. That's why 'e left me with enough o' the ready to enjoy myself. Why should oi give any o' it to you, eh?"

"I've never asked you for money. For anything," Maggie whispered. "You came to *me* wanting me to take Jeremy off your hands."

"Ma always said you were the good one. The responsible one." Her sister's voice shook with rage. "Well, you ain't so perfect now, are you?"

Rhys had witnessed enough. "You will desist this attack, madam. At once."

Delilah whirled on him. "Who're you to give me orders?"

"I'm the man who will enforce consequences if you do not take yourself off."

The woman blinked, then her sneer returned. "Patron of Foley's, my arse. You're tupping my saintly little sister 'ere, aren't you? She's got you by the cock with her simpering, virginal ways!"

Maggie gasped. Glory let go of his hand and scrambled to her mama's side. She huddled close, offering comfort the best she could, her loyalty and courage plain to see.

Rhys stalked over to Delilah. For once, he didn't mask his emotions. He let his displeasure show—and even the harpy retreated a step.

"Leave now," he said. "You're embarrassing yourself and upsetting your sister and niece."

"Why does everyone always take Maggie's side? What about me?" Her belligerence waning, Delilah sounded like a petulant child. "Why do oi 'ave to put up with bleeding Jeremy—"

"What you do with Jeremy is of no consequence to me. Throw him out, if that's your wish. He's a grown man, and his troubles are his own. What you will *not* do is come here and disrespect your sister. Not in front of her child and in her own home. Not ever. Do I make myself clear?"

Delilah opened her mouth...then closed it.

"You may go." He dismissed her in his most ducal voice.

After shooting one last spiteful look at her sister, Delilah scurried off.

He turned to Maggie. Hypatia and Glory flanked her, and all three were staring at him.

"How did you *do* that?" Maggie breathed.

He lifted his brows. "Do what?"

She waved in the direction that her sister had departed. "Get Delilah to..."

"Stop acting like an ill-mannered hussy," Patty said succinctly.

"Aunt Delilah never listens to anyone," Glory clarified. "And she only pays us a call when her drawers are in a knot. Which they *always* are."

"Glory—" Maggie began.

"But it's true! Aunt Delilah never visits unless she's in a high dudgeon."

He frowned at Maggie. "Never say your husband allowed her

to insult you in this manner? Here, on his own property?"

Maggie bit her lip. Slid a look at Patty. "Paul, um, avoided Delilah whenever possible."

What the devil was wrong with the man? Rhys would not permit his woman or child to be treated shabbily—not that Maggie or Glory were his, he reminded himself hastily.

"Can you blame him?" Hypatia said darkly. "That woman is a disgrace."

"She's my kin." Pain threaded Maggie's voice.

Although it was at times to her own detriment, she was a loyal thing. He'd never met a woman with her sense of responsibility, and he couldn't help but admire it.

"Have you had supper, Mr. Jones?"

Hypatia's question diverted him from his thoughts. "Er, no, Miss Foley, I have not."

"You're welcome to join us, if you like," the spinster said graciously.

"Do say you'll stay," Glory pleaded. "We're celebrating the clearing of the shop's debts. Aunt Patty made her famous mutton stew, and for dessert we're having the apple cake Mama baked."

The mention of food made Rhys's stomach rumble. He realized that it had been hours since he'd last eaten. This was Maggie's home and her family, however, and he was her casual lover. Uncertain of his welcome in her domestic domain, he gave her a questioning look.

"You're welcome to stay, if you'd like." Her smile roused a hunger that was for more than food. For something he'd never had. For something he couldn't resist even though he knew he should.

"If it wouldn't be an imposition," he said.

"Hooray!" Glory skipped over to him, her small hand again slipping into his.

It felt oddly right. He offered Maggie his other arm.

Together, the three of them headed into the glowing cottage.

❧ 14 ❧

"Good afternoon, Quince." Maggie smiled at the butler. "I believe Mr. Jones is expecting me."

"That he is, Mrs. Foley," Quince grumbled as he ushered her in. "Been pacing like a caged tiger waiting for you to arrive."

Maggie was glad that the butler was ahead of her and didn't see her blush as he led her to Rhys's study. Truth be told, it heartened her to know that Rhys was as impatient to see her as she was to see him. She was still bemused at how he'd handled Delilah: no one had ever stood up for Maggie that way.

Supper last night had been a further revelation. Rhys had fit in with her family like the missing piece of a puzzle. Conversation had flowed, punctuated by laughter. Maggie had worried that the homey dishes might not suit his sophisticated palate, yet he'd complimented Hypatia on the stew and Maggie on the apple cake. He'd shown his appreciation by finishing two generous helpings of each.

Moreover, he'd brought out the best in Glory. She'd insisted on sitting next to him, chattering at him for the duration of the supper. He'd listened with surprising patience to the trials and tribulations of an eight-year-old girl. When Glory disclosed that she'd been bullied by an older classmate, Billy Pinkleton—a fact that she hadn't shared with Maggie or Patty—Rhys had given her sound advice.

Glory had actually *listened* to him. Perhaps it was the way he spoke to her, directly and without sugar-coating matters, that made her receptive. After he'd left, Patty, too, had made note of how well Rhys and Glory got on.

Maggie had to wonder if blood recognized blood. The secret she was keeping discomfited her, but she told herself it was for the best. Rhys's presence in her and Glory's lives was temporary. She couldn't get used to having his chivalry, his masculine care in her life. She had to enjoy the moments with him while they lasted —and not yearn for anything more.

Arriving at his study, her thoughts skidded to a halt. It was difficult to think, to even breathe, when confronted by all that was Rhys.

His hair was a dark mane around his handsome-as-the-devil face. He was in his shirtsleeves, his bronze silk cravat an elegant knot beneath the trimmed scruff on his chin. His navy waistcoat hugged his lean torso, and his tan trousers followed the sinewy line of his legs, tucking into tall, polished boots.

And he was, indeed, prowling before the fireplace like an impatient beast.

Quince shuffled off, and before the door had closed, Rhys came straight up to her. His mouth claimed hers in a passionate greeting. She kissed him back with burning eagerness. Their lips and tongues fused, heat pouring through her in waves. It was as if desire had been simmering between them since their night in the cave, and now it boiled over.

Finally, they had to come up for air.

Tracing his thumb over her bottom lip, he said huskily, "Christ, I needed that."

"Me too," she blurted.

His eyes gleamed. "Ah, Maggie, you do know how to flatter a man."

Ruffled by the intensity of her desire, she managed a snort. "As if you need to be flattered."

"There's where you're wrong. We males like to have our manhood stroked."

"Then stroke it yourself," she retorted.

He lifted his brows.

Realizing her unintentional double entendre, she felt her cheeks blaze.

Rhys's laugh was husky. "That's taking self-sufficiency to a new level, isn't it? I, personally, prefer to delegate this particular task. Then again, I'm not as formidable as you."

Maggie was torn between his sensual teasing and his assessment of her. "I'm formidable?"

He playfully tweaked a curl that had come loose at her temple. "You, sweeting, are a force of nature. You run a shop, explore caves, and raise a child. You also somehow find time to bake the tastiest apple cake I've ever sampled. Compared to that, I'm basically a lazy sod."

She couldn't tell if he was pulling her leg.

"I just do what needs to be done. Besides," she averred, "you've many positive qualities."

"Do I?"

"You're honorable and kind, for starters."

"Those aren't qualities I'm generally known for," he said wryly.

"Well, you have been to me...and Glory." Maggie swallowed against a pulse of emotion. "Thank you for listening to her last night. I didn't even know that Billy Pinkleton was pestering her."

Over supper, Glory had revealed that the blasted Pinkleton boy had been calling her names ever since she beat him in a tree-climbing contest. Although Maggie had chastised Glory for engaging in hoydenish behavior, she'd been more bothered by the fact that her daughter hadn't told her about the bullying. And that

Snelling had turned a blind eye to Glory's mistreatment by her classmates.

How could Maggie not know all this? How could she be so remiss in her duties as a mother?

"Don't blame yourself." Again, Rhys displayed his singular ability to read her thoughts. "Glory's a bright child. If she doesn't want you to know something, she'll find a way to hide it."

She stared at him. *How does he understand Glory so well?*

Indeed, he'd given the girl sound advice on how to deal with the unwelcome attention. It had made Maggie wonder at his own experience of dealing with bullies. The time that she'd asked about the pressures of being different due to his mixed heritage, he'd brushed her off. Yet she knew how cruel children could be. Could it be that this handsome, confident fellow had suffered unpopularity in his life?

"Glory looks up to you," Maggie said. "Sees you as a hero for saving the shop."

"I'm no hero." The flatness of his tone took her aback. He retreated to his desk, shuffling through some papers. "I'm just a man and not a very good one at that."

She followed him there, facing him across the desk. "Since your return, you've been nothing but good to me. Honest and true to your word."

"Maggie...there's something I need to tell you."

The alertness of his gaze made her instinctively brace. "What is it?"

"Perhaps you ought to sit for this." He gestured to the chair behind her.

Warily, she complied.

He cleared his throat. "There's something I've been meaning to tell you. I had my reasons for not divulging it straight away, and I must once again ask for your discretion."

"All right." She knotted her cold fingers in her lap. "What is it?"

He crossed to her side, leaning against the front of the desk. "I haven't been entirely honest about my identity."

Icicles prickled her nape. "What do you mean? You...you're not Rhys Jones?"

"I am. That is, it is one of my names," he hedged.

One of his names? He had *aliases*? She could think of only one reason a man would need alternate identities: he was in trouble with the authorities. Blooming hell, her brothers went by different names up and down the Dorset coast to avoid detection by the magistrates.

The chill in her spread. What kind of trouble was Rhys in?

"There are reasons, good reasons, for why I haven't told you who I am," he went on.

"What crime did you commit?" The words rushed from her.

He blinked. "Beg pardon?"

"That's why you're in hiding, isn't it? To evade the authorities..." She trailed off at his baffled expression.

"Devil take it, I'm no criminal," he said, clearly offended.

"Oh." She released a breath that she hadn't known she was holding. "That's a relief."

"What I am is a duke."

It was her turn to blink. "You're a...what?"

"Edward Rhys Hugo Jones Cavendish, the Fifth Duke of Ranelagh and Somerville, Earl of Somerville, Viscount Lorne, etcetera, at your service."

He made a leg. An elegant leg. A *ducal* leg.

Waves of numbness rocked her. She stumbled to her feet, but he caught her by the waist.

"Let me go," she said in a trembling voice.

"Not until you tell me why you're leaving. My title changes nothing."

"How can you say that?" Anger pierced her shock. "You *lied* to me."

Did he think to amuse himself by dallying with a woman of

her class? The humiliation of finding that fifty-pound note years ago roared back. A part of her had always known that he was out of her reach. Now she was discovering just how far above her he was.

Her temples throbbed. *A duke...he's a blooming duke.*

"It was more a sin of omission—but, I agree, let's not split hairs," he said hastily when she glared at him. "Sweeting, I had reason to keep my identity a secret. You know about my debts, but what you don't know is that I owe the money to cutthroats. Two of London's most notorious, to be precise. To the tune of fifty thousand pounds apiece."

This second revelation was no less stunning. Merciful heavens, he owed *a hundred thousand pounds* to cutthroats? Jeremy had once taken a small loan from a shady moneylender. She still recalled his battered face after he'd failed to make the first payment. She'd never seen her feckless brother pay off a debt so quickly.

"Now they're out for my blood." Rhys released her, raking a hand through his dark hair. "That is why I left London, why I sought anonymity here as Rhys Jones."

"But you're a *duke*. Can't you sell off your properties, jewels, horses...?"

Her vague wave encompassed all the riches she'd always associated with the exalted title.

"Everything that isn't entailed or nailed down has been sold," he said bluntly. "The financial troubles did not begin with me. My father, the former duke, lived well beyond his means and mismanaged the estate. It wasn't until his deathbed that he presented me with my true inheritance: a duchy in ruin." His mouth twisted. "His Grace rather enjoyed that moment, I think. Told me I was getting what I deserved. Said a weakling like me would have destroyed the duchy anyway."

"What a horrid thing to say," she burst out.

No wonder Rhys had called his father a bastard.

"He wasn't entirely wrong." Rhys spoke without inflection.

"He created the debts, but I made them worse through my idiotic investments." Self-loathing darkened his eyes. "I had a bequest from my mother, which I used to invest in schemes that promised the highest yields. My initial bets paid off. I was able to reduce the debts and continue to live in the manner to which I was accustomed.

"Over time, however, my investments began to fail. One by one, they pulled me deeper and deeper into the abyss of ruin. The situation got out of control, and I lost my head. I turned to the bottle, spent my days gambling, brawling...whoring."

He looked at her beneath his lashes. She realized he was awaiting her condemnation, perhaps wanting it. She remained silent for no one could judge him more harshly than he clearly did himself.

"Out of desperation, I made the worst mistake of all," he said darkly. "I turned to the cent-per-cents, thinking I would use borrowed money to earn back what I had lost."

She swallowed, knowing the outcome.

"In the end, I lost everything and more. And my failure didn't affect only me. I had to let scores of servants go, some of them long-time retainers at the family seat. When I sold off my residences in London and Paris, the staff there lost their livelihoods as well. With my arrogance and stupidity, I destroyed lives."

His brutal self-condemnation squeezed her heart. She went to him, laid a hand on his arm. Beneath the linen, his bicep was curved steel.

"You cannot be faulted for trying to make the best of a bad situation," she said.

He shook his head. "Not only did I not improve the situation, I made it worse—*far* worse."

"In retrospect, yes, you did," she said frankly. "But if we knew in hindsight what we do in the present, life would be so much simpler, wouldn't it? We all make mistakes. It is how we respond to them that matters. You can berate yourself endlessly, but where will that get you?"

He stared pensively at a point beyond her.

"Now you are making a different choice. A better one." She was determined for him to see that. "Once you find your inheritance, you will restore what you've lost and the livelihoods of those once dependent upon you. The important thing is that you mustn't give up hope."

He suddenly reached out, snatching her against him. Her breath whooshed out as she collided with his hard frame. Her heart thumped as he kept her tucked against him, as he just...held her.

"Thank you," he said gruffly.

"I didn't do anything," she whispered.

"You're you, and you're extraordinary."

She couldn't let that untruth stand. Tipping her head back, she said, "I'm ordinary."

Beneath his mustache, his lips curved. "There's not a single thing ordinary about you, Maggie. Even the fact that you think you are is extraordinary."

"Everything I said was just common sense."

"That is one thing lacking in the *ton*. Or perhaps Society simply enjoyed witnessing my downfall." His expression turned stark. "Because of my mixed blood, I was an outcast at Eton. I learned early on how to deal with bullies. As I became an adult, my "exotic" looks made me popular. But as my fortunes turned, people whom I called friends turned their backs on me. Not one of them offered to lend a hand. They lost interest once I ceased to live up to the image of the devil-may-care rake."

Now that he'd explained why he hadn't told her about his being a duke, she was no longer angry. Her heart bled for the ostracism he'd endured. The cruelty that had been inflicted upon him through no fault of his own. How well she understood that brand of helplessness.

At the same time, her stomach sank like quicksand. Although she'd always known that their affair was temporary, now she *felt* it. A duke and a former bar maid—there could be no happy ending.

"What's going on in that head of yours?" Rhys tipped her chin up. "Regretting your decision to help a man like me? I wouldn't blame you. Failure is not the most attractive quality, is it?"

Despite his sardonic tone, vulnerability lurked in his eyes. She couldn't stand for him to believe that she thought any less of him. That she was any less attracted to him. In truth, his imperfections, his humanity, drew her to him even more.

Don't think about the future. Enjoy this affair for as long as it lasts... for that is all you'll ever have with Rhys.

She summoned a brisk tone. "You're *not* a failure. And wallowing will not help you."

"Strange...that's what Horatio said to me," he said, almost wistfully. "He came to me a year ago, tried to talk me into taking a different path. But I was too far gone to heed his advice. I was angry at myself—and I took it out on him."

"I'm sure your uncle understood that you didn't mean it," she said gently. "After all, he left you an inheritance. He must have cared for you."

"When I was twelve, I stayed with him for a summer. Those were the best months of my life...then my mama died shortly afterward. My father packed me off to Eton. I wrote countless letters to my uncle, never receiving a reply. Being an explorer, Horatio was always off on a grand adventure, and I understand that now, but back then..." His shrug was self-deprecating. "I hadn't yet learned the lesson of self-reliance."

Maggie had the vision of a motherless boy, sent to Eton by an uncaring father, waiting for letters from an uncle that never came. And her heart wept even more. Yet her practical nature told her it was too late for pity or sympathy. What she could offer Rhys now was support.

"You are not alone now. You have me," she said resolutely, "and we have a treasure to find. You say I'm extraordinary, but the truth is I'm just stubborn. When I make mistakes, and I do so often, I pick myself up and try again. You can do the same. I believe in you."

"By Jove...what did I do to deserve you?"

His hoarse reverence curled her toes. She said, "You paid me five hundred pounds."

He blinked—then threw his head back and laughed. "Bloody hell, I did, didn't I? You drove a hard bargain, Margaret Foley."

"Good help is hard to find...um, Your Grace." She wondered if it was even proper to call him by his Christian name now that she knew who he was.

"Showing me proper respect, are you? There's a change." His gaze turned solemn. "To you, I'm Rhys, just Rhys. Always."

She masked her longing, her gaze falling on the scrap of paper on Rhys's desk. The clue they'd found in the cave.

"Since you've retained my invaluable expertise," she said brightly, "shall we get on with the business of solving Horatio's clue?"

"In a moment."

She tilted her head. "Do we have more pressing business to attend to?"

His smile was slow and sensual. Breath-stopping.

Her heart whispered devilishly, *Take what you can...for as long as you can.*

He cupped her face in his palms, bending so that his lips hovered above hers, the heat of his words making her tremble with anticipation. "Far more pressing business."

KISSING HER WAS LIKE HOLDING A MATCH TO KINDLING. No matter that his intention was to worship how extraordinary and rare she was, the mere touch of her lips incinerated his self-control. Desire that was physical combined with something else, something deeper, something he'd never felt before, raged over him.

In a swift motion, he spun her around, setting her on the desk. Objects scattered this way and that, but he took no notice. All that mattered was Maggie.

Maggie who forgave him for not telling her about his title. Who consoled him with her sweetly practical advice. Who made him feel as if he could be more than the sum of his failures.

God, he *had* to have her. Now, now.

Crowding between her legs, he kissed her with gluttonous need. She tasted of sugared tea, lemon, and herself: sweet, tart, with a hint of spice. A flavor that he feared would ruin him for anyone else.

Their tongues twined as he found the buttons on the back of her dress, making quick work of them. As the garment slipped down to her waist, she jerked, tearing her mouth from his.

"We can't do this here," she said frantically.

"Would you prefer to go upstairs?" He kissed the curve of her neck, above her chemise, inhaling the scent of her skin. Who knew that roses and starch could be so arousing?

"Not at this time of day." Her breathy protest tautened his stones. "Everyone would know."

"Then we'll stay right here, sweeting." It wasn't ideal, given that the sheath he intended to use was upstairs, but he would make do. The important thing was to have her—now.

He kissed her bare shoulder next to the strap of her stays. Her skin was softer than swan's down. Far softer than the cheap linen of her undergarments. It was a crime for her to be exposed to such roughness.

"But Quince could come in—"

"He only comes if I summon him. And not always then." He undid the strings of her corset as expertly as any lady's maid. What could he say? He'd had practice. And he was glad for it for now he could employ every skill he'd learned to pleasure the woman before him.

The woman who...mattered.

He tossed aside the corset. "Arms up, love."

She bit her lip. To his everlasting satisfaction, she obeyed.

Unlike the fashionable ladies he'd known, she wore only a single petticoat. Which meant fewer hindrances for him. He divested her of her layers until all she wore was a pair of mended white stockings and plain garters. He plucked the pins from her hair, and the tresses cascaded to her waist, the sunlight from the window picking out the ruby glints. Perched on the mahogany desk, her hands covering her breasts and legs crossed, she was that most beguiling of contradictions: a prim yet sensual goddess.

"Christ, you're a sight to behold," he said huskily.

Her gaze darted to the windows overlooking the gardens. "What if someone looks in?"

As scintillating as their encounter in the cave had been, having her in the light would be even better. He couldn't wait to watch her in the throes of passion.

"That's the one advantage of being impoverished: less nosy servants about. There's no one to look in, sweeting." He pried her hands from her chest, his nostrils flaring at the sight of her exposed breasts. "Did I ever mention that you have the most delightful tits?"

"Your language." Her reproving tone didn't hide the fact that her nipples puckered at his naughty praise.

"Might as well get used to it. You bring out the randy devil in me." He nuzzled her neck, her shiver causing his erection to strain against its confines. "In fact, I have a game in mind."

Her brow pleated. "What sort of game?"

"One inspired by all your talk of striving and self-improvement." He ran a hand along her side, past the dip of her waist to the swell of her hip. God's teeth, he liked her shape. "The last time we made love, how many times did you spend?"

She flushed, squirming on the blotter. "That's hardly proper—"

"More than once?"

A heartbeat passed. She mumbled, "Thrice."

He adored her honesty. "I'll aim to do better this time."

"Better?" Her eyes widened. "I don't think that's possible."

"Ye of little faith." Before she could argue, he kissed her.

Within moments, he had her sighing beneath him on the desk, her hair a fan of spicy fire against the mahogany. He caught a cherry-ripe nipple between his lips, sucking hard. Her moans resonated in his ears as he rolled its twin between his finger and thumb, plucking and tugging until she writhed delightfully. He alternated between her plump mounds, giving each breast an equal share of his attention. When he gently used his teeth, her back arched, her tit pushing into his mouth as she came.

One down, three to go. His gaze roamed hungrily over her breasts, the tips swollen and glistening from his kisses. Seeing the reddened patch on the top of her breast, he rubbed his thumb over the slight abrasion.

"You have sensitive skin. Did I hurt you?" he muttered.

It took a moment for her glazed eyes to clear—and he loved that.

"No, it just tingles." Her smile was both shy and sultry. "I like it."

Fire licked his insides. "In that case..."

He returned to her breasts, circling her nipples with his tongue, teasing the erect buds to rise even higher as he slid a hand between her smooth thighs. His blood thrummed with satisfaction: she was drenched for him. Still sucking on her breasts, he found her pearl, diddling the bold bud. Stroking the center of her sensation until her limbs began to quake. Her legs suddenly clamped around his wrist, and she climaxed with a breathless sigh.

He straightened from the desk. Holding her gaze, he brought his hand to his mouth, licking her honey from his fingers. Her taste shot to his erection, making it throb against the taut ridges of his abdomen. And the way she was looking at him, in all her despoiled primness and awakened sensuality? He was so aroused that he feared spilling in his trousers like an untried lad.

"Ready for round three?" he asked.

He hoped to God she was. Because he wasn't certain how much longer he could play this game.

Despite two powerful orgasms, the desire in Maggie hadn't abated. The need smoldering in Rhys's eyes filled her with feminine power, unleashing a hunger she'd held in check for years. Seeing him take pleasure in pleasuring her unspooled her inhibitions, made her want to give back to him what he gave to her.

Beauty, bliss...a sense of rightness.

Of knowing that, in this moment, this was where she belonged.

"I'm ready," she said in a throaty voice she didn't recognize. "But..."

"But what, love?" His eyes were intent upon her face. "Tell me what you want. Always."

"I want you to undress," she blurted. "Would you mind?"

"Mind?" His grin was slow, sensual. "As much as a drowning man minds being thrown a rope."

She sat up for a better view as he unbuttoned his waistcoat. He tossed the costly navy silk to the floor as if it were no more than a rag, and his cravat and shirt soon followed. The sight of his bare torso made her breath catch. In the years since she'd last seen him, he'd grown even more leanly honed. His golden skin made her think of a lion's, smooth and sleek, stretched tautly over his powerful musculature. Slabs of muscle adorned his upper chest, his abdomen rippling as he bent to remove his boots.

Her gaze followed his hands as they moved to his waistband.

He undid his trousers, shoving them down lean hips girdled with a prominent vee of muscle. Despite her recent climax, her sex quivered at his virile splendor. She'd felt him, of course, that night in the cave, but in the daylight, he was even more imposing, more unapologetically male.

His cock was massive, long and thick. It was as stiff as a lance, the fat rosy head pointing at her. Her gaze traced the length of the wide shaft down to the base, where his bollocks hung like a dusky plum against a dark whorl of hair. He fisted his member, and heat pooled in her belly as she saw how it throbbed, testing the limits of his grip.

She wetted her lips, and he exhaled sharply. A droplet of dew leaked from the slit in his cock, dribbling down the shaft into his slowly stroking fist.

"Is everything to your liking?" he said.

His purring arrogance told her he knew the answer. She gave it to him anyway.

"You're magnificent. I can't believe you're..."

"That I'm what?" he prompted.

"That you're here. With me," she said honestly.

His nostrils flared. "My beautiful Maggie, there's no other place I'd rather be."

His kiss ravished her. She wrapped her arms around his neck, luxuriating in the fit of his ridges against her curves. As he plundered her mouth, she trailed her fingertips over his granite-hard chest, his corrugated abdomen, his muscles leaping beneath her touch. When she lightly brushed his broad cockhead, he groaned.

She jerked away, her cheeks flaming. In their previous encounters, she'd never initiated touching him. Was she being too brazen?

Before she could apologize, he caught her hand and wrapped her fingers firmly around his cock. "Frig me like this, sweeting."

His hand atop hers, he guided the motion. Her fingers scarcely fit around his girth, and the pressure he exerted was far more than she would have dared. His cock was a study in contrast, supple skin dragging over a core of iron. Its eager pulse filled her with heady feminine power.

"Am I doing this right?" she said.

"Too right," he said thickly. "I'm about to come in your palms like a damned greenling."

The idea shivered through her. "I want to feel you come...the way you felt me."

In answer, he crushed his mouth to hers. As his tongue stabbed into her mouth, he guided her to masturbate him harder, faster. She sucked on his tongue, and his flesh reared, straining against her hold. She frigged him strongly, his growls of pleasure egging her on. He grew so engorged that she had to use two hands. She jerked on his meaty staff until he suddenly shuddered.

His hot seed pulsed again and again, spilling like lava over her fists as he panted her name.

Pleased with her efforts, she leaned back to smile at him…only to find his palm on her chest, pushing her firmly back down on the desk. He went down on one knee, and before she knew what was happening, slung her legs over his shoulders.

"My turn again," he said.

He buried his face between her legs, and it was her turn to pant. To sigh his name as he devoured her flesh like a man starved. He pushed her legs back, opening her to his kiss, swirling fire over her senses. When he licked and sucked at the peak of her sensation, her desire went from a simmer to a boil. His tongue circled her opening…then thrust inside.

"Rhys," she gasped.

"You're like a profiterole," he said thickly. "I want to lick up all the cream."

His tongue drove into her. Again and again, taking her like a cock. Unbelievably, she felt ecstasy crash over her again. The waves were slower, deeper this time. Languorous and sweet.

"One more to go."

Floating in aftermath, she barely registered his words before she found herself turned onto her belly. The position was wicked, her breasts and palms pressed against the hard desk, her toes hovering helplessly above the ground as he stroked her swollen flesh.

"Such a sweet, wet pussy." His gravelly tones rasped over her satiated nerves, stirring them to life. "You're going to come one more time for me, aren't you, darling?"

"I don't know if I can," she whimpered.

"Not even if I do this?"

His finger pushed inside her. The sensation was exquisite. Filling an emptiness that had been aching to be filled.

"So tight and hot, I can feel you stretching around me," he rasped. "You can take more, can't you?"

"Yes, give me more," she breathed.

The slick sound of his driving fingers billowed her pleasure. Need reignited, not as desperate as before, but somehow deeper, stronger, tautness building in the core of her. Her fingers curled against the desk as his palm smacked against her sopping sex. Light and steady, his touch was masterful. Designed to drive her mad. Sweet heavens, she needed just a bit more friction...

"Does your love-knot throb, my sweet? Does it need to be frigged?" he said.

He was sinful. Beyond wicked. Right now, so was she.

"Yes," she sighed.

"Then do it," he commanded. "Touch yourself while I fuck you with my fingers."

Lost in sensation, she obeyed. She wedged her hand beneath her sex, searching out the center of her wanting, moaning as she gave herself what she needed. His thrusts rocked her against her own touch.

"You're so juicy you're dripping onto my blotter." His voice was an aphrodisiac in her blood. "You're taking three of my fingers now. Taking them deep into your tight, hungry cunny. I'm watching my fingers fucking you and thinking how bloody good it'll feel when I finally bury my cock inside you..."

Tremors started at her center, spreading outward in torpid waves. Her culmination was endless, deep, nearly painful in its intensity. The instant her spasms stopped, he pulled from her, turned her over.

His cock was hugely erect once more. Leaning back with her elbows on the desk, her breath caught at his sensual grace: the way his biceps flexed, the veins bulging as he handled his rampant flesh. His rod pulsed, wetness dripping. Seeing his jaw clench, she felt an answering tightening at her center.

Their gazes met and held.

"Do you want to feel me?" he growled. "To take my seed on your skin?"

She nodded, breathless. His fist flew faster along his rod. The tendons prominent on his neck, he clenched his jaw—and exploded. His essence rained upon her breasts, belly, and thighs. Marked by the silky-hot proof of his desire, she felt a primal satisfaction. His gaze smoldered into hers as he wrung himself of the last drop.

Chest heaving, he touched his forehead to hers.

"See?" she murmured. "I always knew you could rise to a challenge."

He lifted his head and his brows. "Sweeting, I rose to the challenge *twice*."

She giggled. He smirked, his gaze flicking beyond her—and he went stock still. She twisted her head to see what had captured his attention. She'd been so engrossed in their lovemaking that she hadn't noticed the mess they'd made: papers scattered to the floor, knick-knacks knocked over on the desk. Then she saw what he was looking at.

A red glass bottle shaped like a heart had toppled over, its contents spilling. The liquid had reached the scrap that contained the clue, soaking it, revealing *more words.*

Rhys snatched it up. "*See with the heart...*my uncle meant that literally. He wrote something on this paper in invisible ink, and the stuff in the heart-shaped bottle made it visible."

"What does the new message say?" She leaned closer.

"*I came home to Dorset, but my heart lives on in Bermuda.* Another damnable riddle."

Even as Rhys shook his head in frustration, recognition forked through her like lightning.

"I understand," she breathed. "I know where to find the next clue!"

§ 16 §

Given that the location of the next clue would involve a drive to the nearby village of Whitchurch Canonicorum and Maggie had to return home to her family, Rhys agreed to postpone the journey until the next morning. He arrived at her cottage at nine o'clock. It was an ungodly hour, and he'd already made a stop at the flower shop in town before coming here.

At least he'd gone to bed early last night: the interlude with Maggie had worn him out.

The memory of her delicious climaxes seared through him. By God, she was a lusty wench. Her appetites matched his own to perfection. One of these days, he would get her into a proper bed and truly test both their limits. They'd probably tup each other to death.

What a bloody glorious way to go.

"Down, boy," he muttered to the part of himself that was only too eager to find that certain kind of death with Maggie.

He'd woken with a florid cockstand, which wasn't exactly unusual—a morning screw was his favorite way to start the day—but the fact that his first thought had been of Maggie was unprecedented. He couldn't recall another woman having such a profound effect on him. Who consumed his thoughts even when he wasn't with her. Who incited his lust at the same time that she made him feel...good. Lighter.

Happy.

The realization stunned him. By Jove, he was *Ransom*, a jaded, worldly rake—not some moonstruck calf. Happiness was so...bourgeois.

Yet he couldn't deny that, with Maggie, things were different. *She* was different. Hell, he couldn't tell what had horrified her more: her mistaken assumption that he was a criminal or her discovery that he was a duke. Either way, she'd taken him as he was.

Him...Rhys. Just Rhys.

Her acceptance humbled him, made him want to give her more. More than two weeks, at any rate. If they succeeded in finding the treasure (and it was worth what Horatio had promised), then Rhys would be a free man. No debts, no threat of marriage hanging over him like a guillotine.

He and Maggie could be together for as long as they both wanted. He could take her to London, show her the sights. He'd buy her a house in Town, a proper wardrobe, jewels—

She's a respectable widow, you idiot, not some fancy piece, he chided himself. *And what about Glory? She's not going to leave her child behind and frolic about with you.*

One of the things he most admired about Maggie was her stalwart sense of duty and her love of her family. And the truth was he'd grown fond of Glory. Although he didn't usually care for the company of children, there was something about the girl's mix of brashness and vulnerability that he found endearing. He wouldn't mind having more cozy suppers with Maggie and her family...

Holy hell, did I just have a...domestic thought?

With a shudder, he shut down the line of thinking. His past had taught him that home and hearth were not for him. Better to focus on bedding Maggie, he told himself, and the unlimited, uninhibited fucking they could do once he absolved himself of debt.

Parking the gig, he gathered the bouquet he'd purchased for Maggie and went to knock on her door. The door flung open, revealing Glory's beaming freckled face. She was dressed for an outing, a straw bonnet over her plaits.

"Guess what, Mr. Jones? I cut my finger!" she announced.

He hid a smile at her dramatic declaration. "Not badly, I hope."

"I broke a cup and cut myself on the edge." She held up her index finger, the tip bandaged with a strip of linen. Luckily, the damage looked minor. "Mama washed and wrapped it. She says I'll survive. Are those flowers for Mama?"

"Yes. Do you think she'll like them?"

"Roses are her favorite. And those are the *largest* I've ever seen." Before he could reply, she peered around him to his conveyance. "Is that your carriage?"

"It was my uncle's."

But he was talking to air because she'd skipped past him to the sporty, open-air gig. Opening the door, she clambered right in. While Horatio hadn't paid attention to his property, he'd liked his vehicles. Both the driver's and back benches were lined with velvet cushions, the lacquered sides glossy in the sun.

"Your carriage is very comfortable," she called cheerily from the back seat.

"Oh dear, I am sorry." Maggie appeared in the doorway, her expression flustered as she tied on a dark bonnet. "Hypatia developed a megrim this morning, and I couldn't find anyone on short notice to mind Glory. If I leave her here, she'll pester poor Patty who needs to rest—"

"I understand completely," he assured her. "Glory is welcome to join us."

"She won't be trouble. I've brought her a book, and she's good at entertaining herself. And I didn't tell her the real purpose of our trip to Whitchurch Canonicorum. She thinks I'm giving you a tour of the local sights—"

"Calm yourself, my dear." He wanted to kiss that worried line between her curving brows. Kiss other parts of her, too. Mindful of their audience, he settled for holding out the bouquet she'd been too overset to notice. "These are for you."

Her eyes widened at the cluster of hothouse roses. The vibrant blooms ranged from creamy pink to deep crimson in hue. The florist had added lush foliage and an intricate wrapping of ribbon.

"How beautiful," Maggie breathed. "But these must have cost a *fortune*. With your debts, you oughtn't to spend money on frivolous things."

"I don't consider you frivolous."

Her cheeks turned rosy. "That's not what I meant."

"I know what you meant. While I appreciate your concern, a few roses aren't going to put me farther into dun territory," he said. "If they please you, I would consider them a worthy investment."

"They're the most splendid flowers I've ever seen," she said in a rush. "Thank you. I'll go put them in water and be right back."

Her smile was so sweet that his heart tripped in his chest. Watching her carefully carry the roses into the cottage, he couldn't help but think of the far more expensive gifts he'd given to other women. His ladybirds had had no compunction about dropping hints about the gewgaws they expected from him.

Maggie dropped no hints. Expected nothing. She was grateful for a few flowers, for Christ's sake...and was *fretting* over the fact that he'd spent a few paltry pounds on her. His throat tightened with an emotion he couldn't quite name.

When she returned, they started their journey to Whitchurch Canonicorum. The road wound through the Marshwood Vale, a scenic landscape of leafy copses and hedgerows, with farms scattered here and there. Framed by the idyllic setting, Maggie looked like a prim pagan goddess beside him, her eyes as verdant as the hills, wind-caught tendrils of her hair catching fire in the sunlight.

She was quiet as he drove. He appreciated that about her: she wasn't the sort of woman to bore a man with inane chatter. Glory, on the other hand, was more than happy to fill the silence.

"Do you recall the advice you gave me over supper, Mr. Jones?" the girl said from the rear bench. "About handling bullies?"

"I told you not to give them any satisfaction. To ignore them until you couldn't," he said. "Then, if needed, go for a direct hit."

"I tried your strategy, and it *worked*," she said gleefully. "You should have seen Billy Pinkleton's face when he called me a name, and I pretended he didn't exist. When he tried it again after school, I told him that only a coward made fun of others."

Rhys slid a glance back at her. "How did he respond?"

"He turned as red as a *beet*." Her skinny face shone with satisfaction. "He said he wasn't a coward, so I challenged him to a tree-climbing rematch. In front of everyone this time."

"Glory, you didn't." Maggie twisted around to bestow a reproving look upon her daughter.

"I did, and I beat him *again*," Glory said triumphantly. "Unlike the last time, I made sure other children were there as witnesses, and they saw me win. Now he can't call me names any more, or he'll be known as a sore loser."

Rhys felt an odd surge of pride. "Well done, poppet."

Maggie's frown swung to him. He wondered if it made him depraved to be aroused by that schoolmistress-like look.

"Glory oughtn't to be climbing trees, contest or no," she stated.

"*You* climb cliffs," the girl pointed out with (he thought) rather solid reasoning.

"I do it because I have to. There's no need for you to be risking your reputation—"

"The other children think I'm tip-top for beating Billy Pinkleton." An edge of belligerence entered Glory's voice. "Why shouldn't I do something I'm good at?"

Why indeed? Seeing Maggie's look of frustration, however, Rhys refrained from interfering.

"Because you have Goode blood," Maggie argued. "You need to curb your recklessness, or it will get the best of you."

"I didn't do anything wrong. Mr. Jones said I should stand up for myself, didn't you, sir?"

When Maggie's gaze narrowed upon him, he shrugged. "I can only speak from personal experience."

"You mean to say people tried to bully *you*?" Glory's head popped up between him and Maggie, her golden green eyes huge in her freckled face. "But you're so big and strong. And a gentleman. Who would make fun of you?"

"I wasn't always big and strong," he said, "and certainly not when I was twelve and sent to Eton. The older boys have rituals for 'welcoming' the new ones—especially the ones who were different."

"How were you different?" Glory asked.

"I looked different, to begin with. When I was younger, I more closely resembled my mama." Maggie already knew about his heritage, but for Glory's benefit, he added, "She was Chinese."

The girl's eyes rounded. "You mean...like tea?"

"Mind your manners," Maggie said severely.

"It's all right." Rhys didn't mind the girl's honest curiosity. "Yes, my mama came from China, where tea is grown. My mixed blood made me a target of bullies at Eton, but I refused to give them the satisfaction of knowing they had affected me in any way. I had to learn to fight. At first, I didn't always win, but I didn't back down. Eventually, I won more often than I lost, and the bullies knew better than to engage with me."

"That is *exactly* what happened with Billy Pinkleton," Glory exclaimed. "Now that I beat him, he doesn't bother me anymore. And if someone else should take up his mantle, I'll do what you did. I shan't give them the satisfaction of knowing they affected me."

He smiled at the girl's enthusiasm.

"One cannot control what others think, at any rate. Only what one thinks of oneself." Maggie's voice had a touch of wistfulness. "One of Hypatia's favorite sayings."

He sensed she wasn't referring only to Glory's situation. Because of her family's reputation, Maggie understood what it was like to be ostracized for reasons beyond her control.

"Sometimes the biggest fight is with oneself," he said.

As he said the words, he felt the truth of them. Despite his efforts to ignore the perceptions of others, they had shaped his view of himself. *Mongrel, weakling, rake…*the images were a maze of mirrors he couldn't escape.

"Well said." Maggie's voice was warm with approval.

"You're so clever, Mr. Jones," Glory added admiringly.

He glanced at them—and his heartbeat stuttered. In their shining gazes, he saw a version of himself different from any he'd seen before. And he didn't know whether he was glad…or terrified.

17

Within an hour, they arrived at their location: a parish church on the northern edge of Whitchurch Canonicorum. Maggie's mama had taken her to St. Candida and Holy Cross on occasion, and it was as she remembered it: modest and proud, withstanding the test of time. Built of local ashlar stone, the building had the patina of age, its wheaten walls gleaming against the surrounding knolls of grass. An impressive tower guarded the entrance.

Alighting first, Rhys handed her and Glory down. When Glory dashed off to examine the tombstones in the churchyard, he murmured, "You're certain the next clue is here?"

"Yes," Maggie replied. "In his clue, your uncle was alluding to Sir George Somers, a local explorer who founded the colony of Bermuda. When Sir Somers died, he left instructions for his heart to be buried in Bermuda, while the rest of him was to be returned to his birthplace. His remains are buried under the vestry in the church."

Sir Somers was a legend in Dorset: all schoolchildren learned about him. His exploits had even inspired a play by the Bard.

"What would I do without you, Maggie?"

He was staring at her, an unnerving intensity in his hazel eyes. Her heart bumped against her ribs. The more he shared of himself, the more her attraction to him grew. His candor on the carriage ride over had felt like a gift—as special as the beautiful roses he'd given her. Even though she'd told herself to guard her heart, she knew it was too late: she cared about Rhys.

And she couldn't bring herself to regret it.

To mask her feelings, she kept her tone light. "Five hundred pounds plus a five percent cut says you won't have to find out."

He smiled slowly. "A woman after my own heart. God bless your mercenary ways, sweeting."

"Let's go find ourselves a treasure, shall we?"

Inside the church, the vaulted nave was empty. Maggie settled Glory into one of the pews with a book for company.

"Promise you'll stay put and out of trouble while I give Mr. Jones a tour," she said.

"I'm not a baby." Glory's gaze rolled up impudently, but she opened her book.

Maggie led Rhys down the aisle. They passed through the chancel lit by stained glass windows and entered the vestry. The space was small and spartan, with wood cabinets lining the walls.

"Since Sir Somers's remains are buried under this chamber, it's a good place to start looking for the clue," Maggie said.

They set about searching the room with methodical precision. Inside the cabinets, they found vestments and ceremonial utensils...nothing out of the ordinary.

"The clue's not here." Rhys raked a hand through his hair. "Where next?"

"We could return to the nave—"

"Good day. I am Mr. Peters, the vicar of St. Candida. May I assist you with something?"

Spinning around, Maggie saw a stout blond man with twinkling blue eyes. Childhood memories of church unexpectedly flooded her, filling her with anxiety. The Goodes had been the constant target of fiery sermons from the pulpit and censorious stares from the pews.

And Maggie was no saint. She'd had a child out of wedlock. She was conducting a liaison with the father of said child and deceiving him about their daughter's parentage. She didn't need to compound her sins further by lying to a man of the cloth.

"We were, um…" she floundered.

"We got turned around," Rhys cut in smoothly. "This is my first time here, you see. My uncle spoke highly of this church, and I wanted to see it for myself."

"Oh?" The vicar's eyes lit with interest. "Who is your uncle, sir?"

"Horatio Jones. He passed away recently."

"Whether we live or die, we are the Lord's," the clergyman murmured. "My deepest condolences. Mr. Jones was an exceptional gentleman and a benefactor of the church."

"You knew my uncle?"

"He came here several times in the last few months. We talked about the life he'd led and his love of travel. He seemed at peace with himself and ready to embark on his final adventure. He mentioned that you might pay us a visit one day."

"Did he?" Rhys said alertly.

"Indeed. He said he had a nephew who took after him, who possessed the same spirit of adventure," Mr. Peters said amiably. "He said that if I were to meet you, I should direct you to see his favorite spot, the Shrine of St. Wite. I'd be pleased to show you there, Mr. and Mrs.…"

"The name's Rhys Jones."

"Follow me then, Mr. and Mrs. Jones. The shrine is in the North Transept." The vicar set off.

Blushing furiously, Maggie said, "Rhys, he thinks we're—"

"Let's just play along," Rhys muttered. "It's better than having to explain our true purpose."

Tucking her hand into the crook of his arm, he led her after their chattering guide.

"During the Reformation, many ancient relics were destroyed," Mr. Peters said. "St. Candida's is one of the few churches to still house a relic, that of St. Wite."

"I am not familiar with St. Wite," Rhys said.

"Wasn't she a Saxon woman?" Maggie recalled what her mother had told her. "She risked her life, holding a lantern on the cliffs during storms to guide sailors home."

"While there are many theories concerning the identity of St. Wite, Mr. Horatio Jones preferred the version you just gave." The vicar's smile was indulgent. "Said he liked the idea of a woman leaving a light on for him."

"That sounds like my uncle," Rhys said.

"Mama, I'm bored." Glory appeared in the nave's aisle, swinging her bonnet by its strings. "How much longer will this take?"

Before Maggie could reply, the vicar said heartily, "Hello there, young miss. Would you care to join Mama and Papa on a tour of the shrine?"

Seeing Glory's brow furrow, Maggie quickly took her hand. "She would enjoy it. Thank you."

"My pleasure." The vicar continued to lead the way, Rhys following behind him. "What a charming family you have, sir. Your daughter takes after both of you."

Blooming hell. Maggie's heart shot into her throat. Was it her imagination or did Rhys's broad shoulders freeze for the briefest instant?

"I am a lucky man indeed." Rhys's bland tones drifted back to her.

He sounds calm. He's just playing along. He doesn't know.

"Mama?" Glory whispered. "Why does the vicar think Mr. Jones is my papa?"

"It's just a misunderstanding." Maggie tamped down her panic.

"Just, um, play along for now, will you, dearest? It will take too long to explain. If you wish to leave, we must get this tour over as quickly as we can."

Glory shrugged. "All right."

Breathing in deeply, Maggie led her daughter into the shrine's chamber where Rhys and the vicar were waiting. To her relief, Rhys appeared intent upon the vicar's lecture; he certainly didn't look shocked or outraged or angry.

He doesn't suspect. Yet her relief was mingled with prickling guilt.

"The shrine itself is believed to predate the thirteenth century." The vicar was pointing to a grey stone altar tomb which stood some five feet tall against one wall. Flanked by narrow columns, the shrine was set below a trio of lancet windows, a flickering candelabrum resting atop its surface. "The lid of the tomb is composed of Purbeck marble, the rest of limestone. The platform upon which it rests is built from stone blocks of later origin."

"What are those holes for?" Glory pointed at three oval openings carved into the base of the tomb.

"Their purpose is for healing." The vicar turned to her. "Pilgrims believe in the relic's ability to mend whatever is placed inside those openings."

Glory's eyes widened. She held up her bandaged digit. "You're saying that if I put my finger inside the hole, the cut will heal?"

"You could try." The clergyman winked at her. "While you're at it, you might say a prayer."

Glory scampered over. Plopping onto the ground, she stuck her hand in the first opening, her eyes closing as she muttered a prayer.

"Would you mind if we spent some time here in my uncle's favorite spot?" Rhys asked.

"Take as long as you want, sir." Mr. Peters discreetly departed.

Rhys looked at Maggie. Her lungs squeezed, emptying of air as his eyes smoldered into hers.

"Horatio made a point of telling Peters to show me this place," he said in a low, pressured voice. "There's a good chance he left what we're looking for in here."

Right—the treasure. He's stirred up over that...not suspicions about Glory's parentage.

"What are you looking for?" This came from Glory. She was unwinding the linen dressing from her finger, her lips pursing as she examined the still-visible cut. "The relic didn't work."

"Maybe you didn't leave it in long enough." Rhys's voice had an undercurrent of humor.

"Or maybe the relic's healing powers are taradiddle." Glory snorted. "Anyway, can I help find whatever you're looking for?"

Maggie raised her brows at Rhys. This was his commission. It was up to him to decide what, if anything, to say.

"Can you keep a secret?" he said after a moment.

"Yes." Glory promptly held out her hand, with her smallest finger crooked. "I'll pinkie swear not to tell another soul."

Rhys's lips quirked. "Your word is good enough. The truth is your mama isn't helping me look for fossils; she's helping me look for a treasure."

"A treasure? Like pirate's gold?" the girl breathed.

"Something like that. My Uncle Horatio was rather fond of games, and he left me a set of clues to find my inheritance. The latest clue leads to this tomb."

"Can I help? What are we looking for?" Glory fired words like bullets.

He ran a gloved hand over the marble lid. "Anything that looks out of the ordinary."

The three of them set to work. Rhys examined the top of the shrine, Maggie the sides, and Glory the base. Maggie ran her fingertips over the time-worn stone, looking for cracks or crevices that might act as a hiding place. The task helped distract her from her roiling thoughts.

"I think I found something!" Glory exclaimed.

Maggie hurried over, Rhys close behind her. The girl was wedged in the tiny space between the shrine and its neighboring column.

"At the back, next to the wall," came Glory's muffled words. "I think one of the stones is loose. It moved when I touched it."

"Nicely done, poppet," Rhys said. "Shall I take a look?"

"No, I've got the stone out now. There's something there behind it..."

Glory popped out of the nook. Her nose was streaked with dirt, an impish grin lighting her face. Triumphantly, she held up a small leather pouch.

Maggie's heart hiccupped when, instead of taking the bag, Rhys removed a handkerchief and wiped the smudge from the girl's nose. The gesture was tender, heart-stoppingly...paternal.

The wings that beat in Maggie's chest were of fear and wild longing. Watching Rhys and their daughter, their heads bent close together, Maggie couldn't stop an impossible dream from entering her head. The one of violins, fancy flowers...and faerie tale endings.

"Will you do the honors?" Rhys asked Glory.

Eagerly, Glory untied the drawstring and upended the pouch into her hand—and let out a squeal of delight. Maggie's breath suspended. She'd never seen anything like the jewel that glittered in her daughter's palm.

"By...Jove." Even Rhys sounded stunned.

The diamond was the size of a pigeon's egg. The light from the window hit the gem, illuminating its flawless depths, scattering colorful prisms over the stone walls. Seeing a scrap of paper caught beneath the jewel, Maggie carefully pulled it free.

"What does it say?" Rhys asked hoarsely.

"Congratulations, dear boy," she read aloud. *"Here's a small crumb to tempt you. The rest of the cake awaits you in the DEATHLESS VEIN."*

❧ 18 ☙

AFTER DEPOSITING MAGGIE AND GLORY AT THE COTTAGE, with a promise to call on the morrow, Rhys returned to Journey's End. Dusk was nearing as he alighted from the gig. Instead of going inside, he headed for the gardens. He needed a moment to himself. The diamond joggled in his inner pocket, a reminder of the day's success, yet his mind was on other things.

Your daughter takes after both of you.

Emotions roiling, he strode into the maze of overgrown hedgerows. He realized now that the ember of knowledge had been there before the vicar's innocent observation. From the first time he'd met Glory, he'd felt an odd yet undeniable connection.

I asked Maggie outright. Thoughts circled his mind like vultures. *If Glory is mine, then why did she lie to me? Why would she deny me my own flesh and blood?*

He balled his hands, gravel crunching beneath his boots. The anger that he'd been keeping in check ignited; he had the wild urge to give into it. To go punch the hell out of something or someone. Drink himself into oblivion. Gamble and fuck like a madman.

But he didn't.

Because he'd gone down that route before. Those behaviors hadn't helped him when he'd lost his fortune, and they sure as bloody hell wouldn't help him now. Instead, he forced himself to peer past the seething anger, into the vortex of the storm—and what he found was far more painful.

Clarity.

If he'd gotten Maggie with child all those years ago, what must she have suffered? He knew first-hand what her family was like; clearly, she would have had no support from that quarter. Which meant she'd have been alone, a serving maid swelling with a bastard, with no way of finding the father, with nothing...

Nothing but the fifty-pound note he'd tossed on the table.

Remorse cut short his breath. If he'd known, he would have taken responsibility—even back then, during his wilder days. He'd have taken care of her and the child...financially, at least.

Arriving at the center of the maze, he sat on the cracked stone bench and stared blindly at the dry fountain, a repository of leaves and moss. He propped his elbows on his thighs and dropped his head into his hands. He wasn't one for introspection, and this was why: he felt in shambles, as tangled up as the garden's weeds and neglected brush.

You're such a selfish bastard. He speared his fingers through his hair. *You've done Maggie irreparable harm. Christ, how can she even stand to look at you, never mind help you, after what you did to her?*

Yet that was Maggie. Sweet and generous to a fault.

Hell, she deserved better than him. A woman like her should be with a man who knew how to be a husband and father. Who was in a place to give her and Glory the kind of domestic bliss they merited. The kind he, himself, had absolutely no experience with. The thought of his own sire filled him with nothing but impotent rage.

Perhaps that was why he'd been quick to accept Maggie's denial of his paternity. To relieve himself of the responsibility and shame, yes, but also because he was...afraid. Given all his failures, could he become the kind of man worthy of her and Glory?

Damnation, Maggie, how can I make this up to you?

He'd failed her in ways he could never make up for. Not if he lived to be a hundred—which was unlikely, given that he had two cutthroats after his blood.

Even now, he couldn't do right by Maggie. With his looming debts, he wasn't a free man. He still might have to marry himself out of trouble. The thought of the Sharpe heiress made him even more disgusted at himself.

Yet, in the darkness, there was a pinprick of light: the treasure. If he found it and if it was all that his uncle claimed it was, then he could pay off his debts...and make Maggie an honorable offer.

Not so long ago, marriage had felt like a death sentence—and would still feel that way if it involved any woman other than Maggie. But he'd known all along that she was different. The truth was that he'd been contemplating a future with her even before he knew he was Glory's father. He'd struggled with the fact that Maggie was too respectable, too *good* to be his mistress.

But she'd make the perfect duchess.

He warmed to his plan. As long as they kept their emotions in check, he reasoned, there was no reason why a marriage between them couldn't work. *Love* was what caused pain. He and Maggie could avoid that unnecessary entanglement. They could build a union based on passion and respect—yes, that was the ticket.

They got on well in and out of bed; why should being married change anything?

The important thing was that they had realistic expectations of each other. God knew he wouldn't be a perfect husband or father. Yet he'd do his damnedest to be the opposite of his sire: he'd be faithful and considerate, strive to protect his own. At the same time, he'd take care to set limits on emotional intimacy so that no one would get hurt.

Indeed, there would be benefits to marriage. The regular sex —God, yes—but also more than that. With Maggie by his side, he felt stronger. Less alone. Together, they were making progress on the treasure hunt. At this moment, he had one of the jewels in his possession: a gem that, by his estimation, had to be worth close to ten thousand pounds.

A drop in the ocean of his debt. Yet it was something.

You're not a failure. Maggie's soft conviction drowned out the other harsh voices. *When I make mistakes...I pick myself up and try again. You can do the same...I believe in you.*

God's blood, he didn't deserve her faith. Didn't deserve *her.* But he wasn't going to let her or his daughter go without a fight. He would find the "deathless vein"—whatever the bloody hell that was—and track down the rest of the gems, by any means necessary.

Until then, although he could not offer Maggie his name, he would treat her like the queen that she was. After some deliberation, he decided not to question her about Glory directly. He would not storm in and demand to know if he was the father. He had no right, given the way he'd had his fun and abandoned her.

Instead, he would do everything in his power to *show* Maggie that he was worthy of her trust. To prove that he was the type of man who was good enough for her and their child. He would earn the right to the truth.

He heard footsteps. Quince appeared from around a hedge, huffing with unusual urgency.

"Your Grace, I saw your carriage but didn't know where you were or else I would have come earlier." The butler paused to catch his breath. "Your man-of-business arrived just before you did."

Rhys frowned. He wasn't expecting a visit from Newton. Unless the man had some pressing news about the heiress situation...

His gut knotted. "Did the matter seem urgent?"

"It appears that Mr. Newton has been beaten, Your Grace." Quince's face was grimmer than usual. "I'm afraid rather badly."

"It looks worse than it is, Your Grace," Arthur Newton said from the wingchair.

Rhys stopped pacing and glowered at his man-of-business. In his forties, Newton was a lanky fellow, his shaggy sandy hair and spectacles underscoring his scholarly mien. At present, however, he looked less like a professor and more like a pugilist, thanks to the shiner he sported. The rest of his face was a collage of bruises.

"Usually when you say that, you're referring to my financial portfolio." Rhys raked a hand through his hair. "It is no more reassuring now when you're speaking about your face. Who did this to you?"

"Garrity's men." Sighing, Newton took a sip of his brandy. "My fault, really. I ought to have been more careful walking at night. They cornered me in an alleyway and demanded to know your whereabouts." He shrugged, then winced, his hand going to his ribs. "I told them I didn't know where you were."

"Devil take it, Arthur, you should have told them."

Yet Rhys wasn't surprised by his man-of-business's loyalty; it was why he'd hired Newton four years ago. Back then, he'd been riding high on a wave of success. He'd been returning from a night of debauchery when he'd literally run into Newton—with his carriage.

Luckily, Newton hadn't sustained any injury, and despite his shabby clothes and emaciated figure, he'd refused money. Rhys had ended up buying the other supper at a nearby tavern instead. Over ale and meat pie, Newton had haltingly told his tale. The youngest son of a viscount, he'd been disowned for marrying against his family's wishes. Earnest and educated, he'd been eking out a living as a solicitor. Honesty, apparently, did not serve one well in the legal profession.

One day, he arrived home to find moneylenders waiting for him. His wife had run up several hundred pounds in his name—right before she'd run away with another man. Fate had paid her back for her perfidy for she'd passed away from an illness not long after.

Honorable fellow that Newton was, he'd nonetheless taken responsibility for the debts incurred in his name. Yet the compounding interest defeated his valiant efforts. He'd miserably confided in Rhys that he'd considered taking his own life...and Rhys had needed to hear no more. The next day, he'd settled the other's loans.

A grateful Newton had vowed to work off the sum despite Rhys's assurances that the money had been a gift. With his diligence, loyalty, and gentlemanly comportment, Newton had made an excellent man-of-business. He'd given good counsel when Rhys's fortunes had turned...and stuck by even when Rhys ignored said counsel. When things had gone from bad to worse and all of Rhys's so-called friends had jumped ship, Newton had stayed on.

Thus, Rhys thought of him not only as an employee but as a friend, which made him doubly furious that Newton had been assaulted because of him.

"The beating wasn't that bad. They went easy on me since I didn't fight back." Newton's grin was even more lopsided than usual due to his swollen face. "Being a pacifist has its rewards."

"You should not have taken that beating for me," Rhys said tautly.

"And you should not have paid off my debts for me, Your Grace. But that is neither here nor there." Newton adjusted his spectacles, his expression solemn. "I came because the situation has come to a head. Garrity is willing to wait no longer—and the same goes for Sweeney. As your man-of-business, I'm advising you to make your decision about marriage now. The Sharpes are willing to sign a contract: delay no longer."

It would have been simple to take the easy way out. A part of Rhys considered it.

It was another part of him that spoke. "There is another option."

He gave a summary of all that had transpired since his arrival in Dorset. He didn't hide his personal interest in Maggie because he trusted Newton...and also because he would need the other to make arrangements for her on his behalf. Despite his uncertainty about his future, he did know one thing: he would provide for Maggie and Glory.

He shared the plans that had been taking shape in his head. He would transfer Horatio's estate to Maggie's name. It wasn't much, but at least she and Glory would always have a place to live. Once he sold the diamond, he would provide her with an annuity so that she never had to worry about money again.

To Newton's credit, he took the instructions in stride.

"You've been busy, Your Grace." The man-of-business finished jotting down notes. "And you believe you are making headway on this treasure hunt?"

Rhys withdrew the diamond from his pocket. "This is proof of it."

"Crikey, that's a sparkler, ain't it?" Newton gave a low whistle. "I'd wager a gem of that size would fetch close to ten thousand pounds."

"My estimate as well. I want you to take it back to London and sell it."

Newton nodded. "Will you use the proceeds to make a deposit to Garrity and Sweeney?"

"At this point, they won't be appeased by a few thousand pounds. They want to be paid in full. I'm better off using the money to fund the treasure hunt. Speaking of which, here's the next riddle." Rhys showed Newton the note that had accompanied the diamond. "Any ideas what 'deathless vein' could refer to?"

The solicitor scratched his head. "Haven't a clue. No pun intended."

"I'm meeting at Mrs. Foley's cottage tomorrow to take a crack at solving it," Rhys said. "Her sister-in-law is a bluestocking who apparently excels at puzzles."

"If you like, I'll come along," Newton said amiably. "I'll return to London the day after."

"I won't turn down the help."

The time for pride was over. Rhys would do whatever it took to claim his inheritance. To earn his freedom...and make Maggie his.

$$\maltese \quad 19 \quad \maltese$$

"You didn't tell me she was beautiful," Newton said in hushed tones.

Rhys frowned. He and Newton were standing by the window of Maggie's parlor, bright afternoon sun streaming through the panes. After introductions, Maggie and Hypatia had gone to the kitchen to fetch refreshments. Glory was at a friend's house, where she would be conveniently staying the night.

While Rhys couldn't fault Newton for noticing Maggie's beauty—he knew as well as anybody that her attractions were impossible to ignore—he did blame the man for lacking tact. Especially since he had made clear his personal interest in her.

His newfound possessiveness surprised him. Although he'd never been a man to share, this primal urge to mark a woman as his own was new. Then again, Maggie wasn't just any woman; she was going to be his duchess.

"Mrs. Foley is off limits," he said brusquely.

"Mrs. Foley?" Newton gave him a blank look before adjusting his ever-slipping spectacles. "Oh, I wasn't talking about her. It is *Miss* Foley who holds my admiration."

"Hypatia?" Rhys felt his brows rise.

"Her intellect is astounding. Do you know she has translated works of Ancient Greek?"

"I did not."

"And her eyes are the clearest blue. Like a glimpse of sky behind the windows of her spectacles." Evidently no poet, Newton said dreamily, "She is unlike any female of my acquaintance."

Privately, Rhys did not think Newton had been acquainted with all that many females. As far as he knew, the other lived like a monk. And the perfidious woman the solicitor had once been married to would surely cure a man of any desire to trust another.

Yet as the door opened to reveal Hypatia with a tray, Newton looked as eager as a newly whelped pup. If he had a tail, it would be wagging. Rhys would have snorted...but Maggie entered the parlor, and his breath lodged in his throat.

He'd brought her a poesy, and she'd pinned one of the violets to her breast. The warmth in her eyes made the world fade. Desire shot through his veins, and he had to restrain the urge to haul her over his shoulder like some troglodyte. To take her to his own private cave and have his way with her...

"Won't you have a seat, Your Grace?" Hypatia's voice broke his reverie.

Given that the spinster would be helping with the treasure hunt, he'd seen no point in keeping his true identity secret any longer. Maggie had vouched for her sister-in-law's discretion.

"My friends call me Ransom," he said. "I think we are well past formalities."

He shared the rather lumpy settee with Maggie, while Patty and Newton occupied adjacent chairs. Refreshments were passed around, and he found himself enjoying the simple ritual of being served tea by Maggie. She prepared the dark brew with the same efficiency she did everything, not spilling a drop and doctoring it perfectly to his liking.

As he took a plate of biscuits from her, their fingers touched.

The spark of contact danced over his skin. He saw the answering awareness in her beguiling eyes.

"We should proceed with the task at hand," Hypatia said.

Rhys glanced at Newton, who was nearly salivating at the spinster's brisk tones. Well, he couldn't blame the fellow. Maggie's pragmatism never failed to get him in a lather.

"Did you bring the note, um, Ransom?" Maggie said.

She was still getting used to referring to him by his title. He preferred hearing her call him Rhys, but that was better suited for intimate situations.

"Right here." Removing the note, he put it on the coffee table for all to see.

Hypatia pursed her lips. "Do you have any idea what the 'deathless vein' refers to, Your Grace? Is there anything that your uncle might have said that could be a clue?"

Rhys had spent time mulling over this very question. "My Uncle Horatio had a brief interest in all things Egyptian. I thought that perhaps 'deathless vein' might allude to the Egyptian belief in the Afterlife. I searched Horatio's collection of Egyptian curiosities, however, and found nothing."

"That's still a good guess," Maggie said.

He smiled faintly at her staunch support.

"What if we were to make a list of all the things that 'deathless vein' conjures up?" she suggested. "We could just toss some ideas out there."

"Capital idea, Mrs. Foley," Newton said.

Hypatia fetched a pen and paper, and they set to work. As a group, they came up with a list of possibilities ranging from a gravestone to a well to a fountain. They went through the items one by one, discussing whether there was a specific location of that item where the treasure or next clue might be found. Unfortunately, none of the ideas seemed to bear fruit.

By the time they finished going through the list, the sun had sunk into the horizon. After lighting the lamps, Maggie announced that all the thinking was making her hungry, and she would fetch them a collation.

Hypatia started to rise, but Rhys beat her to it. "I'll help, Miss Hypatia. You and Newton continue working on that list."

He didn't miss his man-of-business's grateful look. Or how readily Hypatia acquiesced to his suggestion. With their heads bent together and respective spectacles agleam, the spinster and the solicitor looked like a match made in heaven. Or some scholarly institution.

Maggie led the way into the kitchen, Rhys following at her heels. The door had scarcely closed behind them when he clamped his hands on her waist, hoisting her onto the scarred worktable. Her gasp tasted of tea and honey; her moan was even sweeter. He possessed her mouth as he yearned to possess her—fully and completely.

When they came up for air, her hands were curled around his lapels. She wore his favorite look: that of a well-kissed, passion-dazed woman.

"I missed you," he murmured.

"You saw me yesterday."

"I resented every minute that didn't have you in it." He tucked a wayward cinnamon tress behind her ear, just for the pleasure of touching her.

She tipped her head to one side. "You seem different."

"How so?"

"I don't know." A furrow formed between her brows. "You're being charming."

"Clearly I've been remiss if my charm surprises you."

"That's not what I meant. You're the most debonair man I've ever met." Her gaze veered briefly skyward. "What I meant was that after all the dead ends we came up with just now, I expected you to be less...optimistic."

"You thought I'd be a glum jackanapes?"

Her lips twitched. "I thought you'd be frustrated."

"You want to know why I'm not?"

She nodded.

"It's because of you."

"Me?"

"Yes, you." He curled a finger under her chin. "With you by my side, I feel that I can accomplish most anything."

"Oh," she said tremulously.

Looking into her eyes, he felt the rightness of the moment. "There's something else I want you to know."

"What is it?" she whispered.

"Although this started out as an affair, you...matter to me."

"Oh, Rhys—"

"I'm not in a position to make you promises. Not yet. But if I were, I want you to know that I would." Looking into her shining verdant eyes, he felt a surge of longing. "Christ, I wish I could give you more than this. More than mere words. I wish I could offer something more substantial, more permanent—"

Her eyes widened. "*Blooming hell*. That's it!"

Not exactly the reaction he was expecting. "Er...what is?"

"Words *aren't* permanent," she said excitedly.

"Yes, I know. But they're all I can offer at the moment—"

"Not you—I'm talking about the clue. What if 'deathless vein' isn't a place per se, but an impermanent word...a set of changeable letters?"

"Devil and damn—an *anagram*." The realization resonated through him. "That's just the sort of puzzle Horatio would enjoy."

"Patty adores them too." She hopped off the table, and they rushed into the other room.

Hypatia and Newton's heads whipped in their direction.

"Deathless vein—it's an anagram," Maggie blurted.

Hypatia shot to her feet. "*Of course.*" She dashed from the parlor.

Newton rose. "Where did she go?"

"To get her anagram tiles," Maggie said.

Sure enough, Hypatia returned with a box, which she upended on the dining table. Everyone crowded around as she sorted out the wood tiles, each of which had a letter painted upon it. She arranged the letters to spell out DEATHLESS VEIN.

Shuffling the tiles, she rearranged them.

SHETLAND SIEVE.

"Ring any bells?" She looked at Rhys.

He shook his head. "Try again."

Her fingers flashed. HEAVIEST LENDS.

"That doesn't make sense," she muttered.

"How about EVIDENT LASHES?" Newton suggested.

"What would that refer to?" Maggie tilted her head. "A place for public floggings?"

"It could be a place where ladies gather to flirt," Rhys mused. "To bat their obvious *eye*lashes."

"You would think of that," Maggie said wryly.

He winked at her.

Hypatia's fingers drummed against the table. "The solution to the anagram should be an obvious place. One that Ransom would know about. We haven't got the right combination as yet."

She pushed the tiles around, trying out different combinations. After a few attempts, she put together SEVENTH AS LIED.

"That's still not right." She tapped out a frustrated ditty with a tile.

"May I?" Rhys said.

He took her place. Removed the "TH" from "SEVENTH." *Seven...seven...* His gut told him he was on the right track. Slowly, he formed the word "THE," placing it in front of "SEVEN." He studied the results: THE SEVEN ASLID.

The answer struck him like a physical blow.

At the same time, Hypatia expelled a breath. "*The Seven Dials.* That's where Horatio hid the treasure. The jewels...they're in London!"

$$\text{\textpaw}\ 20\ \text{\textpaw}$$

WHEN THE DOOR OPENED TO HER CHAMBER LATER THAT NIGHT, Maggie wasn't surprised. She had left a bedside lamp burning, hoping that he would come.

"Rhys?" she called softly.

"Expecting someone else?" Closing the door with a click, he emerged from the shadows. He'd removed his cravat, the strong column of his throat rising from the open vee. His shirtsleeves were rolled up, revealing his sinewy forearms. Unbuttoning his waistcoat, he slung it over a chair on his way to the bed.

Her heart thumped at the vision of masculinity he made. Sitting up against the pillows, she looked up into his wickedly handsome face as he drew near.

"We have to be quiet," she whispered. "Hypatia and Mr. Newton are downstairs."

After solving the anagram, the four of them had enjoyed a celebratory repast. Hypatia had unearthed another bottle of brandy from Paul's study. Before Maggie knew it, the bottle was empty and the clock striking midnight.

Given the lateness of the hour and amount of alcohol

imbibed, Hypatia had suggested that Rhys and Mr. Newton stay the night. The latter had already fallen asleep on the sofa. As long as the men left early in the morning, none would be the wiser.

"I don't think your sister-in-law and Newton will pay us any mind." There was a hint of amusement in Rhys's tone. "My guess is that they're rather occupied at the moment."

Maggie's jaw slackened. Although she hadn't missed the signals passing between Patty and Mr. Newton, the idea that her bluestocking sister-in-law would engage in impropriety—and with a man she'd just met—was shocking.

"You don't think...that is, they *wouldn't*..."

"Why not?" Lips twitching, Rhys settled on the mattress beside her. Slinging an arm around her shoulders, he murmured, "We are."

His nearness almost distracted her from her point. "That's different. You and I have known each other for longer. And I'm a widow whereas Patty has never been married."

"Hypatia strikes me as a woman who knows her own mind. If it will ease yours, Arthur Newton is one of the finest men I know. He would not take advantage of a lady. The two of them are probably engaged in a heated..."—his lips quirked—"discussion of Plato."

"I do like Mr. Newton." She bit her lip. "I just don't want Patty to get hurt...to do something she might later regret."

"Like you did?" Although Rhys spoke quietly, there was an intensity in his hazel eyes.

She hadn't been thinking about herself just then, but since he'd brought up the past, she couldn't deny that she had her share of regrets. The main one being that she'd lied to Rhys about Glory.

With every moment that passed, the burden of that falsehood grew bigger. And now she and Rhys would soon be parted. In discussing the plans for London, he'd been adamant that she would not be accompanying him. He wanted her to "stay put" in Dorset. Despite her protests, he'd stated unequivocally that he would not risk exposing her to the cutthroats who awaited him in Town.

She'd never seen him so serious. So firm in his resolution. The devil-may-care rake was gone, replaced by a man whose protective stance sent pleasant shivers through her.

And earlier in the kitchen, he'd told her that she *mattered*. Joy spilled through her, warring with doubt. For he'd also said that he was not free to make her any promises. Would he welcome the knowledge that he was Glory's father?

"Maggie, is there something you want to tell me?" Rhys was studying her, and she experienced a strange *frisson*. It was as if he already knew what she was hiding.

You can't let him leave without telling him he's Glory's father. He has a right to know. What's the worst that could happen?

He could be furious at her for lying. He, a bona fide duke, could want nothing to do with the bastard he'd had with a serving maid. Or the most likely scenario: he would feel both honor and duty-bound to provide for her and Glory.

To her mind, the last possibility was the worst of the three. She'd rather deal with his anger than be an obligation to him. She'd gotten along without him just fine; she owned a business, was capable of earning her keep and that of her family. She didn't need his or any man's money. The only thing she wanted from him was...

What you cannot have. This is an affair, remember? Even if you 'matter' to him, there are no strings, nothing to bring him back after he finds his treasure.

He tipped her chin up. "What are you thinking, sweeting?"

"Let me go with you to London." She hated that the words sounded like a plea. "I've been helpful to you thus far. I can help you find the treasure."

"We discussed this." Although his eyes were soft, his jaw had a granite edge. "I'm not risking your neck to save mine. You're far too precious to me."

Her heart leapt at his words. Yet...they were just words. He gave her no real assurances.

Because he's a duke, her inner voice said. *Men like him don't wed former tavern wenches. It is as Mama said: there'll be no faerie tale endings.*

"Maggie, you know I'm not free to make you promises. Not when I have a noose of debt around my neck. But if I could, I—"

"Say no more." She patched up her hurt, covering it with a smile. "You were clear from the outset that this was just pleasure for the moment. Trust me, I have no expectations of roses and violins and happily-ever-after."

He stared at her before dragging a hand through his hair. "This may have started out as an affair, but you and I both know it's become more. Until I find that treasure, however, I'm not at liberty to make you promises."

She told herself to be glad that she meant more to him than his average paramour. "That is kind of you to say. Especially to a woman like me."

"Damnit, Maggie." His voice held the growl of frustration. "I'm not being *kind.* A woman like you deserves everything. I'm the problem, don't you see?"

Emotion frothed like ale inside her. He radiated a similar tension. Out of nowhere, agitated energy swirled between them; she felt as if they were perilously close to having a row.

She heard Paul's voice. *Politeness dictates that if you have nothing nice to say, say nothing.*

"There's no point in discussing the matter further." She faked a yawn. "It's late, and I'm tired. Exhausted, in point of fact."

Rhys's dark brows lowered. He looked as if he might argue.

"Good night," she said tartly, in case he didn't get the point.

The lamp flickered. When the shadows lifted, his expression was again smooth and urbane.

"I am sorry to hear it." He wound a strand of her hair around his finger. "For once, we have a bed at our disposal. I was hoping to put it to a use other than sleeping...but your well-being comes first, my sweet."

Her brain fogged with desire and vexation. She couldn't deny that lovemaking would be a good way to vent her churning energy. If this was just an affair, then she ought to get something out of it, oughtn't she? Yet how could she admit she wanted bed sport when they'd nearly gotten into an argument *and* she'd just claimed she was tired? Her pride wouldn't allow it.

The blighter made a show of fluffing her pillow before pushing her gently to lie back upon it. He kissed her on the forehead, the tender press of his lips making her sex flutter.

"Comfortable, my dear?" he said in a solicitous tone.

"Yes." *Annoying bastard.*

"Then close those beautiful, tired eyes."

Blooming hell. She knew she wouldn't get any sleep tonight. Caught in the web of her own conceit, she had no choice but to shut her eyes.

She felt him get out of bed. Heard the torturous rustle of his clothes being shed. The thump of his boots hitting the ground. She tried not to picture him without his clothes. His carved chest and washboard stomach. The oh-so-sensual vee of muscle girdling his loins...

The mattress shifted, and she felt him get into bed. Need simmered and bubbled in her belly. God, she wanted to open her eyes, to reach out and touch him...

Her nightgown began to slide up her legs. Her eyelids flew open.

Rhys was kneeling beside her. He was naked: all taut, golden skin and sinewy splendor. Smiling, he caressed her bare thigh.

"I thought you were letting me rest," she blurted.

"I am. You rest, my sweet," he said silkily, "and I'll do the work."

"How can I possibly...*oh*." Her hips arched as he reached the apex of her legs. She could feel how wet she was, her dew aiding the marauding path of his fingers.

"Poor little pussy, it's weeping with fatigue." His roguish smirk belied any sympathy for her state. "Don't worry, darling, I'll take care of it. You just lie back and relax."

His thumb circled her pearl, rubbing back and forth over the quivering nub of flesh. She moaned as tingles shot to her womb, her breasts. With his other hand, he swept her nightgown over her head, and she struggled to be free of the fabric. He gave a husky laugh at her eagerness, but she no longer cared. Her pride was butter in the hot pan of pleasure. Her thoughts and cares melted away. There was only her sizzling desire for this man.

Tossing the nightgown aside, he placed a big hand on her right breast. He teased the aching peak even as he skillfully manipulated her sex with his other hand. He penetrated her with one long finger, and she moaned, her passage clutching at him.

"Christ, that's sweet," he crooned. "You want more, don't you? There you go, tighten on me again. Milk my fingers with your little sheath, Maggie mine."

It wasn't his naughty litany that stopped her breath, but his endearment. Merciful heavens, it was true...she *was* his. The care he took with her, his tenderness with their daughter, the aliveness he ignited in her—all of it was a dream come true. A dream so good that even knowing that she would one day wake from it didn't change the reality branded upon her heart.

She belonged to this man. To Rhys. Always, Rhys.

The recognition was tinder to her desire. His hot gaze lay claim to her as did his stroking touch. She whimpered as he plunged inside her, harder, faster, his palm slapping wetly against her petals. He pinched her nipple as his long fingers reached deep inside, curling, massaging an exquisite spot. There was no holding back; with him, there never was.

Her crisis swept over her, and she soared into the golden blaze of his eyes.

Chest heaving, Rhys brought his fingers to his lips. He licked them, savoring Maggie's sweetness. Christ, she was never more beautiful to him than when she was robed in afterglow.

When she forgot to be prim and proud. When she was all flushed, soft, and sated from his loving. When her eyes were drowsy with pleasure...and her defenses lowered.

Earlier, he'd thought she might tell him her secret. God knew he'd wanted her to. It had required all his willpower not to reveal that he'd already guessed that he was Glory's father. After how he'd wronged Maggie, he did not deserve her trust. But he was determined to earn it.

She, on the other hand, seemed just as determined to misinterpret his intentions. It aggrieved him that she mistook his desire to protect her for...snobbery. That she would think, because of his title, he believed that she was not good enough for him. He couldn't give a damn what society thought of their match: Maggie Foley was the best woman he'd ever met.

Far too good for him, in truth.

Given the nefarious reputation of her family, he understood why she looked down upon herself. The most frustrating thing of all was that, here and now, he had nothing to offer her. No promises he could make. No actions he could undertake to show her that he *would* come back for her...as long as he could do so a free man.

Well, there were no actions he could take save one. Here in bed, communication was never a problem for them. Maggie trusted him with her body. Mayhap if he loved her well enough here, she might one day trust him with...more.

For years, he'd avoided attachments, feared the responsibility that went along with them. Yet for Maggie, he would try to be a better man. A man fit to be her husband.

He leaned over to touch his mouth to hers. Her lips parted for him. The hot silk of their kiss slid down his spine. He looked into her eyes, running a possessive hand over her, memorizing her giving abundance. Storing her sweetness for the dark travails ahead.

Her rose scent lured him to the curve of her neck, then the deep valley between her big, rounded tits. He cupped her bounty with both hands, squeezing as he paid tribute to her nipples, circling the blushing areola with his tongue. She wriggled as he tasted the smoothness of her belly. He kissed behind her knees, her toes, relishing her giggles of surprise.

Then he made a space for himself between her thighs. He parted her cinnamon curls, blowing softly on her glistening flesh. Her hips jerked, and satisfaction flooded him. So sensitive, his Maggie.

He spread her with his thumbs. Ran his tongue along her exposed cleft. She was spicy and plump, like a pear poached in mulled wine.

"You are delicious, Maggie mine." The first time he'd uttered the endearment, he'd known that it was perfect for her. "I could eat you all day."

She moaned his name; who was he to resist a siren's call?

He dove into her feminine depths. Lapping, stroking, savoring her. He found her bold little bud, lashing it with his tongue. Her thighs stiffened, yet he held her spread.

"Come for me," he crooned. "Let your cunny cream against my tongue."

His wicked words had the desired effect. Her fingers dug into his shoulders; she gasped as her essence gushed into his mouth. By God, she was sweet, giving him everything.

Being a greedy bastard, he wanted more. He screwed his

tongue into her channel. He thrust as deeply as he could go, her pulsating pinkness driving him wild.

He raised his head, gritted out, "Maggie mine, I want to be inside you."

"I want it too." Her face flushed, she bit her lip. "But the consequences..."

"I brought a prophylactic."

Her brow wrinkled. She looked adorably befuddled. "A what?"

"A preventative measure. I'll be right back." Placing a kiss on her plush thigh, he went to fetch the item that he'd sworn never again to be without in her presence.

Returning to the bed, he showed her the white tube with red strings dangling at the open end. "It's a sheath made of sheep gut. It catches my seed so that it cannot take root inside you."

Her eyes lit with the new knowledge. She breathed, "Why didn't you mention this sheath before?"

"Darling," he said, smothering a laugh, "I haven't had the opportunity. We've made love in a cave and in my study. I may be a rake, but even I'm not that prepared."

Her brows arched. "You brought it with you *this* time."

"Touché." He tweaked her nose. "After the delightful session in my study, I vowed to have the necessary precautions on my person any time I'm with you. Call it wishful thinking. You have a way of arousing my optimism."

"Not just your optimism." Her gaze slid to his erection. The randy beast was rearing, the engorged tip nudging his navel.

"I want to be inside you," he said earnestly, "but only if you want it as well. There are many ways to make love, Maggie mine, and I'll have you any way I can. I'm the luckiest bastard to be here with you; I know that."

Her lashes swept up; her emerald eyes searched his.

Then her hand shot out, his breath hissing from him when her fingers circled his shaft. A quick study, his Maggie. She frigged him like he'd taught her the last time: firmly, from root to tip. Then again, her touch was perfect simply because it was hers.

His hands planted on the mattress behind him, his neck arching as she used her other hand to cup his bollocks. She squeezed, and the gentle pressure pushed pre-seed up his burgeoned shaft.

"You make me so bloody hard," he said raggedly.

"And wet." Her lips had a knowing curve as she rubbed her thumb over his slick cockhead.

Watching her delicately play with his raging meat caused more pearly liquid to seep out.

"Wetness is a good thing. It makes the sheath more comfortable." At her inquisitive look, he explained, "The added lubrication feels good for me. As if I'm inside you and there is no barrier between us."

"Oh." Her brows drew together. "The wetter you are, the better?"

"Precisely. In fact, I'm ready...er, Maggie, what are you...? *Christ*."

The last he bit out because she'd bent over to *lick* his cock. Her warm tongue bathed his shaft. When she mouthed the swollen dome and gave a tentative suck, his eyes rolled back in his head.

"Is that wet enough?" she murmured.

"You're about to get a lot more wetness if you don't stop."

He caught her under her arms, a surprised squeak leaving her as her back hit the mattress. Kneeling between her spread thighs, he quickly donned the sheath. He'd never found the action particularly erotic, but she changed it for him...the way she changed everything. Her eyes were smoky with desire, her tongue darting out to wet her lips as she watched him work the sheep gut over his swollen length.

Tying the sheath in place, he moved atop her, careful to keep his weight on one forearm. Anticipation licked down his spine as he fitted himself to her slick entrance. He pushed in slowly, panting at the closeness of the fit. Her channel had felt snug around his fingers. Around his cock, she was as tight as a virgin.

"Everything all right?" he managed to get out.

"Just go slowly." Her voice was breathy. "It's, um, been a while."

"I'll go as slow as you want." *Even if it kills me.*

Gritting his teeth, he forged on. Inch by inch, until he was hilted in her pulsing heat. The need to thrust clawed at him, but he remained still, feeling her flesh flutter and soften around him. A blissful torture.

"How does that feel?" He searched her half-lidded gaze.

"Good," she sighed. "You can move now."

Praise God. He moved, increasing his pace when he was certain she felt only pleasure. When she began to move with him, the rhythm of her hips matching his, he let desire take over. He took her harder, faster, her tits jiggling deliciously with his heavy thrusts. Her knees notched against his hips. An erotic symphony filled the room: her moans, the creaking bed, the wet smack of their joining flesh.

He felt the warning sizzle at the base of his spine, knew he wouldn't last for long. With his thumb, he delved into her mound, rubbing her slick bud as he shafted her, burying himself to the balls again and again and again. She gasped, her hips bucking. He felt her clench around him...and not a moment too soon.

His bollocks tightened, heat blasting up his shaft. He crushed his mouth to hers, pouring his groans down her throat as his release jetted from him in an agony of pleasure. Shuddering, he continued thrusting, her pussy milking him of every last drop.

He left the bed long enough to take care of the sheath. When he returned, he doused the lamp and took her in his arms. She snuggled against him, warm and lax from their loving.

He thought she'd fallen asleep when her voice came quietly through the darkness. "Rhys?"

"Yes, my sweet?"

"I just wanted to say...you matter too."

His throat tightened. As did his arms around her. "Thank you, Maggie mine."

It wasn't just an endearment but a promise.

MAGGIE STIRRED. A STRANGE SOUND HAD WOKEN HER...THE wind whirring against the window. Was a storm coming? Moonlight spilled through a crack in the curtain, casting an otherworldly glow over the room. She had the disorienting sensation of being in a dream. She was cocooned in warmth, her cheek pressed against...a hard chest?

Rhys.

Leftover sensations of their lovemaking migrated over her body. The pleasurable tenderness between her legs. The tingle of nipples thoroughly suckled. The slight burn of beard-abraded skin.

Contentment suffused her, and she snuggled closer, inhaling his male musk. Just as she was drifting back to sleep, she heard a thump. From below stairs?

Chilly foreboding stirred her nape; at the same time, Rhys came awake.

"Did you hear that?" Although raspy with sleep, his voice had a vigilant quality.

"Yes," she whispered back.

The sound came again. A second thump and perhaps...whispered voices?

He bolted out of bed. She followed suit, her feet tangling with her nightgown on the floor. She picked it up, yanking it over her head. He cursed softly as he fumbled with his clothes. When she reached to light the lamp, he stopped her.

"Don't alert them." He grabbed the poker by the hearth. "Stay put until I come to get you, understood?"

Before she could argue, he was on the move. She heard the slight protest of door hinges, the stealthy pad of his footsteps fading.

The wind wailed. Her heart thundered. Was that the creak of a floorboard?

THUD. A man's shout. Crashing sounds.

She dashed for the stairs, descending as quickly as she could in the dimness. The front door was open, the wind banging it against the wall. Sounds of combat came from the parlor, light flickering beneath the closed door: movements of a brawl in progress.

Sweet Heavens, I have to help Rhys. I need...a weapon.

She ran down the corridor to the kitchen. Inside, she headed straight for the cook stove, her hands closing around the handle of a cast iron pan. Hefting it up, she rushed to the door that connected the kitchen to the parlor. Inhaling, she shouldered it open a crack.

Two brutes held Rhys pinned to the opposite wall. He struggled, but they held him fast. A third villain advanced toward them. His back was to her, but she could see the glint of the blade in his raised hand.

The blighters were ganging up on Rhys. On *her* man.

Instinct took over. She charged through the door and straight at the man with the knife.

"Leggett, behind you!"

At his comrade's shouted warning, the villain spun around... too late. Her weapon was already in motion. She glimpsed Leggett's yellow-toothed snarl the instant before her pan struck home.

She hit him squarely in the face. The contact reverberated up her arms.

With a moan, he crumpled, his blade skittering across the floor. She stared down at the blood pouring over his visage. *Blooming hell, did I kill him?*

"I'll get the bitch! You hold this bastard."

The voice pierced her shock.

"Run, Maggie!" Rhys roared.

Her head snapped up. By the wall, Rhys was scuffling with his remaining captor; a brute built like a brick house was bearing down upon her. She quickly raised her pan.

"I'll use this again," she warned. "Don't think I won't."

Her attacker's eyes roved over her nightgown-clad form. His smile made her stomach twist. "After I teach you a lesson, I'm going 'ave my fun wif you."

He lunged at her. She dodged, but he grabbed a hold of her sleeve. He tore it viciously, exposing her right arm to the shoulder. Seeing the predatory lust in his eyes, she swung the pan with all her might.

He caught it, yanking it from her grip. Before she could run, he had her bodice in his fist. He pushed her backward, the back of her knees hitting the settee. He toppled her onto the cushions.

"I like my bitches wif bite." He grabbed her bared shoulder in a bruising grip. "Let's see what you're 'iding 'neath that—"

"Get your hands off of her!"

Eyes lit with unholy fury, Rhys caught her attacker in a flying tackle. He landed on top, plowing his fists repeatedly into her assailant's face. Just as he gained the upper hand, the bastard's comrade grabbed him from behind. Frantically, Maggie scrambled to her feet, looking for her weapon—when another movement caught her eye.

In the doorway, a newcomer.

"Jeremy?" she croaked.

Her brother took instant stock of the situation. If Goodes had one talent, it was spotting trouble. His gaze shot from her ripped nightgown to the blood-soaked brute on the floor to the two remaining bastards ganging up on Rhys.

Anger blazed on Jeremy's face. Tossing aside his bag, he barreled into the fray with a war cry. He ripped the man off Rhys's back, making the fight even. Just in case, Maggie ran to pick up her pan...and not a moment too soon. The villain she'd knocked out sat up, holding his head.

Oh no, you don't. She stalked over.

He looked up just as she swung again.

He hit the ground with a thud that resounded in the sudden stillness.

Panting, she turned around to see Rhys and Jeremy staring at her. Their chests were heaving, their faces sheened with sweat. Their respective foes lay on the ground, groaning.

Rhys arched a brow at her brother. "Did you teach her to use the pan?"

Jeremy shook his head. "She learned it from our ma. Men might rule with an iron fist but Ma, she did it with an iron pan."

"Remind me not to get on your sister's bad side."

The men exchanged knowing looks.

Maggie expelled an exasperated breath. "When you're finished with your manly jokes, do you think you could restrain these burglars?"

"They're not burglars," Rhys said.

"You know them?" she asked in disbelief.

His jaw clenched, his hands curling at his sides. "They work for Adam Garrity, one of the moneylenders I owe. He's sending me a message: he wants his money...or his pound of flesh."

A cold droplet slid down Maggie's spine. At the same time, another thought struck her.

"Dear heavens. Hypatia and Mr. Newton," she whispered.

Dropping the pan, she raced to look for them.

❧ 2 2 ❧

"It all happened rather quickly," Hypatia said, sipping her tea.

After the magistrate and his men had hauled the attackers off to the local gaol that morning, Rhys had herded everyone back to his estate, picking Glory up along the way. Now he, Maggie, Hypatia, Newton, and Jeremy convened in the drawing room.

Glory had been put in the care of Quince who was, at present, giving her a tour of the curiosities. Strangely enough, the butler hadn't complained when assigned what was, in essence, a nanny's task. In fact, as Glory chattered away, Rhys had caught what might have been a smile on the old curmudgeon's face. Either that or Quince had been passing wind.

"Mr. Newton and I must have fallen asleep discussing the plans for London," Hypatia went on. "The next thing I knew, I was being bound and gagged and dragged into the study. It was a bit of a shock."

"To say the least." His shaggy hair disheveled, Newton gazed at her with puppyish adoration. "I admire your nerves, Miss Foley. They are as formidable as your intellect."

The spinster's cheeks turned pink. "How kind of you to say, sir."

Sitting beside Rhys, Maggie shivered. "I'm just glad that no one was hurt."

The possibility of Maggie or his friends coming to harm made Rhys want to punch someone. Namely, himself. He rose, prowling to the hearth, searching for the right words.

"I must apologize again for putting all of you in harm's way," he said tautly. "If I had had the slightest inkling that Garrity knew my location—"

"You cannot be held accountable for a cutthroat's actions," Hypatia said.

Maggie gave a brisk nod. "And we mustn't allow the attack to deter us from the task at hand: finding the treasure."

Despite his churning guilt, Rhys admired the show of female resilience. Devil and damn, but Dorset produced sturdy feminine stock.

"When be you off to London, guv?" Sprawled in the chair nearest the food-laden sideboard, Jeremy spoke while plowing through a plate of sandwiches.

"Tomorrow." There was no delaying the inevitable. Especially now, when trouble had come knocking. The sooner Rhys found the treasure, the sooner he could pay off his debts. Then he could come back to Maggie. To their daughter. To the life he wanted to build.

This time, I cannot fail.

"I'm coming with you," Maggie declared.

He stared at her. Was she mad? After she'd nearly been *raped* because of him?

"You most definitely are not," he said, jaw clenched.

"I've helped you find the clues and solve them." The mutinous angle of her chin looked familiar; he'd seen it on Glory a number of times. "You need me."

"I need you *alive*," he bit out. "Devil take it, Maggie, I will not countenance you risking your neck to save mine. I am not worth it. You will bloody well stay here where you're safe." For good measure, he said in ducal tones, "That is final."

He might as well have spoken in the tones of a chimney sweep for all that it impressed Maggie.

"What makes you think I am safe here?" She marched over to him. "Garrity's men came to *my cottage* to find you, remember? Garrity knows of our connection. Perhaps that other cutthroat you owe..."

"Sweeney," Newton supplied.

Bloody traitor, Rhys thought darkly.

"...Sweeney does too. What's to stop either of them from sending more men to my cottage? While you're off gallivanting in London,"—she poked him in the chest—"I'll be here like a sitting duck."

The truth of her words sunk into him like a blade. He tried to staunch the bleeding.

"Your brother will keep you safe," he said curtly.

"How's he supposed to keep me safe from a gang of professional cutthroats?" she demanded. "Besides, you know my brothers cannot be relied upon. They're Goodes. The only reason Jeremy showed up when he did was because Delilah kicked him out, and he needed a place to stay."

"Those are the thanks I get?" Jeremy said through a mouthful of cake. "Should've let your toff get pummeled into the ground."

"I was not getting pummeled." Rhys narrowed his eyes at Jeremy. "You and your brothers will look after Maggie, won't you?"

"Stay out of this, Jeremy," Maggie said.

Her brother, probably wisely, held up his hands. "Reckon I ain't the sharpest tool in the box, but I know better than to involve myself in another's spat."

"See?" Maggie said triumphantly. "He doesn't want to get involved."

Rhys recalibrated. "I'll hire men to guard you in my absence. Professional, *reliable* men."

"I'll not have strangers watching my every move. I'll dispatch them from my property, you see if I don't."

His temper snapped because he *could* see her doing it. Just to be difficult. "Bloody hell, woman, why are you being so damned stubborn?"

"Because I don't want my lover marching into danger alone!" she shouted.

Silence blanketed the room.

Hypatia cleared her throat. "Mr. Newton, didn't you say there was an interesting artifact out in the corridor that you wanted to show me?"

"I said that?" At the nudge of Hypatia's elbow, Newton's brow cleared. "Oh, *right*. That artifact. The one out in the, er...well, I don't recall where exactly. But it's out there. Not in here."

Rhys had no idea how the man had made a living as a solicitor.

"Let's go." Hypatia stood, aiming a look at Maggie's brother. "You, too."

"And miss the fireworks?" Jeremy polished off a bun. "Oi ain't been to Vauxhall, but methinks these might be even better."

"Jeremy," Maggie said in warning tones.

"Right-o. On my way." Getting up, he sauntered over to Rhys. "Before oi go, guv, wanted to thank you again for putting me up in this palace o' yours."

"You're welcome. Now get out," Rhys said.

The trio left, leaving Rhys and Maggie alone.

Her emerald eyes formed slits. "You're letting Jeremy stay here?"

"The man fought beside me. It's the least I could do."

"He's Jeremy. He'd fight just to fight."

She had a point. "Don't distract me from the fact that you shared with the world that we're lovers."

"It wasn't the world. Just Hypatia, Mr. Newton, and Jeremy. All of whom probably guessed the nature of our relationship."

"Nonetheless." He braced his hands on his hips. "I didn't want to compromise your reputation."

"But you would make love to me and then leave?"

Her accusation decimated his self-control.

"Damnit, I don't *want* to leave you. I have to. For your own good—Christ, I nearly got you killed!" he exploded.

"Do not tell me what is for my own good! I am not some nitwit."

"Then stop acting like you are," he said acidly, "and do as I tell you."

"Don't you *dare* tell me what to do," she blazed. "For years, I heeded my husband's advice—but I'm *done*. Done with doing what others want of me. If I want to shout to the world that I have a lover, I'm going to shout. If I want to wallop a bastard with a pan, he'd better beware. If I want to go to London, you cannot bloody stop me. I am a grown woman, capable of looking after my own interests!"

Her temper matched her hair, full of hidden fire. He realized that he'd never seen her unleash her anger before. Not in full force. Devil and damn, but she was a spitfire—and it aroused him. To see her lose her temper because she didn't want to be parted from him. Because she was fighting for her own interests...for him.

A fierce ache throbbed in his chest. His cock, too.

Hell, he was getting hard from their row.

"I know you're capable. In point of fact, I'm in awe of your competence." He reached for her, but she jerked away. In a placating tone, he said, "What you are not capable of, however, is taking on cutthroats. Have no doubt that I want you with me, Maggie; I just want your safety *more*."

"You can hire guards in London to keep us both safe." While she still kept her distance, the entreaty in her eyes would have melted a stone. "We're stronger together than apart, Rhys. I *know* we'll find the treasure. The sooner we do that, the sooner we'll all be safe."

He dropped his hand. Stared at her broodingly. Never had he felt so torn between his own desires and what he believed to be right—to be better for her. His teeth ground together as he fought to make the right choice...

"There is something else you should know," she said.

He cocked his head.

Looking him in the eye, Maggie declared, "Glory is your daughter."

❧ 23 ❧

WHAT HAVE I DONE?

Maggie hadn't planned to vomit out her secret. Yet the truth was out; she couldn't take it back. And she couldn't read Rhys's reaction. He'd gone still. So still that she could see a dust mote hover above his shoulder before landing on the silver-grey wool.

His expression was cool. Composed. Ducal.

In contrast, she felt like a former serving maid who'd just blurted out that she'd had a child out of wedlock. Oh, wait—that *was* her.

The demons of doubt swarmed her. *What if he repudiates Glory? What if he wants nothing to do with me or the bastard he sired? What if I've just been a convenient bed warmer for him…the way I was nine years ago?*

Her throat tightened. "Say something," she croaked.

"I know," he said.

She blinked, not understanding. "What do you know?"

"That Glory is mine. I think some part of me knew it the moment I met her," he said slowly. "The vicar's pointing out of the family resemblance confirmed what I'd secretly suspected."

She moistened her dry lips, not sure what to say.

His gaze was steady. "I asked you about it, if you'll recall."

And I lied. To your face. With thumping guilt, she whispered, "I...I'm sorry."

"Why did you lie to me?"

She expected him to be furious. Instead, he was calm, inscrutable, his lack of emotion ratcheting up her anxiety more than his anger would have done.

"At first, it was to protect Glory. She was raised as Paul's, the daughter of a gentleman. I didn't want anything to threaten her respectability." She swallowed. "I didn't know how you would react and couldn't stand the thought of her paying for my mistake."

"Do you think I would hurt her?" The tautness of his jaw betrayed his tension.

"No. That is, not now. When you first came back, I didn't know you," she said candidly. "Didn't know if you would care about Glory's well-being. Since then, I've seen you with her, and I know you would not harm her."

"No, I would not." His hazel eyes blazed with emotion. "Nor would I hurt you."

"I know." In truth, she'd known for some time, yet she'd continued lying to him.

Why, oh why, had she been so stupid? Insight seared through her.

"The truth is...it wasn't you I didn't trust," she admitted. "It was myself."

His brows lowered. "Explain."

"I didn't think you'd want to have a child with me. With the serving maid you'd tupped on the first night that you met her." She dropped her gaze, the shine of his boots almost blinding. "With a...No Goode."

"It's true that I don't want you to have my child."

Why are you surprised? The onslaught of pain was slowed by numbness. *Of course he doesn't want* you *to be the mother of his child. You're a No Goode. A nobody.*

His finger curled beneath her chin, lifting her gaze to his. What she saw there made her breath stick in her throat. His brilliant eyes were sheened...with remorse.

"I got you with child and then just *left*," he said gruffly. "I cannot imagine the suffering I caused you. The pain and fear. There are no words to express how sorry I am for what I've done. What I did because I was a selfish, irresponsible bastard out for my own pleasure."

His apology spread through her like sunlight. Her numbness melted as she saw the genuine regret on his face, heard the harsh anguish in his voice. All traces of the debonair duke were gone. In his place was a man, his sins exposed, his repentance real.

And she knew that it wasn't fair for him to assume the entire burden for what had happened. For two of them had engaged in that reckless, life-altering night of passion.

"It was my fault too. I went with you willingly." There was no longer any reason to keep secrets, and she said in halting tones, "It was my...first time. Being with a man, I mean. I didn't think of the consequences—"

Rhys's oath cut her off. Before she could react, her cheek was pressed against the plush silk of his waistcoat, his arms tight bands around her. He did nothing more...just held her. His heart thundered beneath her ear. Given the uncertainty of the situation, it was odd how safe she felt.

"Not another word. You are not to blame, sweetheart, and, by God, I'll not let you think that you are." His voice was grittier than sandpaper. "The fault is entirely mine. I should have sensed your inexperience. Bloody hell, I'm a blackguard. I told myself that because you were working in a dockside tavern, you knew what you were about."

"It's a common assumption about us serving maids," she said wryly.

"Common doesn't make it right." His hand continued its comforting stroke even as his voice dripped with self-condemnation. "I was a careless sod. If I could go back and do it over, I would."

She tipped her head back. "You wouldn't have approached me?"

"I've done many things I'm not proud of." His eyes darkened. "But I've never to my knowledge dallied with a virgin. And the fact that I did so with you and didn't even realize—"

"Because I didn't act like a virgin, did I?" She squirmed at the memory of her wantonness. "I went with you, and we didn't even get to the bed..."

"My God." His eyes shut. "Your first time. Against a bloody *door*."

"It was fine," she said quickly. "I, um, enjoyed it. Didn't you?"

His lashes lifted, revealing his glowering stare. "That's hardly the point, Maggie mine. It's not *right* for your first time."

Now that the truth was out, she felt lighter. Relieved. While she appreciated that Rhys clearly felt responsible for their tryst—and was reassured by the respect he expressed for her—she was ready to move on.

"Regardless, it happened, and we are where we are," she said prosaically. "Now about London—"

"Maggie, you've paid a heavy price because of me," he went on in a determined manner. "While I admire your strength and courage more than I can say, I want you to know that you're no longer alone. From here on in, I will take care of you and Glory. I will see that you want for nothing ever again."

Wariness crept over her. She extricated herself from his arms. Took a step back.

"*How* will you take care of us?" she asked. "What exactly are you offering, Rhys?"

A heartbeat passed. A muscle in his jaw leapt.

"If I could offer you marriage, I would," he said. "But I cannot."

Rhys thought he could not hate himself more. But he was wrong.

Seeing the pain darken Maggie's eyes, he cursed himself for being a bastard. "Maggie—"

"No, it's all right. It's what I expected." Her smile was as taut as a steel wire as she gestured first to him, then to herself. "You're a duke; I'm me. Of course marriage isn't a possibility."

"My rank has nothing to do with—"

"You don't have to explain. In all fairness, you were clear about the terms of our affair from the start," she said as if he hadn't spoken. "At any rate, I have no need to marry again. I have my independence, the means to support myself and my daughter."

"*Our* daughter."

"She doesn't have to be." Maggie's cool correction slithered down his spine. "She had a doting papa in my husband. To the world, she is a gentleman's daughter. Better that than an unwanted bastard."

"I do want her. I want *you*." Even as his chest knotted with frustration, he *felt* the truth of his words. For the first time, the notion of a family didn't make him feel as if he were about to be buried alive. Instead, it felt...right. "But I can't be a father or a husband if I'm a dead man. Until I resolve my debts with Garrity and Sweeney, I cannot, in good faith, make you an honorable offer."

"I understand."

He could tell she didn't, so he cut to the chase. "Newton has found an American heiress. If I fail to find the treasure, I'll have to barter my title for a dowry. To undertake a marriage of convenience, for that is all that it would be."

He saw the truth sink in. She wrapped her arms around her waist.

"I will not be the mistress of a married man," she said in trembling tones.

"I would not ask you to be." The fact that she believed he would demean her in that fashion made his gut clench. "I know that if I have to marry someone else, I will lose you forever. Regardless, I want you to know that I would provide for you and Glory financially."

"I don't need your money."

Pride burned in her like an eternal flame. And he knew that if he lived to be old and grey, he would still never meet another woman with her mettle. With her indomitable spirit.

A duchess's spirit.

"I know you don't, but you'll have it anyway. Christ," he said in frustration, "I wish I could give you more. If I could, I would give you everything."

She gnawed on her lip. "If it weren't for the debt, you'd truly want to marry me?"

"I told you...you matter to me." Words he'd never said to any woman before her.

Her gaze was searching. His heart thudded. Did she not believe him?

"I care for you too," she whispered.

Hearing her say that a second time didn't lessen its impact. Emotion flooded him, foreign but not unwelcome. It took him a moment to recognize the feeling as...happiness.

His throat raw, he said, "I'm going to find those jewels so that I can make you mine."

"If that's what you want, then take me with you. Let me help," she pleaded. "*Prove* to me that you think I'm worthy."

"You are worth ten of me." In his heart, he knew she'd already won.

His main reservation about taking her was safety. But what

she'd said earlier was true: now that Garrity and Sweeney knew about her, she'd be no safer here than in London. In fact, she might be safer with Rhys keeping an eye on her—him and the coterie of guards he planned to hire for protection. He had already compromised her well-being, and there was no going back.

Only forward...to London.

And, damn him to hell, he *wanted* her by his side. The woman he cared for. With her holding the light for him, he felt as if he could navigate the darkest waters and find the way...home.

"Rhys?" she pressed.

He prayed that he was making the right choice.

Hoarsely, he said, "How long will it take you to pack for London, Maggie mine?"

$$\text{✻ } 24 \text{ ✻}$$

GETTING READY FOR THE TRIP TOOK MAGGIE LONGER THAN expected. Not that she had much basis for comparison: this would be her first excursion beyond Dorset. She tackled the requisite packing, the hardest part of which involved saying "no" to the assorted sundry that Glory wished to bring...which appeared to be *everything*.

When Glory dragged in her rock collection, Maggie had to put her foot down.

As Hypatia had declared her intention to go on the trip as well—and no one could dissuade her once she made up her mind —the shop had to be temporarily closed. Truth be told, Maggie didn't mind one bit.

The excursion began at dawn three days later. Rhys had sent Newton ahead to prepare for their stay, and they made the journey by private mail coach. They stopped only to change horses, but the luxurious conveyance made the hours pass quickly. Lulled by the plush cushions and well-sprung ride, Maggie slept most of the way.

Before she knew it, the coachman announced that they were approaching London. Darkness had long fallen; her first view of the city was the twinkling of lit windows, a miasma of grey fog weaving around the dark silhouettes of buildings. She didn't have the heart to wake Glory, who was asleep between her and Hypatia. Rhys occupied the opposite bench, an ankle propped on his knee, his expression pensive in the dim carriage light.

In the frenzy of preparation for the trip, she and he had not spent much time alone. She knew he still had his reservations about taking her to London. In truth, she had forced the issue—and she wasn't sorry about it.

You matter to me.

She hugged his words to herself. From a man with Rhys's past, they meant everything. At a young age, Rhys had lost his mother, suffered mistreatment by his father, been bullied by classmates and abandoned by the uncle he'd loved. As an adult, he'd been shunned by those who ought to have stood by his side. Was it any wonder that he was wary of relationships?

She was beginning to understand that, contrary to his devil-may-care image, he wasn't an unfeeling rake wedded to his freedom. He was the opposite: a man who cared too much. A man who longed for connection but feared getting hurt.

I'll never hurt him. Tender resolve filled her. *I'll take care of him... as he's taken care of me.*

Her feelings were strong, undeniable. She cared about Rhys... had fallen in love with him. Despite the risks, the likelihood of pain worse than she'd ever known before, she'd lost her heart. The time wasn't right to tell him; she didn't want to burden him with her feelings...or scare him off. But she *had* to come to London—so that they could fight for their future together.

She cleared her throat to get his attention. "Will we be going straight to the Seven Dials?"

He slanted her an amused look. "Much as I admire your stamina, we'll be checking into our accommodations first. I had to let the lease on my usual townhouse go, so we'll be staying at Mivart's hotel. I think you'll like it."

Maggie had never stayed at a hotel. To her, the notion sounded rather exotic.

"We'll start our hunt for the treasure tomorrow then?" she asked. "If we're to search the Seven Dials, we have much ground to cover."

"From what I recall of London," Hypatia said, "the Seven Dials is not the most searchable of places."

"You have a knack for euphemism, Miss Hypatia. Seven Dials is located in the rookery of St. Giles, a hotbed of thieves, drunks, and cutthroats," Rhys said. "We will not venture into the slum without reinforcements."

"Do you mean to hire guards?" Maggie asked.

"That was one of Newton's assignments. While guards will provide protection against casual cutthroats, they will not suffice against more serious enemies." Rhys's mouth formed a tight line. "Before we venture forth into London, I will need to negotiate an armistice with Garrity and Sweeney."

Thinking of the ruffians that had besieged them, Maggie swallowed. "Aren't you afraid they'll attack first and ask questions later?"

"Indeed. That is why I need an intermediary, one with the power to keep Garrity and Sweeney in check. Newton has arranged for me to meet with her tomorrow."

"*Her?*" A woman had the power to control the cutthroats?

"Tessa Black-Todd—now Mrs. Harry Kent. She's the granddaughter of Bartholomew Black, a powerful cutthroat who rules over the London underworld."

"How do you know her?"

"It's a long story." Rhys lifted the curtain. "It appears we've arrived."

Seeing as how Maggie was a Goode and the mama of a trouble-prone child, she knew evasion when she saw it. She made a mental note to ask more about the mysterious Mrs. Kent later.

For now, she peered eagerly out at the accommodations—and her breath lodged in her throat.

This was Mivart's? Sweet heavens, it looked like a *palace*.

Lit by street lamps, the Palladian façade gleamed white as the moon against the night sky. It stood four grand stories, and the entrance was flanked by fluted columns, gleaming conveyances jostling for prime parking space. Liveried footmen dashed forward to assist well-dressed patrons from their carriages.

Entering the hotel was like stepping into a faerie tale castle. The marble floors gleamed so much that Maggie feared she might slip on them. For once, even Glory was quiet, her jaw slack and gaze wide as she took in the opulent lobby. Everywhere was polished wood, silver, and shining glass. Red carpeted stairs flowed up a grand stairwell.

As Rhys was met by the hotelier, who bowed low and greeted him as "Your Grace," Maggie couldn't help but stare at the guests milling about the lobby. Even though it was nearing midnight, people were heading out, draped in velvet, jewels, and finery so resplendent that Maggie thought they must be royalty. She gave a self-conscious tug at her traveling cloak, which was twice dyed over and fraying at the seams.

Glory's hand crept into hers. "Are you sure Mr. Jones...um, I mean, Ransom, has the correct hotel, Mama?" she asked, her voice hushed with wonder. "Are we really staying here?"

Maggie and Rhys had agreed that it would be best to share his true identity with Glory but to withhold the fact that he was her father for now. It was for Glory's safety. If the cutthroats discovered that she was Rhys's child, she might also become a target.

Moreover, too much was unsettled between Maggie and Rhys. She didn't want to confuse Glory...or raise the girl's hopes.

Learning that Rhys was a duke seemed to have no quelling effect on Glory's affection for him. Instead, she'd pestered him with questions. How many servants did he have? How many houses did he own? Did he sup with the queen?

As per his style, he'd provided matter-of-fact answers. He'd lost his houses and servants because of bad investments. And yes, he had been at Court, but it had been quite some time since his last visit. He was trying to rebuild his fortune by locating the inheritance left to him by his uncle, the diamond they'd located at St. Candida being part of that trove.

Being part of a grand treasure-seeking adventure had sent Glory into paroxysms of delight. She'd given Rhys her word—and a pinky swear—to carry on with discretion. It wouldn't do for others to catch wind of the missing treasure; the last thing they needed were rivals for the prize.

To prevent undue scrutiny about Glory's presence, she would be presented as Uncle Horatio's former ward and now Rhys's. As the widowed mother of Rhys's new "ward," Maggie would have a socially acceptable reason to be there as well, one that would not cause undue gossip and speculation.

Now she squeezed her daughter's hand.

"Ransom knows what he is about," she said. "We'll be in our chambers soon enough."

The hotelier himself led their party to rooms on the third floor. Rhys went to attend to some business, leaving Maggie, Hypatia, and Glory to explore their accommodations. They began with Maggie's sitting room. Done in shades of cameo blue and cream, it was fit for a queen. And Maggie *felt* like a queen when she discovered that Rhys had arranged a lady's maid for her. Bertha, a cheerful, no-nonsense sort, greeted her with a curtsy and told her she would get to work unpacking.

"I didn't bring much," Maggie said ruefully, thinking of the two black dresses, one nightgown, and set of plain unmention-ables in her trunk.

"Oh, I wasn't talking about what you brought, ma'am, but what came for you earlier. It's all in the bedchamber." A twinkle lit Bertha's eyes. "A mountain of boxes from some of the finest shops in London."

Entering the bedchamber, Maggie saw that the maid hadn't exaggerated. Stacks of boxes stood by the canopied bed. Although she didn't know the names of the establishments stamped on each, the gilt curlicues and flourishes left no doubt that they were exclusive. Lifting the lid of a flat dress box stamped "Maison de Rousseau," she parted the tissue wrapping... and her breath caught.

The dress was the finest she'd ever seen. It was a ball gown, wholly impractical given that she would have no occasion to wear it, but she couldn't stop herself from reverently stroking the rich emerald silk.

"Oh, Mama, that color will look beautiful on you," Glory said with a sigh.

"But how did all this get here?" she murmured.

"His Grace instructed Mr. Newton to order the very best for you and the Misses Foley," Bertha said. "Gowns, hats, all the accoutrements. The modiste will be by to ensure that everything fits properly."

"Hooray!" Glory raced out of the room to find her loot.

"How generous of His Grace." Even Hypatia sounded impressed.

Maggie didn't know what to say. The elegant suite, the finery... it all seemed unreal. As if she, Maggie Foley, would wake up any minute now from some fantastic dream.

Yet it was real; Rhys had made it real.

If I could, I would give you everything.

She felt heat press behind her eyes. Not because of the expensive trappings...but because Rhys thought her worthy of them. And, for the first time, she felt she was.

Bertha took charge of the unpacking with the zeal of a general leading a war campaign. With nothing better to do and too awake to go to bed, Maggie and Hypatia settled in Maggie's sitting room. Hypatia had her own separate suite, and Glory's room was attached to Maggie's by an adjoining door. Distant whoops could be heard from the girl, who instead of sleeping, was clearly testing out her featherbed.

"Do you think she's being too loud?" Maggie asked apprehensively.

Her feet up on a velvet footstool, Hypatia sipped contentedly at her beverage, which she hadn't bothered to mix with tea. "Mivart's has seen far worse, I'm sure. No one revels like the Upper Crust."

"It feels strange being here."

"You'd better get used to it." Over her spectacles, Patty gave her a pointed look. "Now that we are alone, it is time for a *tête-à-tête*. Has His Grace made clear his intentions toward you?"

Guilt gnawed at Maggie. Hypatia was her kin and closest friend, yet there were confidences she hadn't shared. She knew that Patty had guessed the nature of her relationship with Rhys and seemed to bear no ill judgement. She was less certain how the other would react to the news that Rhys was Glory's father.

Rhys...and not Patty's own brother.

Rhys had once called her "formidable"—God, she wished she had the same confidence in herself. Yet here was a chance to test her courage...with the woman who was a true sister to her.

"Rhys and I are lovers." Then, before she lost nerve, "And he is...he's Glory's father."

Hypatia's cup clattered onto its saucer. "I think you had better start from the beginning."

Maggie did. She left nothing out. Not even the lack of marital intimacy between her and Paul.

When she was done, her hands were trembling. She clasped them together in her lap, awaiting her sister-in-law's edict. Would Hypatia condemn her?

"My poor dear." Leaning over, Hypatia squeezed her hand. "What a burden you've carried."

Relief dampened her eyes. "Glory was never a burden. But I hated lying to you. Paul thought that it was best for everyone to believe that Glory was his—even you."

"I understand my brother's decision. He was lucky to find a wife like you, Maggie, and a daughter like Gloriana."

"You don't hate me?"

"Hate you? Why on earth?"

"Because I was...impure before my wedding night," she said in a small voice.

"If I judged you for that, I would be a hypocrite. And you know how I hate hypocrisy."

Maggie blinked. "Are you saying...?"

"I was young and impetuous once," Hypatia said. "He was a soldier, and he never came back from the war. I was more fortunate than you: all I suffered was a broken heart. And how could I possibly hate you when you've been so good to us Foleys?"

A tear slipped down Maggie's cheek. "I owe so much to Paul. To you."

Hypatia handed her a handkerchief. "The truth is Paul and I owe *you*. You took care of him, his shop, and his household. You gave him a child to dote upon. You accepted what he could offer in a marriage, which not all women would." The understanding in the other's eyes made Maggie flush. "As for me, I could not ask for a more sensible, loyal, and bosom friend."

Maggie sniffled.

"There, there. Don't turn into a watering pot on me now," Hypatia muttered.

Smiling through her tears, she said, "Thank you...for accepting me as I am."

"I always have. 'Tis self-acceptance that eludes us all," Patty said wisely.

Maggie knew the other was right. "Do you think a future is possible for me and Rhys? He's a duke, after all, and I'm..."

"You're the woman who will help him win his future back. He needs you as much as you need him." Hypatia gave her a searching look. "You do love him, don't you, dear?"

"I do." It was a relief to admit it aloud. "So very much."

"Then don't wait another minute." Hypatia picked up her brandy. "Life is far too short and precious to waste."

Her sister-in-law was right, Maggie realized. She didn't know what the future held for her and Rhys, but they had tonight. Every moment counted. Her mind flashed to the luxurious wardrobe he'd had made for her, lingering on a particular item.

Lips curving, she knew what she would do.

IT was nearing two o' clock in the morning when Rhys returned to his suite. He was tired yet satisfied with the outcome of his meeting with Newton down in the hotel's private lounge. The man-of-business had proved his competence once again. Everything had been arranged to Rhys's instructions.

The diamond had been sold for a tidy sum. Guards had been retained. Rush orders of new clothes for the women had arrived and been sent to their rooms, along with a lady's maid.

And a meeting had been set up with Tessa Kent for the morrow.

He winced at the thought of facing the woman he'd once thought to marry. Egad, but that whole business had been a mistake. He felt only relief that he'd escaped that particular disaster as he and Tessa had never suited. Nonetheless, they had not parted on the best of terms, and knowing her cunning and devilish ways, Tessa might make him pay the piper tomorrow.

As much as it galled him, he needed Tessa's protection if he wished to find the treasure without Garrity and Sweeney breathing down his neck. For the sake of keeping Maggie and

Glory safe, he would eat the humble pie Tessa served him. Or take a drubbing from her over-protective new husband.

Ah, well. Whatever would come would come.

Removing his jacket and cravat, Rhys slung them over a chair in the sitting room. His valet would take care of the garments...by God, it was good to be flush in the pocket again. He poured himself a glass of Scotch, savoring its fine burn as he stared out into the velvet-framed view of Mayfair. In this playground of luxury, he was back in his element.

Yet the money from the jewel wouldn't last forever. The sooner he could start scouring the Seven Dials for the next clue, the better. Which meant he'd better get his rest.

Tossing back the rest of the drink, he headed to the bedchamber. He paused at the adjoining door to Maggie's suite. Thinking of her on the other side of that barrier sent a swirl of heat through him. But his desire wasn't just about sex; his feelings for Maggie were different from anything he'd experienced with other women. He craved her company, wanted to be near her, to hold her close even if all they did was sleep.

Given the long journey, she must be exhausted and asleep by now. Moreover, with their child in the mix, he had to carry out their affair with the utmost discretion. What if Glory suddenly awoke fearful in this strange new place and went to search out her mama...only to find him sharing Maggie's bed?

No, he wouldn't risk it. He would confer with Maggie tomorrow about the sleeping arrangements and come up with a foolproof plan. It struck him that this could be the most prudish thought that he, an established rake, had ever had.

Bemused, he went onto his chamber.

A bedside lamp had thoughtfully been left burning. His pulse leapt when he saw an even more thoughtful gesture: cinnamon waves spread deliciously across his pillow and a familiar curvy form beneath the silk coverlet. The smooth rise and fall of

Maggie's breathing indicated that she'd fallen asleep waiting for him.

He couldn't help his smug grin. *Leave it to my Maggie to take matters into her own hands.*

Quietly, he stripped off his garments. He wouldn't wake her if she was sound asleep; it would be enough just to hold her through the night. With care, he tugged aside the coverlet...

Bloody. Fuck.

A ragged breath left him. Along with all his good intentions.

She stirred, stretching sleepily. Each movement pulled the form-fitting white satin negligee more tautly over her luscious curves. He was treated to a peek-a-boo view of a cherry nipple through a deep vee of lace.

Her lashes fluttered. Her emerald eyes were dreamy. His heart stuttered at the vision she made: an awakened siren warming his bed, keeping the fire burning for him. A fantasy come true.

"Waiting long?" He tried to sound casual. It wasn't easy when all the blood had plummeted from his brain to his cock.

"Long enough that I fell asleep." She smiled ruefully. "I wanted to say thank you for the gifts."

"You're welcome. Now that I see you in that negligee, however, I think I should be the one offering thanks. Maggie mine, I cannot tell you how happy I am to see you."

He crawled onto the bed. Her gaze sparkled with feminine appreciation as she took in his naked form. The part that her gaze lingered on swelled even more.

"Very happy, I should say," she said with a laugh.

The perfection of the moment struck him. The two of them, in a comfortable bed. His Maggie, relaxed and beautiful, laughing over a sensual joke. For the first time in a long time, he felt...free. Blessed to be alive in this moment. He knew the feeling wouldn't last, so why waste it?

Yet he had to ask. "What about Glory? What if she wakes and..."

"Not to worry." Maggie's smile warmed the depths of him. "Hypatia is sleeping in the room next to hers tonight and will keep watch."

"You've thought of everything."

"I believe in planning," she said demurely.

They simultaneously reached for one another. Their kiss was carnal, uninhibited. They rolled on the bed, a tangle of lips and bodies and tongues. She somehow ended up on top, and when she pushed him back against the pillows, he raised his brows in question.

"Tonight, I want to have my way with you," she said.

Well. He didn't think it possible, but his cock got harder.

Folding his hands behind his head, he said, "Have at it."

Just because he was accustomed to taking the lead in bed didn't mean that he couldn't enjoy some variety. And the way Maggie was looking at him, with such sweet feminine hunger, made him want to encourage her newfound confidence.

After a sweet touch of her lips to his, she began to taste her way down his body. It didn't escape his notice that taking charge sexually was likely a new experience for her. There was a shyness to the way she licked his earlobe and nibbled down the tendon of his neck. In fact, she was pretty much mimicking what he'd done to her...and damn, if it wasn't working.

When she traced one of his nipples with her tongue, he couldn't hold back a groan.

Her head popped up. "Is that all right?"

"I'm not certain. Keep doing it, and I'll let you know."

A smile tucked into her cheeks. Then she lowered her head again, and his chest heaved as she slowly, deliberately licked his nipple. Lapped at it like a delicate cat. Right before she used her teeth.

His pulse spiked. His erection jerked against the rigid muscles of his belly.

She repeated the action on his other nipple, the soft scrape of teeth driving him wild. It took everything in him to keep his hands behind his head, to not give into the impulse to take over. The primitive part of him that wanted to flip his naughty enchantress onto her back and bury himself in her snug, lush hole.

Experience had taught him that prolonging the pleasure would make it even more intense. All he had to do was not unload his cannon like an untried lad.

Easier said than done.

Through hooded eyes, he watched as she nibbled her way between his ribcage, stopping here and there to pepper kisses over the twitching ridges. It wasn't just the pleasure of her touch that he savored: it was her enjoyment of what she was doing. The sultry fun sparkling in her eyes, her growing awareness of her own sensual power. When she made a place for herself between his legs and wrapped her fingers carefully around his turgid flesh, he thought he might die from the anticipation.

"You're so big," she murmured. "I can hardly fit my fingers around you."

She wasn't being coy; his rod did strain the limits of her grip.

He wanted to strain other limits of her as well.

"How about your sweet lips?" he suggested silkily.

He adored the determined tilt of her head. She had a prim, business-like look as she sized up his throbbing prick the way she might a specimen in her fossils shop. Thank God his Maggie was never one to back down from a challenge.

Prying his rampant flesh gently away from his stomach, she put her mouth on him. His breaths grew shallow as she licked him the way she did last time, only with more surety and feminine resolve. It was, undoubtedly, the most arousing, torturous fellatio he'd ever received. He watched avidly as the tip of her pink tongue followed the bulging vein on the underside of his cock, all the way to his balls. When she mouthed his aching stones, a hot sizzle shot up his pole.

She kissed her way up his length, licking up the dribbled pre-seed.

"Mmm," she said with a flirty smile.

Christ. Her sensual teasing drove him wild. He couldn't hold back any longer. His hands wove into her silky hair, positioning her mouth over his burgeoned crown.

"Take me into your mouth," he said huskily. "As deep as you can, love."

Understanding lit her eyes. He would have laughed at her endearing innocence if she hadn't plunged down, surrounding his cockhead in a hot, wet kiss. A tattered breath left him as she followed his instruction to the letter, impaling her mouth on his prick. He guided her head, and she got the rhythm quickly, bobbing up and down, taking him deeper with each pass.

"God, yes, just like that," he rasped. "You suck my cock so well, Maggie mine."

Her reply was muffled against said cock. Her hands had found an intuitive rhythm, one frigging him as she sucked, the other cupping and squeezing his balls. He had to stop her soon, or he would shoot himself into her mouth. When she dove too deeply, she gagged a little, and he groaned as her throat clamped his sensitive tip.

Lungs straining, he dragged her off his cock...just in time. He erupted in searing blasts. He shuddered as his release rumbled through him, shaking the foundation of his being, of everything he'd thought he knew about pleasure.

Catching his breath, he saw Maggie watching him with languid eyes. He'd managed not to come in her mouth, but her cheeks and tits hadn't escaped the deluge. He couldn't help the primal rush he felt at seeing her marked with his seed.

He swiped his thumb down her cheekbone, wiping away the droplet. "Sorry about that."

"You're not *that* sorry." Her eyes had a teasing glint.

By Jove, he adored this blossoming sensual side of her. She was made for him. In his gut, he knew he'd never find a woman who suited him half as well.

"All right, I'm not. You look ravishing wearing my pleasure." He hooked his finger into the neckline of her negligee. "And you looked ravishing in this as well."

"Looked?" Her brow furrowed.

In a smooth motion, he tore the white satin down the middle, baring her succulent curves.

"Rhys," she rebuked in horrified tones, "that must have been expensive—"

"I'll buy you another."

He caught her by the hips, hauling his scolding minx upward until her cunny was positioned over his mouth. He growled with appreciation at the sight of her plump pinkness. He pulled her down onto his face and proceeded to eat her pussy until she gasped his name. Until she was grasping onto the headboard and riding his tongue. Until her honey gushed upon his lips and he was wearing her pleasure as well.

Only then did he flip her onto her back, don a sheath, and drive into her still spasming passage. Groaning, he slammed into her, deeper and deeper, wanting to get to the heart of her. When she cried out her completion once again, he lost himself in her generous heat. And for that one incendiary moment, there was no yesterday or tomorrow, only the now that fused them.

❧ 26 ❧

"STOP FIDGETING, MAGGIE MINE," RHYS MURMURED.

"I'm not fidgeting."

All right, she *was* fidgeting. Who could blame her after the morning she had? It had been unexpected, to say the least.

The day had begun pleasantly enough. Just past dawn, she'd awoken in Rhys's bed—or, more accurately, had been awakened by Rhys in his bed. She'd been tucked up against him like a spoon, his lips skimming the curve of her neck, his hands playing with her breasts.

She'd twisted her head and looked into his sensual, slumberous eyes. "Again?"

Not that she'd been averse to the idea. Far from. But by her last count, he'd spent three times throughout the night and she a great many times more. The man had limits...didn't he?

In answer, he'd smiled, wedging his thick erection against the cleft of her bottom.

The man's stamina was truly remarkable.

After a frisky bout in bed, they'd discussed the plans for the day. Rhys would breakfast with her, Hypatia, and Glory before leaving to call upon Tessa Kent. Mr. Newton would arrive with their new guards and keep them company until Rhys's return.

Those had been the plans...until Mrs. Kent threw a wrench into them.

There'd been a knock on the door just as they sat down to breakfast. A Chinese man with a long braid, beard, and wiry figure had entered. Introducing himself simply as Ming, he'd announced that Mrs. Kent had sent him to escort them to the meeting. When Rhys had stated that he would be going alone, Ming had returned, "Mistress will see woman and girl, too. All come—or none."

Seeing Rhys's countenance darken at the ultimatum, Maggie had taken him aside and convinced him to go along with Mrs. Kent's plans. Thus, the three of them had been conveyed to the Kent residence, which turned out to be a Palladian mansion on a leafy Mayfair square. At present, Maggie was seated on a napped velvet divan in the sitting room, Glory beside her, and Rhys standing behind them both. Light streamed in through the tall windows, glinting off the gilt-framed landscapes and mahogany furniture.

What kind of woman is this Tessa Kent? Maggie wondered. *How can she be mistress of such an elegant house...and belong to the criminal underclass?*

Curiosity brimming, she wished she'd had time to milk more information from Rhys about their mysterious hostess. All he'd told her was that Tessa was considered royalty amongst the London underworld and that her husband was some sort of scientist.

The door opened. Maggie got to her feet, Glory doing the same.

The woman who ambled in was not what Maggie expected.

In her head, she'd conjured up a fiercer-looking, older woman. An Amazon who could wield a sword and defend her territory. Instead, Mrs. Kent looked to be in her mid-twenties, around

Maggie's age. She was slight, her maize cashmere walking dress accentuating her tiny waist and diminutive figure. With her ebony hair arranged in ringlets and decorated with silk leaves, she was a pretty contrast to the tall, athletically-built gentleman at her side.

His unruly dark hair and spectacles gave him a scholarly air. The scientist-husband, obviously. His would be an earnestly handsome, pleasant sort of face—if he weren't directing a fierce scowl at Rhys.

Rhys stepped forward. His expression was a smooth mask, and his eyes were wary.

He bowed. "Mr. and Mrs. Kent. Thank you for receiving us."

"If I'd had my way, I would have received you in a back alley," Mr. Kent growled.

Maggie swallowed. What was the source of their bad blood?

"Now, Harry, we discussed this," his wife reminded him. "Let me take care of this, please?"

After a smoldering glare at Rhys, Harry Kent turned to his wife. Then his look was smoldering in a different way, and despite the situation, Maggie felt a little swoony seeing the obvious attraction between the two. Kent kissed his wife's hand, and her cheeks turned rosy.

"All right, sprite. But one misstep,"—he aimed another warning look at Rhys—"and I'm calling the bastard out."

"Now that that's settled," Mrs. Kent said brightly, "introductions are in order, are they not?"

She came up to Maggie and Glory, her clear jade eyes regarding them with frank interest. Maggie was glad that she'd worn her new lilac carriage dress. It had fit her perfectly out of the box; when she'd asked Rhys how he knew her measurements to the inch, he'd merely given her a rakish grin. The stylish garment had full bishop sleeves and a draped flounce. Bertha had tamed her hair into a fashionable chignon, securing it with a pair of ivory combs.

"Good day, ma'am. I'm Margaret Foley. This is my daughter,

Gloriana." Maggie dropped a curtsy, but Glory failed to follow suit. She nudged her frozen daughter, whispering, "Mind your manners."

"But, Mama," Glory said, her eyes wide, "there's something *moving* around her neck!"

Maggie blinked because her daughter was right. Out of nowhere, a length of champagne-colored fur had appeared, circling itself around Mrs. Kent's neck like a muff. When it stopped moving, she saw that it was a...a ferret?

"This is Swift Nick Nevison," Mrs. Kent said, as if presenting ferrets was a perfectly normal thing to do. "Say hello to everyone, Swift Nick."

His paws on his mistress's shoulder, Swift Nick had inquisitive eyes that peered out of a dark, mask-like strip of fur. A second later, his head bobbed in a distinct bow.

"Aren't you the cleverest?" Giggling, Glory curtsied in return. "I'm pleased to meet you too, Swift Nick."

The animal visibly preened. Then it looked in Rhys's direction...and bared its fangs.

"Still haven't traded him in for a spaniel, I see," Rhys said dryly (and, Maggie thought, somewhat cryptically).

"Swift Nick is an excellent judge of character. Neither he nor I have forgotten your distaste for ferrets." Mrs. Kent's pretty eyes turned flinty. "Shall we have tea and discuss the matter at hand?"

Refreshments were brought in. Mrs. Kent gave Glory a dish of liver biscuits to feed Swift Nick, and the girl and the ferret were now "having tea" in a far corner of the room while the adults faced off around the coffee table. Mrs. Kent had gestured for Maggie to take the seat beside her while the men occupied adjacent chairs.

"Now to business," Mrs. Kent said. "You have something to ask of me, Ransom?"

Rhys straightened his shoulders, as if bracing for something unpleasant. "Indeed. But first, if I may, I'd like to offer my sincere apologies for any past,"—he cleared his throat— "misunderstandings."

"By misunderstanding, are you referring to the fact that you kidnapped my wife and held her hostage?" Harry Kent snarled.

At the accusation, Maggie's head swung to Rhys. "You *did* that?"

A muscle clenched in his jaw. "I did nothing of the sort."

"Liar," Mr. Kent said darkly.

"I believe I will take you up on that offer of the back alley," Rhys clipped out.

"Gentlemen, please." Mrs. Kent held up a hand. "We are not here for the two of you to engage in bloodshed."

"Only one of us will be bleeding," her husband said, "and it won't be me."

Mrs. Kent sighed and looked at Maggie as if to say, *See what I have to deal with?*

Strangely, Maggie felt a surge of kinship with her hostess. She didn't want the men to duel either. Yet she was burning to know what Rhys had done to offend the Kents.

"Let's get the facts straight, shall we, Kent?" Although Rhys spoke calmly, his voice was honed steel. "Tessa was not yet your wife when she left with me. Secondly, she accompanied me back to London of her own accord. Indeed, she gave me her word that she'd marry me."

Maggie sucked in a breath.

Rhys's gaze shot to her, softening. "I'll explain later."

"There's not much to explain," Mrs. Kent said. "Ransom wanted my dowry. I agreed to marry him only because I was angry at Harry—a lover's spat, you know how that goes."

The forthright explanation made Maggie feel a little better.

"He held you in his townhouse against your will." Harry Kent scowled. "You had to escape out a bloody window."

"You do have a point," Mrs. Kent said coolly. "That *is* a debt that must be paid."

Rhys shifted in his chair, muttering, "I did apologize."

"Hmm. We'll leave it at that—for now." The lady gave her yellow skirts a precise flick. "Now onto the reason you're here. You want me to hold Garrity and Sweeney at bay for you while you look for a treasure in London."

Rhys stiffened; Maggie blinked in surprise. *How does she know?*

"I have eyes and ears everywhere." Mrs. Kent's smile was smug...and a wee bit menacing. "The only question that remains is why should I help you?"

"Would money be an enticement?" Rhys returned.

"It depends on how much."

"Say, a thousand pounds?"

Their hostess rolled her eyes. "Please, Ransom. Don't insult me."

"Two thousand, then. That is all I can offer you at the moment."

"At the moment." Mrs. Kent's gaze was keen. "How much is that treasure you're after worth?"

"I cannot say for certain."

She tapped a finger against her chin. "Well, if the diamond alone was worth ten thousand pounds...how many gems did you say there were?"

Maggie couldn't help but be impressed and terrified by the extent of the lady's knowledge. This was a clever, diabolical female. And, by Maggie's estimation, not one to be trifled with.

Apparently, Rhys agreed for he said in a resigned voice, "I can make no guarantees, but Uncle Horatio claimed their total value was half a million pounds."

"I'll take thirty percent," Mrs. Kent said.

"The devil you will." Rhys's gaze thinned. "That's outrageous."

"Watch how you speak to my wife," Harry Kent warned.

"I'll speak to her any way I wish when she issues such bloody cutthroat terms."

The two men looked ready to spring from their chairs and brawl right there in the sitting room.

"Surely," Maggie blurted, "a negotiation is in order?"

All eyes turned to her.

She summoned up her most diplomatic smile, the kind she used to deal with difficult patrons.

"Both parties have something the other wants," she said in a soothing manner. "There is much to be gained from working together. It is merely a matter of deciding upon the terms."

Mrs. Kent raised her dark brows. "What do you suggest, Mrs. Foley?"

"Maggie." Rhys's terse shake of the head indicated that he didn't want her involved.

Ignoring him, she said, "While the importance of your support cannot be underestimated, Mrs. Kent, thirty percent is a trifle high."

"The cost reflects the rarity of what I have to offer." Mrs. Kent studied her nails. "Unless you know someone else who can negotiate a cease-fire with two of London's most infamous moneylenders."

The woman had a point. Instinct told Maggie that it would be best to respond with equal candor.

"Your power cannot be questioned, ma'am," she said. "At the same time, we have possession of the clues and are doing all the work to find the treasure. In all fairness, the split must reflect the division of labor." Pausing, she went with her instinct. "The truth is His Grace hired me to assist in the treasure hunt because of my fossil-finding skills. At the rate of five percent of the find."

"Five?" Mrs. Kent scoffed. "My dear, you could have done much better."

"Perhaps. But five is fair," she said firmly.

Mrs. Kent's gaze narrowed upon her; despite her *frisson* of fear, she kept her expression bland.

"Twenty percent," her hostess said.

"Ten," she returned.

"Fifteen and you have a deal."

"Agreed."

Mrs. Kent held out her hand, and Maggie shook it.

"When the two of you are finished divvying up my fortune," Rhys inserted dryly, "might I get a word in?"

"Don't see why that's necessary," Mrs. Kent said. "Mrs. Foley here just solved your problem. If you have anything to add, it should be your thanks for her intervention."

"I intend to show Mrs. Foley the full extent of my appreciation at the first opportunity."

Maggie flushed at the very admiring, very *male* look in Rhys's eyes. Darting a quick glance around, she saw that the other two didn't miss the subtext. Mrs. Kent was fighting a smile; Mr. Kent looked bemused.

"I'll set up the meeting with Garrity and Sweeney." Mrs. Kent rose, and everyone followed suit. "I cannot promise a long armistice, but I can buy you some time to find your inheritance. In addition, I do not believe either Garrity or Sweeney knows about your treasure; if I were you, I'd keep it that way."

"Thank you for your assistance. And your advice." Rhys bowed.

"We are most grateful, Mrs. Kent," Maggie said.

"Do call me Tessa. All my friends do."

Touched by the lady's unexpected warmth, she smiled back. "And I'm Maggie."

"Capital. Now that we are friends, Maggie," the lady said brightly, "I'm having a ball in three days. Will you come?"

Later that night, Harry found his wife sitting in front of the vanity. She was dressed in a peach peignoir, her maid brushing out her long, glossy black tresses. He was a scientist not a poet, but to him she resembled a faerie creature, robed in petals and dew.

Dismissing her maid, he placed his hands on her shoulders, savoring her shiver of awareness. His loins heated beneath his dressing gown. His wife never failed to stir him up—in more ways than one.

"What are you up to, sprite?" he murmured.

"I'm just getting ready for bed, darling." In the mirror, Tessa's beautiful jade eyes were wide and incredibly innocent.

He knew her too well. His pretty little wife had a diabolic mind. "I mean with regards to Ransom. Why are you helping that bastard?"

"He's not a bad sort."

"He's a conscienceless rake," Harry said flatly. "After everything that he did—"

"Nothing happened, really. You saved me in time."

"Seeing you dangling from that window shaved years off my life." He didn't like to even think of that time when he'd almost lost her. Tessa, his love and his wife. His entire bloody world.

"I hope not." Turning around on the bench, she smiled up at him. "Because I want nothing more than to grow old with you, my love."

How the devil was he supposed to resist her?

Instead of continuing his lecture, he swept her into his arms and took her to their bed. Their passion had only grown more intense during the months of their marriage, and tonight was no exception. Harry loved watching his wife climax, her expressive face showing every bit of what she was feeling. Thus, he made sure she went over...three times, by his reckoning.

He, himself, was no slouch. He'd blown his seed twice, needing no recovery in between. That was Tessa's effect on him.

When they were done, he cuddled her against him. His hand rested possessively over her belly, only now beginning to swell with their babe.

"Love?" he asked.

"Hmm?"

Good, she sounded sleepy. In this state, she was more prone to tell him what she was scheming. Tessa's mind was more complex than the scientific problems he worked on as a member of the Royal Society. And more dangerous than the blasting devices that were his expertise.

"Why are you helping Ransom?" he asked.

She snuggled against his chest. "Oh, Harry. You're not jealous, are you?"

"Of course not." He was jealous of anyone who looked at her. "But I don't understand why you wouldn't abandon him to his justified fate."

"Seventy-five thousand pounds?"

"We don't need the money."

"I feel sorry for him?"

He snorted. "Your tenet is an eye for an eye."

"You know me too well." She sighed. "What if I told you this isn't about Ransom?"

"Go on."

"You know that, after the attacks on Grandpapa, things have been unsettled in the underworld."

He did know. Those nefarious events had nearly cost both him and Tessa their lives. Since then, Tessa's grandfather, Bartholomew Black, King of the Underworld, had been rebuilding his kingdom, but alliances between cutthroats were always tenuous.

"I want to help Grandpapa maintain the peace," she said.

"You are helping him," Harry countered. "You're doing splendidly as the Duchess of Covent Garden."

To reward Tessa for her loyalty, Black had given her one of his underworld territories to oversee and the ceremonial title that went with it. Tessa took the responsibilities to heart. She protected her people, especially the women and children who would otherwise have no one to look after their interests. While authorities might turn a blind eye to the suffering of the lower orders, blaming the poor for their own misery, she did not.

She stood up against the drunken lord beating the whore. The pimp who lured children into his den. The man who beat his wife in the street. Thus, Harry had his hands full keeping *her* safe. But it was worthy work, and he admired Tessa for her mettle...most of the time.

"I do my best," she said modestly. "I've heard rumors of a possible new uprising, however."

His shoulders tensed against the pillows. Goddamnit, would peace ever last?

"Involving whom?" he asked tersely.

"That's just it: I don't know." In the dimness, her eyes glowed with frustration. "My sources say the leader has deep pockets and controls many in society because they are indebted to him."

Harry understood. "A moneylender. You think it's Garrity or Sweeney?"

She nodded. "Garrity has fought on our side, but he's a snake —no offense to Gabby."

Adam Garrity's wife, Gabriella, was a friend of Tessa and Harry's. Neither understood the match between the sweet, guileless redhead and the wicked usurer. Yet it was clear that Gabby adored her husband.

"And Sweeney?" Harry asked. "What do you know about him?"

"Not enough. But his sudden rise to prominence worries me. He arrived in London just over a year ago, and tales of his cruelty and violence already abound."

"Thus, you want to invite Garrity and Sweeney to a parley," he concluded, "because you want to see which one of them could be instigating a rebellion?"

"I need to know who is loyal to my grandfather and who is not."

"These are dangerous men, sprite. In your condition—"

"You know I'm indelicately hale and healthy. And I'll have you to protect me."

It was true that pregnancy hadn't affected Tessa very much. She ate like a horse and carried on as usual—that is, with a surfeit of feminine energy. Since that energy was beyond delightful in bed, Harry couldn't complain.

"All right," he decided. "But at the first sign of trouble, you'll withdraw from this and leave Ransom to deal with his own problems."

"Thank you, darling." She kissed his jaw, then his neck. "I knew you'd understand."

"What about Mrs. Foley? Is befriending her part of your scheming as well?"

"Oh no." Tessa's hand was wandering in an interesting direction.

"Then why,"—he had to pause to think when her fingers trailed delicately over his flexing abdomen—"did you invite her to the ball?"

"Because she seemed perfectly lovely. I liked her. Didn't you?"

"Didn't I...what?" *God*, his wife's touch. He was already stiff and throbbing.

Tessa giggled when he rolled on top of her. "I thought you wanted me to say more."

"You have a more pressing matter to attend to," he told her.

He dragged his erection along her drenched petals. Her laughter melted into a moan. And thoughts of dukes and cutthroats were temporarily abandoned as they took care of more important matters.

27

WHILE TESSA KENT HAD AN UNDENIABLY DEVIOUS STREAK, Rhys had to admit that she was a woman of her word. Her note the next morning indicated that she'd arranged a meeting with Garrity and Sweeney for two o'clock that afternoon. They were to convene at Nightingale's, a Covent Garden coffee house that also served as a meeting place for the underworld.

Rhys searched out Maggie to tell her the news. She was in her sitting room with Hypatia and Glory. The two women called absent hellos from the far end of the table, where they appeared to be poring over a sheet of paper. Rhys went first to Glory, who had a paintbrush in hand and pots of watercolors scattered around her.

He hid a smile at the smudge of paint on her freckled nose. Taking out his handkerchief, he handed it to her, gesturing to her pert appendage. She wiped it off and gave him a smile so infectious that his lips tugged upward. Tenderness jolted him as he looked into her eyes and saw a reflection that combined the best of Maggie and himself.

The desire to claim Glory burgeoned day by day. Not for the first time, he wondered how she would receive the news. Would she be glad…or would she mourn Foley, the only father she'd ever known? Regret and frustration sat like a boulder in Rhys's gut.

The notion of fatherhood had never appealed to him because he'd never wanted to be like his own sire. Yet by not acknowledging Glory, by not doing his best to care for her, wasn't he being a bastard, just in a different way?

He was beginning to glimpse a new possibility: what if he could be the kind of father he, himself, had secretly longed for? A father who wouldn't hurt or belittle his child, who'd instead protect and guide her through life's labyrinth. Rhys might not have the requisite experience, but the instinct to shield Glory—from bullies, from any pain or discomfort—burned within him.

He cleared his throat. "What are you working on there, poppet?"

"Can't you tell? It's my pet."

"I wasn't aware you had a…" He studied the brownish blob. It looked like a deposit made by a not altogether healthy horse. "Er, dog?"

"It's not a dog, it's a ferret. And I don't have one…yet." Glory slid a sly look in Maggie's direction.

"You're not getting a ferret," Maggie said without looking up.

"Did you know ferrets are even smarter than dogs?" Glory went on, undeterred. "Mrs. Kent said they understand all sorts of commands. Swift Nick is ever so smart."

"You don't want a ferret." Rhys was no fan of Swift Nick, and the feeling was mutual. "Nasty rodents."

"They're not rodents. They belong to the weasel family. Mrs. Kent said so."

"I'd take anything Mrs. Kent said with a grain of salt."

"Why?"

"She's not the sort of lady you should be associating yourself with," he said.

Indeed, he was wary of Tessa's friendly overtures to Maggie, including the invitation to the ball. Last night in bed, Rhys had tried to warn Maggie about Tessa's machinations. Maggie had responded that she couldn't refuse for fear of offending the other woman, whose goodwill they were dependent upon. She also admitted that she found Tessa rather charming.

Then she'd asked Rhys about his past dealings with the duchess of the underworld.

He'd answered her truthfully. That he'd once been rather intrigued by Tessa's originality and even more so by her dowry. Their "engagement" hadn't even lasted a day and had been undertaken solely for practical reasons.

"She's very pretty, Rhys." Maggie had kept her gaze fixed on the coverlet, where she traced an embroidered vine with a finger. "Clever and very...dainty."

Surprised, he'd tipped up Maggie's chin and saw that she was serious.

"She can't hold a candle to you." In his eyes, no woman could.

"I'm hardly a delicate female."

"Aren't you?"

He'd run a thumb along the silken stem of her throat, over her petal-soft lips, his fingers winding into her rose-tinted hair. She'd shivered in that way he adored. Her vulnerability and passion never failed to bring out his possessive instincts.

"I think you are. As delicate and sensual as a rose," he'd murmured. "The most desirable woman I've ever known..."

In case words hadn't convinced her, he'd showed her just how desirable he found her. Several times throughout the night. And first thing this morning. Heat unfurled in his gut...until he realized that their daughter was studying him.

Head tilting, Glory said, "Why shouldn't I associate with Mrs. Kent?"

"She's, er, not your usual society lady. I don't think she's a good influence."

"Mama's not a society lady." Glory gave him an innocent look. "And you like her, don't you?"

I more than like her.

Seeing Maggie bent so industriously over whatever her project was, her hair spiced by sunlight, he felt a host of intricately woven desires. They were intertwined, impossible to separate from one another. To him, she was sex, companionship...home.

The realization struck him. *Christ. I'm falling in love with her.*

By all rights, he ought to have been terrified. He'd gone and done what he'd vowed not to do. Yet within the trepidation budded a fierce joy—and he couldn't regret it. He wouldn't regret it. Wouldn't let the past stop him from finding a different future.

The sooner he found the damned treasure, the sooner he would be free. To build the life he wanted. With Maggie and Glory...his girls.

"I do. Very much," he said softly.

"I'm glad." In a conspiratorial whisper, Glory said, "I think she likes you too."

Ruffling her hair, he went over to Maggie and Hypatia.

"What are you up to, ladies?" Up close, he saw that the two were studying a map.

"Hypatia purchased this map of London," Maggie told him. "We're planning how to go about searching for the treasure in the Seven Dials."

"The logical place to begin would be here." Hypatia tapped her finger at the junction of the seven streets, the heart of the Seven Dials. "We begin at the center and work our way outward."

"We'll go to all the businesses, look for anyone who knew Horatio," Maggie added.

"As always, I am in awe of your competence, ladies," he murmured.

"That is why you hired us." Maggie's eyes had a saucy sparkle. "Although I'm told we are a bargain at five percent."

"You would be a bargain at any price." He meant it. "May I steal you for a moment? There's something I'd like to discuss."

Rhys led the way to his own sitting room. Closing the door, he took Maggie into his arms and gave her the kiss that had been burning in him.

"Devil and damn, I've missed you," he rasped.

Pressed against the door, her hair a tangle of fire in his hand, she murmured, "We were together less than two hours ago."

He traced her plump mouth with his thumb, recalling the exquisite pleasure of feeding her his cock this morning. Of possessing her sweet holes, one after the other.

"Two hours too long. How did I manage without you, Maggie mine?"

"Um, you floundered about rakishly? Possessed the habits of a spendthrift?"

God, he adored this woman.

"My fault for asking." With a husky laugh, he kissed her forehead and let her go. "Now stop distracting me so I can get to my news."

"Which is?"

"I heard from Tessa. The meeting with Garrity and Sweeney is this afternoon."

Excitement and dread chased across her features. "I'm ready to leave at any time."

"You're not coming." He was appalled that she'd think he'd allow her to take such a risk. Before she could argue, he said firmly, "These are cutthroats, Maggie. I will not put you in any more danger than I already have."

"What about your safety?" she burst out.

"The Kents will not allow any bloodshed to happen under their watch." He hoped. "I'll take two of the guards with me."

The four guards had started work yesterday. Newton had chosen well: they were a strapping and intimidating bunch.

Maggie wrapped her arms around her middle. "I don't like this."

"Neither do I. But we can't have Sweeney and Garrity on our

backs while we search for the treasure. Negotiating a truce with them is the only way."

He knew he'd won when she fell silent, gnawing on her lip.

"Everything will be fine." Pressing his advantage, he curled a finger under her chin. "Besides, you'll be of more use here. By the time I return, I expect that you and Hypatia will have solved the remaining clues and the treasure will be waiting for me."

"Very amusing." Maggie sighed. "You will be careful, won't you?"

With her and Glory to come back to? The life he longed to have with them within reach?

"Always, Maggie mine."

Nightingale's was not what Rhys expected. Coffee houses had reached their heyday in the last century, and the ones that remained carried the burden of time. Yet this one looked newly constructed: its name was proudly painted in fresh gilt, and pristine windows looked onto the busy Covent Garden street. As Rhys approached the entrance with his hired protection, he was met by the Kents.

"Weapons and guards stay outside," Tessa said. "Same rules apply to all guests."

Rhys looked at her entourage, which included Ming, all of whom were armed to the teeth.

"Except you, it seems," he said.

"I'm not a guest." She lifted her brows. "I called this meeting; I set the rules."

"Point taken," he muttered.

Sans his pistol and guards, he followed Tessa and her husband into Nightingale's. Although the interior had the dark, dated look he associated with coffee houses, the shaved wood floors and paneled walls showed little wear. The rich scent of coffee permeated the spacious room; serving boys dashed around with silver pots, refilling the cups of customers chatting around long trestle tables.

"Grandpapa rebuilt the place after a fire," Tessa said. "We'll be meeting in the new wing."

They arrived at a set of doors manned by a pair of guards. At Kent's nod, the guards pushed open the heavy oak, and Rhys found himself entering a chamber with a soaring ceiling. A massive round table sat at the center; his pulse sped up when he saw that the others had already arrived.

Sweeney rose from one of the chairs. He was exactly as Rhys remembered: fat, pasty-skinned, with eyes a chilling ice blue. Next to him, Garrity stood as well. In some ways, Garrity was Sweeney's opposite. Tall and lean, he was undoubtedly an elegant man with his ruthlessly slicked dark hair and eyes so dark they appeared black. While Sweeney had a sneering countenance, Garrity's was impassive...but no less menacing.

Tessa directed everyone to their seats. Her husband took the seat to the right of her, Rhys to the left. Garrity was one chair over from Rhys, but the size of the table separated them by a safe distance.

"Thank you everyone for coming," Tessa said. "I shan't beat around the bush. I wish to negotiate an armistice on behalf of His Grace, the Duke of Ranelagh and Somerville."

"The bastard owes me money," Sweeney snarled. "Don't see as how that's any business of yours. Best keep your nose out of my affairs."

"I'm the Duchess of Covent Garden. What happens in my territory *is* my affair." Tessa's hard gaze circled the room. "While Ransom is in Covent Garden—nay, in London—he is my guest. I am asking you to respect that fact."

Her tone was more of a command than a request. For once, Rhys appreciated her strong-willed nature.

"Pardon, duchess," Garrity said in smooth, cultured tones,

"but I must ask why you wish to intervene on behalf of His Grace?"

"My reasons are my own. Now do we have an agreement?"

Sweeney slammed his hands on the table, rising. "The bugger owes me blunt. Got his vowels that say so. Been chasing him for months—and I ain't waiting no more!"

"I must concur with my...esteemed colleague." Garrity's tone held a hint of irony. "Ransom and I had a business agreement, and he has reneged. In addition, he has caused me no small amount of trouble." His predatory glance fixed on Rhys. "I am, at this moment, having my men bailed out from a Dorset gaol."

"They assaulted my man-of-business," Rhys bit out.

He wanted to say more: that the bastards had broken into Maggie's house, terrorized her and her family and deserved more than gaol...but he held himself back. If there was even a chance that Garrity or Sweeney didn't know about her, he would keep it that way.

"They were following orders." Garrity steepled his hands. "I expect loyalty from my men—and those I conduct business with."

"I'll get you your money," Rhys said.

"When?"

"Give me a month and I'll—"

"A tune I've heard before," Sweeney cut in. "Your promises ain't worth the paper they're written on."

Rhys's gut clenched. He couldn't stop the thoughts from rising. *You're a failure, a bloody disappointment...*

"A fortnight then." He strapped down his demons. "Fourteen days, and I'll give you what I owe. Or you can take your pound of flesh another way."

"I don't believe I need your permission for that, Your Grace." Garrity's razor-sharp smile sliced through Rhys, fear bleeding in its wake. "Let me put it another way. What is in it for me to extend your debt yet again?"

Rhys looked at Tessa. Her shoulders hitched slightly as if to say, *It's your treasure.*

"An extra ten percent interest," he said.

Sweeney's laugh grated against his eardrums. "You can't even cough up the original sum, guv. Now we're supposed to believe you can produce five thousand quid more apiece?"

At least it didn't appear that the moneylenders knew about Rhys's inheritance. A small mercy, but he'd take it.

"Yes," he said firmly. "Because I will."

"Give Ransom another fortnight." This came from Tessa. "If he doesn't come up with the blunt, you're no worse off than you are right now—and you might be richer. You will also have earned a boon from me." She paused significantly. "For your loyalty."

The silence in the room felt as oppressive as a tomb. Rhys's heartbeat thundered in his ears. *Please God, give me one more chance to make things right...*

"One week," Garrity said. "Twenty percent interest."

"Or your head," Sweeney added.

Seven days to find the jewels. Seven days to earn his freedom and place with Maggie and Glory...or be sent straight to hell.

Rhys exhaled. "Agreed."

"I await your good news, Your Grace." Rising, Garrity withdrew his pocket watch. He flicked open the solid gold disc and smiled thinly. "The clock starts ticking now."

❧ 28 ❧

Upon Rhys's return, he gathered Maggie, Hypatia, and Mr. Newton in his sitting room to share the results of his meeting with the moneylenders. The new deadline sent a chill over Maggie's nape. Seeing the tension bracketing Rhys's mouth, however, she firmed her resolve.

"We have an entire week to find the jewels," she said. "That is ample time if we get started now."

"Perhaps we should involve the guards in the search?" Mr. Newton suggested.

Maggie liked the four guards who were keeping watch in the hallway even now. Despite their intimidating size, the men were courteous. In particular, Victor, a blond giant, had been friendly and patient when Glory had fired a fusillade of questions at him about his job.

"Methinks the little lady wants to be a guard when she's grown up, eh?" Victor had teased.

An unholy spark had lit Glory's eyes.

Now Rhys shook his head. "As much as we could use the extra hands, we cannot risk it. The fewer who know about the jewels, the better. If news of the treasure were to leak out, all of London will be looking for it. As for safety reasons, with the present armistice, we should be under no threat from Garrity and Sweeney."

"Then the four of us will leave straight away," Maggie said.

"It's not safe for a woman in the Seven Dials at night," Rhys said. "You can help tomorrow. Tonight, Newton and I will go."

No matter how she argued, he would not be moved.

When he returned in the wee hours of the morning, she was waiting for him in his bed. One look at his haggard expression told her that he hadn't found what he was looking for.

"Tomorrow's another day," she said.

After he bathed, they made love. Their pleasure had a desperate, hungry quality. Afterward, she stared into the shadows of the canopy after he'd fallen asleep, praying that they would have better luck tomorrow.

The next morning, Glory was left securely in the care of Bertha, Victor, and the other guards, and Maggie, Rhys, Hypatia and Mr. Newton set off.

When the carriage deposited them at the center of the Dials, the point from which the seven streets extended like the spokes of a wheel, Maggie couldn't help but gawk. This neighborhood was a far cry from the elegant enclave of Mayfair. Having worked in a dockside tavern (and being a Goode), she was no stranger to iniquity, yet this was eye-opening even for her.

Sleeping bodies littered the area. Pigeons flocked, pecking at pools of detritus, left over from the previous night's revels. No squeamish miss, Maggie nonetheless took the perfumed handkerchief Rhys handed her and held it to her nose. They traversed the dirty streets teeming with playing children, staggering drunks, and paint-smudged whores returning from a night's work.

"Newton and I covered two streets last night," Rhys said briskly. "Castle, Queen, Lion, St. Andrew's, and Earl Streets are what remain. Maggie and I will take Castle Street. Newton and Miss Hypatia, will you take Queen?"

"Gladly, Your Grace," Newton said.

"Excellent. We'll reconvene here in two hours."

Rhys led the way to their assigned street. Taverns, pawn shops, and other businesses hardy enough to survive in the slum crammed both sides of the narrow way.

"Stay close to me," Rhys said. "And watch out for sticky fingers."

He lifted his chin at a group of urchins playing across the street. As Maggie watched, one bumped into a well-to-do gent. While the boy doffed his cap, offering a profuse apology, another of his brethren casually plucked away the unsuspecting victim's coin purse.

"Shouldn't we do something?" Maggie gasped.

"We don't want to stir up the mob. First rule of the rookery: each man for his own."

She drew her reticule closer as they began the arduous task of canvassing the businesses one by one. They were met with responses ranging from annoyed to threatening. After discovering no credible leads, they met up with Hypatia and Newton, who also had nothing to show for their efforts...except for some unexpectedly delicious kidney pies.

After a quick snack, they were off again.

Exiting yet another pawn shop some time later, Maggie was surprised to see that darkness had arrived, along with a cold, steady drizzle. She and Rhys stood beneath the awning, watching as rough-and-ready men roved in packs heedless of the rain, fueled by copious amounts of blue ruin.

"Let's go back to the hotel," Rhys said.

The tautness of his jaw betrayed the frustration that she shared. Their grueling search had yielded naught, and the clock was ticking.

"We have Earl Street yet to search," she said.

He shook his head. "It's wet and dark—"

"The first day's almost over, darling." She touched his sleeve. "We must press on."

"Did you just call me darling?" Some of the brooding tension left his eyes.

"Whatever it takes to get the job done," she said prosaically.

His lips twitched. "Half-hour more and that's it."

Rhys purchased an umbrella from the pawn shop, and under its cover, they dashed toward the nearest tavern. The Sailor's Arms was dark and smoke-filled, smelling of ale and roasting meat. Maggie's expert eye noted that it was better kept than most establishments they'd visited thus far. The floors were swept and the tables wiped; framed paintings of exotic locales added some flair.

Rhys navigated them through the crowded room to the worn but polished bar. The barkeep was a hulk of a man with bushy side whiskers and an apron tied over his protruding belly. He would have looked quite intimidating...if it hadn't been for the life-sized painting of a peacock that hung on the wall behind him. He was positioned so that his bald head was crowned by a burst of feathers.

"What'll it be, guv?" he rumbled.

"We're looking for some information," Rhys said.

The barkeep scowled. "Got ale and mutton on the menu. Anything else, you'd best look elsewhere."

"Please, sir," Maggie said, "it's a matter of vital importance—"

"Ain't a rat and won't e'er be a rat," the man stated.

"We're not looking for that kind of information," Rhys said. "This concerns a personal matter. My uncle Horatio—"

"Horatio?" The man's bushy brows shot up. "Horatio Jones?"

Excitement jolted Maggie.

"Yes," Rhys said alertly. "Do you know him?"

"What did you say your name was?"

"Edward Rhys Hugo Jones Cavendish."

"Blow me down, so you're the nephew. Horatio said you'd be coming. 'Ow is the old codger, anyway?"

"He passed away."

The barkeep's gaze softened. "May God watch o'er 'im on 'is final journey."

"Pardon, but I didn't get your name," Rhys said. "And how did you come to know my uncle?"

"Seamus O'Flaherty, at your service. Was a seaman in my younger days and met Horatio Jones on a voyage to India. Now your uncle, 'e ne'er met an adventure 'e didn't like. We got to talkin'—trip to India ain't exactly short, mind—and came to be friendly. After I retired from the sea, I started this 'ere establishment. Horatio paid me a visit whene'er 'e come to London." The barkeep paused to fill two tankards with ale. "'E was last 'ere 'bout six months ago. To be 'onest, 'e didn't seem all 'imself. But we shot the breeze as usual...and 'e mentioned you."

"What did he say?"

"That you were a good man. But one in sore need o' adventure."

To a stranger, Rhys might appear impassive, but Maggie saw a myriad of emotions chase through his gaze. Pain, sorrow...regret. As she'd guessed, he'd loved his uncle despite their conflicts and felt the loss deeply. Given the trouble that his uncle had taken to arrange this treasure hunt, she suspected his love had been returned.

"After his death, Uncle Horatio left me some instructions," Rhys said. "One of them led me here. Did he perchance leave something with you to give to me, Mr. O'Flaherty?"

"Indeed 'e did."

Maggie's breath held.

"May I see it?" Rhys asked.

O'Flaherty's brows rose. "Why, sir, you're lookin' right at it."

~

"Why on earth would your uncle give you a painting of a peacock?" Hypatia asked.

"I have no idea," Rhys said.

It was later that night. The four of them had returned to the hotel, and now, with the addition of Glory, were sprawled on the furniture in his sitting room. The painting that Flaherty had given them was propped up against the wall in front of them. They'd already removed the frame and found nothing hidden behind the painted canvas.

Rhys pensively contemplated the bright, detailed swirls of paint. The peacock seemed to stare back at him with belligerent yellow eyes, its mass of feathers raised in threat or mockery.

Sitting beside him, Maggie was also studying the painting. "Could the peacock have any symbolic significance?"

Feathers do not make the man, my boy. Horatio's words, amongst the last he'd said to Rhys, banded Rhys's chest with regret. He wished that they had parted on better terms. That he'd been more willing to forgive his uncle for the earlier desertion. That he hadn't continually pushed Horatio away when the other had tried to make amends.

Aloud, he said, "Other than Uncle Horatio taking a sly jab at my vanity, I don't think so."

Yet there had to be something there. Something more. Why would Horatio lead them on this wild goose chase otherwise?

Glory approached the painting in a purposeful stride. Tender amusement melted away some of Rhys's tension. With her bottom lip caught beneath her teeth, she looked like a miniature Maggie.

"Why is there a three in that feather?" she asked.

"A what?" Maggie said.

"A number three." The girl pointed to a swirl of paint. "Right here."

All the adults crowded in front of the painting.

"By God," Rhys said, astounded. "That *is* a three."

The number was hidden in the eddying strokes of navy, royal blue, and green...but it was there. A tiny yet distinct number three.

Squinting behind her spectacles, Hypatia said, "Leave it to the young eyes to catch that."

"Well done, poppet." He gave a playful tug on one of Glory's plaits.

She grinned at him.

Newton brought over a lamp while Hypatia went to fetch a notebook. Rhys, Maggie, and Glory began scouring the painting, calling out letters and numbers.

"By Jove, there's a two in this feather over here," Rhys said.

"Is this an "N" on the bird's throat?" Maggie said simultaneously.

"I see an "F" right here!" Glory exclaimed.

"Is there a sequence to this?" Hypatia mused. "Or will this be another anagram?"

"We ought to be marking where we see the letters and numbers on the painting," Maggie said. "Ink won't work on the oils—but I know what will. I'll be right back."

She returned a few moments later with a pincushion studded with pins.

"Never say I came unprepared," she said.

Rhys felt his lips quirk. "Knowing you, you'd be prepared if there was another Great Fire."

"Planning is essential." Her words were prim, her eyes sassy.

Smiling, he took a handful of pins. Between him, Maggie, and Glory, the painting was soon dotted with the metal heads. He stood back to look at their handiwork, putting together the numbers and letters left to right...

"32 Lincoln's Inn Fields." Satisfaction rolled through him. "That's our next stop."

$\maltese$ 29 $\maltese$

RHYS, ACCOMPANIED BY MAGGIE, HYPATIA AND NEWTON, arrived at 32 Lincoln's Inn Fields early the next morning. The modest brick townhouse bordered a square, the front door visible to all passers-by. This could prove an inconvenience for Horatio hadn't left them a key, and Rhys might have to gain entry through other means.

Thanks to the bullies at Eton, however, he'd found himself on the wrong side of a locked door more than once. Indeed, he considered lock-picking to be the most useful skill he'd gleaned from that hallowed institution.

"Should we go around back?" Newton darted nervous glances around. With his red, sweat-sheened face, he looked like a guilty schoolboy called to the carpet. "We might garner too much attention here."

"Perhaps if you didn't look quite so anxious, Mr. Newton," Hypatia said, "we would be less conspicuous?"

She gave him a reassuring smile and her handkerchief, and he gratefully mopped his face.

"I fear our presence has already been noted." Rhys nodded

toward the gated park in the center of the square, where a pair of strolling matrons had stopped to peer over suspiciously at them.

"Why don't we first find out if anyone is at home?" Maggie suggested.

He nodded, raising his gloved fist to knock.

To his surprise, the door opened a minute later to reveal an elderly woman in a housekeeper's uniform. Her face was wrinkled like an apple left in the sun, her grey hair bound in a knot.

"May I help you, sir?" she said.

"Good morning," Rhys said. "This may sound strange, but I am the nephew of Horatio—"

"Oh, Mr. Rhys, is it?" Her eyes lit up. "You've arrived at last. Come in, come in."

She ushered them into a small antechamber. The townhouse was as modest inside as out. A plain stairwell led upstairs and a narrow hallway to the back of the house, with two closed doors along it.

Ascertaining that the housekeeper was one Mrs. Ingle, Rhys introduced Maggie and the others.

"Uncle Horatio said that I would be coming?" he asked.

Mrs. Ingle nodded, her expression sad. "The master's last instruction to me was to keep an eye out for your arrival. *Look for a handsome lad dressed like a pink of fashion,* he said. *His facial hair is more manicured than a hedge.* No offense, sir—those were the master's words, not mine."

"None taken," Rhys said wryly.

"Mr. Jones also said that when you arrived, I should take you directly to his study."

Mrs. Ingle led them to the second door along the hallway, opening it. The study was a cramped, condensed version of the one at Journey's End, with dark paneled walls and cabinets crammed with curiosities. A large desk carved with an oriental motif sat beneath a painting of a peacock identical to the one they'd found at the Sailor's Arms.

"I haven't touched anything in here since the master's death," the housekeeper said.

"Out of curiosity, Mrs. Ingle," Newton said, "how did Mr. Jones arrange for your wages to be paid after his death? Was it through a solicitor...or a bank, perhaps?"

Rhys caught onto Newton's thinking. Knowing what financial institutions Horatio had patronized could prove useful. As whimsical as the notion of a treasure hunt was, Horatio was no fool: he would have stored the jewels somewhere safe—like a bank.

"The master didn't trust solicitors or banks," Mrs. Ingle said stoutly. "He set up an account for me with Mr. Gruenwald, the goldsmith on Fleet Street."

"Ah. Thank you," Newton said.

"If there's nothing else, I'll leave you to your business. Ring if you need anything."

When the door closed behind Mrs. Ingle, Rhys said, "Good thinking, Newton. Now we know where Uncle Horatio secured at least some of his funds. Perhaps the jewels are there as well."

"A goldsmith would be a secure place to store a treasure," Newton agreed. "After so many private banks have failed of late, taking the fortunes of investors with them, many have returned to old-fashioned methods of safeguarding their wealth."

Already at the desk, Maggie called, "There's a letter for you here, Rhys."

Going over, he took the letter she handed to him, which bore his name and his uncle's seal. Exhaling, he broke the wax.

Dear Rhys,

Congratulations for making it this far! I did not doubt for a moment that you would. The love of adventure burns brightly in our bloodline: no matter how your papa, my brother, endeavored to dim that flame, the fire lives inside you. Even if you try to hide it behind those fine feathers of yours (pardon an old man's sense of humor!).

All jests aside, don't be afraid of your fire. Be guided by it. Life's greatest rewards go to those who stray from the beaten path and carve their own.

Now you have one final clue to conquer—one last hurdle between you and the jewels.

Sometimes to get to the future, we must face the demons of the past. The treasure awaits you in London, and you'll find the key here: 梅林

Good luck and God speed, my boy.

Your loving uncle,
Horatio

Rhys fought the surging pressure in his veins. He had his demons in check; he didn't need his uncle stirring them up.

At his side, Maggie peered at the letter. "What does he mean by *demons?*"

The fact that I failed my mother. That she died...because of me.

"My uncle has a fanciful way of expressing himself," he said tersely.

To his relief, Maggie gave him a curious look but didn't press him on the subject. "And those symbols? Do you know what they mean?"

"They're Chinese characters, I believe." *Concentrate, man. Don't get distracted by things you cannot change.* "When Horatio says I must look to the past, I think he's referring to a place that has something to do with my mother."

"We need to find someone who can tell us what those characters mean," Hypatia said.

"A visit to Limehouse might be in order?" Newton referred to the dockside district which was home to many Chinese sailors and laborers.

"Or how about Tessa Kent's man, Ming?" Maggie suggested. "He's closer. The fewer new people we need to involve, the better."

"Good thinking," Rhys said. "I'll send her a note and ask to meet with him today."

As he set the letter on the desk, his gut told him he was missing something.

Life's greatest rewards go to those who stray from the beaten path and carve their own.

He was damned tired of following Horatio's trail of crumbs. He had no desire to face his past; what if there was a way around it? What if he could circumvent this stupid game?

Reaching out, he jiggled the desk drawers. Locked.

"Pass me that penknife, would you?" he said to Maggie.

When she handed him the mother-of-pearl-handled blade, he inserted it, jimmying the lock until he heard a satisfying click.

"You have some hidden skills, Your Grace." Maggie's brows rose.

"Eton," he said by way of explanation.

He opened the top drawer and found a jumbled mix of writing implements and assorted odds and ends. Finding nothing of import, he repeated the process with the middle drawer. It wasn't until the bottom one that he made a discovery: Horatio's appointment book.

He placed the leather-bound journal onto the desk and began to flip through the pages. His pulse accelerated as Horatio's spiky handwriting revealed the dates, places, and people he'd interacted with in the last year.

"Look here." With simmering excitement, he showed Maggie several pages. "In the weeks prior to Horatio's death, he made five visits to Gruenwald's."

"That seems excessive if he were only making arrangements for Mrs. Ingle," Maggie said.

"My thoughts exactly." Rhys leafed through the rest, including blank pages, and came to the end of the book. He was about to go through it again when his thumb encountered a ridge on the inside of the journal cover. "There's a bump in the back cover."

Maggie peered over. "Yes, I see it. A raised line. As if the book wasn't properly bound or..."

"Or someone inserted something inside the cover."

He used the penknife again, this time to carefully slice through the binding. The leather separated easily from the paper board. He slid his fingers into the narrow pocket...and fished out a thin card made of hammered gold. Gruenwald's logo was embossed on the gleaming surface, along with the words *Edward Rhys Hugo Jones Cavendish*.

"Sweet heavens," Maggie breathed. "What is that?"

The thrill of discovery sizzled through Rhys. "A membership card to Gruenwald's—and, if I'm not mistaken, the key to the treasure."

After sending off a note requesting a meeting with Ming, Rhys and the others made the short trip to Gruenwald's. The goldsmith occupied an unassuming brick building on Fleet Street next to a publishing press. Inside, Rhys noted the iron bars over the elegantly dressed windows and the armed guards stationed discreetly throughout the showroom. The place was as fortified as a citadel.

He led the way past impressive displays of gold and silver plate to the counter, manned by a clerk in a leather apron.

"Good afternoon." The fellow bowed. "How may I be of assistance?"

"I am the Duke of Ranelagh and Somerville." Rhys took out the gold card. "I have come to collect something left to me by my uncle."

"Very good, Your Grace." The clerk's tone was deferential. "Beg pardon, but house policy permits only two visitors at a time to the Vault."

Vault. Rhys looked at Maggie, a charge of excitement passing between them.

"Mr. Newton and I will wait here," Hypatia said.

Taking out a large keyring, the clerk unlocked the door behind the counter and ushered Maggie and Rhys through.

The next room contained a large workshop where some dozen goldsmiths were hard at work fashioning tableware and decorative objects. Tools of the trade lined the tables, and one of the smiths was smelting metal over a large brick hearth. The clerk unlocked yet another door, ushering them through.

In the small chamber, a wizened man wearing rich maroon velvet sat at a desk. He was overshadowed by the pair of hulking guards flanking the massive iron door behind him.

"Your Grace, this is Mr. Gruenwald," the clerk said. "He will assist you from here."

With a respectful bow to Rhys and his employer, the clerk left, closing the door behind him.

It took Gruenwald several minutes to rise, the action accompanied by the creaking of old bones. Standing, his height was not much changed.

"May I see your credentials, Your Grace?" the goldsmith asked.

With thrumming anticipation, Rhys handed over the gold card.

Gruenwald perused it with care. "And the key?"

"Pardon?" Rhys asked.

"The key that is required to access the locked box inside the vault," the old man said.

"I do not have the key. You see, my uncle recently passed, and he left me this card—"

"I'm afraid I cannot help you, Your Grace. Card and key must both be present in order for accounts to be accessed. Those are the terms."

Rhys's elation was replaced by frustration. Devil take it, the treasure was *literally* within reach. He could feel it in his bones.

"My inheritance is within that vault," he said in ducal tones.

"You will not get it without the key." The old man's manner was immovable. "There are over five hundred locked boxes within the vault. You will need the proper key to open the proper box. The security at Gruenwald's is such that even I do not have the ability to open patrons' boxes, only the door to the vault."

"There's nothing you can do to help us, sir?" Maggie asked.

"Nothing, I'm afraid." The old man's bones creaked like rusty hinges as he slowly lowered himself back into the chair. "Come back when you have the key."

Bloody hell. Disquiet merged with Rhys's frustration for it was clear that he had no choice: to find the treasure, he would have to face whatever ghosts Horatio had resurrected.

❧ 30 ☙

That evening, Maggie stepped into the sitting room at the hotel. Nervously smoothing her black satin gloves, she asked, "What do you think?"

"Oh, Mama, you look ever so beautiful!" Glory clasped her hands together.

"You are in splendid looks this eve," Patty agreed.

"Feathers make the bird." Relieved, Maggie smiled at her lady's maid, who'd followed her in from the bedchamber. "And I have Bertha to thank as well."

"It's a pleasure to dress you, ma'am." Bertha gave the elaborate skirts of the ball gown an expert twitch. "You do look a treat."

"I don't feel like myself," Maggie admitted.

Seeing her reflection in the wide oval mirror above the hearth, she hardly recognized herself. The lady in the looking glass wore an exquisite dress of emerald silk embroidered with floral sprigs. The décolletage was low but tasteful, leaving her shoulders bare, and the sleeves were two delicate puffs. The bodice fitted closely to her waist before flaring into full skirts overlaid with fine gold netting that added subtle sparkle to her movements.

Her dark auburn hair had been parted in the middle, soft

braids dangling over her ears and woven into a coronet at the back of her head. As she had no jewelry, her only adornment was the thin gold ribbon Bertha had artfully woven into her coiffure.

Maggie had never felt more elegant in her whole life.

"I wish I was old enough to go," Glory said wistfully. "I would love to see the beautiful gowns and the dancing."

"It'll be your turn one day."

Even as Maggie said the words, she wondered what her daughter's future would hold. The closer they came to finding the treasure, the more her hopes climbed. Although they'd hit a snag at Gruenwald's, they'd had a reply from Tessa: Ming would be available to talk to them tonight before the ball. Once they knew the location the Chinese characters were referring to, Maggie was certain that they would find the key to the goldsmith's vault.

The nights of passion and days of companionship had only strengthened her love for Rhys. Her heart was unalterably and forever his. Perhaps it was the optimism of a woman in love, but she couldn't help but hope that his feelings for her might go beyond caring one day...that he might come to love her in return.

Even if she could win his heart, there was still the fact that he was a duke and she the commonest of commoners. She couldn't lie: the idea of living in his world intimidated her. But, for Rhys, she'd work her hardest to be the sort of woman he'd be proud to have as his duchess.

Tonight would be a test. Rhys had explained that while Tessa wasn't *bon ton* (a fact that actually made Maggie more at ease with the lady), her husband came from a family with aristocratic connections. Apparently, Harry Kent's sisters were infamous for marrying well, and since the Kents were a close-knit clan, some of them would likely be at the ball. Therefore, Maggie knew she would be rubbing shoulders with the *crème de la crème*, and she didn't want to let Rhys down.

At that moment, Rhys entered the room; by all rights, Maggie ought to have been accustomed to his male perfection, but the sight of him in formal evening attire made her feel swoony. The stark black and white emphasized his height and virile leanness. His hair gleamed in tamed waves, his mustache and beard trimmed to dashing perfection. A diamond stick pin glittered in the snowy folds of his cravat. He was every inch a duke.

But he still had a pirate's eyes. The smoldering possessiveness in them made her heart stutter.

"How stunning you are," he murmured, bending over her hand.

"You look rather fine yourself," she said breathlessly. "Very, um, ducal."

His smile flashed white against his beard. "One tries."

Glory ambled over and looked up at him. "Will you be dancing with Mama tonight, Ransom?"

"Only if they play the waltz, poppet."

Maggie froze. "I've never waltzed before." She only knew some simple country dances.

"I'll lead, and all you need to do is follow," he reassured her. "Now, if you have a moment, I'd like to speak to you in private before we go."

"We were just leaving, Your Grace." Hypatia ushered Glory out.

Alone with Rhys, Maggie said, "Do you really think I'll do?"

"Now that I take a good look at you, your ensemble *is* missing something." He stroked his chin. "The dress needs adornment."

She flushed. "I don't have any."

His eyes smiled at her. "Could it be that, for once, I'm the one who is prepared?"

He withdrew a flat box from his jacket. When he opened it, her eyes widened: nestled against black velvet was the most beautiful and striking necklace she'd ever seen. Translucent green stones carved into exotic blooms were held together by intricate links of solid gold. The clasp, a blooming golden chrysanthemum, was a work of art itself.

"The necklace was my mama's," he said. "The jade is antique and of the highest quality."

"It's too much, I couldn't possibly—"

He twirled a finger. "Turn around."

She did as he asked, swallowing as she felt the weight of the necklace against her skin. She shivered when his lips touched the back of her neck just above the clasp. His hands on her bare shoulders, he turned her to face the mirror on the wall.

"Now your ensemble is complete." His gaze met hers in the glass. "How magnificent you are."

Eyes on the gilt-framed image, she *felt* magnificent. The extravagant collar of stones brought out the color of her eyes, the creaminess of her décolletage. It elevated her ensemble from fashionable to regal. Yet what truly made her feel special was the man standing behind her.

Any woman would feel beautiful belonging to Rhys. He was so sophisticated and sinfully handsome. The fierce possession in his eyes made her feel like...a duchess.

The thought reminded her of Horatio's letter and the reference to the demons of Rhys's past. She'd seen how that letter had shaken him. Being no idiot, she knew that he had evaded her question about the demons. Her intuition told her they had something to do with his family. With the parents he didn't like to discuss. With the woman whose necklace she now wore.

She hesitated, not wanting to intrude upon his privacy. At the same time, he had helped her...and given her many other gifts besides. Her fingertips brushed over the carved jade. Perhaps she could give something to him in return.

Hesitating, she said, "Rhys, I've been meaning to ask..."

"Yes, Maggie mine?" He tipped her chin up. "You can ask me anything."

You wanted an opening; here it is.

"What demons was your uncle referring to?"

His hand dropped. Beneath the black velvet, his broad shoulders tensed. "I told you Horatio was just being fanciful."

"That is what you said. But I think there is more." She searched his hooded gaze. "Will you not share it with me, Rhys? You know about my family, warts and all. Will you not trust me... the way I've trusted you?"

"Trust has naught to do with it." He raked a hand through his dark mane. "It's unpleasant business, Maggie. There's no use dredging it up."

"I want to hear it," she pressed. "Since Horatio brought it up in his letter, perhaps this is information that will help us find the treasure. He wants you to face these demons, whatever they are. But you do not have to do so alone; I am here."

He gave her a brooding look. "Scotch is necessary for this conversation."

She waited for him to return with a whiskey for himself and a glass of ratafia for her. He sat next to her on the divan, taking a long swallow of the amber liquid before he began.

"By demons, I believe Horatio was alluding to my parents. I'll start with my father, Phillip. You know he and I did not get on."

"He was dreadful to you," she said hotly. "Blamed you for his mistakes and called you weak when you are anything but."

"He did more than call me weak." Rhys's mouth twisted. "He tried to train the weakness out of me."

The hairs shivered on her nape. "Train?"

"It was his belief that a man should depend on no one. From the time I was born, he kept me separated from my mama. Whenever he felt that I became too attached to a servant, he dismissed them immediately. I can't remember all the names of my nannies, governesses, and tutors: there were too many."

Maggie's heart squeezed. "Oh, Rhys."

"I was not permitted to have friends. The closest I had to a playmate was a foxhound...Bailey." A muscle ticked in his jaw, as if he were trying to contain some powerful emotion. "Bailey had been born the runt of the litter, so I got to keep him. For five years, he was my constant companion. One day, when I was eight, I was playing with Bailey and accidentally broke a vase. My father flew into a rage. He dragged Bailey outside, and he...he shot him."

Stunned by such cruelty, she didn't know what to say.

"I just stood there—didn't do anything. Just watched as he killed my dog." Rhys's tones were flat, terrifyingly devoid of emotion. "He told me it was my fault, that I should have had Bailey under control. When I started crying, he called me a pathetic weakling. Said that my mongrel blood was a taint to the Cavendish name."

"The bloody *blackguard*." Rage overcame her shock. "It was *not* your fault. Your father is entirely to blame. He took his anger out on an innocent animal—and hurt you, his own son, in the process. If he were here, I'd take a pan to him!"

At her passionate declaration, Rhys smiled faintly, but the humor didn't reach his eyes. He took another drink of whiskey before continuing.

"The irony of it is, Phillip extolled self-sufficiency but never achieved it for himself. As a young man, he gambled away the family fortune and had to leave for foreign lands to try to regain it. He ran into trouble in China; a dispute with dockside ruffians nearly led to his demise. A powerful local merchant witnessed the altercation and offered to intervene. In return, my father promised to marry the merchant's daughter, Yu-Yan. He returned to London with my mother, and I was born a year later. By then, he'd already removed her to the country seat. To keep her out of sight."

"Why?" Maggie asked.

"He was ashamed of her. Of tainting the Cavendish blood with a 'foreign element'." Rhys stared at the half-empty glass in his hands. "I think the truth was that she was the symbol of his desperation and failures, and he hated her for it."

What a bastard. Controlling her anger, Maggie said cautiously, "What was your mama like?"

"I don't know. Phillip restricted my contact with her; I was permitted to see her a few times a year, and the visits were brief, chaperoned by him. He prevented her from learning English, so she and I never spoke, really. She'd just look at me, and her eyes, they were always...sad." His own gaze took on a distant look. "She didn't leave her room, couldn't walk far...because of pain. She'd brought a young maid with her, a girl whose name was Show Me—well, that wasn't her real name, but that was what it sounded like to me. Show Me had picked up a little English and told me once that my mother's feet had been broken and bound since she was a girl in order to keep them as tiny as possible."

"That is barbaric," Maggie gasped.

"It's customary, apparently, in my mother's culture. Small feet are prized as signs of beauty and femininity. My father despised what he called her 'deformity'...along with everything else about her." He tossed back the rest of the Scotch. "What I can say for certain is that the pain my mother suffered in her homeland was far surpassed by what she experienced at my father's hands."

His cool, detached tone raised the hairs on her neck. Instinctively, she knew that he was approaching the worst of the demons his uncle wanted him to face.

Although she feared the answer, she forced herself to ask, "What did he do to her?"

"He beat her. Regularly. As a child, I didn't understand what was going on between them, only saw my mother's sadness. Her quiet despair. Well, that's not entirely true." His throat moved, the diamond stick pin in his cravat glittering like a tear. "I did sometimes glimpse the bruises on her. My father said she was clumsy, a disgrace who couldn't even walk properly on her damaged feet. And I believed him until the day I saw..."

"What did you see, Rhys?"

"I was twelve and beginning to feel rebellious. I'd decided to defy my sire and seek out my mama. She wasn't in her bedchamber when I arrived. But then I heard my father's voice, and in a panic, I jumped into the armoire and hid. I was there when he dragged her in."

Apprehension whipped through Maggie like a tempest. While she wanted to say something, do something, she knew that the best thing was to remain silent. To let him purge what was festering inside him.

"Through a crack, I saw her crying, and he shook her so hard that her head snapped back. *Shut up, you bitch. You are my property, do you understand? You will do your duty and provide my spare.* He tore at her clothes, and when she wouldn't stop crying, he...struck her. Again and again." Rhys's voice was gritty. "I burst out of the armoire—I don't know why I hadn't moved until then. Why I'd been hiding like a coward that whole time. I finally came to my senses, and I ran to the duke, tried to pull him off my mother. I think I was shouting something, telling him to let her go, and he threw me across the room."

"Dear God," Maggie whispered. *What kind of monster would abuse his wife in that despicable fashion—and his son?* As drunk as her father got, he'd never raised a hand to her mother. Probably because her mother would have walloped him right back.

She put a hand on Rhys's arm. His muscles quivered beneath her touch, like that of a stallion ready to bolt. But his voice remained steady, unnaturally calm.

"My head hit something hard. For an instant, I lay on the ground, dazed. Then the duke came at me. I'd never seen him like this before. He was enraged—angrier than when he shot Bailey. He told me to get out, and he raised his fist as if to strike me again. I readied myself for the blow—but my mother got between us."

"What...what happened next?"

"She said, *Go, Rhys, go.*" He slammed the empty glass onto the coffee table in front of him. His elbows planting on his thighs, he dragged his hands through his hair. "And like a bloody coward, I did. I left her there. And she died...because of me."

"Rhys, how did your mother die?"

Maggie's voice seemed to come from a distance. It was muffled, filtered as if through a wall of ice. He dug his fingers into his scalp, tugging on his hair, the small pain keeping him anchored as the undertow of the past threatened to suck him under.

"I've never spoken about it." Didn't like to think about it. "It was a long time ago."

"Tell me anyway."

Her gentle coaxing reached through his numbness. As much as he wanted to resist, he couldn't. Because this was Maggie, and he could never resist her.

"After that incident, the duke sent me to stay the summer with Horatio. That was my first visit to Dorset."

"Did you tell your uncle...about what happened?"

"No. I didn't." *Why didn't I?* He'd asked himself the question a thousand times, and there was never a good answer. Stomach churning, he said, "I should have. I know I should have. As incredible as it sounds, it was like I...I forgot what happened." Frustration roiled along with the shame. "I can't explain it."

"Our mind can shut out the things we're not ready to cope with. It was that way for me when my mama died." Maggie's soft words encouraged him to go on.

"The summer with Horatio was a grand adventure. He told stories of his trips abroad, and we played games, hunted for fossils on the beach and in the caverns. Then my mama died, and I was sent home." His throat felt hot and itchy. "She'd had a miscarriage, the duke said. Died when the bleeding wouldn't stop. But I knew."

"What did you know?"

"That she died because I didn't protect her." *Because I failed her*.

The darkness in him spread. Suffocating. Relentless.

He felt a touch on his jaw. Maggie turned his head to face hers.

"That's not true," she said firmly. "What happened to your mama is not your fault."

"I should have stopped him." His hands curled, fingernails biting into skin. "I should have *stayed*. Fought. Or, at the very bloody least, told someone."

The options were so obvious. Only a fool would not see them. Only a dastardly weakling would not act upon them.

"Let us say you're right. That you ought to have done those things."

Maggie's acknowledgement made his gut clench. At the same time, that was why he trusted her. She was never one to mince words.

He gave a heavy nod.

"What do you think would have happened if you had?"

Her question took him aback. He didn't usually look beyond his failures.

"My mother..." He faltered. "She wouldn't have died."

"Really?" Maggie gave him a skeptical look. "You think that you could have fought off your father? You, a twelve-year-old boy?"

"I should have tried," he insisted.

"You did. You got knocked across the room for your efforts."

His chest burned. "Then I should have tried harder."

"Let's suppose you told someone. Your uncle, say. What would Horatio have done?"

Frowning, he said, "I assume that he would have..."

He trailed off because, bloody hell, what *would* Horatio have done? He could have spoken to his older brother...but what would that have accomplished? The duke had never taken anyone's counsel, let alone his younger brother's.

And the fact was Horatio had never been one to interfere. He did not like conflict and entanglements; he'd avoided family and duty, preferring the freedom of travel and exploration. He hadn't even responded to Rhys's letters, and Rhys knew that his uncle had been fond of him, in his own way.

"What would Horatio have done?" Maggie repeated.

"Nothing." The truth plowed into him like a bullet. "Not a damned thing. And even if he had been moved to try, he didn't have the power to stop the duke."

Because no one could have stopped him. Not even...me.

The realization spread through him like cracks through ice. His chest and eyes grew hot. When Maggie said nothing more, he pulled her into his arms. Held her. Let her strength and care wash through him, cleansing him of his past.

After a while, she drew back, but only to look at him with a steady emerald gaze. "You're not alone any longer, Rhys. You have me. And Glory. We won't leave you."

He couldn't find the words, so he kissed her. A sweet, lingering kiss that expressed what was in his heart, now that she'd cracked it open, shown him what was inside, and patched it up neatly again. All with a pragmatism that was so utterly Maggie that he wanted to smile.

Instead, he continued kissing her. His Maggie. His.

❧ 31 ☙

After Rhys's dark revelations, Maggie wished that they'd had more time to be alone. The fact that he'd trusted her with his painful secrets felt like the most precious of gifts. At last, she understood his demons, and she wanted to help him fight them. To comfort and support him—show him that he was no longer alone. That the brutality of his father and tragedy of his mother need not be his burden to carry.

But there hadn't been time. The need to meet with Ming and discover the meaning of those Chinese characters had to take precedence.

As it was, they arrived late to Tessa's ball. The strains of an orchestra and hum of guests indicated the party was already in full swing. They were led upstairs to a sumptuous private sitting room, where Ming awaited them. His wiry form was clad in a long Chinese-style tunic, his hair bound in a braid. His eyes were watchful as Rhys spoke.

"We think my uncle has hidden the key to the treasure in London." Rhys showed Ming the letter they'd found in Horatio's flat. "These Chinese characters—can you tell me what they mean?"

Ming glanced at the letter. "Of course I can."

Visibly bridling his impatience, Rhys asked, "What do the characters mean? Is it a place in London?"

"*Mei-Lin*. Means Plum Forest." Ming raised his brows. "There is such place in London."

"Where?" Rhys demanded.

"Why uncle send you to this place?"

A brief hesitation. "I believe he wanted me to discover something about my past. My mother...she was Chinese."

"Hmm." Ming stroked his beard and said nothing more.

Rhys narrowed his gaze. "Do you have something to say, sir?"

"Not me. But you, yes. You half-Chinese, half-English duke and now conflict between China and Britain over opium trade, what have you to say?"

"Not that it's any of your business, but I do not dabble in politics," Rhys said coldly.

"Maybe should do more than dabble. Maybe take up cause like Gladstone." The Chinese man's eyebrows winged. "Maybe make a difference."

While Maggie wasn't well versed in politics, Hypatia read the newspapers and kept her informed about current events, including the conflicts with China. According to Patty, William Gladstone, a prominent politician, opposed Britain's policy of using opium to barter for the much sought-after Chinese goods. Although the Chinese Emperor had banned the drug, the British continued to find ways to import it into China, causing widespread societal harm.

Tensions were high between the two countries, a possible war brewing.

Maggie looked curiously at Rhys, wondering what his views on the subject were. Now that she knew more about the tragedy with his mama, she wondered how he felt about that part of his legacy. About belonging to two cultures.

Or, in his case, she thought with empathy, neither one.

"I shall consider it," Rhys said stiffly. "Now are you going to help me or not?"

Ming shrugged. "Plum Forest around long time. Restaurant in Limehouse, known only to Chinese. Serve sailors, mostly. Good food."

The new information filled Maggie with excitement. She blurted, "Should we go now?"

Ming frowned in disproval. "Mrs. Kent put effort into ball. She wishes to entertain her family and *friends*."

"Forgive me, I meant no offense." Abashed by her rudeness, Maggie added, "Mrs. Kent has been kindness itself to us. We would not miss her ball, of course."

Ming appeared mollified. "No use going now anyway. Plum Forest not open late. Give you address; you go tomorrow morning."

"We will." Rhys bowed. "Thank you, sir."

Ming returned the courtesy. "Enjoy the evening."

"Maggie, there you are! I've been looking all over for you."

Maggie, who'd just found a quiet spot beneath a potted palm, turned to see her hostess approaching. Tessa Kent looked like an exquisite doll in an ivory satin gown trimmed with a feather fringe, diamonds at her ears and throat. In her tow were three other ladies: a brunette, a golden blonde, and a redhead. All were as uniquely beautiful as she.

"I wanted to introduce you to some family and friends." Tessa turned first to the buxom brunette dressed in claret taffeta. "Emma, Duchess of Strathaven, may I present to you Margaret Foley?"

"A pleasure, Your Grace." Maggie curtsied low.

"As Tessa has told me we have dispensed with formalities, you must call me Emma."

The lady's warm smile and no-nonsense manner put Maggie at ease.

"And I'm Polly," the golden blonde said shyly. Her aquamarine jewelry matched her stunning eyes. "Another of Tessa's sisters-in-law."

"She's also the Duchess of Acton," Tessa said.

When Rhys said the Kents married well, he wasn't joking, Maggie mused.

"And I'll just introduce myself since I'm always nervous meeting people for the first time and when I'm nervous I tend to chatter nonsensically." The torrent of words came from the voluptuous redhead, whose eyes were the pure sky blue of her flounced and ruffled gown. "May I say how much I admire your necklace? It's unusual and ever so lovely. Oh, and I'm Gabriella Garrity."

Blooming hell. Maggie jolted. Gabriella couldn't be related to *that* Garrity...could she?

"And I forgot to mention how I know Tessa. She is a *dear* friend. My husband has business dealings with her and her grand-papa all the time," Gabriella added ingenuously.

Apparently, this friendly chatterbox *was* married to the infamous moneylender. The one who had sent the ruffians after Rhys. Who had set the clock ticking on the hunt for the jewels.

Warily, Maggie said, "I'm pleased to meet you, Mrs. Garrity."

"Gabby, please—that's what my friends call me, and I do wish for us to be friends," Gabby said earnestly. "You seem ever so nice. I can always tell with people: a sixth sense, if you will. In point of fact, I met Emma at a ball years ago and knew straight away that she and I would be bosom friends. And the same with Polly and Tessa." Her smile was as bright as the chandeliers overhead. "I suppose I have an affinity for Kents."

"We have one for you as well, Gabby dear," Emma said. "But perhaps we should ask Maggie how she is enjoying the evening?"

"Oh dear. There I go again." Gabby's dismay was so sincere that Maggie couldn't help but find her charming.

"It's quite all right," she said. "I was enjoying the evening and even more so now that I've made your acquaintances."

"Where is Ransom?" Tessa asked. "Why is he not paying you escort?"

"He is on the dance floor at the moment. But we shared a dance earlier," she said quickly.

Upon arriving at the ball, Rhys had been besieged by admirers—mostly of the female variety. Apparently, his absence from London had made their hearts grow fonder, and his dashing reappearance had caused excited speculation to ripple through the mirrored ballroom.

Despite being swarmed, Rhys had made a point of dancing with Maggie twice, both times waltzes. He'd been right: with him leading, dancing had been effortless...and divine. She could have floated in his arms forever. With the violins swelling, his hazel eyes focused only on her and intimacy pulsing between them, she'd felt like a princess in a faerie tale.

After their last dance, he'd been surrounded yet again. Maggie left him to attend to his social duties while she took a break. At present, he was on the dance floor, partnering a ravishing brunette. He looked sophisticated, dashing...and bored.

Over the brunette's head, his gaze met Maggie's. She sucked in a breath at the flare of heat in his eyes. He gave her a subtle but undeniable wink.

"His Grace may be dancing with another, but his attention is certainly on you," Emma said knowingly.

Realizing that the by-play between her and Rhys was not lost on her new friends, Maggie blushed. "He's being kind as he knows that I'm not at ease in high society." She gave a self-conscious smile. "The truth is I'm just a country mouse."

"Polly and I grew up in a village in Hampshire," Emma said. "We're country mice at heart."

"I didn't grow up in the country, but I'm a mouse too," Gabby blurted.

They all laughed.

"How is Glory enjoying her first visit to London?" Tessa asked, still smiling.

"She wishes to see more of it." Maggie hesitated. "Unfortunately, I've been rather, um, busy."

As much as she liked the ladies, it was vital to keep the treasure hunt a secret: especially from Gabby's husband, Mr. Garrity. She hoped that Tessa had practiced discretion, even with her close friends.

"Oh, yes, Tessa mentioned you have a daughter. She was the ward of His Grace's uncle, I believe, and that is how you and His Grace know one another?"

Gabby's innocent question showed that Tessa hadn't divulged that Maggie was helping Rhys find his inheritance. Her worries allayed somewhat, Maggie nodded.

"Is there anything we can assist with?" Emma's tea-colored eyes had an unaffected kindness. "If you're busy, we would be happy to show your daughter the sights. All three of us have children, and the more, the merrier, I always say."

"That is very kind of you." Maggie wished she could take the duchess up on the offer; Glory could use some friends. "But we may not be staying in town for long."

"Let us know if you change your mind," Polly said, a soft smile tucked into her cheeks. "Acton and I plan to take our boys and some of their cousins to Astley's Amphitheatre next week. There's always room for more."

"I've signed up my hellions for the outing, haven't I?" Gabby asked worriedly.

"Yes, dear."

"Thank *heavens*."

Gabby's sigh was so heartfelt that they all laughed again.

"In the meantime, I have just the thing to keep Glory occupied. I shall send it over tomorrow morning," Tessa said.

"Oh, that is too kind. You needn't—"

"I insist."

"What are you insisting upon, sprite?" Harry Kent joined the group. He wasn't alone.

Two exceedingly handsome gentlemen accompanied him. They shared his tall, broad-shouldered, narrow-hipped build. The three were the epitome of male virility, and Maggie noticed ladies eyeing them covetously, though the men had no eyes for anyone but their own wives.

The newcomers were introduced as the Dukes of Strathaven and Acton. Strathaven was ebony-haired and debonair, his pale green gaze warm and possessive as it settled upon Emma. Acton, a bronze-haired Adonis, also wasted no time in claiming his duchess; his arm slid around Polly's waist, his stormy blue eyes taking her in as if the rest of the world ceased to exist.

Maggie's breath caught at the love and passionate attraction that sizzled between the men and their wives. It was clear that these marriages were love matches...the sort of relationship she dreamed of one day having with Rhys. And if Emma and Polly, professed country mice, could become duchesses adored by their dukes, could it be possible for Maggie too?

"We were just sharing a chat between ladies," Tessa said blithely.

"Are you too busy to have a dance?" her husband asked.

"Never too busy for you, darling."

"Excuse us," Harry Kent said, sweeping his wife off to the dance floor.

The Dukes of Strathaven and Acton followed suit with their ladies.

"I guess it's just you and..." Gabby trailed off, her gaze catching on something behind Maggie. Pivoting, Maggie saw the gentleman approaching them. Tall and lean, he radiated an air of ruthless elegance, from his slicked-back black hair to his sharp features.

"My dear." He bowed to Gabby, who looked as besotted as a newlywed.

"What are you d-doing here?" she stammered. "I thought you had another event tonight."

"I left early and thought you might like a ride home." A black brow winged. "Unless you would rather stay with...your new friend?"

"Oh, where are my manners!" Clearly flustered, Gabby turned to Maggie. "Mrs. Foley, I'd like you to meet my husband, Mr. Garrity."

A chill snaked down Maggie's spine as Garrity's fathomless gaze met hers. She had the distinct feeling that he already knew who she was. That, unlike his sweet, rather naïve wife, he knew entirely too much.

"A pleasure, ma'am." He bent over her hand.

All of a sudden, Maggie felt a solid masculine presence behind her.

"Garrity." Rhys's greeting sounded more like a warning.

"Your Grace." Garrity's smile was razor-sharp. "I don't believe you've met my wife."

After a brief hesitation, Rhys bowed. "How do you do, madam?"

"I hope you are enjoying the ball, Your Grace." Seemingly oblivious to the tension, Gabby spoke in cheery tones. "I must confess my evening was ever so improved by meeting your lovely Mrs. Foley."

"I am glad to hear it, Mrs. Garrity." Rhys's gaze remained fixed on her husband.

The moneylender held out his arm. "My dear, are you ready?"

"Yes, of course." Gabby gave him a look of pure adoration. As she was led off, she abruptly turned and waved. "I hope to see you both soon!"

Maggie waved back.

Rhys muttered, "What was that about?"

"I don't know," Maggie said, bemused. "Tessa introduced me to her sisters-in-law, and Mrs. Garrity was with them. She seems quite lovely."

"She's married to Garrity." Rhys's jaw was set. "Did Tessa let news of the treasure leak?"

"Her sisters-in-law and Gabby didn't seem to know anything about it." Seeing his grim expression, she said tentatively, "Shall we leave now?"

His gaze softened. "Are you ready to go?"

"I was ready hours ago," she confessed.

"I'm sorry this was a bore, sweeting. I suppose I'll have to entertain you better...in private."

The wicked glint in his eyes made her intimate muscles flutter. She was about to answer when a new voice cut in.

"I say, is that you, Ranelagh and Somerville?"

Rhys stiffened at the harsh accents—American, Maggie guessed. They came from a portly man outfitted in ostentatious luxury. The gold of his multiple fobs, cufflinks, and buttons was blinding. He was accompanied by a beautiful, ethereal blonde in white.

"I thought that was you, Your Grace. It's me, Thomas Sharpe. This is my daughter Gretchen," the man said in booming tones that carried. "Why wasn't I informed that you were in town?"

"Good evening, Mr. Sharpe. Miss Sharpe." Rhys's bow to the pair of Americans was rigid. "I am here unexpectedly."

Maggie wondered at his curt tone. And why he, who had flawless manners, made no effort to introduce her.

"Now that you are here, you must pay us a visit," Sharpe said forcefully. "Surely Mr. Newton has given you our address? Lord knows we've been communicating with him long enough. We've leased the largest residence on Berkeley Square and have been awaiting your visit so that you and Gretchen may become better acquainted." He nudged his daughter. "Isn't that so, Gretchen?"

"I welcome the opportunity to get to know you better, Your Grace," the blonde said archly.

Rhys's voice played in Maggie's head. *Newton has found an American heiress. If I fail to find the treasure, I'll have to barter my title for a dowry...to undertake a marriage of convenience...*

The truth slapped her in the face. She knew who these people were.

She looked at Rhys and saw the confirming guilt in his eyes.

"Maggie—" he began.

Her vision blurred, the ballroom disintegrating like a dream.

"I have to get some air." *I need to get out of here.*

Burning with humiliation and pain, she fled.

❧ 32 ❧

"MAGGIE!"

Ignoring Rhys's voice, she continued blindly on. She didn't know how many blocks she'd gone, hadn't even bothered to get her velvet mantle. The night was chilly and damp, but she felt nothing. Rhys caught up to her. He shrugged off his jacket, tried to put it around her shoulders, but she dodged him and walked on as fast as her silk slippers and bulky skirts would allow.

"You'll catch cold." He matched her stride.

"Why do you care?" she asked bitterly.

She didn't know who she was angrier at: him or herself. Once again, he hadn't lied to her. Once again, she'd gone into this with her eyes wide open. She'd foolishly lost her heart knowing what the outcome would be. Yet knowing about the heiress and seeing her in person...

Two different things, her heart cried.

"I care because I love you," he said.

The declaration halted her. Momentarily stemmed the tide of pain. The intensity of his hazel gaze made her longing surge...but what was the point? By the sounds of it, he'd already made arrangements with the Sharpes. With the beautiful, blonde, virginal, and *rich* Miss Sharpe...who was everything that Maggie wasn't.

Pain and jealousy clawed at Maggie's insides.

She managed, "You'd do better courting your fiancée with that flummery."

Perhaps he already did. Perhaps that is what took him so long to catch up to you.

"She's not my fiancée. And it's not flummery. It's the truth: I love you, Maggie mine."

"Apparently love isn't enough." She stalked on.

"It is with you." He caught her arm, stopping them beneath a streetlamp. "Can we stop this damned chase?"

"We can—if you stop following me."

"I'll never stop. I can't." In the lamplight, determination and desperation blazed on his face, making him even more impossibly handsome. "God help you, Maggie, but you're the one for me, and I'll have no other. That is why it took me so long to find you: I had to tell the Sharpes that negotiations are over."

She swallowed. "You told them that?"

"Unequivocally. There'll be no more talk of engagements for me—unless it involves you."

Relief shivered through her. In the next instant, he slid his jacket over her shoulders.

"You're going to catch cold," he said quietly. "Come, we'll talk more inside."

It was then that she noticed his carriage following behind them. She allowed him to help her up into the cozy velvet-lined cocoon. After instructing the groom to simply "Drive," Rhys sat beside her. Took her hand in his.

"I'm sorry," he said in a low voice. "Sorry you had to witness that. Sorry that I've involved you in this mess. Most of all, I'm sorry that I can't let you go."

"I don't want you to let me go."

"It isn't fair that my love should endanger you." His eyes had a feverish glow, his voice gritty as ash. "If harm should befall you because of me, I couldn't stand it. I can't fail you too. Not you, Maggie."

In a flash, she understood why he'd been hesitant to commit to her all along. His fear of not being able to protect her...it was tied to his loss of his mama. The other woman he'd loved—and lost in a devastating manner.

The realization melted away her anger.

"Nothing is going to happen to me," she said firmly. "Tomorrow we're going to find that key in Limehouse and then the jewels. All will be well."

"Promise you'll never leave me." He gripped her hand as if she were driftwood and he a drowning man. "Promise that when this is over you'll be my duchess, my wife, my love for as long as we both shall live."

"I promise. Oh, Rhys,"—her voice broke a little—"I love you so."

He exhaled, and it was then that she realized that he'd been holding his breath. The joy glowing in his eyes overflowed her heart.

"Maggie mine," he whispered.

Their kiss was slow, tender, and soul-altering.

Then he lifted his head, his brows drawn. "Christ...I just realized. I don't have a ring."

He—her urbane duke—looked so sincerely flummoxed that her heart melted even more.

"I don't care about the ring. All I want is you," she said softly. "And I'm sorry...for overreacting earlier. For not giving you a chance to explain before I ran out."

"I don't blame you. If the situation were reversed, I'd have lost my bloody head." He brushed his knuckles against her cheek. "I've never been in love before, Maggie. I don't know how good I'll be at this—at marriage. You'll have to teach me how to be a proper husband."

His boyish earnestness was beyond endearing. It also reminded her that, while he'd spilled his heart out to her, she'd not done the same. She'd held back a truth, and she didn't want to any longer. Didn't want anything between them.

"Rhys...about my marriage," she began hesitantly.

"Yes, my love?"

"It wasn't a proper marriage."

He blinked. "You mean..."

"There's never been anyone but you," she said tremulously.

He went still. So still that she began to worry.

"It was how my husband wanted it," she said in a rush. "It was a good union in many respects, and I'll be forever grateful to—"

He placed a finger across her lips, stemming the flow of words.

"You don't owe me any explanations," he said quietly.

He was right. Yet she felt compelled to ask, "You're not... upset, are you? Because it doesn't change anything. I just didn't feel right *not* telling you."

"The only thing that upsets me is the time we've lost." He cupped her face in both his hands, as if she were the rarest treasure. "What we can never get back because I was too much of a fool to see what I found that night we met. To see *you*. Everything that you are."

Although his words wrought a quivering pleasure, she said honestly, "We weren't the same people we are now. Maybe we had to be apart to grow. Maybe this was the only way for us to find each other again."

"Perhaps." He paused before saying gruffly, "I know this makes me a selfish bastard, but I'm glad. Glad that you're mine and mine alone."

She gave him the truth in her heart. "I've always been yours."

"I don't deserve you, but I am never letting you go," he declared with passionate conviction.

Heavens, this man. What was she going to do with him?

Spend the rest of my life with him, that's what.

Never had she felt more wanted, more seen, more *loved*. There would be no more hiding, no more loneliness. A heady sense of freedom washed over her...and with it a powerful rush of desire.

She brought her lips to his ear and whispered, "Why don't we make up for lost time?"

~

He turned instantly hard.

What man wouldn't when the woman he loved—and who loved him back, Praise Jesus—was looking at him as if she wanted to tup him then and there in a moving carriage? His misgivings that she deserved better than him fled, replaced by a surge of love and lust.

"What do you have in mind?" he murmured.

Her smile, that of a siren aware of her power, made his cock jerk to attention. He could feel his pre-seed dampening his smalls. Then her hands slid into his hair, bringing his head down to hers.

Their mouths fused in a kiss so hot it was a wonder they didn't set the carriage afire.

When she broke the kiss, he growled at the deprivation...but she only smiled and sank onto the floor between his legs. Her gown was getting crushed, but she didn't seem to care. She was too busy working on the placket of his trousers; his chest heaved as his heavy erection fell into her hands.

Her emerald eyes shone with excitement, with feminine hunger, and he adored it. Adored that their love had unlocked her vibrant sensuality. Just adored *her*.

His love, who was his and had only been his. He didn't care if his possessiveness was wrong, it just *was*. He would kill anyone who tried to take her away from him.

It seemed she had similar thoughts.

"If I'm yours, then you're mine too." She frigged him firmly. "Only mine."

"There'll be no other for me," he vowed.

"Good." She sounded so satisfied that he laughed.

Then she licked him from root to tip, and he moaned at the decadent caress. The little tease did it again and again, lapping delicately at his veined meat. Making him stiff, wet, and aching from her kisses—but withholding what he craved. What she'd given to him with regularity ever since he'd instructed her on the finer points of fellatio. He counted it one of life's blessings that his future duchess enjoyed oral pleasures as much as he did.

When her tongue lightly investigated the slit on his tip, he tangled his fingers in her coiffure.

"Suck my cock properly, wench," he said in mock command.

She gave him a playfully pert look. "Like this, Your Grace?"

His hips bucked at the sudden, scorching bliss of her mouth surrounding him.

"God, yes." His breath turned ragged. "Exactly like that."

She came up then plunged upon him again, her head bobbing in a rhythm that made him pant. His fingers dug into her scalp as she took him even deeper, faster, the wet sounds of her sucking arousing him beyond belief. When he felt himself nearing the edge, he tried to pull her off.

"Sweeting, I'm going to spend," he grated out.

"Good." Her hungry eyes and lush, swollen lips mesmerized him. "I want to taste you. Drink your pleasure as you've drunk mine."

He hissed out a breath as she impaled her mouth on his rampant prick. She took him deeper and deeper still. So deep that her lips met his swollen stones. Feeling the intimate massage of her throat, he could hold back no more. He let go, blowing his seed with a roar, giving himself over to her loving kiss.

Maggie barely had time to savor the taste of Rhys before she found herself hauled onto his lap. He shoved her skirts up, and there was a distinct tearing sound when the fabric didn't cooperate. She should probably care that the emerald silk was being ruined beyond repair, but she didn't.

Desire heated her Goode blood, and she welcomed it. Reveled in the wanton excitement that pulsed through her when her pussy came into contact with his cock.

Despite his recent ejaculation, he was still hard.

"Rub your pussy against my cock." His voice had the hungry, commanding tone that she loved. "Slide your petals along my rod, make it wet, but don't put it inside you."

Shivering with excitement, she did as she was told. Pleasuring him had fed her own arousal, and her movements dampened the thick, pulsing length of him. Her hands on his shoulders, she gyrated her hips, moaning as she found the right angle, the one that made her pearl glide against his steely bar. The friction made her wetter, desperate, the need for release coiling in her core.

"Frig yourself on my prick." His eyes were hot, hooded. "Come on me."

With a breathless cry, she did. Her culmination was lightning in her pussy, blissful shocks sizzling into her limbs, making them boneless. Then he was driving inside her, his massive girth opening her, prolonging the rapturous tremors and setting off new ones. She was coming, coming, the pleasure unending.

"Ride me," he rasped.

His hands gripped her hips, guiding her to rise up and down on his fleshy pole. Their gazes held, and she found it unbearably erotic that they were both fully clothed, yet intimately connected: eyes to eyes, cunny to cock, heart to beating heart. Their fit was tight, lush perfection. As he drilled upward on her downward glide, desire gushed between them.

"God, I'll never get enough of this. Of you," he growled. "I want to get so deep inside that you'll never get me out..."

She soared over the peak again. He caught her against him,

holding her close even as he drove toward his own finish. He uttered love words, dirty words, his rod slamming into her again and again. Suspended in bliss, she took what he had to give, wanting it, loving him. At the last possible instant, he pulled out, crushing his mouth to hers. His groan rumbled down her throat as his satisfaction pulsed hotly against her bottom.

His lips brushed her temple, his voice hoarse. "My duchess, my Maggie. Just mine."

Cradled against his chest, suffused with love, she smiled.

"DID YOU SLEEP WELL, MAMA?" GLORY ASKED.

At her daughter's innocent query, Maggie nearly choked on her tea. She, Glory, Rhys, and Hypatia were having an early breakfast in her sitting room. She made the mistake of looking at Rhys, whose twitching lips and gleaming gaze betrayed that he, too, was thinking of the nocturnal activities that had kept them up half the night.

Not only had they made love again upon returning to the hotel, but he'd awoken her at dawn, his ready cockstand tucked against the curve of her bottom. Not an uncommon state for Rhys, she'd discovered.

Merciful heavens, but the man liked his mornings.

"Bonjour, my love," he'd murmured. "I have a question."

"Is that what that is?" She'd twisted her head to look at him, eyebrows raised.

He'd grinned. "We'll get to that later. But first my question. While you were married, how did you take care of yourself?"

It'd taken her a minute to comprehend. When she did, unholy heat had risen up her face.

"I'm not discussing this with you," she'd muttered.

"That's fine." He'd nuzzled her ear, his bristle scraping the tender lobe, his wicked tone raising goose pimples everywhere. "Because I'd much rather you show me."

She couldn't believe what he'd talked her into doing. Or how much she'd enjoyed it. Or how much *he*'d enjoyed it. His pupils flared, he'd interrupted her halfway through her performance, positioning her on her hands and knees, shafting her from behind until she'd cried her pleasure into the pillows...twice.

"You do look a bit peaked." Hypatia peered at her.

"I'm fine." Maggie drained her cup and avoided Rhys's laughing eyes.

"Mr. Newton should be arriving any moment now," Patty said, reaching for the silver toast rack. "We'll get to the Plum Forest restaurant right when it opens."

"Why can't I go?" Glory wheedled, not for the first time.

"It's no errand for children," Maggie said, also not for the first time. "You'll have more fun here with Bertha and Victor."

Luckily, the girl had taken a liking to the brawny blond guard, and she wasn't the only one. Maggie thought she'd caught sparks between Victor and her lady's maid. Perhaps being a woman in love made her recognize the emotion in others, she thought giddily.

"I'm tired of staying in the hotel. It's boring." Glory turned pleading eyes to Rhys. "Say I can go, please, Ransom?"

"Your mama's right, poppet. Your place is here, where you're safe."

Glory's bottom lip jutted out. "You're just as bad as mama."

"We both want what is best for you." His tone was firm yet warm. "How about this? Once our business is done, we'll go on a full tour of London. We can visit any attraction you like."

"Really?" Glory asked, wide-eyed. "Even Astley's Amphitheatre?"

"When I said anything, I meant anything."

"*Hooray!*" She threw her hands into the air.

Maggie exchanged an amused glance with Rhys just as a knock sounded on the door.

"Ah, there's Newton now," Rhys said. "Punctual as ever."

Bertha went to get the door, returning alone moments later.

"Where's Newton?" Rhys asked.

"That wasn't Mr. Newton that came, Your Grace," the maid said. "It was a delivery from Mrs. Kent. The guards have it out in the hallway."

"Tessa mentioned that she'd send something by for Glory," Maggie said. "How kind of her."

"For me?" Glory shot up from the table.

"Manners, dear," Maggie said.

"May I be excused?"

"Yes—"

Glory dashed past Bertha toward the door. Moments later, whoops of joy sounded.

Smiling, Maggie said to the maid, "What did Mrs. Kent send?"

Bertha looked oddly wary. "I think you'd best go see for yourself, ma'am."

"I can't believe Tessa gave Glory a ferret of all things," Maggie said.

Beside her on the carriage bench, Hypatia replied, "It is a rather odd gift, I must say."

"That's because it's not a gift," Rhys said.

"It's not? Then what is it?" Maggie asked.

"Revenge," he said dryly.

The bloody thing—which Glory had named Ferdinand the Ferret or F. F. for short—had already hissed at him thrice before they left the hotel. As F. F. was the descendent of Rhys's nemesis, the infamous Swift Nick Nevison, this hardly came as a surprise.

Shaking her head, Maggie said, "Well, at least Glory and Ferdinand took to each other. And she was so over-the-moon to have a pet that she was happy to stay behind at the hotel."

"Small mercies," Rhys muttered.

The carriage came to a sudden stop. Parting the curtain, Rhys saw that they'd arrived in Limehouse, the dockside neighborhood east of London. Tall ships crammed the thriving commercial docks, a jungle of masts and sunburned sails as far as the eye could see.

Rhys opened the window. "Why are we stopped?"

"Beg pardon, Your Grace, but there's a collision up ahead," the groom said. "Two overturned carts blocking the thoroughfare and no way around it."

"How far are we from our destination?"

"Just three blocks east, Your Grace. Not five minutes away."

Rhys turned to the others. "Would you mind walking?"

The ladies readily agreed, and he and Newton helped them alight. The driver would meet them at the address as soon as the road cleared. Rhys offered his arm to Maggie, keeping her close as he led the expedition down the dockside street. The buildings were dilapidated, leaning together and appearing to prop each other up. The businesses they housed catered to sailors and dock-workers—taverns, lodging houses, and supply shops, mostly.

Barrows crammed the dusty pathway, hawkers shouting out their wares. The scent of meat pies mingled with the sewage-tinged brine of the Thames. Limehouse was home to seafarers from all over the world, and they passed men from Africa, Spain, and China speaking in their native tongues.

"According to Ming's directions, Plum Forest should just be around the corner," Rhys said, leading the way around the bend. "He said it's next to a boarding house..."

He came to a halt, his heart thudding.

Beside him, Maggie gasped, "That—that can't be it."

He stared at the charred remains of the building. Most of it was rubble. A small section of the front wall remained standing, a sign hanging crookedly from it.

Stalking over, Rhys pulled out his uncle's letter, holding the Chinese characters next to the sign. A match. This *was* Plum Forest—or had been.

The final clue to the treasure was now nothing more than a pile of ash.

"We'll think of something else," Maggie said to Rhys as they climbed the carpeted stairs at Mivart's that evening.

"Yes," Rhys agreed, but his expression was not hopeful.

They'd spent the entire day in Limehouse trying to pick up the scent from the ruins of Plum Forest. From a helpful hawker, they'd learned that the restaurant had had a kitchen fire a few days ago. The owner, a Chinese man, had been killed in the blaze; he had no known relatives in London. Maggie and Rhys had tracked down two of the servers who'd survived the fire, and neither recalled anyone resembling Horatio visiting the restaurant, nor did they know anything about a hidden key.

While Maggie and Rhys had hunted down those dead ends, Hypatia and Mr. Newton had gone through what little remained of the building. What hadn't been destroyed by fire had been taken by scavengers. The pair had even asked around to see if there were other businesses and/or places named Plum Forest; no one knew of any.

"Tomorrow is another day," Hypatia said. "We'll get cleaned up, have a good night's rest, and tackle the problem afresh in the morning."

Maggie appreciated her sister-in-law's optimism. It was needed at the moment. For doubt had taken root, and she battled the spreading vines of panic. After tonight, they would only have four more days to produce the treasure to the cutthroats.

And they had no leads, no clues...nothing.

"Miss Foley makes an excellent point." Newton's spectacles were askew, his face dirt-smudged, yet he still managed to look chipper. "We could make a list of new strategies tonight. For instance, perhaps we could go back to the bank, try to negotiate our way into the vault..."

"Perhaps," Rhys said.

They arrived at Maggie's suite, and Rhys took the key to open the door.

He aimed a wry smile at her. "Let us hope that Glory and F. F. had a better day than we did."

She appreciated his attempt at levity. "I'm certain we'll hear all about it."

He opened the door—and the gaping darkness filled her with instant fear.

"Why are the lights off?" she said in a rush.

Rhys held her back. "Newton, guard the ladies."

With those terse words, he withdrew his pistol and entered the darkness.

Newton prevented her from following. "You'll only distract him, Mrs. Foley. I'm sure everything is fine, and there's a perfectly good explanation. Perhaps Bertha and the guards took Miss Glory downstairs for supper—"

Unable to stand it any longer, Maggie pushed past Newton, who tried in vain to stop her. She stumbled through the dark sitting room, toward the faint light coming from her bedchamber. In the doorway, she stopped short, frozen by the terrifying tableau.

By the bed, Bertha and three guards lay trussed and gagged on the ground. A lit lamp on the floor beside him, Rhys was crouched next to their unmoving forms, trying to rouse them.

"Where is Glory?" Maggie asked through suffocating panic.

He turned to her; in the glow of the lamp, his expression was grimmer than she'd ever seen it.

Her heart lodged in her throat because she knew. She already knew.

Stark anguish blazed in his eyes. "She's been taken."

❦ 34 ❦

AN HOUR LATER, RHYS WENT TO FIND MAGGIE IN HER bedchamber.

She was on the settee by the hearth, staring into the flames. She'd changed into an old flannel robe; Hypatia must have helped her undress. God knew Bertha had been in no shape to do so. When Rhys had managed to rouse the lady's maid and three guards from their drugged state, the last thing they remembered was having tea with Glory. Then...nothing.

Given that the fourth guard, Victor, had disappeared and Bertha tearfully recalled that he'd been the one to wheel in the tea cart, it wasn't difficult to figure out that he'd taken Glory. The ransom note had spelled out who was ultimately behind the kidnapping and why.

Your daughter for the treasure. You have two days. Tell anyone and she dies...painfully.

   J. Erasmus Sweeney

A vortex of helpless fear and fury spun in Rhys. Sweeney had

had a man on the inside the entire time; the cutthroat knew about Glory and the treasure...knew everything.

Now Rhys had two days to come up with the jewels, or his girl would pay the ultimate price.

His throat closed. *Two days...and all I've got is a dead end.*

As if sensing his arrival, Maggie whipped her head in his direction. He'd have rather taken a bullet than be responsible for the agonized panic in her eyes.

I did this to her—to our little girl. I knew this would happen. I knew I would hurt them, fail them...yet I went ahead and loved them anyway.

Darkness welled. It was the color of his father's rage, his mama's bruises, Bailey's blood. It came for him just like the bullies always did. The darkness spread through him like pitch, coating his throat, until he thought he might drown in it.

"Did you find out anything from the hotel staff?" Maggie asked anxiously.

The numbness that set in felt both familiar and foreign. Familiar because that cool, disconnected feeling had been his companion for most of his life. Foreign because the weeks with Maggie, the warmth and vitality of her love, had made him forget how he'd existed before her.

But now his detachment was back, and he was grateful for it. Grateful because it pushed aside the darkness and cleared his head. He knew what he had to do—had known it from the moment he'd found the ransom letter.

I can't let anything happen to our daughter. I will not be my father, he thought fiercely. *This time, I'll do whatever it takes to protect the ones I love.*

"Did you discover anything?" Maggie asked again, sitting up straighter.

Shaking his head, he took the chair across from her. He didn't dare sit beside her. Being close to her would only make doing what he had to do—the right thing to do—more difficult.

"None of the staff remember seeing Victor or Glory," he said tonelessly.

Maggie gave a disappointed nod. "I tried to question Bertha further, but the poor woman is beside herself. She blames herself even though she's not at fault. She did recall that Glory drank the tea, and Ferdinand was in the hidden pocket of her skirt. I'm glad because if Glory was asleep when she was taken and F. F. was with her, then she wouldn't have been quite as..."—Maggie's voice cracked—"...alone and afraid."

Rhys caged his emotions; he had to stay focused. Level-headed. The notion of Glory alone and terrified, her life in peril—it could not be condoned. Something had to be done. And he could only think of one feasible option.

"What are we going to do?" Maggie whispered.

"We're going to get Sweeney his money," he stated.

"But how? He's given us only two days, and we have no leads, no clues...nothing."

Seeing her despair, her terror, he hated himself. For doing this to the woman he loved. And now he would have to hurt her even more.

He forced himself to go on. "There is one other option."

"What option?" Hope flared in Maggie's gaze.

The notion sickened him. But it was his best shot at getting Glory back safely, and time was running out. Exhaling, he said, "I am going to speak to Sharpe tomorrow morning."

He saw the instant when understanding hit her.

Pain darkened her eyes; she shook her head in denial. "No, Rhys. There has to be...some other way. Perhaps we could talk to Tessa—"

"*Tell anyone and she dies painfully*. Those were Sweeney's words," he said harshly. "I'm not willing to take that risk, are you?"

Maggie stared at him silently, her eyes glistening.

"Like you said, we're out of clues and out of time. There is no good choice but one. If I can manage to mend fences with Sharpe tomorrow and procure a special license," he said in a flat voice, "then I can go to Sweeney with the dowry. Or the very near promise of one. It won't be as much as the jewels, but a bird in the hand is worth two in the bush. Miss Sharpe's dowry is worth over a hundred thousand pounds: Sweeney will not turn it down."

A tear leaked, trailing down Maggie's cheek, and agony clawed through his cool resolve. He wanted to wipe away that tear, her pain, and the best way to do it—the only way—was to extricate himself from her life forever. To leave her...so that their daughter could be safe.

There was no better alternative.

And Maggie, his practical, no-nonsense love, had to know it too.

She said nothing when he took her hand in his. Her fingers were cold and lifeless.

How he felt inside.

"I want you to know that I..." What good would it do to make this harder? Why say the words when they were not enough? When his love was, once again, not enough.

"I'm...sorry," he said roughly. *I love you, Maggie mine. I'll never stop.* "For everything."

"Just go." She pulled her hand away, her eyes drenched anew. "Please. I want to be alone."

Her distress, and knowing that he was the cause of it, spread like acid through his veins. Yet, in the long run, there was only one way for him to ease her pain and get their child back. Knowing that he was doing the right thing, the honorable thing, didn't lessen the torment.

He forced himself to go...again.

～

Alone on the settee, Maggie gave into tears. She hadn't cried, not like this, not in a long time. Not since she'd discovered she was with child, unwed and alone. But she surrendered to the sobs that wracked her because she was too tired to fight any longer.

Too tired to hope any longer.

She wept for Glory, her beloved girl, whose fate hung in the terrifying balance.

She wept for Rhys who, in doing the right thing, was destroying their love.

She wept for herself. For not being a good enough mama and failing her daughter. For losing her heart to a man who would never be hers. For believing in violins and roses and faerie tales even though her own mother had taught her better.

When she was done, her insides dry as bone, she sat up. She wiped her eyes, blew her nose, and took several hitched breaths. Then she did what a Goode always did when her back was against the wall.

She found a way to survive.

❦ 35 ❦

THE NEXT MORNING, RHYS SENT A NOTE TO THOMAS SHARPE and received a prompt reply. After stopping at the Archbishop's to procure the document that was essential to his plan, he presented himself at the Sharpes' townhouse on Berkeley Square. He was ushered into a lavishly decorated study, where Thomas Sharpe awaited him with coffee and a surfeit of smugness.

"Well, can't say I'm surprised you came to your senses. One look at my Gretchen and most men would fall to their knees in gratitude. After your shabby treatment of her last night, it might take just that." Sharpe's glee was that of a man who enjoyed watching a worm wriggle on a hook. "A bit of groveling never hurt a man, did it?"

"I'll do what it takes," Rhys said flatly.

Clearly misinterpreting the cause of his determination, Sharpe smirked and took a slurp of coffee. "Glad you came to heel after all, Ransom. Was looking forward to adding a title to the family tree. After you're wed, you and Gretchen must visit us in New York so that we can show you the sights."

And parade me like a prized blue-blooded stud from Tattersall's in front of your friends. Yes, I know what I'm signing up for.

As revolting as the notion was, Rhys was here to close a deal.

"Before we discuss the future," he said evenly, "I wish to finalize the present negotiations."

"Finalize? Your representative Newton and I put together an agreement, which I understood had your approval." Sharpe's jolly façade evaporated, revealing his industrialist's keenness. "There'll be no last-minute changing of the terms, no sirrah. I wasn't born yesterday."

"Nothing of the essence will change. I do, however, wish to speed up the process. I've procured a special license from the Archbishop which will allow Miss Sharpe and me to be wed forthwith."

"My wife's got her heart set on a grand wedding." Dark brew sloshed over Sharpe's cup as he set it down with undue force. "One at St. George's or another of the venues you and your circle use for such occasions. She wants our daughter to have the very best, and so do I."

"We can have a ceremony after the wedding and invite the entire *ton*, if you wish. But I want to get married as soon as possible."

"Why?" Sharpe asked bluntly.

"I need your daughter's dowry tomorrow."

"I'm not signing over anything until the ink is dry on the wedding certificate."

"I understand. In that case, I will need a signed statement from you guaranteeing the amount of the dowry and when it will be delivered. And I will expect to receive the funds the day I wed your daughter."

"This haste is unseemly," the American blustered. "And all this talk of funds—"

"Is why you and I will be related," Rhys said coolly. "My title and connections for your money. As I said, nothing in our arrangement changes."

Sharpe's fingers drummed on the arm of his chair. Perhaps his conscience had finally kicked in, and he regretted the loveless marriage to which he was consigning his only child.

With a stark pang, Rhys thought of Glory. How he loved his cinnamon-haired poppet, feared for her well-being. If he'd had a chance to be her father, he would never barter her off like chattel. He'd care only for her happiness. It killed him to think that he would have no part in her future—but the most important thing was that she would *have* a future.

He'd do anything to protect her, including going through with this despicable arrangement.

Once he had the money to pay Sweeney, she would be free. He had to believe that. Because the alternative...he shut out the mind-numbing terror. Forced himself to concentrate.

"I'll agree to your revised terms," Sharpe said, "but I have an addendum of my own."

Of course you do. Rhys arched a brow.

"I want a grandchild within a year."

The idea of touching any woman other than Maggie sickened Rhys. Yet this was what he was signing up for. A lifetime without the woman he loved...the only woman he would ever love.

"That is not under my control," he said.

"I want your word that you'll put in the effort on your part."

He made no effort to hide his distaste. "You have it."

"Capital." Sharpe all but rubbed his hands together. "Let me summon Gretchen and Mrs. Sharpe to share the good news."

"Now that we have a moment alone, Your Grace," Miss Sharpe said, "I should like to come to an understanding."

Rhys roused himself from his moody contemplation. They were outside, taking a stroll in the garden after luncheon. They had no chaperone. Mrs. Sharpe had slyly said, "You'll be wed in a few days. I'm sure you'll behave yourselves in the meantime, hmm?"

No problem from Rhys's quarter.

"I was under the impression that we had an understanding," he said.

Miss Sharpe regarded him with cool blue eyes. She wore a white satin pelisse edged with white fur, and it heightened her aura of frostiness. "You and my father have an understanding. You and I, however, do not."

He'd suspected that beneath his intended's simpering coyness lay a calculating nature. He found it relieving. Neither of them would be going into this marriage with any illusions.

"What would you like to clarify?" he asked as they continued to stroll.

"I would prefer not to have to mince words."

"By all means, let us abandon any pretense of civility."

"That woman you were with at the ball. Is she your mistress?"

The question ripped open his wounds. The ones he'd patched up with denial in order to get through the present deed.

"Not my mistress, no," he said tightly.

"Your lover, then."

He saw no point in denying it. "The affair will not continue after our marriage."

His torment broke through his resolve. *I'm going to lose Maggie...forever.*

"Well, don't end it on my account," Miss Sharpe said.

Somehow, he wasn't surprised. "You don't require my fidelity?"

"I require your title, which Father purchased for me and himself at no small cost." Her smile showed small, pointed incisors. "In addition, your respect for my independence and freedom, both of which I shall enjoy exercising as a married woman. Living in one another's pockets is so provincial. I daresay you'll find me as sophisticated as any one of your London ladies."

When he made no comment, she added, "All of this will occur after I have provided you with an heir and a spare, of course."

"Of course," he said tightly.

This sort of bloodless union was prevalent in his circles. He should be grateful for Miss Sharpe's worldly attitude. Yet the weeks with Maggie had altered him, made him long for more.

For everything.

Knots of yearning tightened his chest. Maggie would probably wallop him with a pan if he carried on with another woman. He understood those feelings for he would surely wring the neck of any bastard who dared to even look at his Maggie.

She's not yours. She'll never be. Your duchess is going to be the walking icicle beside you.

The memories he'd been holding at bay flooded him, penetrating his numbness. He couldn't stop reliving the moments with Maggie, how she made him feel alive with her sweet primness and hot passion. Her vulnerability and strength. Her laughter made his life worth living...and her tears—he'd do anything to stop them.

Remembering the way she'd cried made his throat hot and scratchy.

Her happiness was everything to him—he'd fight for it, lay down his life if necessary.

The thought stopped him. Maggie's happiness...it *was* everything.

Then why in bloody hell was he here, proposing marriage to another woman?

Realization prickled through him like awareness returning to a sleeping limb. As his detachment began to dissipate, he saw that it hadn't cleared his head—quite the opposite. The numbness had been a panicked response, a fog that had obscured his true path. He'd beaten a hasty retreat rather than advanced as he should have.

He should be *fighting* for Maggie—for the family that she, he, and Glory were meant to be.

The truth freed his brain from paralysis. Devil and damn, he *did* have options. He could go to Tessa; she was devilish and cunning...perhaps she could help him deal with Sweeney. He could even beg her and Kent to lend him money to ransom Glory. The Kents were decent people—surely they wouldn't let a child come to harm? And there must be a way that he could get word to Tessa without Sweeney knowing...

"Are you listening, Your Grace?"

Miss Sharpe's shrill voice pierced his inner flurry.

Distracted, he looked at her. "Pardon?"

"I asked you if we are in agreement that we will go our separate ways after the birth of the children," Miss Sharpe said. "I hope my candor does not disquiet you. I prefer clarity in communication. Words can have so many nuances, and I want there to be no misunderstandings between us. Especially as it pertains to our future."

Something she said struck his newly awakened brain. *Words can have so many nuances...*

Nuances were meanings...words can have so many meanings...

Even...Chinese words?

The realization flashed like lightning. Bloody hell, why hadn't he thought of it before? What if the Chinese characters "Plum Forest" referred to something other than the restaurant? True, they'd asked around about other businesses...but maybe there was some hidden meaning to the characters they didn't understand.

Or, he thought with escalating excitement, what if the two symbols could be *reversed* in order like the anagram they'd solved earlier...and lead them to a different place?

What if the trail wasn't cold? What if he'd simply gone *on the wrong trail?*

"Are we in accord, Your Grace?"

His gaze jerked to Miss Sharpe, who was regarding him with a tilted head. Her slight smirk conveyed that she thought she held all the cards, that she had him where it counted: by the purse strings.

He realized that she represented what he'd allowed himself to become. The man whom Horatio had rightly said had lost the joy of adventure...the love of living. The love that Maggie and Glory had brought back into his life.

I am not my father. I will not hurt the woman I love. I won't give up on Maggie...or our girl.

I'll find a way to deserve their love—or I'll die trying.

The truth whipped through him like a storm. It tore off the shutters of fear and panic. He stared straight into the ferocious squall—and didn't flinch.

"I have to go," he said.

"What?" Miss Sharpe exclaimed.

"Pardon for the inconvenience. Best wishes on finding a title to wed."

He took off toward his future, praying he wasn't too late.

On Rhys's way over to the Kent residence, he took steps to ensure that he was not followed. He dodged through crowded streets and buildings, keeping close watch behind him. When he arrived, luck was on his side: Tessa was at home, Ming with her. Rhys was led into the study where she sat at the desk, flanked by her husband and the Chinese guard.

"To what do we owe this surprise?" Tessa lifted her brows. "If you're here to thank me for Glory's present, no need. The pleasure was all mine."

During his journey over, Rhys had debated his best course of action. He knew the present one had its risk: Sweeney had threatened to harm Glory if Rhys told anyone of the kidnapping. Yet if

Rhys's past had taught him anything, it was that silence gave evil men their power.

He would not be silent again.

"Sweeney kidnapped Glory," he said before he could change his mind. "He's holding her ransom. He has given me two days to find the treasure and exchange it for her freedom."

He gave a succinct summary of the events leading to the kidnapping, even as doubts hovered, circling. Was he making the right choice? Could he trust these people to help him?

"That *despicable* bastard," Tessa spat. "How dare he involve an innocent child—and an innocent ferret?"

Harry Kent's jaw clenched. "When did this happen?"

Their genuine outrage eased some of Rhys's apprehension. "Yesterday. We were in Limehouse looking for the final clue. When we returned, she was taken and a ransom note left with Sweeney's signature." He paused, then said quietly, "He's figured out that she's my daughter."

Tessa looked at her husband. "See? I told you."

"So you did, sprite."

"You knew?" Rhys asked.

"She has your eyes and adores you, God knows why." Tessa's gaze was shrewd. "And you're in love with her mother."

Were his feelings that obvious? His neck heated, but he didn't bother denying it. "Sweeney also instructed me not to tell anyone about this—or he'll hurt my daughter."

Both Harry and Ming swore.

"By 'anyone,' the bounder is clearly referring to me." Slapping her palms on the desk, Tessa rose. "You did the right thing coming to me, Ransom. You needn't worry: I know Sweeney, and he's bluffing about harming your girl. Until he gets the treasure, she is his only leverage—which means she's safe for the time being."

Her words confirmed Rhys's own theory. He nodded, the knots in his gut easing.

"But Sweeney hasn't just committed an unforgivable crime by taking Glory," she continued hotly, "he has insulted me as well. He has attacked those under my protection and called my authority into question. If he wants to poke the bear, he'd better be prepared for the consequences."

"Now, love," Kent said, "remember your condition."

Rhys's gaze shot automatically to Tessa's midsection. Was she increasing...?

She glowered at her husband. "I thought we talked about not referencing my condition."

"You talked about it. I was noncommittal." Clearly not afraid of poking bears, Kent chucked her beneath the chin. "Count yourself lucky that I'm not shouting it from the rooftops."

She rolled her eyes.

After a moment, Rhys offered his hand to Kent. "Congratulations."

Chest puffed with pride, Kent shook it. "Thank you."

"Now can we get on with the business of saving Glory?" Despite her brisk words, Tessa's cheeks were pink. "Where is Maggie, by the by?"

Rhys explained the temporary insanity that had led him to seek out the Sharpes.

"What a *stupid* plan," Tessa said.

"Ever the diplomat, aren't you?" her husband said dryly. "But you can't blame the man for trying to do the right thing."

"The plan was stupid, and I acted out of panic," Rhys admitted. "Now I don't want to go back to Maggie without the last clue, which is why I'm here. I was hoping Ming could be of help."

He took out his uncle's letter and put it on the desk.

Addressing Ming, who'd been watchful all this time, he said, "Sir, could the characters have another meaning other than Plum Forest? If they were reversed in order, for instance...like an English anagram?"

"Hard to believe, but not everything like English." There was a hint of irony in Ming's tone. "Plum Forest is not anagram." As Rhys's gut pitched, he added, "But Plum Forest not just name of restaurant, either. Also name of woman."

Holy Christ. "Why didn't you mention this earlier?" Rhys blurted.

"You not ask." Ming shrugged. "You say, *Is Plum Forest a place in London?* You not say, *Do you know woman named Mei-Lin?*"

Rhys inhaled for patience. "Well, I'm asking you now. Do you know this Mei-Lin?"

Ming shook his head.

"There must be a reason your uncle wanted you to find this woman, Ransom," Tessa said. "She must have some significance. Are you certain you've never met her, even in passing?"

"My mama was the only Chinese woman I knew. Her name was *Yu-Yan*," he said, his tongue tripping over the foreign syllables.

"You don't know any other Chinese females?" Tessa pressed.

The memory struck. "The only other one was my mother's servant who accompanied her from China." He tried to summon the faded details of the past: a round-cheeked girl, twinkling brown eyes, jet-black hair worn in twin coils above her ears. "I knew her when I was a child. I'm not sure what her actual Chinese name was, but I called her *Show Me*. That's what it sounded like when my mother said her name."

"Do you mean *Xiao Mei*?" Ming asked alertly.

At the echo from his past, the hairs tingled on Rhys's nape. "Yes. That sounds right."

"*Xiao Mei* means Little Plum. What mistress might call servant girl."

At Rhys's blank look, Ming added, "Short form for *Mei-Lin*."

"Bloody hell," Rhys said hoarsely.

"Apparently your uncle wants you to find your mother's servant." Tessa paced in front of her desk. "Any idea where she might live?"

"I heard the servants gossiping once," he said with growing

excitement. "After my mother's death, Mei-Lin didn't want to return to China and instead went to London. *By Jove.*" He balled his hands into fists. "I'm going to find her."

The hunt is on.

"I will ask. Not many Chinese women in London," Ming said.

"We'll put the word out as well," Kent said. "We have contacts throughout the city—we'll find her soon."

"I am in your debt. I must also ask that everything be carried out with discretion—"

"Sweeney won't know that we're onto him," Tessa said.

Emotion swelled in Rhys; he covered it with a deep bow. "If ever I am in the position to return this favor—"

"You will be returning it. To the tune of *twenty* percent," Tessa said sweetly.

"You agreed to fifteen," Kent said under his breath.

"The extra five is for the extra trouble," she returned.

"You have a deal." Rhys would gladly pay any price to have Glory—and Maggie—back. "Now, if you'll excuse me, I wish to tell Maggie the new plans."

"Bring her here when you're done," Tessa said. "We have much to discuss."

"Such as?"

Her green eyes had a distinctly bloodthirsty gleam. "Such as what we're going to do to that blackguard Sweeney once Glory is safely returned."

Rhys's journey to Mivart's was fraught with anticipation. He'd made a muck of things with his impulsive decision to wed Miss Sharpe. He'd caused Maggie undue pain—and at the worst possible moment, when her world had been crumbling from the loss of Glory.

He deserved to be horsewhipped. He could only hope that

Maggie would forgive his stupidity the way she'd forgiven so many of his shortcomings. He prayed that his love—and the new lead he'd found—would be enough to earn her trust again.

Upon arrival at the hotel, he all but ran the entire way to their rooms, attracting not one but several shocked glances. He heard someone titter, "That cannot possibly be *Ransom*—the devil-may-care duke?"

They could all go hang.

"Maggie, I'm back!" Rhys strode into her suite. "I have some news..."

He trailed off at the sight of Hypatia and Newton on the settee. Their heads both whipped in his direction, and ice coated his gut.

Hypatia's eyes were red-rimmed, Newton's framed by lines of worry.

"What's happened?" Rhys demanded. "Where's Maggie?"

"She left," Hypatia said faintly. It was then that he saw the note crumpled in her lap. "She's gone to look for the treasure on her own."

❧ 36 ❧

WITH HER CHILD KIDNAPPED AND LOVER GONE OFF TO WED another woman, Maggie supposed she could have given into despair. Or had a fit of the vapors. Neither, however, was in her nature.

When the going gets rough, a Goode keeps going.

Ma had lived and died by those words. By God, so would Maggie.

She didn't blame Rhys for his decision; she understood why he had to do what he had to do. Ultimately, she agreed with it. If it came to choosing between Glory's life and her own happiness, she knew what she'd choose...even if it meant losing the man she loved forever.

Even heartbreak couldn't distract her from the reality, however: Rhys's plan was not foolproof. If Sweeney knew about the treasure, then he might also know its supposed worth—which was well beyond what Rhys could get by marrying the American heiress.

As a former businesswoman, Maggie understood about costs and benefits. By reneging on the armistice, Sweeney was openly disrespecting Tessa and risking her wrath. The cost to him was great...which meant the benefits had to be bigger.

What if Sweeney wouldn't settle for less than the jewels?

Thus, the treasure remained the key. And Maggie still had two days to find it.

After Rhys left for the Sharpes' this morning, she pleaded a megrim to Hypatia and went to her room. She'd changed into one of her old dresses and departed the suite discreetly, hailing a hackney to take her back to Limehouse.

She didn't have any new ideas. What she had was some money, a copy she'd made of the Chinese characters, and determination fueled by a mother's love.

She started canvassing the neighborhood again, going beyond what they'd covered earlier. She would go through every tavern, lodging house, and, yes, brothel in order to get her daughter back.

She worked for hours and had no luck. The men she spoke with either told her what she already knew—"Plum Forest burned down"—or they didn't speak to her at all. She continued onward.

As dusk fell, the darkening streets filled with dockside laborers and sailors out for an evening's entertainment. Whores paraded through the throng, their painted faces and scantily clad figures drawing unsavory types like magnets. Maggie kept her head down low as she scouted the next street.

It was crammed with bawdy houses and lodging houses that looked like they rented chambers by the hour. Some couples didn't even bother with privacy; she could see figures doing the upright in the shadowed alleyways off the main way. Steeling herself, she prepared to go forth.

A ruckus stopped her.

Turning, she saw a pair of adolescents ganging up on an elderly Chinese vendor a few yards away. They pushed over his chestnut cart, and he shouted at them in his native tongue as his long-handled pan flew to the ground, his livelihood spilling from it and scattering over the dirt-packed street. They jeered at him, shoving him as he tried to collect his fallen goods.

The wise thing to do would be to move on, mind her own business like all the other passers-by were doing. Yet a dam of rage broke inside her: she was *done* with bullies and bastards. With those who'd hurt and take advantage of others just because they could. Most of all, she was done with feeling powerless.

She ran toward them, picking up the fallen pan along the way.

She arrived at the old man's side. "Leave him *be*."

One of the youths, a husky brute-in-the-making, laughed. "Look 'ere, now we got a pretty dove. Maybe we should pluck 'er as well as the Chinaman."

"You're not plucking anyone." Her grip tightened on the handle of the heavy pan. "You ought to be ashamed of yourselves, picking on an old man."

"Yes, Mama." The mocking reply came from the second youth, who had a case of spots and a belligerent attitude. He pointed at the vendor. "Now 'and o'er your purse, Chinaman, if you know what's good for you."

"Leave him *alone*," Maggie hissed.

"Thank you, miss." The hawker's wrinkled face had a kindly demeanor, and his English accents were precise. "I don't want trouble."

"Eno' jabbering. I'm taking that purse."

The first bastard dove for the chestnut seller. Maggie swung on instinct. She'd only intended to ward him off, but he lowered his head into the trajectory of her pan.

Iron and skull collided; iron won.

"She broke my noggin," the brute moaned, clutching his bleeding head.

Oops. She couldn't bring herself to feel sorry for him.

"You're going to pay fer that." Spotted-Face pulled out a blade.

Maggie swallowed, raising her pan in readiness.

Click. Both she and her opponent looked in the direction of the sound.

The old Chinese man held a cocked flintlock; it was pointed between his attacker's eyes.

"I am a good shot." His gaze and aim were steady. "Do not make me prove it."

Maggie could see the ruffian teetering between violence and self-preservation. The latter instinct won out. Cursing, he pocketed his knife and gestured for his injured crony to follow him. Within seconds, they disappeared into the throng.

"Why didn't you take the pistol out earlier?" Maggie asked.

"Didn't want trouble." The old man shrugged. "But if trouble comes to find me, I have an answer. One doesn't survive in Limehouse as long as I have without being prepared."

He put his pistol away and began cleaning up the mess. Hastily, Maggie set down the pan and between the two of them, they managed to right the cart. The man, who introduced himself as Mr. Jiang, set a fresh batch of chestnuts over the coals.

"Chestnuts on the house," he said. "Best in Limehouse."

Maggie's stomach growled at the mention of food. Yet she had work to do and she'd tarried long enough. "Thank you, Mr. Jiang. But I must continue on an important errand."

"The errand must be important indeed to miss these beauties." He stirred the nuts, releasing a mouth-watering sweet and smoky aroma.

"It is important. Actually, perhaps you could help?" On impulse, she took out the Chinese characters. "I'm looking for a place called Plum Forest."

He looked at the paper she held out. "Ah, you're too late. *Mei-Lin* restaurant burned down."

"Yes, I know." Maggie fought her rising resignation. "I was hoping that there might be another place by that name."

"Can't think of any." The man gave the nuts another good stir. "But I do know Mei-Lin."

She frowned. "I don't understand. I thought you didn't know a place—"

"Not a place, a woman. Most people know her as Madeline Smith, but since I'm as old as the hills, I knew her back when she was Wong Mei-Lin. She and her husband own a rope-making shop not far from here."

Excitement shot through Maggie. "Mr. Jiang, could you direct me there?"

It took her twenty minutes to find Smith & Co. Ropemakers, which was located on a tiny lane off Three Colt Street. The shop was closed, but light seeped into the darkness from the curtained window on the story above. Seeing no entrance to the upper flat, Maggie surmised it must be behind the shop and made her way there.

Her nape tingled as she entered the back alley. Its darkness enveloped her, muting the distant sounds. The smell of rotting refuse curled in her nostrils, and she jumped as something brushed against her skirts.

Just a rat. Keep going. You're almost there.

She wished she'd thought to bring a lamp; instead she had to make do with the shifting moonlight. She counted the buildings, trying to find Smith & Co. A shuffling sound made her spin around. In the darkness, she saw only vague outlines, a sudden flash of yellow eyes.

Her heart thumping, she hurried along until she found Smith & Co., the back entrance guarded by a gate.

She lifted her hand to open the latch...and an arm closed like a steel band around her waist. Fear sliced through her. She opened her mouth, but a gloved hand muffled her scream.

❧ 37 ☙

"Maggie mine, it's me." Rhys's deep voice entered her ear.

Rhys...it's Rhys.

Even as her mind recognized the fact, her body remained rigid with fright. He removed his hand from her mouth but continued to hold her against him as the tremors faded.

"Wh-what are you doing here?" she finally managed.

"I was looking for you."

She could see the stark lines of worry on his face. One moment...she could see his face. Where was the light coming from?

She peered beyond him. Ming stood there, holding a lamp.

"Hello, Ming," she called softly.

He bowed.

Her gaze returned to Rhys. "How did you find me?"

"You're not exactly inconspicuous, sweetheart. A beautiful woman wandering around Limehouse on her own. Asking questions, knocking out hooligans with a pan." His mouth twitched as he tenderly brushed a stray curl from her cheek. "I met your friend, Mr. Jiang. He told me where you were headed. I have a team of people searching for Mei-Lin...but, as usual, you're one step ahead of everyone."

Questions filled her head. *What team of people? How does he know about Mei-Lin?*

She pushed away from him, blurting out the foremost question. "Are you married?"

"No, love. I gave up on that plan." His eyes held hers. "Right or wrong, I realized I couldn't marry anyone but the woman I love."

Heat pushed behind her eyes. "Do you mean...me?"

He blinked. Then, on a groaning laugh, he pulled her close. "Yes, Maggie mine. I love you. Only you and forever you."

Joy unfurled in her, bright petals pushing through the darkness.

Yet darkness pushed back.

She whispered, "But the dowry..."

"Damn the dowry—we're going to find the jewels. For Glory. For us." Fierce conviction shone in his eyes. "We're going to get our daughter back from that bastard Sweeney, and then the three of us are going to be a family. Do you trust me?"

"Yes, darling. Always." Hearing the crack in her voice, she pulled herself together. There wasn't time to fall apart. "We need to speak with Mrs. Smith—"

The gate swung open.

A mountain of a man appeared. He held a wooden club, slapping it into his beefy palm.

"Who wants to talk to my wife?" he boomed.

"Thank you for seeing us," Rhys said.

"I was expecting you, Your Grace. Mr. Horatio said you would come." Madeline Smith, the former Mei-Lin, spoke in accented but clear English.

Smiling, she poured tea into Chinese-style cups with no handles and passed them out to him, Maggie, Ming, and her husband. They were sitting around a circular table in the small flat, biscuits laid out in the middle.

Rhys recognized Mrs. Smith from his childhood memories. She had the same smooth, round face, and her clear, brandy-colored eyes still twinkled with a youthful exuberance. Instead of the double coils, her jet-black hair was now worn in a single braided bun. As a boy, he'd thought that she, an adolescent girl, was much older than him, but now he realized she was probably only in her late thirties.

Sampling the tea, Rhys discovered it was an excellent oolong. "My uncle visited you?"

Mrs. Smith nodded. "About six months ago. He told me he had been searching for me for some time, and he was glad to have found me before his time ran out. As you are here, am I to offer my condolences?"

"Thank you," he said gruffly. "Why was Uncle Horatio looking for you?"

Her clear eyes darkened. "He wished to talk about the past."

"If you don't wish to talk about it, pet—" her husband began.

"I am fine." She smiled at him, and the brawny fellow turned ruddy. "The events are over and done with, and the living must go on. Mr. Horatio believed that I had information that could be of use to His Grace. The key, he called it, to understanding your past."

Rhys braced, his heart pounding like a fist.

Beneath the table, Maggie's hand found his, and he drew from her strength.

"What information?" he asked.

"About your mama, my beloved mistress." Mrs. Smith's expression was troubled. "About what happened...between her and the duke."

"I know what happened." His gut churned. "I was there once when my father abused her."

Maggie's fingers laced tightly with his.

Mrs. Smith let out a sigh. "Such things were not for a boy to see. Nor for a lady to endure. Yet endure them she did, my mistress."

"I don't know how she managed." His throat thickened as he saw the bruises spreading over his mother's pale skin like ink over paper. "She was so delicate and frail."

"Your *mother*, frail? *Ai-yah*," Mrs. Smith exclaimed, "where did you get that foolish idea? My mistress was the strongest woman I ever knew!"

"I only meant...physically she..." He swallowed. "She was slight, and even walking was difficult for her."

"Because of her feet," Mrs. Smith said matter-of-factly. "In China, small feet are prized, considered a sign of feminine beauty. Her Grace's feet were bound since she was a young girl. The bones were broken over and again, her toes folded under the soles." She spread her fingers on the table, folding them into her palm to illustrate. "I changed the bandage daily, and I know it caused my mistress great pain."

"How cruel to inflict such a deformity," Maggie burst out. Then her eyes widened. "Oh, beg pardon, Mrs. Smith. Are your feet...?"

The lady laughed. "Goodness, no. I was a servant and needed my big feet to run around on."

"Your feet aren't big," her husband muttered. "We Englishmen like our womenfolk to be able to walk."

"But not to breathe. Have you ever worn a corset?" Mrs. Smith's eyes flitted heavenward. "But that is neither here nor there. My point is that my mistress met her suffering with fortitude and grace. And I don't mean just the pain of her feet. She did not want to leave China, to leave her home and dearest mother behind. But her father insisted she marry the duke to fulfill his ambitions, and she did so without complaint. For the honor of her family, she would do anything. Endure anything."

Rhys's chest tightened. He had never thought of his mother in this way. Yet Mrs. Smith's words shone a new light behind his mother's porcelain façade, illuminating an unexpected core...of steel.

"I wish she didn't have to suffer what she did," he said, his voice raw. "I wish I could have stopped my father, protected her—"

"You were a boy. What could you have done?"

Mrs. Smith's response echoed what Maggie had told him. Yet a part of him couldn't let go of his responsibility. His failure to defend his own mother. "I could have done more. Something." Agitated, he stood, raking a hand through his hair. "I could have told someone, encouraged her to leave—"

"I see now why Mr. Horatio wanted you to find me," the former servant interjected softly. "To help you see the past clearly. You think you failed your mama, is this true?"

He jerked his chin in assent.

"You did not. The truth is, you were the source of her strength," Mrs. Smith declared.

Shame welled. "I cannot see how that is true."

"Because you still see with a child's eyes. Your mother cherished you. You were the one good thing that resulted from her marriage, and even though the duke prohibited her from spending time alone with you, she found her happiness in those rare moments she had of your company. When she and I were alone, she spoke with pride about you. About what a handsome boy you were. How quickly you learned to speak, even though she didn't understand the language. About how brave you were to stand between her and your father." Mrs. Smith's eyes had a sudden sheen. "She was proud of you; you brought her *joy*."

His chest burned with emotion. He didn't trust himself to speak.

Mrs. Smith leaned forward, her hands flat on the table. "The duke forbade your mother from learning English, the same way he forbade her from teaching you Chinese. But she secretly gave you a name in Chinese. Did you know that?"

He shook his head mutely.

"*Nan-Di*," Mrs. Smith said. "Literally, it translates as 'difficult to fight against'. It is a name given to a boy who is strong and brave, who perseveres in the face of overwhelming odds. That is how your mother saw you."

Her words dislodged the arrowhead of his past. Pain and sorrow bled in its wake, but it was staunched by an excruciating beauty. One that began to heal him even as it rocked his very foundation.

Maggie came to him, wrapping her arms around his waist, and he held her. He anchored himself in her embrace, the succor offered by the woman he loved, as the past flowed through him, out of him...and he finally let it go.

Composing himself, he turned to face Mrs. Smith, who'd also risen.

"Thank you, madam." He bowed over her hand. "For your kindness and service to my mama. And to me."

"It was my honor to serve the duchess. And if it wasn't for her journey, I would not have found my own." She smiled at her husband, who stood protectively by her side.

"I must ask one more thing of you," Rhys said. "My uncle, did he perchance leave you something to give to me?"

"Ah, yes. He told me to give it to you after we talked. I will fetch it."

She returned moments later. Rhys's heart thudded as he saw what lay in her palm.

"Thank you for seeing us at this late hour," Rhys said.

"We are sorry if we disturbed your rest," Maggie added.

"I am old." As if to prove that point, Gruenwald rose creakily from his desk by the vault. "As my grandmama used to say, I shall sleep when I am dead. Do you have it?"

Rhys took out the key that Mrs. Smith had given him. The polished gold bow bore the stamp of Gruenwald and the number 108.

"Excellent," the goldsmith said. "And the card?"

Rhys handed over the thin piece of embossed gold.

After a thorough appraisal, Gruenwald nodded. "Everything appears to be in order. Follow me, if you please."

He led the way slowly to the massive door of the vault. The guards unlocked the sliding metal gate that protected the vault door, stepping aside deferentially as Gruenwald removed a key from his pocket.

Rhys saw that there were two key openings; the goldsmith inserted his into the bottom one.

"Place your key in the top slot," Gruenwald said. "We will turn together, on the count of three."

Rhys followed the instruction; there was a click, and the heavy door opened into darkness.

Gruenwald waved his hand at one of the guards, who entered the vault. A moment later, light flared inside the space, revealing rows of iron boxes.

"You'll find the safe box with the matching number on the wall to your right, middle of the stack," Gruenwald said. "I'll close the door behind you for privacy."

Thanking the goldsmith, Rhys entered the vault, Maggie by his side. The spacious cavern was hushed as they made their way through the iron hedgerows. The boxes were square, about five feet wide, and stacked three high. Rolling ladders were supplied to reach the higher boxes.

Each box had a bronze plate engraved with a number, and they found Number 108 where Gruenfeld said it would be.

Rhys's gaze met Maggie's. "I hope my uncle wasn't exaggerating about the treasure."

"There's only one way to find out," she said.

Despite his roiling tension, he had to smile at her matter-of-factness.

With a breath and a prayer, he slid the key into the lock. He twisted it, and the door swung open...revealing a large wooden chest. Propped against the chest was a note, scripted in his uncle's hand:

Congratulations, lad! You've earned what's inside.

I'm proud of you, nephew...but then I always was.

In your quest for the jewels, I hope you have found the true treasure: love. You always had it, my boy—your mama's love...and mine. May you use your wealth wisely, and let it guide the adventures ahead.

Your loving uncle,
Horatio

"He loved you," Maggie said softly.

"Yes." His throat swelled. "I wish I'd told him that...I loved him too."

Thank you, uncle. For everything.

He carefully dragged out the case, which was promisingly heavy, and set it on the floor.

"You do the honors," he said to Maggie.

With trembling hands, she undid the latch and flipped open the lid. She gasped.

The array of jewels was stunning: diamonds, emeralds, sapphires...a dazzling rainbow of huge, flawless gems nestled in neat rows. Each one of them was a fortune on its own, but together, they were a treasure beyond imagination.

And this was only the top tray of the box.

"This is a king's ransom," Maggie breathed.

"And our daughter's." Determination roared through him. "Now let's go get Glory back."

❧ 38 ❧

AFTER A QUICK INVENTORY OF THE JEWELS, MAGGIE AND RHYS decided to leave the treasure in the vault for safekeeping. They returned to Mivart's; after sending off a note to the Kents, they caught a few hours of sleep. Then, at eight o'clock, they presented themselves at the Kent residence. Tessa and Harry were waiting for them in the drawing room...and they weren't alone.

The Garritys were also present.

As Rhys and the moneylender eyed one another, the tension in the room grew thicker than a fog on the Dorset coast. Maggie was wondering why on earth Tessa had invited Rhys's enemy to the meeting when Gabriella Garrity rushed up and surprised her with a hug.

"It's ever so dreadful what happened to your daughter, Maggie," Gabby said.

The pain Maggie had been holding at bay broke through, her next breath hitching.

Gabby stepped back, her blue eyes filled with genuine worry. "Oh, that was tactless of me, wasn't it? I'm ever so *sorry*. Since Tessa told me about it, I haven't been able to sleep a wink. When I think of my own children..." Her voice wobbled. "I hope you don't mind that we're here. My husband and I want to lend our *unconditional* support, don't we, Mr. Garrity?"

The moneylender's dark eyes were unreadable. "As you say, Mrs. Garrity."

"There, you see?" Gabby gave Maggie a reassuring smile. "Mr. Garrity is ever so clever and adroit in sticky situations. With our combined efforts, we will get your Glory back."

It was then that Maggie understood why Tessa had involved Gabby. The redhead was sweet-natured and tenderhearted...and, most importantly, she held sway over her powerful husband. Maggie didn't quite understand the match between the cutthroat moneylender and his guileless wife, but undeniable currents flowed between the unlikely pair.

If the Garritys wanted to help secure Glory's return, Maggie would not look a gift horse in the mouth. She would reciprocate Gabby's goodwill.

"We're grateful for your assistance," Maggie said. "Aren't we, Ransom?"

Rhys's gaze remained locked on the usurer. "I wasn't aware that Mr. Garrity was in the business of helping people. When he throws a rope, it's usually just enough for one to hang oneself with."

Garrity's smile resembled a bearing of teeth. "Your Grace is correct in that I do not run a charity. My motivation in this case is more along the lines of retribution: Sweeney intended to steal my portion of your treasure. The insult cannot go unanswered."

"So your goal is to destroy Sweeney, not help me," Rhys shot back.

"Think of it as killing two birds with one stone."

"Given your ulterior motive, don't think to chalk me up further in your debt."

Garrity's brows arched. "I will not...as long as you fulfill your obligation to me. You owe me sixty thousand pounds, I believe?"

Maggie cast an anxious look at Rhys. Back at the vault, Mr.

Gruenfeld had provided a rough appraisal of the gems' worth: close to six hundred thousand pounds, he'd reckoned, and perhaps more. Even with Garrity's share deducted, the loot would be impressive. Sweeney should be none the wiser and well content with the ransom paid.

"Done," Rhys said.

"A pleasure doing business." Garrity extended a manicured hand.

Rhys shook it, and Maggie felt a jolt of relief.

One obstacle down. One step closer to saving Glory.

"Now onto the business of dealing with Sweeney," Garrity said.

A shiver ran through Maggie. She had a feeling that Garrity's version of "dealing" with Sweeney might result in the other cutthroat being buried six feet under. But since Sweeney had kidnapped her girl, she wasn't going to mourn for him: the bastard deserved whatever was coming.

"We'll discuss the plans over breakfast," Tessa announced.

Carts were wheeled in, and they all filled their plates before settling in to discuss strategy.

"Once I notify Sweeney that I've found the treasure, do you have any idea where he'll carry out the exchange?" Rhys asked.

"He has significant interests in Bluegate Fields. Took them over from the bastard who ruled there before him," Tessa said. "My guess is that he'll set the meeting there."

Rhys gave a terse nod. "If you would be so kind as to provide security, I'll transport the treasure from Gruenwald's to make the exchange."

"It won't be that simple." Garrity took the coffee Gabby had doctored for him with sugar and cream. Tasting it, his lips curved with satisfaction. "I know Sweeney. He lacks honor: the fact that he involved an innocent child in his scheme is a case in point. Once he has the treasure, there is no guarantee that he will set your daughter free."

A cold droplet trickled down Maggie's spine. "Then what do we do?"

"We surround the place. Ensure that Sweeney cannot escape with Glory," Tessa said.

"But won't that be dangerous? If Sweeney is angered, he might hurt her," Maggie protested.

Rhys's hand engulfed hers. "Once Sweeney has the treasure, Maggie mine, there's nothing preventing him from hurting her anyway. At least this way we have troops waiting in the wings, ready to fight for Glory if he doesn't set her free."

"I should point out there is nothing preventing Sweeney from harming His Grace after he hands over the jewels," Garrity said.

"I'll go in with Ransom," Kent said. "Be his second."

For once, even Tessa looked worried. "Harry, darling, I'm not sure—"

"I'll be fine. Besides, with me there, Sweeney will be less likely to make a false move."

"Thank you, Kent," Rhys said.

"This is too dangerous," Maggie fretted.

"Don't worry, love." Rhys's expression was resolute. "Sweeney will be the one in danger if he stands between me and our daughter."

~

Rhys sent the note.

Sweeney's reply came swiftly.

Ten o'clock tonight. Underhill & Son Cabinetmakers, Bluegate Fields. Come alone.

~

That night, in the dim light of the carriage, Rhys's eyes bored into Maggie's.

"Promise me that you'll stay in the carriage with Tessa," he said for the umpteenth time. "You will not leave her side for an instant."

They were nearly at the meeting place, a warehouse in the heart of the dockland slums. Maggie had insisted on going: with her daughter and her lover's lives at risk, there was no way she'd be left behind. She was to wait with Tessa who, along with an army of guards, would be monitoring the situation from a discreet distance.

"I'm not the one who is meeting with a cutthroat." As the carriage slowed, she clutched his lapels. "Rhys, promise me that you'll be safe."

"You have my word I'll get Glory back safe and sound," he said fiercely.

"Get yourself back safe and sound as well."

He cupped her cheek, his thumb running along her cheekbone. "With all I have to come back for, can you doubt that I will?"

"I love you, Rhys," she said, her voice hitching.

"And you hold my heart. Never forget it. Your light will guide me home."

Their kiss was one of heated promise and desperation. They clung to each other, to the preciousness of the moment, for neither knew how the next hours would unfold. They were still in each other's arms when a knock sounded on the door.

"It's time." Harry Kent's voice filtered through the wood.

"I have to go, Maggie mine." Rhys's gaze roamed possessively over her.

She closed her eyes as he pressed his lips tenderly against her forehead.

When she opened them, he was gone.

❧ 39 ❧

UNDERHILL & SONS WAS SITUATED IN ONE OF THE WORST warrens of Bluegate Fields, on a street so wretched that its occupants slept or lay in a drunken stupor on the dirt, and piles of vermin-infested rubbish were everywhere. Sitting precariously on the banks of the Thames, the warehouse was a brick building with boards nailed over the broken windows. Faint lines of light escaped from the spaces between the slats.

"Is everyone in place?" Rhys muttered.

Kent nodded, his spectacles glinting in the moonlight. "We scouted the warehouse earlier and have eyes on all the exits. Garrity and his men are guarding the dock behind the building in case Sweeney plans a water escape."

Rhys tightened his grip on the bulky leather satchel containing the jewels. "Then we'd better get this over and done with."

"Before we go." Kent pulled out what appeared to be a large, folded handkerchief. "For you."

Rhys raised his brows. "What for?"

"Insurance," Kent said succinctly. "You'll know if you need it."

If I happen to have an urgent need...to blow my nose?

Puzzled, Rhys nonetheless took the handkerchief, stuffing it into his greatcoat pocket.

They continued to the warehouse, where a gang of ruffians paraded around the perimeter. The guard at the entrance divested them of their weapons—no surprise there. Rhys dumped his pistol into the waiting sack. His brows raised as Kent's contributions included two pistols, a small bludgeon, and an assortment of small knives.

"Wot's this?" The guard shook a flask he found in one of Kent's greatcoat pockets.

"Spirits," Kent said easily. "Brewed it myself. You're welcome to try it."

The guard took a sniff and grimaced. Screwing the cap back in place, he peered at the next object retrieved from Kent's pockets. "And this?"

"Just a matchbox."

After a brief inspection, the guard returned the objects and opened the door.

Inside the warehouse, Sweeney stood waiting flanked by another pair of armed men—including Victor, who smirked at Rhys. Rhys ignored the blond bastard, his gut clenching as he saw no sign of Glory. Scanning the room, he spied no exits save for the door that the guards were closing behind him. Cabinets in various stages of construction had been pushed up against the walls, their silhouettes ghostly in the flickering light of the wall sconces.

Where were they keeping Glory?

"You made it, Your Grace." Sweeney's smile was oily as he advanced toward them, dragging shadows in his wake. "But you failed to follow instructions, I see."

"Kent is here to see that the exchange goes smoothly," Rhys said.

"It will." Sweeney's gaze fixed on the leather satchel. "Once you give me the treasure."

Rhys's fist gripped the handles. "Show me my daughter first."

Sweeney snapped his fingers.

One of the guards went to the far wall. He opened a cabinet, fumbling inside it. Suddenly, the section of the wall behind the cabinet separated from the rest. It rotated on a spinning platform, the cabinet turning out of view and on the other side was...*Glory*.

Rhys's heart thundered as he saw that she was trussed to a chair, a gag over her mouth. Her plaits were disheveled, her eyes dark pools in her pale face. Something moved on her lap...Ferdinand. The light brown ferret hissed, jumping up and down.

"Don't be afraid, poppet," Rhys shouted. "I'm coming to get you."

The wall continued rotating back to its original position, Glory disappearing from view.

"There, you see? Safe and sound." Sweeney's gaze narrowed. "Now hand over the treasure."

With boiling rage, Rhys strode over. "You want this? Have at it."

He tossed the bag to the ground. It landed with a loud thunk by Sweeney's feet.

Crouching, the cutthroat opened the bag, rummaging through the protective layers of velvet. He let out a gasp as he dug through the contents with both hands, the look on his face one of pure, unadulterated greed. He took out an emerald the size of a pigeon's egg, holding it up: even in the dimness, it flashed with green fire.

"Remarkable," he chortled.

"You have your jewels," Rhys said, his jaw clenched. "Now give me Glory."

The cutthroat closed the bag and rose. "These jewels are fine indeed, and I want to live long enough to enjoy them. I don't doubt you've got Tessa Kent's men out there waiting to pounce. To ensure my safe journey, I believe I'll take the girl." He took out a pistol, waving it at Kent. "And you'll come too."

"That was not the deal," Rhys grated out.

"The terms have changed, Your Grace." Sweeney's expression was cunning. "He who holds the pistol makes the rules. Count yourself lucky that I don't put a hole through you before I leave."

Out of the corner of his eye, Rhys noticed that while Sweeney was talking, Kent had been subtly fiddling with something in the pocket of his greatcoat. Knowing Kent—and recalling the other's earlier comment about "insurance"—Rhys decided to buy him more time.

"Surely you are not afraid to commit murder?" he taunted.

"I am afraid of nothing, and certainly not of you," Sweeney said with a sneer. "But why go to the trouble of committing murder when there isn't a bloody thing a useless fop like you can do to stop me?"

"You've been ahead of me every step of the way, haven't you?" Rhys egged him on.

"Every *damned* step. Did you know my men tracked you down in Dorset? Oh, aye, they arrived just after you left, but it wasn't a wasted errand. They heard some drunk bragging in the tavern that his sister had landed herself a duke, and they'd gone to London to find his inheritance: a treasure from a sunken ship, with a worth beyond measure."

Bloody Jeremy. If Rhys lived through this night, he was definitely killing Maggie's brother.

Seeing Kent furtively take out the matchbox, Rhys goaded Sweeney on. "If you knew I was in London, why didn't you capture me immediately?"

"Because, you bloody *dolt*, I wanted the treasure." Sweeney gave him a superior look. "I made sure to infiltrate your little band of guards from the start. Victor, here, was eavesdropping at every opportunity; what he heard confirmed what you were hunting for—and that you were close. All you needed was a little motivation."

"Kidnapping an innocent child—that's your version of motivation?" Beneath his lashes, Rhys glanced at Kent, who gave a barely perceptible nod.

Rhys readied himself for whatever would happen next.

"It worked, didn't it?" With a smug smile, Sweeney said, "Now enough talking—"

At that moment, Kent moved. He lobbed something in the air —the flask, a lit fuse trailing from its opening. An instant later, a blast sounded, thick black smoke billowing through the room.

Rhys launched himself at Sweeney. He tackled the cutthroat to the ground, heard the other's weapon skitter across the floor. The smoke obscured his vision, but he managed to land a punch in the other's face. Sweeney howled in pain. Rhys drew his arm back, readying to pummel the bastard, but he was knocked aside, landing on his back.

Victor had jumped on him. Rhys grappled blindly with the brute, rolling across the ground. Victor's hands closed around his throat, choking off his air. Desperately, Rhys swept the ground with his hand, his fingers brushing against...*Sweeney's gun*.

He grabbed the handle, jerked the gun up, and fired.

A strangled cry...and a dead weight slumped onto him.

Coughing, he pushed off the guard's body and jumped to his feet. Remembering the handkerchief, he tore it out of his pocket and tied it over his mouth; it helped to filter out the choking smoke. Through the fumes, he glimpsed Kent taking on two guards and sprinted over to help. Between the two of them, they defeated the bastards, grabbing their weapons and holding them at bay.

Chest heaving, Rhys tried to see through the smoke. "Where's Sweeney?"

"Over by the revolving wall!" Kent's voice was muffled by his own handkerchief. "He and one of the guards are making a run for it!"

At that instant, the front door slammed open. Through the swirling smoke, Rhys saw more of Sweeney's guards pouring in.

"Get Glory," Kent shouted. "I'll keep them at bay."

Torn, Rhys hesitated. "There are too many—"

At that instant, a battle cry went up. It didn't come from Sweeney's army—but that of the Kents. Ming led the charge through the entrance, he and his men swarming inside, closing ranks around the enemy.

"We have this in hand." Kent cocked his pistol.

Not wasting another second, Rhys raced to the far wall. He shoved his hand into the cabinet like he'd seen the guard do earlier. His fingers closed around a lever, and he pulled down on it. He heard the creak of the wall separating. Pushing through the widening crack, he found himself in a dimly lit space, surrounded by...himself.

He was in a room where looking glasses were fabricated. Freshly silvered mirrors covered the walls and hung on tall drying racks that turned the space into a disorienting maze. He advanced, pistol in hand, muscles tensing as movement skated across the mirrors. He heard a scuffling sound and spun around—only to be confronted by his own image.

His heart beating a rapid tattoo, he continued on. About to round a drying rack, he caught a metallic glint in one of the mirrors—a firearm. He dodged, a bullet whizzing by his ear. Shards of glass rained around him as he whipped around, returning fire.

With a moan, the brute crashed to the ground.

Rhys stepped over the fallen body, tossing aside the empty pistol. He saw himself in endless reflections, stripes of blood on his cheek where the glass had hit him. The images were designed to distract and disguise—to lure him away from his path.

All of a sudden, he knew what to do.

Placing his hands on the closest rack, he shoved with all his might. The heavy frame teetered before falling, knocking into the one behind it, the pattern continuing like a line of dominoes. Images exploded, shattering as he went to the next rack and the next, sweat dripping down his face as he toppled the maze. As he smashed the false reflections into dust.

Surrounded by glittering ash, he saw his enemy at last. At the far end of the room, Sweeney was bent over, struggling to open a heavy trapdoor. Beside him, Glory lay awkwardly on the ground. She was crying, trying to reach the ferret who was sprawled a few feet away, unmoving. She writhed helplessly—and that was when Rhys saw that Sweeney had her trapped, his boot pinning her plaits to the ground.

He had Rhys's daughter pinned by her *hair*.

He's a dead man.

Rhys stormed over, his boots crunching over debris. Sweeney had an instant to look up before Rhys barreled into him. They crashed into the ground, rolling, wrestling for the upper hand. Rage surged through Rhys as he held down the other man.

"You want to fight? Pick on someone your own size," he roared.

He plowed his fist into the bastard's face.

Then he did it again and again.

"Rhys. Darling, *stop*. He's unconscious."

Her arms securely around Glory, Maggie called to her lover, but he didn't seem to hear her. In fact, he didn't seem to notice that the fight was over. Escorted by an army of guards, she and Tessa had rushed into this room a few minutes ago, and Glory had run straight to her...but Rhys had been too busy beating the life out of Sweeney. He still was.

She started forward, but Harry Kent stopped her.

"Better let him get it out of his system," he advised.

"When he's through, it's my turn," Tessa said darkly.

But now that Glory was safe, Maggie didn't want Rhys to be charged with *murder*.

"Mama?"

She instantly looked at her daughter. Glory had her ferret cuddled against her chest. Ferdinand was still woozy after sustaining injuries defending her against Sweeney. Tessa had examined F. F., and luckily the bump on its head didn't appear too serious. The heroic animal gave Glory's bruised cheek a weak lick.

Seeing the battered pair caused anger to smolder in Maggie's chest.

Maybe Rhys has the right of it: Sweeney deserves to pay.

She put a protective arm around Glory's shoulders. "Yes, my dearest?"

"The bad man, Mr. Sweeney...he told me that Ransom is my father. Is that true?"

Maggie sucked in a breath. Confronted with Glory's eyes—Rhys's eyes—she couldn't lie.

Nor did she want to.

"Yes, it's true. I knew Ransom before I married your father... the one who raised you I mean. But Ransom didn't find out about you until he came to Dorset a few weeks ago." Anxiously, she searched her daughter's face. "I know how confusing this must be. It all happened a long time ago, and—"

"I understand."

She blinked at the steady reply. "You do?"

Glory nodded. "Does Ransom want to be my papa now?"

"He does, dear heart." Hesitantly, Maggie asked, "Do you think...you'd like that too?"

In answer, Glory called out, "Papa! Papa—stop fighting!"

Rhys's arm froze mid-swing. He twisted toward them.

Maggie saw the haze of bloodlust slowly fade from his eyes.

"Did Glory just call me...Papa?" he asked hoarsely.

"She did." Her heart full to bursting, Maggie smiled tremulously. "Now that we have your attention, would you mind leaving off the killing and joining your family instead?"

Rhys surged to his feet, rising from the ash of pulverized glass.

Dark hair waved over his sweaty brow. His cheek was cut, his jacket torn, and his fists dripped blood.

He was the most beautiful sight she'd ever seen.

"Anything for my girls," he said.

He started over.

She and Glory met him halfway, running into his arms.

❦ 40 ❧

THREE DAYS LATER, MAGGIE WAS RETURNING TO MIVART'S IN Tessa's carriage. The two of them had been keeping vigil with Gabby. For in the victory against Sweeney—who was now in the custody of Tessa's grandfather and awaiting underworld justice—there had been a casualty.

During the battle, Adam Garrity had taken a bullet.

As the physician had explained, the shot had gone cleanly through, not injuring any essential organs. Garrity would have healed without issue...had the shot not knocked him off his feet. He'd hit his head on the dock before tumbling into the water.

Luckily, his head guard, a fellow by the name of Wickham, had witnessed the accident and dove in after him. According to the physician, the brave action had saved Garrity's life: a minute later and the moneylender might have perished.

Nonetheless, his recuperation would not be an easy one.

Maggie and Rhys had visited the Garritys every day. Garrity had been injured fighting on their behalf, and it was a debt they would never forget. Moreover, Maggie had become fond of Gabby, and she was determined to support her new friend through whatever challenges lay ahead.

"Mr. Garrity looked better today, don't you think?" she asked quietly.

"He didn't look any worse." Tessa sighed. "I do hope he recovers quickly. For his sake as well as Gabby's. The poor dear is keeping up a cheerful front but..."

She didn't have to finish. Anyone who spent a second in Gabby's company knew how utterly devoted she was to her husband.

"Perhaps I should bring Glory tomorrow," Maggie said. "She might hit it off with the Garritys' children. At the very least, she could bring F. F. to entertain them."

Glory and the ferret were inseparable. Given that Ferdinand had protected Glory from Sweeney, even Rhys had taken a liking to the creature. Yesterday, Maggie had caught him sneaking the ferret a morsel under the table.

"I knew F. F. would be the perfect gift," Tessa said smugly.

Maggie gave the other a wry look. "Gift...or revenge?"

Mischief danced in Tessa's eyes. "Speaking of gifts, when is the wedding? I need time to prepare something special for you and Ransom."

"Please, there's no need for gifts," Maggie said sincerely. "We already owe you more than we can ever repay. Besides, the wedding is going to be a small, quiet affair."

Discussing the matter with Rhys, she'd suggested that a no-fuss ceremony with a few simple refreshments would be the most practical plan, and he had agreed.

"That's why Ransom had to leave early from the Garritys today," she added. "He had to see about a special license."

"A small wedding? But you're to become a duchess," Tessa protested. "You deserve some grand society affair."

Maggie smiled. "I'm to become Rhys's wife. That's enough for me."

"Hold up. How small is this wedding going to be? Harry and I are invited, aren't we?"

She laughed at Tessa's stricken expression. Perhaps it had been the intensity of the events that had bonded them, but she'd become inordinately fond of this roguish duchess of the underworld.

She leaned forward, squeezing the other's hand. "Of course you are."

They arrived at Mivart's, and Tessa invited herself up to tea. They stepped into the lobby—and Maggie stopped short. There were roses. *Everywhere.*

Red, pink, white, and every blushing shade in between. Massive, exquisite bouquets covered the counters and tables, lush garlands winding up the sweeping stairwell and festooned from the ceiling. A trellised arch sat at the foot of the stairs, bursting with hothouse blooms.

Fellow hotel guests were exclaiming over the extraordinary display. A lush, floral scent filled the air. It was joined by the lilting strains of violins.

"What on earth...?" Maggie murmured.

Her breath caught as Rhys appeared on the top landing of the stairs. He was dressed in formal elegance, so dazzling and princely that several of the female guests sighed aloud. He descended the steps, his pirate's eyes never leaving Maggie.

Her heart beat like a bird's wings.

He stopped beneath the trellis...and held a gloved hand out to her.

"Go to him." Grinning, Tessa nudged her forward. "Before one of these other ladies does."

Like a sleep walker, Maggie went to where Rhys stood waiting. It felt like a dream...until his hand closed around hers. His grip was strong and warm—real.

She stared up at him in wonder. Then he went down on one knee.

"Margaret Goode Foley," he said in clear, deep tones that carried, "your beauty enchants me more than I can say. But more than that, *you* enchant me: with your strength, determination, and grace. You are the beginning and end of all my journeys, the only adventure I'll ever need. With you by my side, I am never lost, for you are my home."

She was so overwhelmed that she couldn't speak.

Feminine *oohs* and *aahs* went up around them.

"The truth is that I need you by my side," he went on in solemn tones. "Now that I have wealth to manage, estates to properly run, and long-neglected responsibilities to attend to, I require a wife who will keep me in line. One who will lecture me on the practicality of no-fuss weddings while I plot to spoil her silly with everything she professes not to need but most certainly deserves."

Maggie let out a watery laugh.

His eyes smiling, Rhys pulled out a ring. A tear rolled down Maggie's cheek as she recognized the center stone. He'd chosen a huge, brilliant emerald from his uncle's treasure. The peerless stone was set in a frame of flawless white diamonds, creating a ring beyond compare.

A ring fit for a duchess.

"I love you, Maggie mine. My heart, my respect, and my devotion—they are yours until my last breath." Rhys's voice hoarsened with emotion. "Will you also do me the great honor of taking my name...of being my wife?"

"Yes." She half-sobbed the word.

He slid the ring on her finger: a perfect fit. The emerald shone with the lessons of the past, joy of the present, and promises of their storybook future. Rising, he swept her into his arms. Violins soared and the audience erupted into cheering as he kissed her and she kissed her duke back with all the love in her heart.

EPILOGUE

EIGHT WEEKS LATER

"Rhys, we can't. The guests will be arriving at any moment..."

His new duchess's reprimand melted into a moan as he drove his cock inside her. They were standing, and she was naked except for her garters, stockings, and the pearl necklace he'd given her as a wedding gift. Her back was against her dressing room door, one of her stockinged legs hitched over his hip. Her wet, tight pussy clutched him lovingly.

"The guests can go hang themselves," he rasped.

They'd returned from their grand wedding at St. George's an hour ago, where several hundred well-wishers had braved the cold winter day to be in attendance. Now that Rhys's fortune had been restored—and rumors of an epic treasure hunt added to his mystique—the *ton* was once again at his feet. He didn't give a damn, but he wanted to show Maggie how proud he was to make her his wife. The Upper Crust had been all agog to see the wedding of the Duke of Ranelagh and Somerville and the mysterious widow who'd stolen his heart.

Maggie did not disappoint. An admiring hush had settled over the crowd as she'd glided down the aisle toward Rhys in a celestial blue dress adorned with thousands of seed pearls, her manner serene and regal. Ahead of her, Glory had tossed petals like a charming sprite, F. F. trotting beside her.

Rhys's daughter had beamed at him; he'd winked back.

Then Maggie had arrived at the altar. Lifting her veil, he'd looked into her smiling eyes and known that he was the luckiest bastard in the world.

After the ceremony, they'd returned to their recently acquired townhouse in Mayfair. They would be throwing an intimate supper party for a few selected guests. They'd gone upstairs to change, and after he'd finished, Rhys had gone to find Maggie in her dressing room. He'd caught her wearing nothing but her necklace and the fine silk hosiery.

One look at him, and Bertha had scurried out the door.

Hence, Rhys's present position with his wife.

One hand braced against the door, he drilled up into her. Into her snug, giving softness. When he saw her gaze grow unfocused, the telltale flush spreading over her bouncing breasts, he knew she was close. He delved into her nest, finding the key to her pleasure, diddling and shafting her at the same time.

Maggie cried out his name as she came.

He groaned as her convulsions milked his prick. It was too much, not enough. He wanted all of his duchess—to bury himself into the heart of her. So deep she would feel him always, the way he felt her.

Gripping her hips, he hoisted her off the ground, holding her aloft against the door. With her feet above the floor, she was impaled completely on his cock. They both gasped when he nudged the opening of her womb.

"All right?" he asked.

"You're so...*deep*," she said, her words slurred with pleasure.

"I want to get deeper." The need was primal, irresistible. "I want to come inside you, Maggie mine, and fill you with my seed."

He hadn't done that since their very first time. But now she was his, and he was hers, and he wanted everything. She shivered, the reflexive squeeze of her cunny telling him she wanted it too.

He needed no other encouragement. He lifted her, then brought her down hard onto his shaft. The depth of the penetration set fire to his blood. He drove up inside her over and again, her pussy wetly kissing his balls, her sounds of pleasure egging him on. Flames licked his insides, and finally he could hold back no more.

"Take me, my love. All of me," he growled.

"Come inside me," she beckoned sultrily. "I want to feel you."

They came together, looking into each other's eyes, and the rapture was beyond anything he'd felt before. He groaned as his duchess wrung him of his seed, as he emptied himself into her sweet, generous keeping.

Panting, he set her on the ground and touched his forehead to hers.

"That is what I call a wedding celebration," he said huskily. "Now tell me again why we invited all those damned people?"

"It was your idea," she reminded him. "I wanted a small wedding, remember?"

"Hoisted by my own petard."

Reluctantly, he withdrew from her in a warm, moist rush. The sight of his seed trickling down her silken thigh made him regret the party more than ever. What he wouldn't give to continue their festivities...

"Oh no, you don't." Maggie slapped his hand away with mock severity.

The problem was that her primness had the opposite of its intended effect. Her eyes widened as she took in his renewed interest. Well, not renewed exactly: it had never subsided.

He gave her his most rakish grin. "I can make this one quick."

"There's no time." Clearly trying not to smile, she retrieved his trousers from the floor and handed them to him. "Get dressed."

"The guests can entertain themselves," he cajoled.

Giggling, she slipped out of his reach, pulling on her chemise. "I'm not talking about the guests. I want to give you your wedding present."

He waggled his brows. "Didn't you already?"

"This one is from Glory and me. She's been waiting all day to give it to you."

The mention of his daughter caused a kick of warmth in Rhys's chest. Day by day, the bond between them had grown even stronger. He'd had the adoption paperwork readied before the wedding; now that he and Maggie were married, he would legally adopt Glory. The world would officially recognize what was already in his heart.

Sighing, he got dressed and waited while Maggie's lady's maid set her to rights.

Together, they headed to Glory's chamber.

As his wife had claimed, their daughter was waiting for him. Glory's eyes were as bright as new guineas as she presented him with the gift. Rhys's throat swelled at the sight of the pup, a foxhound with floppy brown ears and a big red bow tied around its neck.

Crouching, he put out his hand, and the pup bounded over. Tail wagging, it sniffed and licked his fingers.

"Do you like him?" Glory asked eagerly.

He had to clear his throat before speaking. "Very much. Thank you."

"You're welcome. It was my idea," she said. "Mama thought I just wanted a dog for myself, but I don't need one any more since I have F. F."

As if hearing its name, the ferret came running, zipping up Glory's arm and winding around her neck. From its perch, it eyed the puppy with great suspicion.

"What are you going to call him?" Maggie asked softly.

Looking at his wife and daughter's smiling faces, his dog's fur soft beneath his palm, Rhys said the first thing that came to mind. "Lucky."

~

JOURNEY'S END, A FEW YEARS LATER

Rhys knew he would find his wife in the garden.

The Duchess of Ranelagh and Somerville had gained a reputation for her flower gardens, visitors coming to their flourishing estate in Northumberland and here in Dorset to see her exquisite designs. One society paper had even raved that her mingling of native wildflowers with cultivated roses was "a wildly original ode to the marriage of nature and man."

He and Maggie had shared a chuckle over that. Just as they had when the wags had given Rhys a new moniker after a well-received speech he'd given in the House of Lords against the Opium War. Now the *ton* called him Ransom the Rhetorician—which was patently ridiculous, but he supposed they'd needed to give him another sobriquet after his former one had fallen out of use.

His devotion to his duchess had become something of a legend.

Rhys strode with purpose through the lush maze, Lucky following faithfully at his heels. He found Maggie at the center with their children. Even after the years of marriage, the sight of her never failed to stir him. She wore a stylish white taffeta gown and had left off her bonnet, the sunshine picking out the ruby glints in her casual yet elegant coiffure. She was pointing out a flower to their three-year-old son, Horatio, while Glory read to their newborn, Theo, on a nearby blanket.

Everyone turned at Rhys's approach.

"Papa!" Horatio was the first to run over.

Rhys hoisted the dark-haired child onto his shoulders. "How's my boy?"

"Hun-gwy," Horatio confirmed.

He was always hungry.

"We're ready to have luncheon," Rhys said.

"Have Hypatia and Arthur arrived?" Maggie came up to him.

Rhys brushed his lips against her temple, relishing her sweet fragrance and sensual shiver. "Yes and your brothers as well. We'd better get back before all the food is gone."

"And the silver," she muttered.

Smiling because her assessment wasn't wholly inaccurate, he went over to Glory. "What are you reading, poppet?"

"I'm teaching Theo Chinese," she said seriously.

Since learning about her heritage, Glory had developed a love affair with all things Chinese. Rhys had hired a tutor for her, and she'd soaked everything up like a sponge, showing a natural aptitude for the language. Even Ming had looked impressed when Glory had carried on a conversation with him in his native tongue.

"I don't think he's old enough to understand, dear," Maggie said.

"He smiles when I count to him. Watch." Glory turned to her baby brother. "*Yi, er, san*—see?"

Sure enough, Theo was smiling and blinking his wide hazel eyes.

Maggie looked doubtful. "Are you sure he's not just passing wind?"

Rhys didn't know if it was the Chinese or his sister's love that the baby was responding to, but what did it matter?

"Well done, poppet," he said. "Now it's time for lunch."

"I'm hun-gwy," Horatio reminded them all.

Glory got up, and Maggie took Theo.

Rhys put his arms around his wife and daughter, and they all headed in together.

AUTHOR'S NOTE

Fans of the great Bruce Lee will recognize this book's nod to his kung-fu classic, "Enter the Dragon." Bruce Lee was my husband's childhood hero (the nunchuks made by Mr. Callaway's thirteen-year-old self still reside in our closet) and one of the few Asian men portrayed as strong and masculine in the popular media of that time. Lee's legacy lives on not only in his martial arts movies but in his many writings about philosophy and life. To learn more about him, check out the Bruce Lee Foundation.

ABOUT THE AUTHOR

USA Today & International Bestselling Author Grace Callaway writes steamy and adventurous historical romances. Her debut book, *Her Husband's Harlot*, was a Romance Writers of America Golden Heart® Finalist and a #1 Regency Bestseller, and her subsequent novels have topped national and international best-selling lists. She's the winner of the Daphne du Maurier Award for Excellence in Mystery/ Suspense and the Passionate Plume Award for Historical Novel. Her books have also been shortlisted for numerous honors including the National Reader's Choice Awards, the Maggie Award of Excellence, and the National Excellence in Romance Fiction Award.

Growing up on the Canadian prairies, Grace could often be found with her nose in a book—and not much has changed since. She set aside her favorite romance novels long enough to get her doctorate from the University of Michigan. A clinical psychologist, she lives with her family in Northern California, where their adventures include remodeling a ramshackle house, exploring the great outdoors, and sampling local artisanal goodies.

Keep up with my latest news!
Newsletter: gracecallaway.com/newsletter

facebook.com/GraceCallawayBooks
bookbub.com/authors/grace-callaway
instagram.com/gracecallawaybooks
amazon.com/author/gracecallaway

ACKNOWLEDGMENTS

To my readers: thank you from the bottom of my heart for joining me on this journey. Your support means the world. I'm grateful and humbled that I get to call writing my profession.

A shout out to my editor, Veronica Nelson, for her keen insight and ability to know where I'm trying to go...even if I get a bit lost in the woods.

Special thanks to my parents (who also fall in the next category) for help with all things Chinese. Any mistakes are mine.

Finally, this book would not be possible without the support of my village. You know who you are. And I hope you know that I love you endlessly.